P9-BYU-497

Road Trip

Buffy, Angel, and Micaela were approaching the door when they heard the sounds of a struggle outside.

"God, what now?" Buffy asked.

The door tore off its hinges as two acolytes slammed against it. They fell to the floor, one dead, one nearly so. Framed in the open door, in the moonlight streaming in from outside, Buffy saw three Sons of Entropy attacking the tall, lithe, familiar figure of Spike. He'd grown his white-blond hair out a bit, but there was no mistaking him.

"Look, boys, I'm here for the Spear, and I mean to have it," he said, sounding entirely reasonable, just before he snapped one acolyte's neck.

Yep, Buffy thought. *Same old Spike.*

"You've gotta be kidding me," Angel said, his voice raspy and dangerous.

Spike looked up, blinked in surprise, then laughed as he crushed the face of another acolyte beneath his boot heel.

"Well, isn't this lovely," he said, "it's a bloody reunion. Not that it doesn't give me grand spasms of pleasure, but what brings you lot here?"

Buffy the Vampire Slayer™

Available from ARCHWAY Paperbacks and POCKET PULSE

Buffy the Vampire Slayer adult books

Available from POCKET BOOKS

For orders other than by individual consumers, Pocket Books grants a discount on the purchase of 10 or more copies of single titles for special markets or premium use. For further details, please write to the Vice President of Special Markets, Pocket Books, 1230 Avenue of the Americas, 9th Floor, New York, NY 10020-1586.

For information on how individual consumers can place orders, please write to Mail Order Department, Simon & Schuster Inc., 100 Front Street, Riverside, NJ 08075.

The Gatekeeper Trilogy
Book Two

BUFFY
THE VAMPIRE
SLAYER™

GHOST ROADS

CHRISTOPHER GOLDEN and **NANCY HOLDER**
An original novel based on the hit TV series created by Joss Whedon

POCKET BOOKS
New York London Toronto Sydney Tokyo Singapore

The sale of this book without its cover is unauthorized. If you purchased this book without a cover, you should be aware that it was reported to the publisher as "unsold and destroyed." Neither the author nor the publisher has received payment for the sale of this "stripped book."

This book is a work of fiction. Names, characters, places and incidents are products of the author's imagination or are used fictitiously. Any resemblance to actual events or locales or persons, living or dead, is entirely coincidental.

An *Original* Publication of POCKET BOOKS

POCKET BOOKS, a division of Simon & Schuster Inc.
1230 Avenue of the Americas, New York, NY 10020

™ and copyright © 1999 by Twentieth Century Fox Film Corporation. All rights reserved.

All rights reserved, including the right to reproduce this book or portions thereof in any form whatsoever. For information address Pocket Books, 1230 Avenue of the Americas, New York, NY 10020

ISBN: 0-671-02749-2

First Pocket Books printing March 1999

10 9 8 7 6 5 4

POCKET and colophon are registered trademarks of Simon & Schuster Inc.

Printed in the U.S.A.

This one is for Lisa Clancy and Caroline Kallas, who make it all possible

—C.G. and N.H.

Acknowledgments

Our deepest thanks to Joss Whedon, the cast and crew of *Buffy,* and to assistant editor Liz Shiflett. Chris would also like to thank his agent, Lori Perkins, and his wife, Connie. Nancy would like to thank her agent, Howard Morhaim, his assistant, Lindsay Sagnette; her husband, Wayne, and the Babysitter Battalion: Bekah and Julie Simpson, Ida Khabazian, and Lara and April Koljonen. Also, Stinne Lighthart and Leslie Jones.

The Gatekeeper Trilogy

Book Two

BUFFY THE VAMPIRE SLAYER™

GHOST ROADS

Prologue

THE GHOST ROADS.

A place of madness.

A limbo, a vacuum of nothingness: no sound, not even Buffy's gasps of shock, no light, just a dull gray that formed no boundary, met no horizon. No heat, no cold. Simply . . . nothing.

Oz and Angel had tried to prepare her for the terror of the experience, but Buffy Summers, the Chosen One, knew now that there was no way to prepare. By instinct and by training, vampire slayers fought *against*—against a target, an enemy. While every cell in her body screamed at her to defend herself, there was no enemy to focus on. And yet she sensed overwhelming danger.

Fists clenched, she took a breath and calmed herself. She released the tension from her body, dangling her arms at her sides. As contrary as it was to everything she knew, the only way to conquer this place was to do nothing. The only defense was passivity. She had to find a way to accept the lack of form and structure, the storm-colored, endless gray, and know that it was . . . what it was.

It was the ghost roads.

As soon as Buffy had the thought, she felt solid ground beneath her boots. Everything snapped into focus and she heard a strange *shushing* sound. She blinked and saw Oz and Angel standing beside her in their travel clothes—Angel in black jeans, a black turtleneck, and a duster, with a duffel bag slung over one shoulder; Oz in a flamingo-pink bowling shirt, jeans, and a denim jacket, with a canvas backpack—both of them looking at her with deep concern.

The sight of Angel's dark, deep-set eyes was like a steadying rock as he put his hand on her shoulder and said softly, "Buffy, are you okay? Are you with us?"

Awkwardly she moved her head, feeling something like a puppet minus vital strings. "That'd be a yes," she said uncertainly. "Unless you're figments of my imagination."

Both Angel and Oz visibly relaxed. She wondered how she had appeared to them during the time she hadn't been able to see them. They had both traveled the ghost roads before, and it made sense that they would be able to adjust to it faster than she. Oz had been the first, going to Sunnydale to retrieve Angel when they needed him for the Ritual of Endowment at the Gatehouse. When he and Angel had returned to the house together, Angel's face was smeared with bloody tears, shed for someone here, someone who walked the ghost roads.

Buffy wasn't sure who she herself might see.

Then she snapped her gaze left, right, and tensed. An aura of menace wrapped around her, stealing in like a coastal summer fog. It caressed her cheek and touched her heart. It chilled her to the core, and she shivered.

"Something's here with us." She assumed a fighter's stance. "Something evil."

Oz said, "I gave this part a lot of thought. I think it's the shadow of death." He cocked his head at Buffy and put his hands in the pockets of his denim jacket. "Interesting. When the shadow crossed my path, I wanted to wander off the road and go to sleep. Give in. Seemed peaceful. To you, it's dangerous. You want to fight it."

Because she is a Slayer, came a voice. *As I was.*

All around Buffy, the gray dissolved into a blinding white flash. The road beneath her feet crumbled into dust, white and searing through her boots. She covered her eyes, blinking, as crimson glowed on her retinas. She remembered Angel's tears of blood and wondered, briefly, if they had been tears at all.

Slowly she opened her eyes, squinting through the afterburn.

Before her stood a barefoot girl about her age, in a long white robe knotted at each shoulder. It was covered with dried blood. The girl was chalk white, her eyes almost black, and her deep red hair tumbled over her shoulders like a waterfall.

She stood alone against a field of black, her outline quite distinct. Buffy had the feeling that if she reached out her hand to the girl, she would touch solid flesh. But there was a strange quality about her, something

3

ethereal, otherworldly. Something that spoke of a land of ghosts.

She raised a hand and extended it toward Buffy. *Slayer, know me. I am of your house.*

"Then you must be one of the Southern Summers," Buffy retorted. "Our side of the family tends toward blonds." She cleared her throat and asked, far more seriously, "Why are you here?"

I was a Vampire Slayer, like you.

Though the girl's lips moved, it was as if a thousand people were speaking. Buffy glanced around and saw brief, blurred images of faces and bodies. People. Some stared at her, some averted their gazes. Many wept. Others were whispering, laughing, almost crazily.

When those faded, others took their place. There was a vast multitude of them. The dead who still wandered, seeking journey's end. Blurring and fading, like a great creature breathing. Like hopes rising and ebbing.

Angel stiffened, took her hand, and squeezed hard. Buffy searched the crowd to see what he saw. The only face that remained distinct for her was the dead girl's.

Buffy glanced at Oz, who in turn looked back at her. He said softly, "What do you see? Who are you talking to?"

"What do *you* see?" she asked.

He shrugged. "No one I know." Then he lowered his voice and added, "But the last time I was here, I saw Kendra."

Buffy frowned. Was this where dead Slayers ended up? After all the struggle and the relentless fighting, the nothing world of the ghost roads was what lay ahead?

"Why are you here?" Buffy asked the girl again.

The girl raised her chin as tears welled in her eyes. But she wasn't sad; by the set of her jaw and the pulsing vein in her neck, Buffy realized she was seething with anger.

I was careless. There was a lad I liked. I thought he was just a stable boy, a nothing. He betrayed me to Fulcanelli and his devils. She raised her chin as the voices emanating from her mouth whispered and echoed the name, Fulcanelli. *He was one of them.*

"Fulcanelli," Buffy said slowly.

"The Sons of Entropy. He founded them, acted as their first leader," Angel supplied. "Giles read about them in the Gatekeeper's grandfather's diary. The first Gatekeeper, Richard Regnier, was a rival of Fulcanelli's in the court of the French king, Francis I. Fulcanelli engineered Richard's fall from favor, and they hunted each other all over Europe." He looked curiously at Buffy. "What's going on? What do you see?"

So she and she alone could see the dead Slayer. That creeped Buffy. What was the reason each of them saw different dead people?

"What's your name?" Buffy asked.

Maria Regina served me in my lifetime.

"I'm looking at Maria Regina," Buffy told Angel. "Fulcanelli killed her." She looked at the dried blood. "With a gun, I'm guessing."

A knife. I was murdered in the year of Our Lord 1539.

And she had been here ever since? Buffy shuddered. Four hundred sixty years of wandering the ghost roads but never reaching a destination, not heaven, not hell. Just nothing. So *not* what she wanted in an afterlife.

I was called. To warn you, Slayer.

"By the Gatekeeper?" Buffy asked.

I know not. She shrugged in the exact way Buffy shrugged. That distinctive Buffy gesture was something Xander had pointed out to Buffy just the other day, so now she noticed it.

"Warn me about what?"

Death walks these roads with you. It would be better for you to turn back.

Buffy scowled at her. "And you call yourself a Slayer?"

I was killed.

Buffy huffed and gave a short little laugh. "Well, I don't intend to get killed."

Then turn back.

"Angel," Buffy said, "do you know how to change the channel?"

But his attention was elsewhere. He was staring in the distance, his eyes lidded, a strained expression on his face. In his black duster and turtleneck, he reminded her of a sailor longing for the sight of land.

"Angel, what is it?" she asked quietly.

He shook his head. "Nothing. I thought I saw someone." He returned her intense gaze. "But I didn't."

"Jenny," she said slowly.

He looked away. "Yes."

He was tormented by the memory of her death,

6

which was exactly the way Jenny Calendar's Gypsy clan, the Kalderash, wanted it. When, as the evil vampire Angelus, he had killed a beautiful Kalderash Gypsy girl, the Gypsy shaman restored Angelus's soul to him, along with the knowledge of every foul act, every drop of blood that stained his hands. Then he was Angel, the only vampire to possess a soul, perpetually remorseful, finding no peace . . . until he lay in the arms of Buffy. There was love, happiness, and bliss . . . the very things the Gypsies swore always to deny him. So his soul was ripped away once more, until Jenny died trying to restore it one last time.

Buffy tenderly touched his cheek as sympathy and longing swept through her. They could never be together in that way again, never express the love they still felt for each other. It was over. It had to be over. There was no choice.

As there was no choice for Angel but to bitterly regret everything he had done and accept with as much grace as he could manage everything that had been done to him.

He gritted, "It's all right."

Buffy slowly lowered her hand and turned back to Maria Regina, the dead Slayer.

But she was gone.

"Hello?" Buffy called.

Then Oz said, "Whoa."

The space around Buffy, Angel, and Oz filled with wailing as the dead rushed toward them, arms extended, hands open. In rows they came, wave after wave of indistinct bodies and faces, silver tears coursing down their cheeks.

Help us. Show us the way out, they pleaded, crushing against each other in their anxiety to get close to the three travelers. *Free us.*

"You hear that?" Oz asked, as the three backed away. "Intense."

"Loud and clear," Angel affirmed.

Oz looked at Buffy. "What do we do?"

Angel said softly, "Walk away. There's nothing else we can do. Not today."

Buffy bit her lower lip. Much as she hated to admit it, Angel was right. This was not their battle.

The wailing rose as the three turned their backs on the sorrowful dead.

The *shushing* noise returned, like surf or . . .

"A car," Buffy said. "Look. We made it."

She pointed to a distant night landscape, a boxy black car wound along a country road.

Angel said. "Welcome to England."

Rupert Giles felt mortally sorry for Joyce Summers, who sat in an overstuffed chair opposite the couch in the living room on a brilliant mid-afternoon in her home in Sunnydale, the sun splashing the walls like egg-yellow paint. On the coffee table an astounding array of junk food, courtesy of one Xander Harris, was being devoured by same, while Willow and Cordelia sipped their iced teas and nodded at every word Xander said.

The Slayer's mother was clearly terribly confused about what was going on and where her daughter was at the moment. And Xander, unfortunately, was not helping.

"Okay, Mrs. S., one more time," Xander said, leaning forward and spreading his fingers, as if he were about to wade knee-deep into his explanation. "We went to this place called the Gatehouse. This old guy—and we are talking *old,* not just Giles-old—"

"He's, like, a hundred and forty," Cordelia piped up, "and he looks terrible. I mean, if you even tried a chemical peel, all his skin would, like, peel off." She made a face.

Xander looked exasperated as he turned to her. "Which is the point of a chemical peel, no?"

"Not down to your bones. Not a skull-peel. Eew." Cordelia folded her arms. "And you should have bought fat-free potato chips. There's nothing on this table I can eat."

"Oh, I'm sorry," Joyce said, rising. "Let me see—"

"Please, Mrs. Summers. Joyce," Giles said kindly. "We don't need refreshment." Which was not entirely true, judging from the frowns the others gave his words. He himself had been so concerned about what was happening that he had not been able to eat much since being released from hospital back in New York.

He was also very worried about Micaela Tomasi, the beautiful young Watcher who had flirted with him at the librarians' convention, then revealed her identity to him while he was in hospital. She'd brought him a volume of Sherlock Holmes and a huge bouquet of flowers.

Now she was missing, and presumed dead. Many Watchers were, these days. If she was dead, it was a terrible pity. And for him, another loss to mourn.

Xander, Cordelia, and Giles had just returned, days late from their supposed "history competition" in Boston. There would be hell to pay, elaborate explanations to be made, and, possibly, the necessity for the Watcher of the current Slayer to find a new job. An unsettling prospect, to say the least. Sunnydale was not exactly a bustling metropolis, and new employment such as would suit Giles's requirements—that it be solitary, and easily accessible for Buffy—would be difficult to find.

"Well, the Doritos are low-fat," Xander offered. "And the cheese balls are little."

Cordelia shot him a look. "Want to talk about little?"

Xander drew himself up and said, "Hey."

Willow rolled her eyes.

Giles hastened to soothe over the moment. "What I believe Xander is trying to explain is that for centuries, the masters of the Gatehouse, always one of the Regnier line of sorcerers, have been collecting and binding the monsters and demons that escape from breaches into the Otherworld, a sort of other dimension."

"Like the Hellmouth?" Joyce asked, looking dazed.

Giles was pleased. "Very much so. Sunnydale sits upon the Hellmouth, and it both attracts and disgorges various and sundry manifestations of the dark forces of evil. But there are a great many things and people and places which are believed to be myths, and yet also did once exist on earth. All the things which this world doesn't have room for in its collective imagination—legends and extinct species, abominations and such—they all exist in the Otherworld. But from time to time, there is a breach in the barrier between there and here, and they escape.

"It is the role of the Gatekeeper to capture these

escapees and bind them into rooms in his endless home."

"And it's such a smashing little madhouse," Xander drawled in a fake British accent. "Just loaded to the gills with wicked bad juju."

Joyce blinked her deep blue eyes. "Where does he keep them all?"

"It's astonishing," Giles answered, warming to the subject. "His house is magickal, you see, and there are thousands of rooms into which he binds all these many diabolical creatures. The house shifts according to the dominant personality within its walls. It's fascinating."

"More like scary," Willow offered. She leaned forward and plucked up a handful of cheese balls. "They're little," she said to Cordelia.

"You'll balloon," Cordelia warned her. "A couple nibbles here, a couple there . . ."

"Where?" Xander asked sassily, raising and lowering his brows at her.

"Stop it," Cordelia said, sighing at Joyce, as if to say, *Can you believe this?*

Buffy's mother nodded slowly. "And something got out of the Gatehouse."

"A whole lot of somethings," Xander cut in. "See, the heir to the Gatehouse got kidnapped, and if Buffy doesn't get him back to the Gatehouse before the old man croaks, well, you can probably say good-bye to Family Fun Evening at the Pitch 'n' Putt."

"Oh," Joyce said slowly.

Giles pushed his glasses up. He was tired, and trying to put a word in edgewise was more tiring still. But he owed it to Joyce.

"I must tell you, the world is in grave danger, and Buffy, Angel, and Oz may be its last hope."

"How new," Cordelia said.

"How different," Xander added.

Willow sipped her tea.

"Seriously," Giles insisted. "And the Hellmouth has been badly compromised. All sorts of terrible things have emerged from it. They're held at bay thanks only to Willow's excellent binding spells—" he smiled in Willow's direction as she sat up straighter and preened a bit—"but I'm not sure how long they'll last. In short, perhaps it would be best if you got out of Sunnydale for a time."

Joyce looked shocked. Then she said, "We live here."

Giles inclined his head. "Fair enough. But Buffy—"

And then it happened.

There was a low rumbling very like an earthquake. As everyone jumped to their feet and hurried to the doorways in the room—thank goodness for California's community earthquake preparedness training— the walls of the house began to shimmy, then to shake violently. A crack ran diagonally from the upper left-hand side of the window behind the couch all the way across the opposite side. The coffee table bounced up and over, scattering Xander's junk food everywhere.

Joyce fell to the floor, bumping her head. The room went pitch black, and for a moment, she thought she was losing consciousness. Then, as her eyes adjusted, the sun shifted behind the curtains, casting an eerie glow over the tense faces in the room.

"Look," Cordelia said, pointing.

Something dark formed in the floor, a blackness darker than anything Joyce had ever seen. It collected the wan sunlight, and yet she could still make it out on the carpet. It looked like a puddle of shiny tar.

A high, frigid wind whistled through the house, so loud Joyce had to cover her ears. Books and knick-knacks slammed against the wall.

"Willow," Giles called.

Buffy's redheaded friend got to her knees and pointed at the puddle as it began to rise into the air.

"Hurry, Will," Xander said.

"To the gods I give supplication, and all deference, and honor," Willow said in a loud, booming voice.

The black circle began to rotate so that it now hung vertically in the center of the room. The air around it seemed to shimmer like a pool of water broken by a stone or the movements of life beneath the surface.

"Snap it up!" Cordelia shouted.

Willow raised her other arm. *"Pan, hear my plea."*

"What's happening?" Joyce cried.

"It's a breach," Giles explained. "Running might be wise."

Joyce stayed rooted. "You aren't running. And neither are they."

"And therefore, and henceforth, with all the power of the Old Gods, I bind thee!" Willow shouted. She threw back her hair and raised a fist at the puddle.

It contracted like the iris of an eye exposed to brilliant light, and then it disappeared. The wind died down, then stopped. The rumbling ceased.

Xander groaned. "Twelve dollars and sixteen cents' worth of fat-laden tasty treats down the drain."

"That was close, Willow," Cordelia said sternly.

Willow nodded and made a face. "I was caught off guard."

Buffy's Watcher smoothed back his hair and pushed up his glasses. It was a habit of his that Joyce now found oddly comforting, a reassurance that she hadn't just gone completely insane.

"That was a breach," she guessed. "A portal." Her heart was pounding so hard she was surprised she wasn't having a heart attack.

"Yes. What we've been trying to explain." Giles regarded the area where the circle had appeared with obvious apprehension. "Willow successfully bound it."

"Well, good," Joyce said uneasily, avoiding the area as she moved to pick up the mess on the floor. Giles dropped to his knees to help her, clearing his throat meaningfully as the kids stood by. At once Willow grabbed an overturned bowl and started gathering up the vast array of cheese balls and potato chips. She sighed softly and handed a broken terra-cotta statuette of a donkey to Joyce, who cradled it gently. Perhaps the girl knew that Buffy had bought this for Joyce on Olvera Street, a touristy Mexican shopping district back in Los Angeles, many years ago.

"Well, yes, the thing is," Giles said, coming up beside her with a double handful of spilled food, "Willow's done this spell many times all over Sunnydale, and what we've discovered of late is that the spells may not be permanent. They are overtaxed, shall we say, and there's no telling if this breach will reopen. Or if so, when."

"Oh." Joyce gazed uneasily at the spot.

"And so, I must restate my suggestion that if you feel you can't leave Sunnydale, nevertheless you simply must leave this house."

Joyce frowned at him. "What if Buffy calls?"

"Call forwarding," Xander said. "We have a guest room." He looked at the others. "So we tell people they've got roaches. They're fumigating." He smiled at Joyce. "With bunk beds and a desk lamp shaped like a cowboy boot."

"Thanks, but I don't think so." Joyce gazed down at the donkey. "I need to be here. This is Buffy's home."

"Buffy would not want you to be in danger," Giles said.

"Well, I don't want her to be in danger, either. But she has to be. And she's my daughter. So I guess I have to be, too."

With that, she burst into tears. She couldn't help herself. She was so terribly, terribly frightened for her daughter.

"I'm sorry," she said. "It's just that, why does she have to do this until she *dies?*"

"If you please," Giles said to Buffy's friends. They stared at each other, then shuffled out of the room.

Then Giles did something for which Joyce was unprepared. He took her into his arms and laid her head on his shoulder.

"Joyce, I know it's difficult," he said, and suddenly, they were very alike, she and this man who had shouldered the burden of knowing that Buffy was a Vampire Slayer, and had kept that secret from Joyce for two years. She sometimes hated him for it even though she understood the reason: her ignorance had allowed Buffy to do what she had to without moments like these.

"When I was her age, I thought I might like to be an archaeologist," she said, her voice muffled against his shoulder.

"Really? I was, for a time," he said. "But I had something else to do. Something more important."

"You were called to be Buffy's Watcher."

"Even so."

She pulled away from him. "And I'm her mother. I guess what we want doesn't really matter. We have to help her." She took a deep breath. "Help her survive."

"Yes." He looked at her steadily. "I wish it weren't so, but it's true."

Tears spilled down her cheeks. "When you have a baby, you have so many hopes and dreams. You never want them to be sad or hurt. Just wrap them in cotton wool and keep them safe forever. I can't help but feel that I've failed her in some way."

"You haven't. She loves you so much." He smiled gently. "She's always going on about your chocolate chip cookies. I must say, they are quite delicious."

"I'll make some tomorrow," she said. "I'll have them ready in case she comes home." Then she finally managed a smile. "And I'll make a double batch."

"Triple?" Xander said from the doorway.

Joyce laughed. This boy in his baggy shirts and corduroy pants was such a mixture of man and puppy dog. Then there was Cordelia, always so overdressed in her high-fashion clothes—today's black-and-gray chiffon dress was no exception—and sweet Willow, in her overalls and sweaters. They were all a combination of seasoned adults who had faced terrors she could scarcely imagine and wide-eyed children learning to deal with the world outside their families and homes.

"Quadruple batch," Joyce said.

Willow smiled sweetly at her and came to her side as Xander said, "If it helps, Mrs. Summers, we're all pulling for her. We'll do anything for Buffy. We'd die for her."

"Hey," Cordelia said, then shrugged. "Well, maybe I would consider getting seriously hurt."

Somehow, amid all the stress and fear, that got them all laughing.

In the little house in Sunnydale. Situated on the mouth of Hell.

Chapter 1

JUST AS ANGEL, BUFFY, AND OZ WERE ABOUT TO LEAVE the ghost roads, the suffering and pleading and furious wraiths of the dead swarmed around Angel, desperate to be set free. In spite of their translucence, for a brief moment he lost sight of Buffy and Oz. With the ghosts whipping past him, lashing out, hurting him—here on the ghost roads, they had the power to do that—Angel felt his face change. His brow began to protrude and his eyes shifted to feral yellow. His fangs extended, and he hissed at the spirits of the dead.

For the merest fraction of a second, not even an eyeblink, he wondered if this was where his soul waited during those times it had left his body. When his soul returned to him, he had no real memory of any afterlife, but some part of him knew that if his soul had somehow ever reached paradise, the curse on him would have allowed him to retain that memory, in order to torture him even further.

"Angel!"

With a bellow of rage and fear for Buffy's safety, Angel spun, his eyes searching the ranks of the gossamer dead for something solid. Something flesh and blood.

There. The Slayer.

Intangible and yet brutal claws raked his back. It made no sense. He could hardly fight them, and yet it seemed they would be able to kill him. Kill them all. Buffy included. Or perhaps not Buffy, for as he watched her now, she spun and with a snap of one wrist, she cracked a ghost into pieces and it dissipated in front of her.

Angel's eyes were wide as he watched her in that tiny moment. She was truly extraordinary. And as he moved to her side, to risk damnation once more with the Slayer, the vampire felt the dread and sorrow of the dead, just a little.

"They're like smoke!" he snapped. "It's almost impossible to connect!"

"Focus on one at a time," Buffy said, her blond hair flying as she spun into a high kick. Her eyes flashed as she glanced quickly at Angel. "I'm all turned around. Where's the breach? Where did England go?"

Angel stared hard at the face of a spirit that reached out for him. Stared into its eyes. Then he shot out his arm, palm flat out, and crushed its face. Buffy was right, but he could take no pleasure or relief from that. Instead, he merely defended himself, and then gazed around, hoping to see the breach, the shimmering portal through which they had seen the British countryside before the ghostly tide had swept them away.

"There!" he yelled, and pointed to show Buffy the way.

They'd been forced away from the breach, the gray nothing of the ghost road flaring white and the firmness of the path beneath their feet giving way to something more nebulous. Now Angel reached out for Buffy and began forging his way toward the breach again.

"Angel, stop!" Buffy shouted. "We can't leave!"

A ghost entwined tendrils of nothing in Angel's hair and snapped his head back, staring into his yellow, blazing eyes.

You must take us with you, take us out of here! We wander here forever, it said, with the voice of the multitude, a chorus of lost spirits. He knew then that these were souls that had been unable to move on to their final rest. But he also knew that whatever happened, the land of the living was not the place for the shades of the dead.

Focused on the ghost's eyes, Angel slammed both palms against its chest, then crushed its face with a hard-knuckled backhand. He whirled on Buffy, who was in a fierce struggle with several other lost souls.

"We've got to get out of here, Buffy," he snarled. "What's the . . . ?"

Then he paused, his eyes darting around the misty nothingness, even as his lips moved and he answered his own question. "Oz. Where the hell is Oz?"

"We can't leave without him!" Buffy shouted.

"Damn it!" Angel roared.

With Buffy at his side, Angel waded through the spirits of the dead off the straight path of the ghost road and into the void of limbo.

Oz crouched, protecting his face and eyes. He whipped his jacket around like a madman, and though it passed right through the spirits who had hauled him roughly from the path, it seemed to disrupt them. Apparently, if you paid enough attention, it didn't take much to take on a single one of these specters. The problem was, there wasn't just one, but an infinite number of them. And they seemed to be diverting him from the path, shoving and scratching and herding him farther and farther from the road.

"Back off!" Oz said furiously. For the first time since the curse of lycanthropy had fallen upon him, he wished that he could force the transformation upon himself. As a werewolf, he'd tear through these things in no time. But he wasn't a werewolf. Not right now.

He could hear nothing but the rustling of the spirits, like the sound of someone slipping beneath their bedsheets, or the soft shush of a woman's stockings as she walks by. His eyes were almost twilight blind, everything around him washed out by the wan, gray light of the Otherworld that was all the illumination available on the ghost road. Only the spirits were visible to him. He could see no sign of Angel or Buffy.

Nor of the ghost road itself. The path that would take him back to the breach. The spirits dragged at him, pushed and prodded, scratched deeply—and yet he didn't bleed. They were moving him somewhere, and wherever it was, Oz knew he didn't want to go there.

"No offense," he muttered, "but I've never been much of a joiner."

With no sense at all of where the ghost road might lie, he had only one choice. It seemed obvious that they were trying to move him away from the others. Oz determined to change course, to move in a direction exactly opposite the one the ghosts were trying to force him into.

Normally, he was a laid-back guy.

Laid back wasn't going to work this time.

With a twist of his arm, Oz swung his denim jacket so that it wrapped around his right hand. He lashed out, concentrating just enough to connect with a nearby spirit that looked particularly nasty. The spook seemed to shatter. In that same moment, Oz ran toward it. Through it. He shivered with a chill that was colder than anything he had ever felt. It made him want to stop, to lie down in the nothing ether and let the cold take him. But no matter how cold it was, how frozen he might feel, he knew there would be heat again. Knew there would be warmth.

With a tremendous effort, he surged through a scattered crowd of ghosts. They reached for him, scratched his face and arms and back, tried to turn him around in the opposite direction. They wanted to stop him. And Oz figured that, like a lot of authority figures he'd known in his life, if they wanted to stop him from doing it, it was probably something worth doing. In this case, something that could save him from being lost here forever.

"Well, all right," Oz muttered, and nodded to himself.

Then the ghosts swept in, wispy as the fog itself, but tangible enough to grab him and hold him. There were too many of them, and they dragged him down into the misty depths of limbo.

Oz choked on the thick spirit mist that surrounded him and managed one word before his voice was taken from him. He said, "Willow."

Buffy saw Oz just as the ghosts dragged him down. Though the air, or what passed for air here, was thick and filmy, and distance could not be judged accurately, Oz seemed to be only a short way off the path.

Next to her, Angel asked, "Did you see?" The tension in his voice was almost too much for her. Angel was overwhelmed, Buffy knew, by the ghost roads and what they represented. Here were the spirits of the dead—some on their way to their final rest, some so restless that they would walk these roads forever. Buffy knew that he had to have wondered— just as she had wondered—how many of his victims walked here, so abruptly torn from their lives that they might never be able to move on.

Buffy turned and gazed into his eyes. She reached out and grabbed his hands with both of hers. "We're going to be all right," she promised. "Watch my back. I'm going after him."

"No!" Angel snapped.

Buffy stared at him. "We don't have any choice. If we lose Oz now, we might never get him back."

And Willow would never forgive me, she thought,

without a trace of humor. She didn't give voice to that fear, however.

Angel cursed aloud, his vampiric features contorting even further into a snarl of frustration and fear. His eyes seemed to glow, even in the colorless world of the ghost roads. With a grunt, he shrugged out of his heavy duster and grabbed Buffy's wrist.

"Don't untie this," he said, as he knotted one sleeve around her wrist. "And don't let it get untied."

With spirits whipping around, lunging in for an attack, only to be rebuffed, Angel wrapped the bottom edge of his coat around his own wrist and held on to it with both hands. He sat on the path and gazed up at Buffy.

She shivered as he looked at her, for he looked like little more than a wraith himself. When he'd sat down on the path, the limbo mists had moved in, and now they wreathed Angel's head as though he himself were a ghost. Only those blazing yellow eyes gave him away.

"If you have to go any farther than the length of this coat," Angel said, staring into her eyes, "then we leave. The world is hanging in the balance, Buffy. I don't want to leave Oz behind either, but if we don't find the heir, it'll just mean he was the first one to go, and the rest of us won't last much longer."

Buffy looked at Angel, turning away only to crush the spiderweb skull of another ghost. When she glanced back at him again, his eyes were narrowed and he was urging her on.

"Hurry," he said, and then he grunted as a dark, hulking ghost swung something that struck Angel in the head.

His gaze never wavered.

Stop! the multitude whispered. *He is ours, now. We will give him back to you once you have aided in our release. Stop now, or we will kill him. The boy is ours by right. We only want to be free!*

Oz felt as though he were falling. The spirits held him aloft, but how high he truly could not have guessed. Altitude might not even be a concept this place was ready for, he considered. His coat now hung loosely in his right hand. Since he had no leverage, no purchase beneath his feet, Oz could barely swing a punch. Still, he tried. He flailed one way and then the other, trying to keep the angry spirits of the lost and lonely dead away from him.

Enough! screamed the multitude. *If the Slayer will not aid us . . .*

Even as the chorus of voices boomed in Oz's head, a ghostly man who looked enormous, as though he might once have been a circus strongman, wrapped frozen fingers of icy mist around his throat—wisps, but wisps of steel. Oz could not breathe. The gray light of limbo began to dim even further as his eyes went wide. He struggled, striking out once more but now losing focus so that the ghosts became immaterial to him again. Nothing but shadows.

Something gripped his wrist. It took him a moment to realize that these fingers were not ice, but warm, human flesh. Then he was yanked roughly away from the ghost who had been choking off his air. Oz gasped, wheezing in whatever was passing for oxygen on the way to the Otherworld.

"Trust me, you wouldn't have wanted him anyway," Buffy said, her voice coming to Oz from out of the gray nothing. "He isn't housebroken."

Then his butt slammed down onto a hard surface and he sprawled sideways. He glanced up and saw Angel sitting next to him, his face bleeding, his hair nearly standing on end. Ghosts swirled around him in the gray mist. The vampire held onto the end of his duster, and the other end was in Buffy's hand—the one that wasn't wrapped around Oz's wrist.

"Thanks." Oz nodded, eyes still wide with amazement. "Part of me would like to respond to that housebroken crack, but do you think maybe we should go now?"

Buffy hauled Oz to his feet. Angel jumped up next to them. All of them were badly scratched and bruised. Angel pointed and shouted something Oz could not hear over the moaning of the angry ghosts, and Oz looked up to see the breach not far away. Through it, they could see a small British village across a green hill. He thought he could hear a train whistle, but then thought it might just be the despair of the wandering ghosts.

"Back off!" Buffy barked at the ghosts. She turned to Angel and Oz and snapped, "What I wouldn't give for a cattle prod right now!"

Without a word, she got them both moving toward the breach. Granted, it didn't take much. The ghosts began to gather at the breach to block their path. There were so many of them, Oz didn't think they would have any chance at all of breaking free. Even through the spectral forms, he could see the world through that breach, the darkened hillside out there, and he wanted so badly to smell the night breeze that blew the scents of earth across the land.

You'll go no farther unless you agree to hold the breach open for the rest of us, cried the multitude.

"Look," Buffy snapped, angrily, "maybe you've got a raw deal. I don't know. But if you're trapped here, the way to get out is to move on to where you're supposed to be. Out there? That's not it. Now back off, or you may never rest in peace!"

Angel snarled, fangs bared, eyes blazing color in the land of limbo and nothing.

A ripple seemed to pass through the cloud of lost souls, and the wispy shades of the dead seemed to become even less substantial. They began to fade, like shadows as the sun emerges from the clouds. Oz thought he saw a look of shame on some of their faces, but most of them only seemed very, very sad.

In seconds, all that remained was the enormous spirit he'd thought was a circus strongman, a ghost who was angry enough to dare anything to escape the sameness of the ghost roads. The thing opened its mouth and tried to scream, but without the support of the multitude, it had no voice. In silent fury, it lunged toward them.

"Go!" Buffy snapped.

Oz and Angel, spurred on by the Slayer, ran directly at the specter. The three of them passed through the ghost as though it were nothing but a shadow. There wasn't even the slightest bit of resistance. But the freezing cold was there, and Oz felt numb and slow as he stumbled the final distance to the breach, practically fell through it, and then dropped nearly ten feet from the split in the night sky to land none too gently on a hill in the English countryside.

A moment later, Angel slammed down next to him. Buffy landed hard on top of both of them, and Oz got a boot in the back of the head.

"Ow!" he grunted, then just lay there shivering as the cold finally began to pass from his body.

"Well," Buffy said with a sigh. "That completely sucked."

Oz was about to respond when Angel stood and started to put his duster back on. As he did so, Angel looked at his hands, reached up to touch his face, and quite obviously realized what Oz had just noticed. Angel looked at him, and Oz shrugged.

"What happened to all the blood?" Angel asked.

For it was gone. All the wounds. The blood and bruises.

"Ghost blood?" Oz suggested.

"They didn't feel like ghost wounds," Buffy said. "But I suppose we should be grateful. What ever happened to Casper? That's the kind of ghost I want in my life."

Oz stood and brushed dirt from his jeans. "I don't know," he said offhandedly, "I always thought Casper was a little too goody-two-shoes. I'd prefer a ghost who could tell the difference between a Gibson and a Stratocaster."

That earned him a baffled look and raised eyebrow from Buffy. Angel didn't even respond. He was staring at the sky and sniffing the air.

"Angel?" Buffy asked. Her concern was obvious.

When he turned to face them, his face was smooth and human. Oz was glad. When Angel got all vampy, it freaked him something fierce. But he wasn't entirely comforted. Not with the grave, brooding look on Angel's face now.

"Sunrise is maybe two hours away. We have no shelter at the moment, and no idea where we are, as of yet," Angel said, and slipped into his duster, almost as though it could protect him from the coming dawn.

"Then we'd better go," Buffy said.

But Oz wasn't listening. He was staring up at the space, ten feet above, where they had appeared out of mid-air.

"Oz?" Buffy prodded.

"Sorry," he said. "I was just thinking that there are so many ghost stories around, it must be pretty common for them to escape. They probably wander around the earth looking for something to hold on to, someone to talk to. It can't be easy to pass over. The ones who do must work really hard at it."

He turned to regard Buffy. "Kind of sad, actually."

When the three of them moved off across the hillside toward the town in the distance, and the train tracks that ran toward it, they walked in silence, broken only by the whistling of a cold, disdainful wind.

Boston, January 27, 1882
The city of Boston was covered with snow. It had been falling for nearly two days and showed no sign of lessening in intensity. Jean-Marc Regnier trudged through the cold, wet whiteness that came nearly to his knees. He squinted into the storm, but the fat,

heavy flakes fell in a curtain all around him. He could barely see the house he now passed on his left, never mind the manse his grandfather had built atop Beacon Hill those many years ago.

But he was determined.

With an anger that had not subsided throughout this long trek across the city, Jean-Marc forged on, sweating a bit now beneath the wool. Snowflakes struck his face and melted there, and he wiped them away from his skin and hair.

At long last, he saw the turrets of the Gatehouse looming ahead, crested with white, like some kind of mad confection. The thought prompted a bitter smile from Jean-Marc. There would be nothing sweet about this visit. Not in the least.

With legs as cold and unfeeling as iron, Jean-Marc dragged himself the last few yards to the doorstep of the home in which he had been raised. The madhouse where he had lived his entire life until only a few months earlier. He'd spent his years as apprentice to his father, learning the ways of magick and the paths of shadows. His mother had stood quietly by, tacitly agreeing with her husband's effort to train his son as a sorcerer. She believed that he was meant for great things. Now a man of twenty-one, Jean-Marc realized that this was a belief held by nearly all mothers about their offspring.

The day he'd left them both standing just inside the doorway of the massive house, Jean-Marc had felt the fetters of what he now perceived almost as indentured servitude fall away.

The role of apprentice magician had not been

enough for him. Jean-Marc Regnier wanted to live a life that was all his own. He was a learned man, of course. His father had seen to that. In the months since his departure from the Gatehouse, he had found meager living quarters far from the spying eye of his father's home, met several young ladies, each of whom had instantly stolen his heart, and had obtained a position as an instructor at a prominent boys' school.

He'd been happy.

Until scant hours ago, when he had received a missive carried to him from his father by messenger. Heaven forbid that the old man might actually step down from his perch above the city and sully himself among the people he had sworn to protect from the unseen horrors of another age.

My son, the note had read, *the time has come for you to accept the responsibility that falls to you as scion of him who guards the gate. The years gather about me like shadows now, and the duty falls to you. Return to the house by this evening. If you stay away, the world will suffer for your selfishness.*

Jean-Marc mounted the steps. At the door, he did not bother to reach for the knocker. Instead, he merely lifted his hands, palms together, and then moved them swiftly apart. As a burst of rosy light emanated from his hands, the locks shattered and the doors slammed open with such force that the hinges screamed and the wood slammed against the walls inside with a bang that shook the foyer.

Trailing tumbled piles of snow behind him, Jean-Marc stomped into the foyer of his father's home. The wind whipped snowflakes in behind him, and blew the already substantial drifts over the threshold. Jean-Marc didn't bother to close the door. With melting snow dripping from his already sodden clothes, he tromped up the wide stairwell at the front of the house, calling for his parents to show themselves. Removing his woolen jacket and scarf, he left them on the steps and continued on.

He found his father in a study on the second floor, among arcane volumes and an eclectic collection of talismans and wards. Though Henri Regnier was more than two hundred years old, he looked no more than sixty. When Jean-Marc stepped into the study, his father smiled softly, painfully, and nodded.

"Thank you for coming," Henri Regnier said, in French.

When Jean-Marc spoke to him, it was in English. "How dare you?" he snapped, sensing the presence of his mother, Antoinette, as she came into the room behind him. She remained silent, however. It only infuriated Jean-Marc further.

"I have a life now!" he shouted at his father. "Whatever mantle you want to pass on to your progeny, you'll have to find someone else to give it to. I don't want it. I don't want to live forever. I'm a teacher, Father. It's a glorious profession. Protecting the world from the horrors of another age is the job for someone who is *from* another age. Chaos will not shatter the world around us if I do not follow in your role as Gatekeeper."

Henri chuckled sadly, but even that was enough to start him coughing harshly into a closed fist. When he looked back up at Jean-Marc, the young man winced and stared closer at his father. A trick of the light, perhaps, but he looked older than he had only moments ago.

"I'm afraid you're wrong about chaos," Henri said, capitulating and speaking English. "If you do not do your duty, it will reign supreme indeed. Sadly for you, Jean-Marc, but fortunately for the world, you have no real choice."

Jean-Marc groaned in frustration, threw up his hands, and turned to leave the room. The only reason he stayed was that his mother blocked his way, and no matter how aggravated he might become, he would raise neither voice nor hand to his mother. Not ever.

"Of course I have a choice," he said through gritted teeth, still looking at his mother, who would not meet his gaze. "I can walk away, Father. In fact, in case it has escaped your notice, I have already walked away."

He turned on his father, anger seething within him, but what Jean-Marc saw made him stop short, his mouth open in astonishment. In what seemed to be the span of only seconds, his father had aged perhaps twenty years. He looked ninety years old, at the least.

Blood dripped from his nose down onto his lips. His eyes were yellow and filmy, and his hands were crooked and arthritic. What was worst, however, were the tears that rolled down his cheeks. In his twenty-one years—a trifle compared to his father's magickally sustained life—Jean-Marc had seen many horrors. But he had never seen his father cry.

It gave him pause.

"Jean-Marc," his mother whispered behind him.

"I'll be with you. I can help you, just as I have your father."

For a moment, he considered it. Then he shook his head vehemently. "I will not!" he shouted. "I won't give up my life for this. I can't."

The tears flowed more freely now, and the Gatekeeper had grown much, much older.

"I'm sorry, Jean-Marc. When it was my turn, I had no choice, either. My father told me that when I was just a boy, so perhaps it was easier for me. With you, there were so many dreams I had for you. I suppose I simply didn't expect it to come around so soon.

"It's part of the house. Part of being the Gatekeeper," Henri explained. "It was a spell my father, Richard, placed on the house not long after he built it."

Jean-Marc stared at his father. "What are you saying?" he demanded.

But Henri could no longer speak. His eyes had sunken in his head, and his face drooped as he stared at his son through eyes quickly losing the last of their light. He could not even respond.

"Your grandfather knew how vital this house was," his mother explained. "Essential to the survival of everything you value in the world. Upon his death, his knowledge and vast power passed to Henri, your father. And when your father dies, as long as you are within these walls, those things will be transferred to you. No one else will have the power or the knowledge to be the Gatekeeper. Don't you see? You must do it."

Jean-Marc stared at his mother in horror. He looked at his father, or what was once his father. Only the gleam in his dark eyes and the rattle of his breathing indicated that he still lived.

"No," Jean-Marc said, horrified. "No!" he screamed. "Give it to someone else."

Then he bolted for the door. Down the hall he ran, then to the landing above the vast stairwell leading down to the foyer. Halfway down the steps, he felt as though he had heard his father's last gasp, and he cried out to heaven for deliverance. Like a shaft of lightning, the magick struck him, worked through him, stood him up rigid and infiltrated his entire body. The knowledge. The power.

Jean-Marc cried out in pain and reached for his abdomen, where his stomach seized and revolted. Doubled over, he fell down the rest of the stairs to sprawl, only semiconscious, at the bottom.

The knowledge.

His father, Henri Regnier, the second Gatekeeper, had died. Jean-Marc now understood, for the first time, exactly what horrors he faced, what chaos he held back from the world.

As his mother slowly began to move down the steps toward him, Jean-Marc Regnier, the third Gatekeeper, buried his face in his hands and wept bitter tears of surrender.

The year was 1999, and the third Gatekeeper, Jean-Marc Regnier, lay submerged in the warm water collected within the Cauldron of Bran the Blessed. The ancient iron cauldron held magickal properties, life-giving ones, which were helping to keep him alive.

Immediately after he had risen from the Cauldron,

Jean-Marc was robust once more, as robust as when he'd only half a century of life behind him. He had a secondary source of magickal life support in the legendary Spear of Longinus, which he was now forced to carry about with him whenever he was not in the Cauldron. But even with the Spear, as the hours went by, the strain of keeping the Gatehouse bound to his will, keeping all his charges in check, made the Gatekeeper age and wither and his magick weaken. Twice a day now he was forced to immerse himself in the warm waters of the Cauldron. Soon he would have to increase the frequency, and he wondered how long it would be before the Cauldron ceased to revive him.

It will not be long, thought the Gatekeeper, as the sun began to warm his home. It was morning, and he relished it. For he knew that each passing morning might be his last.

Dawn had come to Boston only minutes earlier. The Gatehouse had gone relatively unmolested in the time since the Sons of Entropy were defeated within it by the combined might of Gatekeeper and Slayer. But now, outside, a figure in a long, heavy coat stood in front of a brownstone apartment building on Beacon Hill and tried very hard to pretend that, like other passersby, he was not aware of the Gatehouse's existence. Ancient magicks had hidden it from view. Those who walked right by the building did not see it.

Brother Antonio did.

He had flown that very night from New York City, arriving too late to be of any assistance to his brethren, the other acolytes of the Sons of Entropy, who had been vanquished in the great battle. But he served the interests of Il Maestro, and Brother Antonio knew there would be other ways in which he could do precisely that—serve.

Turning away from the house so as to avoid the temptation of allowing his eyes to stray to it, Brother Antonio removed a tiny cellular phone from inside his long coat. He flipped it open and quickly dialed a familiar number, which connected him to a villa on the outskirts of Florence, Italy. The city of his birth. Firenze.

"Antonio," a voice said after the ringing had ceased.

The voice of Il Maestro. He always knew who was calling.

"My lord," Antonio said. "The spell was difficult to construct without drawing the attention of the Gatekeeper, but I have done so. Only Regnier himself remains in the house. Excluding, of course, those things which do not belong to our reality. It was simple to scan them out."

Silence on the other end. Antonio had never liked the long silences that were common to Il Maestro at times.

"The Slayer is gone, then?" Il Maestro asked at length.

"I don't know how, Maestro, since I did not see her leave. Some sorcerous means, perhaps. But yes, she is gone indeed."

Il Maestro laughed dryly. Brother Antonio shivered. It was a horrible sound.

"You may go and refresh yourself. Return to that place this evening at dusk," Il Maestro said. "The Gatehouse is nearly defenseless. I will send more acolytes to follow your instructions. Take that house, Antonio. Otherwise, it will be your blood that fills the cup of my sacrifice."

"Well, that was not so fun," Buffy said softly, as she reseated herself across from Oz at the tiny English pub not far from the bed and breakfast where they'd managed to find a room.

"Your mom's okay?" Oz asked, as their steaming plates of shepherd's pie were brought to the table by a young man with an outdated bob and a scraggly goatee.

"I don't know. She sounded defensive about something, but she wouldn't say what. She kept telling me over and over how fine she was. Which she did not sound. She sounded scared." Buffy looked down at her food, a heap of mashed potatoes and peas on top of something that looked like Sloppy Joes. "I thought this stuff was a pie."

"It's called that," Oz offered. "It must be a British thing."

The village they were in was not far south of the Cotswold Hills, east and slightly south of London. Most of the local economy seemed to be agricultural, but there were several beautiful shops in the town— likely for tourists who were just driving around Great Britain—and Buffy and Oz had peeked into every one of them while Angel slept the day away. Buffy had bought a thick wool sweater. No telling how long they'd be here. Besides, it was on sale.

Though she had called Giles even before they'd all gone to bed that morning, Buffy had had to try several times during the subsequent day to catch her mom—

it was eight hours earlier there, after all—and now, all the effort had yielded one strained and very short conversation.

The proprietor of the B and B, a hugely fat man with a crooked nose and just enough hair on either side of his gleaming pate to avoid being labeled "bald," had been none too pleased to see them at just before dawn that morning. But when they brandished their backpacks and explained that they'd been hiking cross-country and got a bit turned around, the old man softened up some. He probably could see how tired they were.

Buffy didn't think she'd ever forget the weirdly absurd sight of Angel whipping out Giles's American Express card. Surreality at its finest. Still, it had achieved the desired effect. A single room with two large beds, one supposedly for the guys and the other for Buffy. Actually, the grumpy but soft-hearted old innkeeper was also, in Buffy's near expert opinion, quite the lech. He hadn't questioned the sleeping arrangements, but he had given Buffy a look of frank appraisal that had caused Angel to squeeze his hands into fists so tight his nails cut into his palms.

It didn't matter. What did matter was that, with the beds shifted properly, and down comforters placed just so, Angel had been able to shield himself from the sun without too much trouble. To be safe, Oz had made a homemade "do not disturb" sign and hung it from the doorknob, then asked the manager to leave their friend to sleep, as he was very exhausted.

"That was really tasty," Oz said casually as they walked from the restaurant. "I mean, I usually like to segregate my meat from my carbs and my veggies.

Not a bigotry thing at all, you know, but it makes it easier to savor each individual flavor. This was different. A glorious mélange."

Buffy glanced sidelong at him as they walked down the village street, receiving curious but generally friendly glances from the townspeople. She smirked slightly, then reached out and gave Oz a small shove.

"Hey!" Oz protested. "In case you didn't get the flyer, I am not Xander's substitute on this trip."

Buffy nodded, smiling. "Okay, but 'glorious mélange'?"

"Glorious mélange," Oz insisted.

"Didn't the Dingoes go up against them in a battle of the bands once?" Buffy asked.

Oz looked slightly chagrined, but his smile told Buffy that he had expected her to catch the reference. "Okay," Oz said, and shrugged. "And we trounced them. It was cool. Shepherd's pie is a glorious mélange. I can't help it if food imitates art."

Buffy just rolled her eyes and laughed, pressing on. Now that the sun was dropping below the horizon, she wanted to get back to Angel as quickly as possible.

"You think he's all right?" she asked, suddenly anxious.

"As long as nobody stole his sheets, I expect he's sleeping like a baby," Oz confirmed. "A vampire baby, actually."

"Don't even go there," Buffy warned.

"Go where?"

"Smart lad." Buffy laughed. She found herself understanding more and more what Willow loved about Oz. He listened. Carefully. And he pretty much let other people be who they were without judging them. Not that he didn't take your measure. But it was more because he was interested in finding out what it was than that it mattered to him.

He wasn't her type, of course. Not at all. She'd already been in love with one creature of the night as it was, and that hadn't worked out very well.

"Buffy, I need to mention something," Oz went on. "It's about that being all right thing."

She looked at him, waiting.

"See, there's a full moon in twelve days."

"Oh." Which meant they had eleven nights before Oz turned into a werewolf. "Okay."

"Just wanted you to know."

"Got it," she said, inwardly sighing. Oz's time of the month couldn't come at a more inconvenient time. Unless it had been earlier.

At the bed and breakfast, she fished out the room key as they went in through the front door.

They quickly climbed the stairs to the second floor. At the back of the house, a tall window showed the last of the sunlight bleaching from the sky. Buffy used her key to open the door to their room. She slid it open quietly, not wanting to wake Angel if he was still sleeping.

"What took you so long?" he asked.

Buffy looked up to see him toweling off hair he'd apparently washed in the sink. He had his black jeans on, but no shirt, and Buffy's breath caught slightly as she saw him looking like that. So natural. So alive. She remembered that part of him so well, the part that made her forget the vampire within him. But the vampire lurked beneath the surface, evidenced by the tattoo on his back: the mark of Angelus. She winced, felt a stab of loneliness and regret, and pushed it all away.

"Shepherd's pie," Oz reported, quite matter-of-factly.

"E.T. phoned home," Buffy added. "To the mother ship."

"Do we have a car?" Angel asked, turning to pick up his turtleneck sweater.

Then Buffy sensed the sudden arrival of a presence behind her. Felt warm breath, and the kinetic energy of another person in close proximity. Even as the new arrival said, "You do now!" Buffy spun, grabbed the British man by the throat and pinned him to the wall.

"You picked the wrong room, freakazoid," Buffy snarled, and hauled back a fist to break his nose.

"Wait," the man said in a choked voice. "I'm . . . from the Council. You . . . you called!"

Buffy glared at him even as her muscles relaxed and she began to draw back. Behind her, Angel slipped into his shirt and turned to look at her quizzically.

"You called who? The Council?"

"You must be the vampire," the shaking man said, and his thin, angular, scarecrow body rattled with his nerves. Still, he was a brave one, for he stepped forward and held out his hand to Angel. "Ian Williams, sir, at your service."

Williams turned to gaze respectfully at Buffy. "And might I say, miss, that assisting you is one of the greatest honors in my brief career thus far."

Oz rubbed a hand across his upper lip. "I'm sorry,"

he said, "this is all very nice, but did I hear . . . Ian, was it? I heard Ian mention a car, and I can't help but have faith that the two of you heard it as well."

Angel moved a bit closer to their new arrival. "Wait a minute," he said. "Haven't we already dealt with a couple of other interested parties supposedly from the Council who didn't turn out to be what they seemed?"

The brown-haired, hawk-nosed Williams smiled gently. "Indeed you have. Which is why I will give you several other contact names you may use if you want to try to get in touch with the Council itself, or certain members. Also, I did bring along the car and supplies you requested, as well as a set of maps . . ."

Williams trailed off and stared at Angel. "But then, of course, you know Britain rather well, don't you?"

"It's been a long time," Angel said simply, unfazed by the insinuating nature of Ian's comment.

"About this car we requested," Buffy pressed, unconvinced. It was true—they had discussed getting a rental. Oz had a fake ID that made him old enough to sign the papers. But they hadn't gotten that far in the game plan, not here in quaint old Brigadoon.

"Well, I'm using *you* in the plural sense," Williams said earnestly. "I had a call from Mr. Giles, who personally requested Council assistance. He said you were coming to England, but we assumed it would be London."

"Well, yeah, that was the plan. But we had a bit of a detour," Buffy said. Though they'd concentrated on London, the lost spirits who attempted to bar their way at the last moment had made them lose focus. It was also possible that what they had come through was the closest the ghost roads got to London, or, considering the unlikeliness of that, the freshest breach. That seemed more probable.

"Yes, and Mr. Giles phoned this morning to tell us where to find you. Which I did. I'm sorry I was unable to reach you. I rang you, but there was no answer."

Angel shrugged. "I must have slept through it."

Buffy said, "You know we can confirm all this with a phone call."

"Absolutely. And I wouldn't be insulted in the slightest," the man assured her. He crossed to the nightstand, picked up the phone, and held it out to her.

Buffy took the phone. "Thanks. Don't be insulted by the fact that I don't care if you're insulted." Then she stared down at it. The restaurant proprietor had dialed her home phone number for her. She regretted now not insisting that he teach her to do it by herself. "Do I press one first?" she asked, embarrassed.

"Allow me," he offered. With lightning speed, he pressed a series of buttons, then paused. "I'm ready for your number," he informed her.

"I'll do it." She took the phone back and punched in Giles's home phone number. There was a moment of dead air, then ringing. And then Giles's phone machine.

She humphed and passed it back to the man. "Please reboot. I'm trying another number." She looked at the guys. "The library."

Giles answered on the first ring.

"It's me," Buffy said. "Did you . . . ?"

"Ah, Buffy, excellent," Giles replied. "Did Williams find you, then?"

"Well, yeah, but . . ."

"Good, good. Have you any word on— Oh." His tone changed. "How lovely. Of course." Into the phone, he said, "Buffy, it appears I have the pleasure of leading a tour of the library for some remedial English students."

"Oh, you'd better go," Buffy said.

"Phone me when you reach London, would you?" he asked, sounding frustrated.

"Sure. Good luck with the tour."

Buffy put the phone back in its cradle and turned to the others.

"Okay," she said. "Let's go."

But by then, Oz was already picking up his backpack. Angel shoved a few things into his duffel, and they were ready.

"So there's a car waiting, but we have no place to take it," Buffy said softly, so that Williams wouldn't hear her.

Ian Williams smiled. Then he reached long, slender fingers into a breast pocket and withdrew a piece of paper with spidery handwriting across it.

"I think I can remedy that," Williams said. "On that paper is the address of a building in London we believe may actually be a safe house for the Sons of Entropy. It isn't the headquarters, we know that. But it's a first step."

Buffy was sorry he hadn't told her that sooner. Giles would have been pleased.

Oz snatched the paper from Buffy's fingers and handed it to Angel.

"You're a native, basically. You're navigating," he told the vampire.

Moments later, they all carried their bags down the

stairs. Williams followed them down to show them the car they'd be driving. In the darkened village street, it started right up. With a last round of handshakes and thank-you's, they loaded into the car, and drove off, the man merely standing there and watching them go.

To London, Buffy thought. To the beginning of answers.

Chapter 2

IT WAS SHORTLY BEFORE ELEVEN O'CLOCK THAT NIGHT AS they sped along on the road to London. Buffy sat next to Angel in the front seat and winced as he burst past another car and screamed back into their lane as an oncoming car approached.

"That was pretty close," she gritted.

"Buffy, don't backseat drive," he chided, suppressing a sad chuckle. For all the world, they sounded like an old married couple. But for all the world, they never would be.

"Everybody's on the wrong side of the road," she said peevishly. "Why don't they drive the same way as us?"

"Just to be contrary." With a slight smile, Angel put his foot on the gas. He supposed he was allowed to be perverse at times. After all, a demon did live inside him.

She folded her arms and squinted through narrowed lids. "Your driving's terrible."

"You want Oz to take over?" he suggested, making as if to pull over.

"No." She looked over shoulder at Oz in the back seat. "No offense. It's just that if we crash, Angel has a better shot at surviving it than you do."

Oz shrugged. "None taken."

"And I'm touched," Angel teased her.

"What's the rush, anyway?" she demanded.

"Buffy, you can stay up for twenty-four hours," he said. "So can Oz. So can I. But I can't stay *out* for twenty-four hours. So we need to be efficient."

"Efficient, not dead."

She scowled and squinted.

He put the pedal to the metal.

Oz said, "Um, now may not be a good time for this, but I have to go to the bathroom."

"Maybe we should eat again, too," Buffy said. "Fuel up." She narrowed her eyes at Angel. "How are you holding up? We haven't exactly seen any O-positive Stop-N-Go's."

He shrugged. "Maybe on this trip we should institute a 'don't ask don't tell' policy about my feeding— I mean eating—habits." He raised a hand. "I'm not going to feed on humans, Buffy. Which means my choices may be rather limited." He decided not to tell her that their quaint little inn in the Cotswolds had a rat problem. Granted, it was slightly smaller than it had been when they'd arrived.

When Whistler had found Angel in Manhattan, he had been surviving—barely—on rats. With any luck, they might run into a butcher shop. And he was currently weighing the possibility of that British delicacy, blood pudding.

"Oz," Angel said, "when do I make that right?"

"Should be in about five miles or so, I think." He tapped the map that was spread over his knees. "Cool. There's Hampstead Heath. Sting has a house there."

"Byron, Keats, and Shelley used to walk there," Angel said, vividly recalling the three wild-eyed poets. Though they had written poems about vampires, they had never realized they had walked with one.

"Also cool." Oz sounded impressed.

"Look, there's a restaurant," Buffy said, happy to see through the windows that there were actually people inside. "I can check on my mom, too."

The restaurant resembled a gray cinderblock. It was definitely lacking in old-world charm, which, Angel hoped, did not mean they were lacking in rodents. He turned off the road and pulled into a gravel parking lot.

"You two go ahead," he said, dawdling over pulling the keys from the ignition.

Buffy pushed open her door. "Okay."

She led the way; Oz brought up the rear.

Angel got out and slipped into the alley, vamp face morphing at the sound of rustling in the restaurant's brimming trash cans.

Slightly disgusted with himself, he moved into the darkness.

Buffy sounded so far away that Joyce wanted to burst into tears. But she kept her cool, determined not to upset her daughter.

"I'm fine," she insisted, flushing, as though Buffy would instantly know she was lying.

She was not fine. She was exhausted. According to Willow and Giles, the breach in their house might be on the verge of reopening at any time. Knowing that a monster might be disgorged in your living room without warning did not make for restful nights.

Neither did constantly worrying about your daughter.

"You don't sound fine," Buffy insisted.

"Well, I'm worried about you."

Joyce glanced at Giles, who had raised his brows slightly, obviously wishing he were speaking to Buffy himself. He'd come by as soon as school had let out, and Joyce had been glad of the company. Even more so, now that Buffy had called.

"Look, Buffy, Mr. Giles is here," she said, knowing full well she was choosing the coward's way out of a confrontation with Buffy. "I think he wants to talk to you."

"Thank you," Giles said, taking the phone without looking at Buffy's mother. And in that moment, she realized he was going to tell Buffy what was going on. She flared and shook her head.

"Yes, hello, Buffy," he said, pushing up his glasses. "You're all right, then? And Williams gave you . . . yes, well, good. Please keep me informed on your progress. Now listen."

He looked up at Joyce as if to ask for her forgiveness. "There's a breach in your house. We've bound it for the moment, but nevertheless, it's here, and your mother is determined to stay here."

He listened, nodding. "Yes, yes, I quite agree." He

looked hard at Joyce. "Yes. With a friend, for the time being."

His mouth formed a perfect *O*. Curious, Joyce leaned slightly forward.

"It's a thought, yes. I do suppose it may the best thing," he said. His face was a brilliant shade of scarlet.

He handed the phone back to Joyce.

"Buffy?" Joyce said.

"Mom, start packing. You're moving in with Giles," Buffy said sternly.

Buffy joined Angel and Oz in the restaurant. Oz smiled at her and said, "Tonight we're having ploughman's lunch. Which has nothing to do with plows. Or lunch. It's the only thing they'll serve us this late, because the kitchen is technically closed."

"This is a very strange country," Buffy muttered.

"Everything all right?" Angel asked her.

She huffed. "Oh, just that my mom's been living in our house, which has a breach in it that Willow bound, but now it looks shaky, so I told her to go live with Giles. And don't even start with me."

Angel held out his hands. "I didn't say a word. But . . . Giles? And your mom?"

"No, not Giles and my mom. Sheesh. You slept in my bedroom and didn't do anything." She looked away, very much regretting having said that. Because it was true that he had slept beside her bed with her full knowledge before she had known he was a vampire. And he had also sneaked into her room many times when he had been Angelus, taunting her in the morning with drawings he had made of her sleeping, letting her know he could have tried to break her neck and was only biding his time.

She looked down and said, "We should hit the road. I'm not hungry after all."

She pushed back her chair and dashed for the exit.

Angel grabbed her elbow.

"Hey," he said.

She caught her breath. "I'm sorry. I hope I didn't make you uncomfortable back there. It was a stupid thing to say."

"No, it wasn't." He slid his hand down to her wrist, and then to her fingers. "Buffy, I know this hasn't worked out the way we hoped. Neither one of us. But I'd like to know that we still mean something to each other. As friends, if nothing else."

She looked down. "As friends," she said dully. "Nothing else. That's all it can be." She looked back up to him. "And the world may be ending, and we may die, or I might—it'll probably be me first." She shrugged. "Your track record's better—"

She waved her hand awkwardly. An ID bracelet she'd been wearing on her wrist beneath her sweater somehow came undone and clattered to the floor.

Angel bent to retrieve it. Straightening, he held it out to her.

"Keep it," she said. "I got it for you anyway."

She walked on, not wanting to be there when he read the inscription: *For Angel. Always. Buffy.*

They got in the car. Oz came soon after, carrying a brown paper sack.

"You got me a doggy bag," Buffy said, touched.

"A hungry Slayer is a cranky Slayer," he riposted.

"And a sluggish Slayer," Angel added.

"All right." She reached for the sack. "Feed me, Seymour."

They followed the map to a place called Hain Mews, which was not inside London proper. They sped down one narrow alley after another, past row houses of red and white brick and buildings of painted wood and darker brick. Oz liked England. He promised himself he'd come back someday with Willow.

"217 Redcliff. It should be here," Buffy was saying to Angel. "Right here."

"Maybe it's magickally invisible," Angel replied.

"Or indescribably delicious," Oz offered, then shrugged. "Sorry. I'm getting a little punchy."

"Maybe we should find someplace to stay," Buffy suggested.

Then they turned a corner, and there it was. Behind large, elaborate wrought-iron gates, a gabled mansion was silhouetted in the moonlight against banks of night clouds. The roof line was a clutter of turrets and chimney tops, reminding Oz of something the Addams Family might winter in. All the arched windows were dark.

Angel doused their lights as well.

"I'll get the gate," Buffy said, hopping out of the car. She strode up to the twin gates. They were chained together, the chain secured by a giant padlock. Buffy snapped it easily and pushed the gates open.

Angel waited for her signal, got it, and quietly slipped from the car as well. Oz followed close behind.

Five seconds later, they were on the grounds of 217 Redcliff. They crept into a copse and watched the house. All was still. Buffy motioned for them to follow her.

"Keep to the shadows," she whispered.

Oz trailed Angel, who caught up with Buffy. They started motioning in shorthand, and Oz was struck by all the history these two shared. It was dark, and he was beginning to tire, so he had a hard time following what Buffy wanted them to do, but basically it had to do with fanning out.

Suddenly Oz had a sense that they were being watched. He cleared his throat, but neither Buffy nor Angel heard him. He tried to look over his shoulder without being obvious, but he could see nothing.

"Guys," he whispered, but they had moved out of range.

Two years ago, Oz would have completely ignored his unease, chalking it up to paranoia. But since he had met Willow, and through her, Buffy and a lot of stuff that Buffy fought and killed, he had learned to take his instincts seriously.

Stopping, he slowly turned.

Swooping at him with lightning speed was what first appeared to be an enormous bird with black, leathery wings. But as it divebombed right for him, he saw that its head was human, with eyes like white-hot coals.

Suddenly, Oz was slammed to the ground as Angel threw him down, and Buffy landed beside them. Oz grunted and said, "I can't breathe."

"What is it?" Buffy cried.

"The Skree," Angel answered, and Oz knew right off there was more to *that* story. "We've been set up."

"Then let's rumble," Buffy replied.

Angel and Buffy got up fast. Oz could breathe again, and then he was right behind them. He wasn't quite as durable as a vampire or a Slayer, but he'd been known to whale on a few monsters in his time.

The Skree emitted a chilling scream that made Oz's eardrums clatter. And, okay, nasty-looking winged beastie. Welcome to England.

"Okay, bird," he said. "Give me your best shot."

"Oz, get out of there!" Buffy shouted.

At the same time, the Skree slammed Oz in the head and dug its enormous, taloned claws into his denim jacket. Before he knew what was happening, the Skree had lifted him into the air. Buffy and Angel stood below, fists raised in his direction.

"Jump, Oz!" Angel cried. "It's your only chance."

Oz looked up at the bird and down at the receding landscape. Jumping did not really appear to be an option.

But then again, neither did dying.

She was tall, she was lanky, and she could gut a fish in ten seconds flat.

Andy Hinchberger was in love again.

Oh, sure, his fiancée, Lindsey, had torn out his heart with her smiles and her promises, but he had finally faced facts. She was not coming back, and it was time to heal and move on.

Her blond hair pulled up into a wild tuft of a ponytail, Summer Simpson wore a pair of overalls, an olive green T-shirt, and a pair of ratty tennis shoes caked with blood and salt water. She was oblivious to

Andy's stare as she stood at the taffrail of the *Lizzie S.* and smoked a cigarette. The orange glow at the tip was like a running light, a tiny beacon in the night sky as the fishing boat plied the black waters. Maybe she was sending out an SOS: *Mayday, Mayday. I need you, Andy Hinchberger. Right here, and right now.*

It occurred to him that he should go check in with his boss and see if there was anything that needed to be attended to. The *Lizzie S.* was doing something illegal, which was nothing new. The *Lizzie*'s skipper, Dale Stagnatowski, had gone all crazy ever since the death of his son, little Timmy. Not death, exactly, but anybody with half a brain knew that when a seven-year-old goes missing for a year, he's not coming back. Maybe Dale knew it, but his wife didn't, and she was pretty crazy by now herself. Her way of dealing with it was to drink—she thought Dale didn't know, but he did, and it grieved him—and help with the Sunnydale runaway shelter. She spent so much time there that Dale didn't bother going home much anymore.

Dale's way to deal was to push his luck.

Andy took a swig of root beer—he had sworn off alcohol when he had met Lindsey and found he liked the clearheadedness that came with twenty-four/ seven sobriety—and leaned his head on the rail. The deep waters off the town of Sunnydale were said to harbor a sea monster. The town wags claimed the *Lisa C.* had met up with it a couple of weeks before and washed up on shore in matchsticks. So had the first mate, Mort Pingree, in pieces like chicken nuggets.

The official story was that the boat got stuck out on

a sandbar or a shoal, couldn't get free, and had been torn apart by the rocking of the waves. Likewise, Mort's body had been battered apart on the rocks, not chewed on by some big rubber monster from Atlantis. The area was declared off-limits until the shallows was located.

Funny thing was, nobody was patrolling the area for a shallows. Andy hadn't seen a single harbor-police vessel, or any Coast Guard cutter, going anywhere near the quarantine zone. Nobody was pulling out the sonar. Nobody was looking for anything.

Dale figured it was time to make a run and grab all the fish they could while the "wusses" obeyed the rules. So here they were, maybe with a great white down there, or even a lost whale. But not a sea monster. And if the *Lizzie S.* got stopped and boarded by the authorities, it was Dale who would get in trouble, not his two lowly assistants.

As Andy lifted his head and watched, Summer finished her cigarette and chucked it into the water. He smiled and wondered if it would be rushing things to ask her what she was doing once they got back to port. He was curious to know what a classy woman like her was doing working a trawler. Maybe she was mending a broken heart, too. With any luck, she was ready for the rebound. He could always hope . . .

He headed toward the stern just as the fog started to roll in from the sea. It was so thick and so white, almost glowing, that it gave him pause. He stopped on his sea legs, riding the deck as the ocean suddenly got choppier.

The thick mist tumbled over itself as it approached

the *Lizzie S.* It was mounding and spilling over like the crest of a tidal wave, and he found himself racing toward Summer as though she needed to be pulled from its path. But it was just mist.

Behind him he heard Dale shouting, "Andy, what *is* that?"

Then Summer screamed, and it all went into slow motion: The fog, boiling and foaming as it flooded the deck up to their waists. Dale joining them, screaming. The three standing, frozen in shock.

The night was cut by the creak and groan of a vessel, long submerged, as it breached the surface—a ship that should be dead now. Was dead now. White water, kelp, and fish poured off the deck as the fog billowed around it. Its hull was a skeletal ribcage of briny, pickled wood encrusted with barnacles and dripping seaweed. A brigantine from the old seafaring days, with two masts and yards of what looked like winding cloth, it could not be sailing, could not be floating.

From the yards hung skeletons in rows, clattering in the glowing fog and the fierce, brittle wind that rose as the ghostly ship righted itself and made straight for the *Lizzie S.* Blood dripped from the lines, splashing on the deck. And from each splash rose a nightmare.

Bodies took form, but severely decayed, the flesh peeling off faces and limbs in strips. The corpses of men, some missing one or more limbs, several headless, worked the lines. A few were nothing but sun-bleached bones. Others wore watch caps with enormous holes in them, striped shirts in tatters, and sailor's trousers that in some cases were mere strips of cloth. Most of the slack-jawed, dead sailors were missing at least one eye; the fog rolled into and out of empty sockets.

At the bow, the figurehead of a lovely woman raised her arms and shrieked, turning into a hideous crone as the trio aboard the *Lizzie S.* tried to take it all in.

Summer was the first to bolt. She ran along the rail as fast as she could, dashed into the wheelhouse, and slammed the door. Andy felt a warm trickle along the inside leg of his jeans and knew that he had lost control of his bladder.

Beside him, Dale stood, not making a sound, but Andy swore he heard the man's heart thundering.

Then a low, eerie voice reverberated on the fog as the wind whistled its own language: *"Vessel, dead ahead."*

High in the crosstrees stood a figure completely coated in green slime, a spyglass to its eye. The glass was pointed directly at Dale and Andy.

"Steady as she goes," came the ghostly order.

"Aye, sir, steady as she goes."

"Andy, look at the helm," Dale gasped.

Andy made out the raised platform of the poop deck where the ship's wheel was manned by a chalk-white man who appeared to be flesh and blood. Huge spikes had been driven through the backs of his hands, nailing them to the wooden wheel. Caked blood covered his hands. His eyes bulged as he stared straight at Andy with a look of agony.

Then, from behind him appeared a figure that towered over the others, dressed in the somber black of a long-ago Dutch sea captain. Andy could see only the shadow of it, no form. Yet when he looked at it, even from an angle, his blood ran cold. Whatever it was terrified him at a deep, primitive level. Deep inside, he knew that this was something very evil, and that he should get the hell away from it right now.

Yet he stood rooted to the spot as the figurehead threw back her head and cackled.

Then the spines of the ship rammed the *Lizzie S.* on her starboard side. As the vessel listed to port, Andy and Dale slid over the deck, fumbling for purchase on a line, a running light, anything. Andy caught hold of a line and held tight, bracing himself for the sound of a splash.

The fog washed over him like a huge, sodden net. Cocooned inside, he saw and heard nothing.

"Dale?" Andy whispered. "Cap'n?"

A hand touched Andy's shoulder. Sagging with relief, he took it. He gripped his other hand around the rest and pulled himself to a half-standing position.

Then he heard the skipper scream.

From far away.

From very far away.

Standing in the fog, he shouted in surprise.

The hand closed tightly over his.

Dead hands held Summer. She was forced to stand upright beside Andy while Captain Dale stared defiantly at the lord and master of the ghost vessel, otherwise known as the *Flying Dutchman*. If she had not been held so tightly, she would have fallen to the deck in a crumpled heap and never gotten back up again.

"This is your last chance," the Captain said. Nothing moved in his blank, gray face to indicate that he

had spoken. He had no mouth, no eyes. He was only shadow.

And he was terrifying.

"Join us willingly. Or die."

Captain Dale's face was pasty. Sweat ran down his forehead. But he raised his chin and said, "No way."

She was very sorry she had ever taken this assignment. These two losers were low-rent schemers, but they weren't drug dealers. Any idiot in the Coast Guard could see that. She figured this assignment was payback for reporting a fellow officer for drinking on the job.

It looked like it was going to be her last.

"You've made your choice," the Captain said. *"You'll serve as an excellent example to your crew. And when you're dead . . ."* The figure gazed up meaningfully at the rows of skeletons dangling from the yards.

Summer gazed at Dale. The man trembled as lines were wound around his wrists and ankles. They meant to keelhaul him. It was a brutal way to die.

"Begin," the Captain ordered.

Flanked by rotting dead men, Dale was walked to the bow. They made him step onto the sprit, lengthening out the line. Then, as he stood at the very front of the vessel, they jiggled the lines, making him lose his balance. He fell from view and splashed into the water.

"Walk him, boys," the Captain said.

Suddenly an accordion began to play. It was discordant; the sour notes played along the bones of Summer's spine and made her teeth ache.

As she watched in horror, about a dozen of the crew turned and slowly began to drag the lines that had been tied around Captain Dale's arms and legs along either side of the ship toward the stern. They sang a hideous parody of a sea chantey as they inched along.

"Faster, faster," Andy muttered beside her, and she realized he was holding out hope that Dale was going to make it. He didn't know there was only one way for this to go down.

After an eternity, the crewmen reached the stern.

"Raise the lines," the Captain commanded.

Though Summer couldn't see what happened next, she wept bitterly at the cheer that rose among the dead men.

The Skree was a horrible creature. Its wings were leathery black and thickly veined. Its breath was fetid and its eyes blazed with a hellish glow. But to Oz, who even now was being carried aloft in its deadly talons, none of those things was half as disturbing as its most prominent feature. For the Skree had a human face, and a hideous one at that. Its teeth were sharp but canted at odd angles in its mouth. Its brow and lips protruded and its eyes were too far to the sides of its head, giving new meaning to the words *peripheral vision* in Oz's personal dictionary.

But what bothered him most wasn't just how ugly the thing was. It was just that juxtaposition: human face, monster body. It gave him what his aunt Maureen always called "the willies." And these were major-league willies.

Oz thought about all these things in the few seconds it took him to recover from the Skree's attack. He'd been a little disoriented, but now the thing was dragging him off into the sky. He struggled in the thing's talons as, below, Buffy and Angel shouted for him to jump, to escape, to fight. Then he stopped struggling. It was a long, long drop to the ground. But if he got any higher, he might never get down.

Without another thought, Oz reached up and grabbed hold of the Skree's feathers and yanked. It screamed just like a human would have, and Oz felt bile rise in his throat. He'd tried to make light of it, even in his own mind, to lessen the horror of it, but the thing was simply awful to look at—perhaps the most unnatural thing he had ever seen.

It dipped a little, in pain, and scowled at him. It screeched angrily and clutched him more tightly. Oz reached up and grabbed a wing and yanked as hard as he could. The Skree shrieked again, then rose up slightly, before dipping into a crazy, seemingly out-of-control dive at the ground.

Oz's heart beat wildly in his chest. He held his breath without even realizing he was doing so. He'd hoped the winged beast would do something like this, but now that he'd gotten his wish, he wasn't quite sure what to do next. It would try to kill him by shattering him on the drive below. When he was a werewolf, he was stronger than the average bear, but at the moment, an abrupt meeting with the pavement, or even the lawn in front of 217 Redcliff, would be very bad for his health.

"Let me go!" he shouted, and began beating at the Skree's chest, then its face. When he crushed its nose, which then squirted blood, the thing's talons released him, and Oz was in sudden freefall.

He pulled his legs around, tucked, and rolled when he landed. He'd be bruised in the morning, but at least he'd make it to morning. Above, the Skree shrieked in fury and swept up on wide, black wings to circle around for another attack. What Oz didn't get was the lack of reinforcements. Buffy and Angel should have come running when he hit the ground.

"Guys?" Oz asked, and glanced around as he got to his feet, anxiously aware of the circling Skree.

"Oz, behind you!"

His heart trip-hammering again, Oz spun with his fists in the air to see a robed acolyte of the Sons of Entropy rushing toward him from the open door of the mansion at 217 Redcliff. Beyond him, Buffy and Angel were being attacked by several other acolytes who had obviously also come from inside the house.

"On the road with Buffy," Oz said, ready to defend himself. "Oodles of excitement."

Angel and Buffy were back to back in the front yard of the aging mansion. The shadows of the night enveloped them, but the Sons of Entropy had no trouble locating them in the dark. Nor did Buffy and Angel have trouble laying hands on the acolytes. The robes were dark, but white symbols glowed on them in some places. It seemed to Buffy as though these goons had two uniforms: business suits and monks' robes.

But they all had breakable bones.

"I'm getting the idea none of this group are magick-users," Angel said, his voice a snarl that reflected the angry yellow glow of his eyes and the feral rage she always saw in his vampire face.

Buffy slammed a high kick into the chest of the man in front of her, and heard several ribs crack. He went down hard, having difficulty breathing. The next one to come at Buffy—a slender, dangerous-looking man who moved with great swiftness and the discipline of martial arts—cried out like an infant when Buffy broke his left arm.

"Okay, whoever doesn't think this was a setup, raise your hand," she muttered.

"At least these guys aren't much of a challenge," Angel noted.

Buffy glanced over to where the Skree had dropped Oz and saw that he, too, was whupping Sons of Entropy butt. Well, okay, one butt. But he was holding his own. Angel was right. They weren't much of a challenge. Then she caught sight of something moving up in the dark sky and realized she'd almost forgotten about the Skree.

"Maybe they were expecting that thing to be enough to punch all our tickets," she suggested, then nodded at the descending creature even as she knocked another acolyte unconscious.

"I'll finish mopping up here," she said, glancing around at those Sons of Entropy still standing. "Why don't you go get pterodactyl-lad off our backs."

Without another word, Angel turned to face the Skree as it dropped toward them. When it got close enough to reach its talons out for Angel, the vampire didn't move. Instead, he reached out his own hands, grabbed the Skree by the head, and twisted sharply, snapping the thing's neck instantly. Its own momentum made it tumble awkwardly along the ground for several yards before coming to a stop not far from where Oz was dusting off his pants after subduing one of the Sons of Entropy.

Buffy backhanded an acolyte and stared at Angel.

She knew what she must look like, knew the horror that was etched across her face, but she couldn't help it. The thing was a monster, but it had a human face. And the casual way that he had done it, just stepped in and snapped the thing's neck . . . just the way the demon within him had killed Jenny Calendar during the time that his soul had been out of his body.

A tiny chill ran up Buffy's spine. His gaze met her own, and Angel turned away. She thought he looked ashamed.

Buffy returned her attention to their attackers, but had barely resumed a battle stance before all the Sons of Entropy there on the grounds, conscious and unconscious, began to scream in unison. The scream lasted only seconds—seconds in which Buffy, Angel, and Oz could only stare at them—and then all the acolytes, as well as the corpse of the Skree, spontaneously combusted. Each body became an inferno, eyes withering in their sockets to blackened cinders, flesh cracking and peeling to drift away on the breeze like so much tapped-off cigarette ash.

Moments later, all that remained were black splotches on the slightly overgrown front lawn of the mansion at 217 Redcliff.

It was Oz who broke the silence. "Is it me?" he asked at length. "Or did those guys just burn up?"

"Yep," Buffy concurred. "Pretty thorough job, too. I'm getting the feeling that whoever these morons report to, he doesn't want them giving us any more information. At least, nothing he hasn't planned for us to find out." After a brief pause, she added, "Did I forget to say 'gross'?"

Oz smiled, fingered a large tear in his jacket, and then glanced at the house. "I guess we should search the place," he said, without much conviction.

"Search?" Angel repeated, then looked up at the sky. "We've only got a couple of hours until dawn. We're camping here for the day."

Buffy thought about that a moment, then agreed. "I doubt the owners are going to be back in the immediate future," she observed.

Once they had settled in—Angel was pleased to discover a very tightly enclosed wine cellar, to which he eventually retreated with a pile of blankets from an upstairs closet—they did end up searching the house. Other than bedding and the clothing of a number of acolytes, they found nothing. No paperwork with any clues, no photographs, no hint whatsoever at where the main headquarters of the Sons of Entropy might be located. Whoever had taken Jacques Regnier was likely the top dog in the group. But there was no record of who that might be, or where he would reside.

At least, not until Buffy ran across a small leather pouch filled with runestones among one of the dead acolytes' things. Sewn into the lining of the pouch was a Paris address. When Buffy showed it to Oz and Angel, both were more than a bit dubious.

"Y'know, far be it from me to question the motives of, well, the bad guys," Oz began, "but, well, y'know . . . trap?"

"What choice do we have?" Angel pointed out.

"Then there's that," Oz replied, with a nod and a shrug.

"Fine. Paris it is," Buffy decided. "But first things first. We go to the Watchers' Council, tell them they've got worse security than Macy's, and find the jerk who set us up for *this* trap."

Angel didn't smile. He barely even glanced at her.

"What is it?" she asked him.

"You've got to wonder," he said calmly. "First of all, they're probably out of spies, or they would have sent others after you, or Giles. Plus, their security can't be *that* bad. There's got to be one person who started it all, who got the ball rolling by infiltrating the Council in some way. If we can find that person, figure out who it is, maybe we could get some of the answers we need."

"That'd be nice," Buffy said bluntly. "But we don't have the time. There's an eleven-year-old kid out there we need to find and get home to his father. We need to stay focused."

Oz handed Angel a pillow, then started moving toward the living room sofa, where he intended to sleep. Before he even began to lie down, he glanced back at them. "The other option being the end of the world," he said calmly, "I'd have to side with Buffy."

Beneath the headquarters of the Sons of Entropy, Il Maestro had built a special chamber. The bricks and mortar from which it had been constructed whispered of unholy histories: they had been gathered from the execution sites of innocent martyrs, the dungeons of the Inquisition, the famed torture chambers of the de' Medicis and the Borgias. The walls were a deep, unending ebony. There were no windows. Candles provided insipid light, and large portions of the room remained in darkness. At the moment, the air was dank and icy. It was a chamber that celebrated misery and despair—and triumph, for Il Maestro would never again know misery and despair.

So he had been promised.

In the center of the chamber, a pentagram had been inscribed with the blood of a dozen virgins who had been tortured slowly to death. Above the pentagram, a portal glowed an unholy indigo, and within it, flecks of hellfire spit and burst. On occasion, shrieks would echo through it—the cries of the damned, followed by the laughter of demons. It was three times as large as when it had first appeared, many years before.

Soon, it would be big enough.

As Il Maestro sank to his knees and chanted, he closed his eyes and waited. Soon the stench of sulfur filled the room. The stones beneath his knees and shins sizzled with heat. Blisters rose on his flesh, but he endured the pain gladly.

He felt the enormous shadow cross his path. Cloaked in the black of the order of the Sons of Entropy, he lowered his forehead to the baking stone floor and murmured, "Welcome, my lord."

Il Maestro's guest said without preamble, *Where is she?*

"Soon," Il Maestro promised, opening his eyes. But as always, his guest had retreated to the shadows. Il Maestro had never actually seen the dark lord he served. "I will have her soon."

She walked the ghost road. You could have taken her then.

Il Maestro swallowed hard. He was waiting to hear

if his followers had achieved their purpose with the help of the Skree.

"She was stronger than I anticipated," Il Maestro confessed. He quickly held up a hand. "Which means her death will bring us all that much more power when it occurs."

There was silence. Then the demon said, *True.* There was glee in his voice. Pleasure.

Il Maestro allowed a single sigh of relief to escape.

Our hour draws near, the Dark One told him. *With the death of a Slayer, we will open all the floodgates of Hell and I shall walk the earth once more.*

"And I alone shall be spared," Il Maestro said nervously. "I and my dearest daughter."

The demon narrowed his eyes. *You treasure her.*

Il Maestro lowered his head. "Indeed, lord, I do."

That imbues her with great power also.

"No," Il Maestro said, thinking to explain. "Since she grew up in the world outside, I chose to limit her access to the energy that I—and you, my lord—so easily shape and dominate. She is aware of the vastness of the dark forces, of course. But in fact, she's rather untried—"

That is an oversight that can be quickly remedied.

Il Maestro shifted his weight. He wanted badly to rise, but he would not until the great demon gave him leave. "Yes, but—"

There are signs and portents we cannot ignore. Our time to act is nigh. Within this fortnight, we must have a sacrifice that will cause the walls of Hell to tumble. And if not the Slayer, then this girl you love so much.

"No!" Il Maestro cried, shocked.

Yes. If you cannot procure the Chosen One, your beloved daughter will take the Slayer's place.

Il Maestro lifted his arms in supplication, oblivious to the heat and the pain. "Lord, please. Not my daughter. I beg you. All of my acolytes believe they will be kings when the barrier to Otherworld falls and all the monsters of chaos roam the Earth. They do not realize that with the death of the Gatekeeper and the sacrifice of the Slayer, the walls of Hell will crumble as well. They love me, give themselves wholly to me, and I, Master, I give them to you.

"All I ask is that you spare Micaela, that I live with her in your kingdom."

Our bargain was for your life, not for hers.

"She had yet to come into my life when I struck that bargain," Il Maestro whispered.

As I said. The demon chuckled cruelly. *She is so very powerful indeed.*

Chapter 3

Willow STOOD ON THE SIDEWALK IN FRONT OF HER house, impatiently checking her watch. Though she felt two sets of glaring eyes burning into her shoulder blades, she dared not turn around, dared not reveal her anxiety. They would be there, at a window or at the door, watching her. She shuddered.

Cordelia's car screeched around the corner, incontrovertible evidence of her dubious driving skills, despite her constant denials. The little sports car sped up the well-manicured suburban street, and not a few lights popped on in windows up and down the street. It was after nine o'clock. The Rosenbergs' neighbors generally liked all life to have gone into hibernation by then.

Not tonight, Willow thought, and smiled slightly to herself as Cordelia brought the car to a jerking halt at the curb. Willow reached for the door handle but paused as her mother's voice drifted down from the house.

"Don't stay out too late, honey. Think about what your father said."

Willow sighed and turned to wave amiably to her mom. She knew her parents meant well, but they were being so pushy and intrusive on the whole postgraduation issue that Willow was starting to get frustrated, almost resentful of them. She didn't like feeling that way. Of course, she figured it didn't help that she had to lie to them all the time. Like tonight, for instance.

"I will," she called to her mother.

Then she pulled open the passenger door and dropped into the low seat of the car. Cordelia looked perfect as usual, in charcoal gray pants and a blue silk shirt so stylish that Willow firmly believed she'd look silly in it. Cordelia didn't look silly at all.

"Love the outfit," Willow told her as she pulled the door shut. "But aren't you a little overdressed for monster patrol?"

"A little elegance never hurt anyone," Cordelia replied. "Well, okay, maybe Xander once or twice. Besides, I told my parents that we'd be helping Mrs. Summers out at the gallery. If Buffy's mom is going to be covering for you, I thought I should be able to take advantage of her, too."

Cordelia shifted into third as she swung out onto a wider road. Then she glanced at Willow and gave a proud half smile. "Aren't these pants screamingly subtle? I was never really a gray, you know? But there's something about it. Gray, that is. It's the new black."

Willow nodded earnestly. "They're very classy, but . . ." her expression became one of bewilderment. "I always thought black was, y'know, black, and gray was not, okay, new black, but old gray." She stared down at her lap. "I'm always so behind on the clothing curve. Once a fashion emergency, now a fashion fatality."

Cordelia glanced at Willow with real sympathy in her eyes. She reached out and patted Willow's hand. "Next week. You. Me. The mall. Cordelia Chase to the rescue."

"Great!" Willow said, actively happy for the first time in days. Though why shopping with Cordelia should give her a happy she wasn't quite sure. Maybe it was just the mere idea of escaping for a few precious hours the battle she'd been fighting on two fronts, one against the monsters and the other against her parents.

As Cordelia took a turn that would eventually lead them to Sunnydale High, where they were supposed to pick up Xander in front of the school, Willow studied her: her face, the way she moved, the confidence that she seemed to have about her nearly all the time. That was the one thing Willow envied about her—the confidence.

The radio began to play the new Cibo Matto tune, and Cordelia began to bop along. If bopping was something any human body could do to Cibo Matto. Willow thought groove, but bop was apparently possible as well.

"Cordelia, have you decided what to do about . . . I mean, what you're going to do after graduation?" Willow asked.

All bopping ceased. Cordelia glanced at her, but Willow was purposely watching the way the lights gleamed on the hood of the car as they drove.

"You mean with Xander?" Cordy asked.

Willow shrugged. "I mean in general." She turned to look at the other girl. "My parents are really putting the pressure on. They're really trying to manipulate my choice of college. To be honest, it's making me kind of wonder if I even want to go."

"You have to go to college," Cordelia said simply, as if there were no place for an argument. "You're Willow."

Willow rolled her eyes. "See, that's exactly the point. That's . . . Have they been talking to you about this? I'm my own Willow, and nobody knows what I want except me. Okay, and maybe Oz."

She blushed at that, and then grew angry again. "Plus, y'know, there's Oz. They don't approve of my going out with him, but he makes me all tingly inside and I don't care if he's on MTV or playing bar mitzvahs, he's just . . ."

"Oz?" Cordelia asked.

Willow smiled, the thought of her boyfriend soothing her. "Yeah," she said. "Oz."

"Hmm. Who was it that said 'love makes you do the wacky'?" Cordelia asked.

"I think that was me."

"Imagine that," Cordy said archly. "That may all be perfect for you, Willow. And, yes, though it makes me one of Earth's lowest life forms to admit it, Xander has taken away every shred of pride and dignity that I've ever had by forcing me to admit that, okay, I'm kind of attracted to him . . ."

"Forcing you?" Willow asked, confounded.

Cordelia gave her a sidelong glare. "Work with me, Willow. We're bonding."

"Oh, okay." Willow nodded.

"All I'm saying is, I don't know what I'm going to do after graduation. What I do know is that I have goals. Xander, on the other hand, not so much. My parents aren't exactly the inspiration I'm looking for in life, and when they bad-mouth my boyfriend, it makes it all the more important for me to disagree completely."

Her face turned a little steely. "But they're right about one thing. Xander and I are two separate people and that may mean we've got two separate lives to lead. I have my path . . . and if he doesn't want to walk down it with me, he's going to have some hard choices to make."

Willow swallowed hard, her eyes wide, and looked at Cordelia. "Have you told him any of this yet?"

Cordelia kept her eyes on the road, her mouth set in a tight grimace. At length, she spoke without turning. "I don't want to," she confessed.

"You don't want to hurt him?" Willow suggested.

With a small chuckle, Cordelia glanced quickly at Willow. "Have I ever been that tactful?" she asked. "All along, it's been a struggle. He was in love with Buffy. He has this weird little fascination with you. Now I think it's just the whole slaying thing, the whole hero thing, that's got him."

Her voice dropped to a whisper now, Cordelia said, "I guess I'm just afraid that when the time comes to choose . . . he won't choose me."

They rode in silence for a moment, and then

Willow said, "What bothers me the most about graduating is that it's such a sham. I mean, all my life my parents and teachers and everyone have told me that graduation and growing up means freedom. You can choose your future, what you want to do with your life, and all that."

She frowned. "But at the same time, they've trapped you and I guess you've kind of trapped yourself with all these weird expectations of what you need to do with your life in order to succeed. Maybe that's why I'm so into Oz. He seems so unaffected by anybody's else's ideas or expectations."

"Yeah, that's Oz," Cordelia agreed.

Willow shrugged. "Graduation's supposed to be all about choices. But I almost feel like so many people are telling me what I'm 'supposed' to do that all the choices are taken away."

"You're just living in the wrong generation, Willow," Cordelia assured her. "If you'd been born a little earlier, you could have just taken a year off and followed the Grateful Dead around America."

Willow brightened considerably. "Yeah. Maybe I could still do that."

"It might be hard. That Cherry Garcia guy is dead."

Depressed, Willow slumped back in her seat. The school wasn't far now, and she thought of Xander.

"What about your boyfriend?" she asked. "What's he going to be when he grows up?"

On the front lawn of Sunnydale High, Xander bounced on his heels, looking out into the darkness for spookables. Every once in a while, in order to feel a little bit more invincible while Sunnydale lacked a Slayer, he whispered to himself.

"I'm Batman."

It didn't really help, but it was fun.

Not too many cars drove by on the road. Very little happened in this part of town at night. Now that he thought of it, Xander amended that thought. Very little happened anywhere in Sunnydale after dark. There wasn't much of a town to speak of. And let's face it, despite the influx of people any sleepy little Southern California coastal community was likely to get in a given year, the population never seemed to go up. Whoever did those surveys to figure out the highest death rates in America was obviously not digging too deep.

A town that sat on top of the Hellmouth needed a Slayer. And as good as Buffy was at her job, she often needed a helping hand to combat the forces of darkness. But Xander was quickly discovering that the Hellmouth without Buffy around was just no damn fun at all.

"I'm Batman," he whispered to himself again, glancing around in the darkness at the front of the school, wondering what was keeping Cordy and Willow. "I'm Batman."

A sudden groan behind him made Xander spin, whipping a stake he'd been carrying out from inside his coat. What he saw made his eyes go wide with surprise and fear. It was ghouls. Five grotesque, green, stooped-over, withered, nasty-looking, flesh-eating ghouls. And he'd seen these particular ghouls before, back at the Gatehouse. Behind them, a breach in reality shimmered in the air, and Xander realized they must have just passed through. Things must have been getting crazy at the Gatehouse again, and the Gatekeeper couldn't contain them. The Hellmouth drew them along the ghost roads, right here to Sunnydale.

Right to Xander.

A white-haired ghoul began to shamble toward Xander. "I . . . remember you," it croaked. "I remember the way you smell."

"Okay! That's the last time I buy Obsession for Ghouls," Xander said nervously, waving the stake in front of him. "Stay back. I'm warning you. You don't even know where you are, guys. This is Slayer country."

The ghouls chuckled to themselves. The white-haired one moved toward Xander and the others started to circle around.

"We know the Slayer's scent from the home of the Gatekeeper," one of the others, a ghoul female, whispered at the back of the pack. "She is far from here."

Xander tensed, glanced around, and realized that in hesitating, he'd allowed them to cut off his chance of an easy escape. If he ran now, they'd be on him in a second.

"Okay," he said, holding up his hands. "Maybe you haven't heard this, but . . . I'm Batman."

He rushed at the ghoul ahead of him, stake ready to strike. The green-fleshed old man gnashed his teeth and reached for Xander's face. With a yell of both fright and rage, Xander knocked his arm out of the way and slammed the stake into the ghoul's chest.

Nothing happened. The ghoul grabbed Xander's

shoulder in an iron grip, and his other hand reached for Xander's hair. Around them, the other monsters moved in.

"Okay, chalk that up to a failed experiment," Xander muttered to himself. "Color me screwed."

The ghoul dragged Xander's face toward its open maw, where gleaming razor teeth lined a rotted throat. It was a view he hoped never to have again. If he survived.

Xander reached out and grabbed the ghoul in a similar hold, slammed his head forward and gave the hideous creature a massive headbutt that echoed with a resounding crack across the lawn. They both stumbled backward, away from their struggle. But Xander merely moved into the grasp of two other ghouls, and now more teeth were reaching for his flesh.

Xander began to panic. He was quite on the verge of screaming when a female voice called out something in what he assumed was Latin.

The ghouls all froze in place, unblinking, unbreathing. If they ever did breathe, of which he was not at all certain. Magick. Someone had cast a spell to stop the monsters, at least for the moment. A huge wave of relief swept over him, and Xander turned toward the school, in the direction from which the voice had come.

"Willow, have I ever told you that you are the greatest . . ." he began, and then he froze.

It wasn't Willow.

In front of the steps leading up to the school's front doors stood an attractive blond girl with whom Xander and Buffy and friends had had several run-ins before. She was a friend, most of the time. She was also Wendy the Good Little Witch. Or she would have been, if her name had been Wendy. It wasn't.

"Go on, Xander," Amy Madison said brightly. "I may not be Willow, but you can still tell me how great I am."

Xander looked away from Amy and glanced at each of the ghouls in turn. He shook his head in amazement, then nodded, mostly to himself. To Amy, he said, "Well, yeah. Pretty great. You get a big a thumbs-up for your timing, too."

"Thanks," Amy said casually, and walked toward him.

He looked at her, not exactly certain what to say. Amy's mother had been a pretty wicked witch, until she ended up exiling herself to parts unknown. Then, last year, it turned out Amy had been studying up on witchcraft herself, and not doing too bad a job of it either. She knew Buffy was the Slayer, knew the whole deal. But she'd never really been part of their group. Just someone they nodded to in the hall or borrowed homework from, when Amy bothered to do her homework.

She wasn't the type to police Sunnydale for creatures of darkness.

"So, Amy," Xander said, as she made her way across the lawn toward him. "What brings you out tonight? Looking for a prince to turn into a frog? A little girl with ruby slippers? Maybe a—"

"Note to self," Amy said wistfully. "Xander still thinks he's funny. What, Harris, you didn't notice that Sunnydale's having a once-in-a-lifetime monster mash, and the Slayer's conveniently out of town? I noticed. I'm not going to lose sleep over it, but if I see something not quite human trying to eat somebody I know . . . well, I figure I have to lend a hand."

Amy came to a stop right in front of Xander, put a hand on her hip, and smiled broadly. "And by the way, you're welcome."

Flustered, Xander said, "Oh, right. Thanks. But what do you mean, *'thinks* he's funny'?"

With a shake of her head, Amy pushed past Xander and kept walking straight out toward the road.

"They'll be coming around in a few minutes," Amy revealed. "You might not want to be around when that happens."

Then she crossed the street, moved into a tall line of shrubbery, and was gone. Xander stared after her a moment. Maybe she wasn't going to join the Scooby Gang, but he thought a lot of what she'd said was just talk. She was out tonight because there was enough insanity going on to endanger the people she cared about. Xander was glad. It was a bit easier to face the horrors now that he knew that—at least for tonight— he and his friends weren't the only ones out there.

A few seconds later, as Xander was looking for something heavy enough or sharp enough to do serious damage to flesh-eating ghouls, Cordelia pulled up in front of the school with Willow in the passenger seat, staring wide-eyed at the odd display on the grounds.

The girls jumped out quickly and slammed the doors. They raced over, just as Xander was walking toward the paralyzed ghouls with a brick in his hand.

"Hey, guys," he said, by way of greeting.

"Xander, what's going on?" Cordelia demanded. "What are those things?"

"What things?" Xander asked innocently.

"Those things!" Willow said, pointing. "They're ghouls, aren't they? Why are they . . . how did you do that?"

Xander glanced over at the ghouls, then looked back at Cordelia and Willow. He smiled mischievously.

"Haven't you heard?" he asked, his expression suddenly turning grim, his voice low and gravely. "I'm Batman."

Both girls sighed and rolled their eyes. They exchanged a glance that had him wondering, but not for long. It was time to take care of Sunnydale High's new lawn ornaments before their stomachs started rumbling again.

The fog rolled into the harbor of the town of Sunnydale. Looking out to sea, Dallas Mayhew wondered if he would be cut from the team if he didn't make morning practice. He was exhausted, and he'd been drinking beer since sundown. He had no idea what time it was, but he'd guzzled a whole six-pack. When he was younger—like last year, when he was just a junior—it wouldn't even have fazed him. Now he was an old man.

And Sunnydale's best running back. Coach would probably overlook another missed practice in his case.

Maybe what he'd do instead is go home and get some sleep.

Then he could come back here tomorrow night with some of the guys and do it all over again.

If he could find his way home in this fog.

In her father's villa in Florence, Italy, Micaela Tomasi stood staring out the window of a room she had once loved but which she now could think of only as her prison cell. She was, indeed, a prisoner here. Her father, the man whose followers called him Il Maestro, had taken her in when she was a young girl and trained her in the ways of chaos. But, as a part of his grand scheme, she had later been raised by a family of Watchers and become a part of the Watchers' Council, only so that she might one day betray them.

Now she had. Not only the Council, but the current Watcher himself, Rupert Giles. Micaela was quite fond of Giles. She had been sent to investigate him, distract him, steal from him . . . but she had no idea that there had been others sent along as well. To kill him. Fortunately, Rupert still lived. But as far as Micaela's father was concerned, his days were numbered.

Her father's dreams for the world had been her primary instruction as a child; they had been the foundation on which the rest of her life had been built. But during her years with the Watchers' Council, first as an apprentice and later as a full-fledged Watcher—preparing for the day when the girl she had been assigned to might be called to become the Slayer—Micaela had learned that the Watchers' Council stood not merely for order, but for a just order. A planet of free people, cleansed of Hellish evil whenever and wherever possible.

Yet it wasn't until she'd recently returned to her father's home and witnessed, firsthand, precisely how savage and brutal he had become, that Micaela truly realized that her father was a part of the evil the Council so vigorously opposed. If she had kept to the path she had been on, she would have been irrevocably tainted. Now . . . it was a life she wanted nothing to do with.

But she couldn't leave. Her father would never allow it. As much as she believed he did love her, despite his profound evil, Micaela knew that he would see her dead before he would see her siding with his enemies.

She was still staring out the window nearly an hour later, sipping a sweet wine made decades earlier from her father's own vineyards, at the magical light cast upon the city, the Duomo lustrous and gleaming in the distance. There was a light knock on the door. Micaela turned and began to walk toward it, but already it was opening.

Suddenly frightened, she stopped in mid-step, uncertain what course of action to follow. None of her father's acolytes would dare enter her private chamber, even after a discreet knock, without express permission. This man made no effort to hide himself. Though he was silhouetted in the doorway, Micaela recognized him immediately.

"Albert," she said, surprise in her voice and in her eyes. "What are you doing here?"

The acolyte magician entered her room as though they had planned some lover's tryst—a thought which did not entirely offend her. She had known and admired Albert for quite some time. But recently, everything had changed. For all of them. Micaela had seen things she never ought to have seen. She had witnessed her father's physical cruelty to others, on an almost inconceivable level, and knew now that, at the very least, despite his many claims, there was nothing holy or spiritual about his work. He was a monster, pure and simple. And the acolytes—the Sons of Entropy he had always called them—were his servants.

But perhaps not all of them. Albert smiled as he came to her and held her hand tightly in his.

"We don't have much time," he whispered. "Not tonight, but soon, I'm going to be leaving here. I'd like to do it with all my limbs intact and my brains still inside my skull."

Micaela only stared, hope rising within her, hope she was afraid might be so easily crushed.

"I have seen your suffering, Micaela," Albert said. "I have prayed that when I flee, you will be by my side. If Il Maestro is an angel of the future, he is the angel of darkness. But you, Micaela. You *are* an angel. I believe . . . I believe I am falling in love with you."

For that, Micaela could not think of a single cogent response. But when Albert came forward to wrap her in his arms, she consented easily, and felt, if nothing else, that she was no longer alone.

Chapter 4

THEY WERE BACK.

The silvery moonlight shining through her gossamer form, the spirit of Antoinette Regnier pulled back the curtains in the window of her son's bedroom in the Gatehouse. Hooded figures swarmed over the lawn of the Gatehouse like vermin. So many, crackling with magick as they looked for a fissure in the protective barriers her son had cast around the Gatehouse. It cast a shudder of dread down her spine, a shudder that was echoed behind her by the rasping cough her son mustered from time to time.

He had crawled into the great Cauldron of Bran to replenish his strength and was lingering there. In his wrinkled, veined hands he limply held the Spear of Longinus, one of the most powerful weapons of all time. It was said that no warrior who held it could be defeated in battle.

Perhaps that was no longer true, for it appeared that death would defeat her son, and very soon. He had been able to replenish his strength by submerging himself in the Cauldron thrice daily, but they both sensed that the time was coming when that would no longer restore him.

Her little boy, now a rapidly aging man, would die.

She began to tremble, anticipating ruin: the end of all that was good, the end of the world as it was known. She told herself to have faith; Jean-Marc would not fail in his duty. He would live until her grandson was brought home. Jean-Marc was his father's son, and Antoinette had loved and trusted Henri Regnier with all her body, spirit, and soul.

She remembered even now the day she had met Henri. Allowing her mind to wander for an instant, she traveled back in memory to the place where her heart had been won with a mere look, and a touch . . .

"They say he's just the wickedest man," whispered Antoinette's lovely American cousin Marie, as they both endured the torturously tight lacing of their corsets by dark-skinned girls who never spoke a word. Marie's blond hair was crimped into ringlets that framed her face like filigree; Antoinette's raven-black tresses hung loose—not the fashion of the day. And yet, the young men of her acquaintance whispered often to her that they preferred her simple, raven coiffure to that of all other ladies. A lie? Perhaps. Did it matter?

Not in the least.

Marie continued, "They say Monsieur Regnier has, you know, a *special friend.*"

Antoinette shrugged, feeling very superior, very French, about such matters. "A handsome man in the prime of his life? Why would he not?"

"Antoinette Cormier, you shock me to my bones!" Marie shrieked, batting her. "Don't you ever let my *maman* hear you talking like that!"

Antoinette grinned. *"Mais non,* I never will. But I say to you now, *chère cousine,* in France we accept that men have appetites that may not be satisfied simply by dining at home."

"Appetites!" Marie was thoroughly scandalized. "How can you talk so!"

"Some women also have large appetites," Antoinette added, delighting in the effect she was creating. "Many women hunger on occasion. Perhaps I. Perhaps even you."

Marie batted at her cousin. "Antoinette! I declare, you are a wanton creature with no morals. I am a lady. I would never *remotely* wish to do . . . what you are suggesting . . . *oh!*"

The corsets done, the petticoats came next, yards of them, and then the superb velvet dresses Antoinette had brought from Paris.

Then—it was crystal-clear in her mind, even now in Boston with the Sons of Entropy gathering below, even with Henri dead over a century—the two cousins, together with Marie's parents, had met Henri Regnier at the fanned wrought-iron gates to his home, aptly named the Gatehouse. How dashing he had looked, all in black, with his dark hair and mustache. How graceful his leg as he bowed in his old-fashioned way, how cultured his beautiful French, although he had assured them he had been born in Italy and had lived much of his life in England.

The party was not to be held inside his home; indeed, he did not so much as invite them inside it, which was odd indeed and, one might venture, very rude. The gathering was most strange and most intimate. For it was a moonlit garden party for only a handful of people. More curious still, the other guests appeared rather nervous in the presence of the cousins and their relatives. From their glances and appraising looks, she had the distinct impression she and Marie were being inspected. And it was then that Antoinette understood precisely that the two girls were being offered as potential brides for the mysterious and charming Henri Regnier.

Marie saw none of this, and she chattered on about the lovely ice sculptures and the petits fours and the champagne. But across the lawn, below the moon's gaze, Antoinette held her head high as Henri Regnier stared at her without moving. There was something about him that held her, captivated her. There was an air about him of something more complicated than high society and the cut of his evening clothes.

She found herself longing for whatever it was, and whatever he was.

Then he crossed to her and bowed over her hand.

"Mademoiselle," he said breathlessly, "I believe that you have come for me. Would you walk?"

"Mais, oui, m'sieur," she had replied, and followed his lead without a thought to taking along a chaperone. Without wondering why none accompanied them.

Ignoring Marie's arch quip in her ear, "Why, dear

Cousin Antoinette, I believe your stomach's growling."

And yes, there was a hunger between them. It was a passion that transcended matters of the flesh and of the earth. For beneath that moon, in a garden scented with roses, he poured out his heart, weeping once, speaking of all the things forbidden for anyone but a Regnier to know. The other guests? Illusions. Aspects of himself, whom he had sought out with his magick, casting runes, gazing into crystals.

"How, I do not know, but you are linked to my house," he said.

Then he took her in his arms, and their pact was made.

Jean-Marc was born three years later. Despite magickal assistance, the birth was long and painful. And on that night, Henri held his infant son in his arms and wept, "I am so sorry. Forgive me. You have yet to speak a single word, but your fate is sealed."

Not long after that, a horror came to Boston Harbor. And it was that horror which sealed Antoinette's fate as well.

Giles stood at the window of his condo, watching the two representatives from the Watchers' Council who were ostensibly guarding him. They had shown up that day, and a quick chat had unearthed several disturbing facts.

The first, that no one had seen Micaela and that the Watchers' Council had officially declared her dead.

Giles grieved, but he did not give up hope. The second, that neither man had ever heard of Matthew Pallamary. A fact that surprised Giles not at all. The man had obviously been sent to retrieve him somehow, rather than to kill him. But for what purpose, he still did not know.

Finally, that only in the last few hours had they received word that Ian Williams—a household servant at the Council headquarters—had disappeared.

But of course he had. After all, since the Council had dispatched guards to watch over Giles, Williams had to realize that they would reveal Pallamary as an impostor.

Williams had personally vouched for Pallamary.

Unfortunately, Williams had also been in contact with Buffy, Angel, and Oz in England and sent them on to London. He prayed it was on a fool's errand and not a trap. Giles had no way to reach them until they phoned in, and he had been on edge ever since. Joyce seemed to sense his unease, but he had pointed out his new "guards" as the source, rather than reveal his anxiety about Buffy's safety.

At last the phone rang. It was Buffy.

Hovering about, Joyce Summers hung on every word he spoke into the phone, and he tried to signal to her that he would give the phone to her once he was finished speaking to Buffy. Her fear for her child was palpable, and Giles wished there were something he could do or say to allay her fears. But it would be dishonest indeed to tell her not to worry.

Buffy said, "So, this Ian Williams guy set us up to be eaten by the—Angel, what was it called?—I don't know, eagle monster thingie, and it nearly ate Oz. And the Sons of Entropy showed up to take care of us in case the eagle monster didn't, only they got burned up on the front lawn."

"Indeed." Giles was deeply troubled.

"Indeed indeed," Buffy said angrily. "Your Watcher buds cannot be trusted."

He sighed and looked out the window. One of the bodyguards hailed him. He gave a wave back.

"Where are you now?"

"The Sons' mansion," she said. "Phone's probably tapped, but hey, let's live dangerously. Since we are living dangerously already, Giles." She was furious, and he didn't blame her.

He pushed his glasses up and considered his next words carefully. "For the moment, we'd best assume that the security of the Watchers' Council is compromised. There may be another leak."

"Their whole roof leaks, as far as I'm concerned," she said.

"So I advise you to steer clear. As shall I," he added. "We'll have to play this close to the vest. Too much is at stake."

"I'm not loving this," Buffy said sourly. "Someone's been killing the great Watchers of Europe—and Japan—and I hate you not having protection."

"Why, Buffy," he began, touched.

She continued, "Because my mom is living with you." Then she actually chuckled, and he found himself admiring her immensely. And not for the first time. Perhaps this Slayer was more unconventional than the others before her—all right, there was no "perhaps" about it—but she was enormously witty and courageous in the extreme. He truly did not believe a better Slayer had ever lived.

"I shall be careful for her sake," he added.

"Good."

"She's quite anxious to speak to you," he added. "Shall I put her on?"

Then he left the condo and took the stairs down through the foyer and into the street.

The two guards regarded him with friendly eyes.

"Lads," he said by way of greeting, "I'm so very sorry to tell you this, but it seems you've been discharged."

Boston, 1875

The fog rolled over Boston town. It smothered the harbor and the Common and Beacon Hill. Mournfully the foghorns warned ships at sea of the danger. But it was not the fog that posed a mortal threat to all who ventured near it.

It was what lurked inside the fog.

One midnight, Henri turned to his wife, Antoinette, as he pulled on his greatcoat and placed a rose quartz in his left pocket. In the right he placed a gilded sphere decorated with Crosses of St. Birgit. Inside lay a piece of parchment on which prayers of protection were inscribed in Latin, Hebrew, and French. It was a talisman that his father, Richard, had taught him to make, and that had seen the Regnier family to the New World.

"So many times I should have been dead," Richard had told him, at the time finally, terrifyingly, on his deathbed. "Such as this protected me." He had sighed. "Had Catherine de' Medici listened to me . . . but she is dust now. As are all the children Fulcanelli finally permitted her to have."

"What comes after for us, Father?" Henri had begged to know. "After all this, are we, too, but dust?"

"We are duty fulfilled," Richard had answered soberly. He looked older than the dead, his lips and hands dust-dry, his face the color of graveyard dirt. "We are a testament to all that is good."

"To a life unlived," Henri had said wistfully.

"To a life given in service," Richard had replied, placing his hand over his son's. "Never forget that to die for others is the highest purpose a person may achieve."

Now, on Beacon Hill, Henri said to Antoinette, "I'm off now. Will you pray for me?"

"As always." She reached on tiptoe and kissed him on the lips.

He closed his eyes and bowed his head, feeling completely unworthy of this woman. "I feel that I misled you, Antoinette. I did not fully disclose to you the misery of your life as the wife of the Gatekeeper. I wanted you so badly. I needed you."

She smiled. "I knew. I saw the agony in your eyes, *mon cher*. The loneliness." Her smile was tremulous. "And I knew you must have an heir."

"That is not why—"

She stilled his mouth with her hand. "Henri, lies are unworthy of us both. You had to marry. I was the fortunate woman you chose."

"Mais—"

"Are you seeing your death tonight?" she asked anxiously. "You speak as though we'll never see each other again."

He turned away for a moment, and then he nodded. "Dearest Antoinette, I must confess that I do."

Tears welled as she shook her head. "Then you cannot leave this house."

"I must. The fog harbors a great evil. If I don't bind it, it will overtake this city, our home."

She looked up at him, begging him with every fiber of her being not to leave her. "Perhaps this time you can find a way to send the monster back."

He put his hands over hers and kissed her forehead. "Believe me, love, always have I tried, and my father before me." He gestured to the house around them. "I have sought for over a century the means to make this place a real home, where laughter echoes down the corridors, and not the enraged shrieks of caged monstrosities. At every juncture I have failed."

The tears came then, hard and bitter. "And if you die tonight, what will happen when the next horror comes?"

He was silent for a moment, and then he looked at her. "Jean-Marc is young, but he is my son."

Her sobs grew harsh. "And mine as well. You cannot leave him fatherless so young. He has too much to learn."

She laid her head on his chest and wept. "I beg of you, *ma vie, mon âme,* he is my only child."

After a time, her sobs quieted, and he said, "Antoinette, there is something I can do for Jean-Marc. But it would be terribly unfair to you."

She looked up at him. "Tell me to pull my living heart from my chest for him, and I will not hesitate."

He took a breath. She saw grim purpose in his expression and for a moment, she was terribly afraid. Then she stilled herself and waited to hear what he had to say.

"I can bind you to this house, for him. When you die, you will not go to the rest you deserve, but care for him beyond the grave. You will walk as an earthbound spirit until his legacy is assured."

Resolutely she squared her shoulders. "And do you need to kill me to make this happen?"

His look of shock reassured her, and she held out her hands. "In any case, I consent, and I insist you perform the ritual before you leave this house."

After it was accomplished, Henri bade his wife an emotional farewell and took himself down to the fog-covered harbor. Alone he rowed, loath to admit even to himself that performing the binding ritual on Antoinette had sapped his strength.

Yet there was nothing to be done for it now. For as he continued to press on into the fog, the lantern at the bow of his little boat cast a beam on something more substantial than the roiling mists.

As he had seen in his runes, it was the rotting hulk of the *Flying Dutchman*.

And the voice of the Captain called to him: *"Henri Regnier, have you come to sail the hellfire seas with me?"*

A chill shot down Henri's spine. He had known that his approach would probably not go unnoticed, but he had not anticipated that the specter would know who he was. This did not bode well. Nevertheless, he rose up in the boat and spread his arms. A soft rose-crystal light glowed around him; tendrils of magick crackled about him and penetrated the fog. His voice steady, he began to intone a spell of binding.

"No!" the Captain shouted through the fog. *"You dare not, Gatekeeper. Join us or die."*

Henri pressed on, concentrating on the words. The rose burned more brightly, and the fog began to stink of smoke. *"Bind this ship and her crew to me and my house. In the courtyard of my manse, trap this hellish vessel and the dead who walk her rotting planks."*

"Ram him," the Captain ordered. *"Bring him aboard."*

The *Dutchman* shoved the rowboat backward. Henri fought to keep his balance. Fog poured down on him and as it touched his flesh, it began to sizzle. Blisters rose on his face and the backs of his hands, and still he sent the rose glow forth, determined to burn away every trace of the fog as he bound the vessel that hid inside it.

"I bind thee. By the gods of light, I hold thee," he said. *"By the power of my name and my house, which is Regnier, I imprison thee."*

The Captain shouted, *"Sing, boys. Drown out the sound of this foolish nursery rhyme."*

The fog ignited, flames shooting like comets across the upending bow of Henri's sailboat. And the vast, decaying cadaver of the *Flying Dutchman* presented itself to him. Dead men—if the corpses of dried gut and bones could be called that—staggered on the canted, filthy deck, their eyes—if they had them— fully fixed on Henri. Jawbones sawed as they sang a chantey, their voices shrieking like a brittle gale:

> *Send these bones to Davey Jones,*
> *Walk him, boys, drag him, boys.*
> *Send these bones to Davey Jones.*
> *Drag him down to hell.*

They came for him then, leaping over the sides of the *Dutchman* and splashing into the water. He fought back with all the forces of his magick, creating a barrier between himself and his adversaries, as he had countless times before.

The *Dutchman* groaned forward, shattering the barrier, and pitched him into the ocean.

He shrieked in surprise and pain as the water chewed like acid through his clothing. Strips of flesh unfurled from his body. He went down, swallowing water that tore holes in his internal organs.

The pain was unimaginable. Unendurable.

"Join us, and it ceases," the captain said in a lilting voice.

Henri closed his mouth and concentrated. Though his ruined mouth could no longer form the words, he said to himself, over and over, *"To the gods I give all deference and honor. For the sake of order, I stake my life."*

Fleetingly he thought of Antoinette and their son and wondered if he would ever look upon them again.

The sun had almost set.

Buffy stood over Angel in the wine cellar and gazed

down at his profile. Asleep, he looked like any young man. No, not just any young man.

The young man she wanted, and loved.

Just as she was about to nudge him gently, he turned over on his back and gazed up at her.

"I'm awake," he told her.

"No rest for the wicked." She regarded him for a moment, and then she said, "You okay in the, ah, food department?"

"I'm managing." He returned her gaze. "You worried?"

She raised her eyebrows. "In the sense of, am I worried about you or worried for Oz and me?"

There was a pause. Buffy realized she had been a little too blunt and hastily tried to repair the damage. "Because I wasn't worried about door number two, there. I just wanted to make sure you were getting enough . . . iron."

"Because I look so darned pale," he drawled.

They both smiled.

"Exactly," she said. Then she frowned slightly. "I don't really want to go there."

"Me, neither. And we've got bigger questions to ask, anyway."

Buffy nodded. "And there's going to be hell to pay if we don't get some answers pronto."

"Pronto." Angel got to his feet. "Your vocabulary never ceases to amaze me."

"I'm that way."

Something was wrong.

Ian Williams stopped pacing and ran his shaking hands through his hair. He had tried to tell himself that the Slayer and her friends might have gotten lost on their way to the Redcliff mansion. They might have had a minor mishap. They might have decided not to go. He tried to tell himself it would take his brothers a long time to kill the Slayer—Skree or no.

But his contact, Brother Ariam, should have called in hours ago.

Hours and hours ago.

Except for one misdialed number, the phone had sat silent for the entire day.

Now, with the sun down, he had to decide what to do. He had to face the probability that they had failed.

The one they served did not permit failure.

The phone rang.

He gave a shout, expelling a fraction of his anxiety, and raced to pick it up.

"What," said the voice, "are you doing there?"

"Maestro," he breathed, for though he had never spoken directly to Il Maestro, he knew his voice, "I am honored. I am speechless."

"What are you doing there?" The voice rose.

"I—I—"

"Go."

Ian trembled. "Go," he echoed, his mind racing. "Go to . . . Redcliff?"

The phone disconnected.

At the last moment, the *Dutchman* was bound.

Though Henri Regnier appeared in the courtyard with the vessel and her enraged crew, the Captain a black shadow of fury, Antoinette did not realize the shambling ruin that staggered toward her was her husband until he spoke in a voice so ruined she could barely understand the words.

"The Cauldron," he rasped. "Hurry."

Numb, she raced for the Great Cauldron of Bran the Blessed. Henri had recently come into possession of it while binding a pack of savages who could transform themselves into animals. The savages had not realized what the Cauldron was and had actually cast it aside because, they had informed him, it made water taste brackish. They had no idea that it could restore vigor and prolong life, or that the water tasted odd because it had been endowed with healing properties.

Henri had been studying the Cauldron, but he had yet to actually employ it. What if it was a sham? Antoinette wondered, as she filled it with buckets of water in the entryway to the Gatehouse while her husband shivered and moaned with pain.

To peel off the vestiges of clothing would have caused him too much agony, and so he climbed into it as he was, in tatters and covered with huge expanses of bloody muscles. Half an hour passed as she knelt beside it, clasping her hands in prayer. And then he spoke.

"I am better."

He lived three more years and died at the age of 216. Jean-Marc, still a mere youth of twenty-one, became the Gatekeeper. Antoinette herself died when Jean-Marc was twenty-nine, and under her husband's binding spell, rose from her own corpse as a ghost scant minutes after drawing her last breath.

At the time of the ritual, she had thought only of her child. But now, over a century later, she thought often and with great longing of her husband. Where did Henri's spirit dwell? There, for her, was Paradise.

She assumed that once Jean-Marc came into his full powers she would be released. Like his father and grandfather, he did not marry early in life, which puzzled Antoinette. If the role of the Gatekeeper was so vital, why did the Regnier men court disaster by waiting so long to have children? And why did they have just one? What if something happened to that one?

All she could assume was that it had to do with their legacy, that this was part of the pattern of their strangely burdened existence, and so she kept her peace as the years rolled by and she remained at his side.

Then, at last, in 1985, he married, and Antoinette prepared herself to move on.

But he married badly. There was no other word for it. His wife, Kathleen, was not made of the stuff to be a proper Gatekeeper's wife. She hated the Gatehouse and all it contained. She couldn't bear the sight of her ghostly mother-in-law. She sought solace in drugs and drink and, when he came, their son, Jacques. She announced her intention to take the baby out of the house and away from "all this madness," but of course she could not, must not.

In the end, believing it to be her only way out, she leaped from the third-story window into the interior courtyard of the house. Antoinette urged Jean-Marc to put her in the Cauldron, but he refused. She had made her choice, and he would honor it. Weeping, he buried her in a Boston cemetery and not at the

Gatehouse, where the other Regniers had been buried.

Though merely a spirit, Antoinette remained to help him raise his motherless son.

Now, tenderly watching over her aged child, she wondered if she would go on when he died. Her charge had been to care for him, had it not? Or did that include taking care of his heir as well?

Only time, she concluded, would tell.

Only time, and they did not have much of that.

Ian was loyal. He was obedient. And he would accomplish what the others had not.

His car sagged beneath the weight of heavy artillery: a rocket launcher, several dozen grenades, a submachine gun. If it took leveling the mansion, reducing it to rubble, he would capture the Slayer for Il Maestro. The others he would kill.

And if Il Maestro sends something after me, I will kill it as well, a tiny voice inside him whispered.

He drove as fast as he could, tires screeching around corners. His heart was thundering; sweat poured down his face. After so many hours of inactivity and indecision, the rush to action disoriented him. He felt as if he were moving in a strange dream that was happening to someone else.

Against the night sky, he rounded a corner and saw the turrets and gables of the mansion at 217 Redcliff. It still stood intact, and he took some comfort in that. It also appeared to be deserted. There was not a light on in the entire building.

At the gates he slowed, then pulled over to the curb and stopped the car. He was scarcely able to breathe.

Then he got out of the car and opened the boot. He took out the rocket launcher and started putting it together.

Suppose some of his brethren were inside the mansion?

He set his jaw. *Then they will die.*

As Angel and Buffy came up from the wine cellar, Oz called softly through the darkness, "Someone's here."

"Good news, bad news, you be the judge," Buffy murmured, dashing up the rest of the stairs. She crept to the side of a window and peered out.

"Wow, Oz. You're Lookout Boy," she said admiringly. The moonlight streamed down on a figure beyond the gates. "I can barely see him."

"He's got something on his shoulder. Looks a little familiar. The guy, I mean. And the weapon. I seem to recall you got one for your birthday. Blew that big blue Judge guy into little pieces with it."

She smiled wistfully. "That was your virgin outing as a Slayerette," she said. Then, catching herself, she added, "Not that I'm assuming that you were, um, well—"

"New to hanging with a Slayer?" he finished for her. "No, Buffy, you were my first."

Angel came up beside Buffy and said, "Rocket launcher."

"Yeah. I'd guess Sons of Entropy," she said. Then she squinted harder. "And hey, look, I'm right. That's Ian Williams."

"Our leak," Oz said.

"Or one of them. With a rocket launcher. I'm saying this means it's time to hit the road." Buffy cast a glance at Angel. "Pronto."

"Pronto is my middle name," Oz said.

"Side exit?" Angel asked.

"Side exit, " Buffy confirmed.

Having scoped out the entire mansion by daylight, Buffy had stacked their backpacks and Angel's duffel by the exit they now ran to. Stealthily they crept outside, conveniently hidden by some thick bushes trimmed into a hedge.

There was an explosion. On instinct, Buffy tucked and rolled, knew Angel would do the same, and lifted her head long enough to satisfy herself that Oz had flung himself to the ground. Several of the Redcliff house's windows blew out. Buffy helped Oz to his feet, but when she glanced around, Angel was gone.

A moment later, he came around from the front of the house, forcing Ian Williams to stumble along in front of him by clutching a thick patch of the man's hair in his fist.

"He's not very well coordinated," Angel said, and gave the traitor's hair a hard tug, eliciting a scream.

"He'd have to be a moron to come after us alone, even with heavy ordnance," Oz added.

Buffy stepped up to stare Williams in the eye.

"You're really getting on my nerves, Ian," she snapped angrily. "What can we do to remedy that?"

Almost on cue, Williams burst into flame. Angel shouted and let him go, and the man was immolated in seconds, burning down to cinder and ash that was blown away by the night breeze.

The three were silent for a moment. Then Oz said, "Whoa, déjà vu."

Buffy grunted. "Let's get the hell out of here."

"We could liberate a small nation with all this stuff," Buffy said, as they finished taking the weaponry out of Ian Williams's car and putting it in the trunk of their own. "And I still have no understanding of why anyone in their right mind would call a car trunk a boot. There's nothing remotely bootlike about it."

Angel half smiled at her as he opened the driver's door and slid behind the wheel. "Well, what on earth is a flashlight? They don't flash."

"Kids, kids," Oz said, as he climbed into the backseat. "My question is this: Are we taking the ghost roads, or are we driving to Paris in this car, with all kinds of illegal, unregistered weapons in the rear compartment?"

"Trunk," Buffy gritted.

Angel started the car and they took off at a nice clip, but not nice enough to cause any notice.

They'd been driving for only twenty minutes or so when something white ran into the road.

Buffy shouted, "Angel, look out!"

He swerved. Buffy caught her breath and stared. Something white had not run into the road. Something white had floated into the road. And it floated there still.

With its head in its arms, like it was carrying a pile of schoolbooks.

"Okay," Oz said. "Ghost."

Buffy got out of the car. She said, "Angel, keep the engine running."

He nodded.

It was a woman dressed in a flowing white garment, hovering about a foot off the ground. She was actually rather pretty in an old-fashioned kind of way. An old-fashioned, detachable-head kind of way.

"Can I help you?" Buffy asked.

Buffy Summers, she intoned. *Listen to me.*

Buffy raised her chin. "Doing that."

I knew your Watcher. I loved him. Charming man.

Oh, really? "We try to let him have his secrets." Buffy wrinkled her nose. "So it wouldn't be nice of you to kiss and tell."

The dead are whispering in their graves that another Slayer is about to lose her life. I tell you this to honor Rupert Giles . . . and because the doors to bad places are opening, and the ghost roads now crawl with evil.

"Those crazy dead," Buffy drawled, feeling a chill. "Is there an office pool on when I'll buy it?"

The ghost raised her hand and pointed at Buffy. *Don't jest. Arm yourself. Guard yourself. You are the Slayer.*

"This just in," Buffy said, leaning toward the phantom. "Don't believe everything the dead tell you."

She turned on her heel. On the night wind, the ghost's voice traveled like a gossamer veil toward her: *Tell Rupert hello from the Countess of Dartmoor.*

"Will do," Buffy said thickly.

And please, stay alive, the Countess added. *For all our sakes. For the sake of the world.*

Buffy glanced over her shoulder. "Thanks," she began, just as the ghost vanished.

Resolutely she walked to the car and climbed in.

Angel looked at her expectantly.

Buffy shrugged. "She was lost. Asked me for directions. I had to tell her I wasn't from around here."

Angel frowned. "Buffy, we could hear her, too."

"Oh."

Oz raised his hand. "Paris? I'm thinking not a good idea," he ventured.

Buffy sighed. "Who's got any others?"

"All right, but it sounds as though the ghost roads might not be very reliable," Angel said. "I know we need to be quick. Who knows how long they might keep the boy alive . . ."

"And Oz is going to be having his monthly cycle pretty soon," Buffy offered.

Oz raised an eyebrow, then glanced at Angel. "Are we going to have trouble getting the weapons and stuff through to France?" he asked.

"I haven't been here in a long time," Angel replied. "But as far as I know, once you're actually in Europe—particularly if you're an American tourist—they're not going to question much."

"All right, then," Buffy said. "Let's go."

Angel put the car in gear, and they were mobile again.

"This is all right for now, but we're going to need a truck or a van, so Angel doesn't get toasted," Oz pointed out. "Plus, if we're supposed to be American tourists, it should be a pretty obvious rental vehicle."

"Car theft," Buffy said wearily. "Giles left that out of Slayer training."

"Not to worry," Angel reassured her. "It's been a while, but I think I can handle it."

Oz shook his head in amazement. "Yeah. Just like riding a bike. Is there anything you haven't done?"

Angel glanced up at the rearview mirror. Apparently, he was looking at Oz, but it was hard to tell, because, of course, Angel wasn't visible in the mirror. "Not a hell of a lot."

Chapter 5

She wore a mantilla over a huge tortoiseshell comb, and her gown was antique black lace. The heavy flamenco train dragged dying rose petals across the hardwood floor as she twirled her fingers and growled to herself. Black was her color, setting off her white skin and dark eyes. A stunner, his baby, if a bit mad.

But that was why he loved her so.

"Bulls," Drusilla whispered, making stabbing motions in the air with her long, sharp fingernails as she dervished to guitar music only she could hear. "Oooh, Spike, how the big bulls bleed."

Then she slowed. She flicked her tongue at Spike and arced in a languid circle with her arms outstretched, as if she held a matador's cape before her body.

"*Olé,*" she breathed. She fanned her nails at him.

"Now, Dru, not in front of the lad," Spike drawled. Perched on the edge of the table in their little seaside flat, he patted the shoulder of the young boy seated beside him in a fatherly way. The dark-haired child tensed, his dangling legs jerking, but he did not shrink from Spike's touch. Spike approved. He liked Jacques Regnier very much. The boy was his sort of person. In other words, not prone to fits of hysteria or pleading for his life.

"What does it matter what we do in front of him?" Drusilla said, dropping her voice to a vicious whisper that thrilled Spike to his marrow, if marrow he still possessed. He was not all that old a vampire, younger of course than Angel, Dru's sire, and that old boy was 240 and change.

Dru's skirts rustled as she made staccato tacks on the floor with her crimson heels. She leered at the boy and made stabbing motions at him. "You'll be dead soon. They'll cut your neck muscles. Make you bleed, little calf."

Jacques raised his chin defiantly as his eyes glittered with fear. Spike chuckled and took Dru's hands in his. He kissed the deceptively fragile-looking little knuckles. "Now, we've no proof of that, have we, poodle. They've not said what they'll do to him."

Dru stood straight and made circles with her fingers over Spike's lips. "They dart forward, you see, and stab the banderillas into all those brawny muscles." She lunged at her man. "That's when the bleeding starts. The bulls suffer. It's all for art."

"The bleeding starts when we say it does," he drawled, nibbling on her little finger. She hissed and smiled with pleasure. "And not a moment before."

"Here. But not in Madrid. Not at the bullfights." Like a jag of lightning, her mood changed and she pulled away from him. Her jaw set and she blazed with anger. The temper caught hold of her, working its way from her forehead down to her temples to her huge, dark eyes. Her lower lip quivered, a frustrated waif deprived of her treat.

"Your eyes are bleeding Spain," she accused. "You promised me Spain. Everything is bleeding there, even the sky." She hissed at him. "You said we'd go. We'd drink *sangre.*"

Spike sat back on his hands and extended his legs. It was a bit warm out, too warm for his duster and his boots. The boy was dressed more reasonably, in a long-sleeved chambray shirt and dove-gray trousers. Some bit having to do with it being a casual day at the posh public school in London where he and Dru had nabbed the cub.

"Well, that was before we knew these Sons of Entropy chaps have their HQ somewhere here in Italy," Spike said reasonably. "This place is nice, don't you think?" He indicated the little room decorated with heavily carved furniture, bookshelves lined with dusty seashells. Sand on the floor. Nature at its most natural. "The sea air is good for you, baby. Keeps your cheeks rosy."

In truth, her cheeks were ashen. They were in a village near Pisa, and Spike thought it rather cozy. There was lots of local wine . . . and no local vampires. Just the place for him and Dru to slake their blood thirst and dicker with the Sons of Entropy, who were proving to be a bit more difficult to deal with than Spike had anticipated. All the blackguards had to do was hand over the Spear of Longinus, and the Gatekeeper's heir was theirs. What was the problem? Probably that they didn't trust him any more than he trusted them. Sound business practice, he'd always thought.

"Spain," Dru pouted.

Spike knew she would keep this up until she tired of it, and the thought wearied him. There was a slight edge to his voice as he said, "We have nice, chubby Italian *mammas* and Tintoretto cherubs here. Do you fancy a cherub, pet? I can go and get you one." He began to rise, and the boy beside him tensed again. The lad was afraid of Dru.

Smart lad.

Spike turned to him and said, "And what would you like, then? Let's get him a tattoo, love. He'd look brilliant with a big snake on his chest, something like that."

"Don't get too fond of him," Dru warned. "That one's bound for the slaughterhouse. "

Spike sighed. "I suppose you're right." He smiled at her adoringly. "You usually are."

Beside him, Jacques Regnier clamped his mouth shut. Perhaps to keep himself from screaming.

Spike patted Dru's arm. "How about getting us something to eat, then?"

"Someone plump." She whirled away and danced toward the door. Then she whirled back around and faced them both. She was in full feeding face, her eyes a beautiful glowing gold, her fangs the sharpest and loveliest in their little Italian hideaway.

Still the boy did not scream. But he wanted to, very much. Spike could tell.

Spike knew quite a lot about human beings and screaming.

Dallas Mayhew pulled the cooler from beneath the ladder in the cabin of his father's thirty-foot boat, the *Walkabout,* and grabbed three beers, one for himself, one for Spenser Ketchum, and one to grow on. Cradling the triplets in his arms, he popped his head up through the companionway just beneath the boom.

"Whoa, dude," Spenser said, pointing. "Check it out."

Dallas climbed into the cockpit and plopped down the beers.

In front of the bow, a thick, white fog boiled up like thunderheads, teetering in a huge mass that threatened to tumble onto the deck of the *Walkabout.*

Dallas shrugged. "It's just fog, man."

"It's glowing, dude," Spenser said. "And there's something in it."

Dallas said, "Have a beer. You'll feel better."

"Dude," Spenser said, *"Look!"*

Dallas looked.

The fog was running them down.

"Dude, point this sucker into the wind!" Spenser shouted at Dallas.

Moments later, the sails were loaded with wind and the motor was smoking it was going so fast. There was nothing more to be done, and Spenser knew it. He was just panicking.

Dallas knew the feeling.

Because Spenser had been so right: there was something in the fog. It was a nightmare, and it wanted them.

This could not be happening. This could not be real. After all, this was Sunnydale, where he had lived all his life, where nothing ever happened.

Only now, something was happening: skeletons aboard a rotting shipwreck were chasing him. The figurehead on the prow was cackling and shrieking, her teeth clacking as she bit the air.

The wind was screaming. In the midst of the shrieking the dead men were singing.

"Hurry up!" Spenser screamed. "Go! Go!"

Tears rolled down Dallas's cheeks. He thought about his mother, who had multiple sclerosis, and his father, who worked an extra job so Dallas and his brother, Cort, could have all the extras. He thought about his stupid dream that one day he would leave this boring town and his sacrificing parents and go somewhere exciting. Somewhere that would change his life.

The harbor loomed ahead of them. From where he crouched behind the tiller, he could see the slip where his father moored the *Walkabout*. It was unbelievably near. But no way was he going to mess with docking. As soon as they hit the shallows, he was jumping out and humping it.

"As soon as we run aground, jump," he said.

It happened almost immediately. Dallas felt the tug of the sand on the hull and leaped out, splashing wildly to shore. He hazarded one look over his shoulder. Maybe it had all been a bad dream. Bad beer. The steroids he'd been taking.

But what he saw made his knees wobble.

The fog was rushing on top of the water like a high

tide. The wreck rode above it, far too high in the water. It shouldn't be there, shouldn't—

"Spense," he shouted, but his friend sat frozen in the cockpit in a fetal position. Dallas wanted to go back for him, he really did.

But he didn't.

Instead, he ran for all he was worth, scrabbling through the water and onto the stone jetty, where once upon a time his mom and he had watched the sand crabs skitter, before she got sick and he got older. He flung himself up the stones, shrieking, and when he reached the pavement of the embankment, he took another look.

That was when the ship launched itself into the sky.

He stared, speechless. Enshrouded with fog, it floated up through the sky, a nightmare riding on the wind. Then the fog thickened and it looked like nothing more sinister than a heavy bank of clouds.

He blinked, unable to believe his luck. He turned back to Spenser, who was slogging through the water.

"Thanks a lot, dude," Spenser flung at him. "Thanks for abandoning me. Wow, you're really a friend, you know it?"

"Spense," Dallas began, but there was nothing he could say in his own defense. He had abandoned his friend.

He hung his head in shame.

"Dallas."

"Spense, if I had it to do over, I—"

"Dallas."

Dallas raised his head and looked at Spense. He was gazing at a point above Dallas's head, his eyes enormous. His mouth was working but no sound came out.

Dallas whirled around.

A net dropped over his head. Dallas screamed as the icy cords wrapped around his body and tightened, cutting into his skin.

The net began to lift back into the sky.

Then, as Dallas gasped for air and struggled against the ropes, something very sharp slammed through his chest. In shock, he stared down and saw the steel point protruding from his body. Blood poured out of him like the open spigot on a keg of beer.

It doesn't hurt, he found himself thinking.

It would a little later.

But just for a little while.

"Ah, Paris. I knew I'd make it someday," Buffy said.

The Eiffel Tower rose dead ahead.

"And I knew I would be there with a werewolf driving a van and a vampire sacked out asleep in the back."

"I'm not asleep," Angel said fuzzily.

Buffy glanced over her shoulder. They had made a sort of tent for Angel, and all she could see was blankets. "You should be. You never know which of the many fun and exciting forces of darkness we'll be battling tonight."

"Or now," Oz said, as a man dressed like someone in *Casablanca* raised his hands and motioned them to one side.

"Oh, great," Buffy muttered. "I knew we should have dumped the AK-47 before we took the ferry."

"Good weapon," Angel said. "We pitched just about everything else. Hard to let go of something like that."

"What are we gonna do if they want us to get out of the van?" Oz said quietly. "We forgot our tube of SPF five million and two for Angel."

Buffy shrugged. "I guess we'll have to make a run for it."

"Okay," Oz said with his infinite calmness. He had the class not to mention the fact that they were stuck in an amazing traffic jam, making running for it one Slayer's pathetic little dream.

"Pulling over," Oz reported. He rolled down the window as the French policeman came over. *"Bonjour,"* he said serenely.

The Frenchman replied in rapid-fire French that left Buffy wondering if she had actually studied French in school or if it had been some diabolical plot on the part of the administration—more specifically, Principal Snyder—to get students to raise the evil dead by chanting in a strange foreign tongue. *Which would explain the cafeteria lady with the vacant stare and the extreme body odor.*

"D'accord?" the cop said, giving the side of the van a little pat.

"Oui, merci," Oz replied.

The man waded back into the traffic jam.

Oz eased onto the gas pedal and started the tortuous return to the traffic. No one wanted to let them in. After all, this was Paris.

When he said nothing, Buffy prodded, "Well?"

Oz glanced in the rearview mirror. "He was telling

me there was an accident up ahead, and we should take a detour." He waved at the car behind them and darted into the lane. Brakes squealed. A horn blared.

"Or else, Camembert cheese is on sale at the mini-mart. Take your pick."

Angel said, "Detour."

Buffy leaned toward Oz. "He was around when they invented French."

Angel said, "I heard that."

Buffy replied, "Go to sleep."

"So, detour," Oz said. He shrugged. "Which could be a good thing."

Nightfall had descended over Paris by the time Buffy, Oz, and Angel reached the address they'd found back in London.

"It just figures," Buffy grumbled, as she led the way, her AK-47 in hand. Oz had a keen revolver and Angel carried a pistol. They'd left the rocket launcher in the van. "Get me involved, and you wind up with spiders and human remains."

They were down in the catacombs of Paris, where the bones of the dead were stacked like calcified Lego blocks: skulls and forearms here, femurs there, hips way, way over there.

"It's not so bad," Oz said, training his flashlight over the walls of bones. "I mean, most people pay money to see this."

"Someday we're going to run up against a monster who likes amusement parks or really good restaurants." Buffy stumbled and caught her balance on the face of a skull. "Sorry," she said to it.

"Speaking of restaurants," Oz ventured, "have you ever noticed how bad guys in movies are always eating? Grapes. Or they're slicing off big hunks of turkey and feeding it to their Persian cats. What's that all about?"

"Gluttony," Angel supplied. "One of the seven deadly sins."

"Right up there with monotony." Buffy yawned. "There's no one here, guys. Let's give it up and go to Disneyland Paris."

"Slayer," came a hushed whisper.

Immediately Buffy ticked her gaze at Angel and Oz, both of whom nodded and began to move in opposite directions, Oz to the left and Angel to the right. It made sense to cover ground as quickly as possible, try to grab the speaker before he knew what was happening. Then she flicked off her flashlight. It was impossible to tell where the voice was coming from. No sense giving him the advantage.

"Slayer."

"That'd be me," Buffy said, looking around as she moved forward in the darkness, listening very hard. "And you are?"

There was a pause. And then the voice said, "A friend."

"Oh, I see. Which is why you're hiding from me. Some of my other friends do that, too. I think it's got something to do with my appreciation for the films of Molly Ringwald. Or my bad taste in friends."

"Please, I beg of you. Listen to me. I haven't much time."

"Are you eating grapes?" she demanded.

"I think I was followed," he said in an underbreath.

"Well, that certainly would be a new experience for me. You aren't by any chance with the Sons of Entropy, are you? And I don't mean the singing group," she added sternly.

"I am, but—"

"But you're a *good* Son of Entropy," she cut in. She scanned the area, detecting nothing but pitch black darkness. Briefly she reconsidered the wisdom of keeping her flashlight turned off. Her finger was on the trigger of the AK-47, and that was better.

There was a strange growl.

"Oh, my God," said Buffy's new friend. "It's coming. Help me."

There was a flash of blue light against the far wall. Magickal blue light. Buffy went on alert. "First, tell me why you're here."

"No. It's coming. *Please.*"

Another flash, followed by a fireball.

Buffy kept her silence: Maybe the guy was trying to trick her. Maybe he would succeed in saving himself. And in the category Slayer's Duty for three hundred, maybe he really did need her help.

Which he, being a bad person, would not get for free.

"It's the ghost roads," he said finally. "There are many of them besides the ones you've used. I know you've had trouble on them, but you mustn't travel aboveground. You're too obvious."

"This is another setup, isn't it," Buffy said dangerously. "The address in the bag . . ."

"It was intended to be a setup, but I learned of it." There was a pause. "I'm working with someone. Someone your Watcher knows."

Her ears pricked up, but Buffy couldn't imagine who this guy could be referring to.

"Just know that we are trying to stop him from within."

"So, wait," Buffy said. "Giles knows someone in the Sons of Entropy? And who exactly is this 'him?'"

"Il Maestro."

There was another growl.

A scream.

Buffy flicked on her flashlight and ran in the direction of the scream. As she came to a fork in the tunnels of the dead, Angel dashed from a side passage, saw her, and joined her as she charged to the left.

"Oz!" she shouted.

"On my way," Oz called back.

Then a roar shook the catacombs. Dirt and pebbles clattered from the wall as Buffy's hand scraped another skull, nubs of teeth catching at her skin. She barely registered the sensation as she dashed on.

"Buffy!" Angel shouted. "Look out!"

From above, something crashed down on top of her. Her flashlight went flying. So did her weapon. She was pinned to the ground.

A shot rang out, but it had no effect on whatever had landed on top of her. Catching her hair in its mouth, it began to drag her beneath its body. It had four legs, and each of them ended in a pad of sharp claws.

Then suddenly, it was half-running, half-falling at a sharp angle.

Buffy reached up to yank herself free, but it was traveling too fast. Angel was shouting her name somewhere above. She heard footfalls.

Somehow, she and her attacker had slipped beneath the path she and Angel had stood on.

"Buffy? Buffy, where are you?" Angel shouted.

"Trap door, or something. Look around."

She flailed with her legs, trying to find purchase against the walls as she was pulled along. Failing that, she pulled her legs up against her chest, struggling to rock backward against the momentum, in an effort to kick the thing in the stomach.

No luck. She straightened her legs back out and dug her heels into the pitted ground. Something stabbed her above the kneecap, and she cried out in both surprise and pain. It bored into her quadriceps and released something into her muscles that burned like a brand.

The thing roared.

Then she heard Oz say, "Hey."

Dim light penetrated the surrounding area. Squinting through the pain, Buffy looked at her attacker. From what she could see, it was a lion.

There was a shot. It burned to the left of Buffy's cheek, missing the lion entirely.

There was another shot.

This time the creature roared and dropped Buffy.

Her head slammed against the earthen floor. Just as the creature sailed on, she grabbed its hind leg. Her grip was bad; it yanked free of her grasp and shook her off like an inconsequential bug.

She caught the tail. White-hot pain pulsed deep into her hands. Gritting her teeth, she held on.

The thing dragged her along, but it was moving more slowly. Buffy crawled hand over hand up the tail, then grabbed at the hindquarters.

"Oz, shoot it again!" she shouted.

Another shot fired. The creature bellowed with fury and turned on Buffy.

She gasped. It had a man's face, except that its mouth was crammed with rows and rows of teeth. The eyes flashed bloodred. Waving above the back of its head like a boa constrictor, the tail darted at her. There was a long scorpion-like stinger attached to it.

"Whoa, camel," she said. Then she pulled back her right hand and slammed her open palm against its jaw. The head snapped back; the creature roared.

She did it again, and as the creature fell backward, she leaped on top and began to pummel it. That it had a man's face barely registered, and she attacked as violently and as viciously as she could. Slamming her fists into it, making a double fist and crashing down on its nose—it was like a frenzy, and she couldn't stop herself.

"Easy, easy," someone said gently, pulling her off the monster.

She whirled around, fists doubled, to find Angel before her, his flashlight trained on the monster's body. It took her a moment to calm sufficiently, and then she dropped her hands to her sides and tried to catch her breath.

"All in the name of survival," he said, and she knew he was talking about the look she had given him when he had broken the neck of the Skree.

"Yeah." She nodded and wiped her mouth with the back of her hand.

Oz came over. He looked down at the creature, then at Buffy, then at Angel. "Sorry," he said. "I'm not such a good shot."

Buffy managed a smile as she massaged her sore leg. "Oh, I think you pretty much saved my life."

He shook his head. "Not me, Buffy. I didn't hit it once."

"Maybe it was the Whisperer in the Darkness," she said. "Which would be nice, and help to restore my faith in mankind. A little."

Of the stranger, however, there was no sign.

"Y'know, it's becoming pretty obvious that, completely aside from whatever's been coming out of the Gatehouse, the big kahuna who's behind the Sons of Entropy also has some monsters working for him."

"Not working for him," Buffy said, remembering the savagery of the Wendigo, which had unwittingly saved her life back in Sunnydale, "but at least under his control. No question, in the nasty sorcery department, this guy makes our old pal Ethan Rayne look like Daffy Duck with a magick wand."

Now Angel knelt over the dead monster and stared at the rows of needle teeth in its mouth.

"Incredible. A manticore," he said. "Face of a man, body of a lion. Reputed to steal babies, cut them up, and eat them. I've never seen one before."

"Another in a limited edition series of monsters with human faces," Buffy said grimly. "Like whoever this Il Maestro guy is." She stared down at the creature, who stared back at her with glassy, blank eyes.

"And when I find him, this is exactly what I'm going to do to him," she seethed.

She glared at Oz and Angel.

"For starters."

Chapter 6

"HERE'S WHAT HAPPENED," ANGEL SAID, SHINING HIS flashlight over a long, ramplike plank covered with dirt and bones that had crashed down under the weight of Buffy and the monster. "This was the entrance to the room we're standing in. The catacombs were used in World War II by the French Resistance. This was probably a secret meeting place."

"And now it's a secret dying place," Buffy said, then glanced around and realized she'd lost track of the AK-47 somewhere. Not that it mattered. It hadn't been her kind of weapon. Not at all.

Suddenly, the manticore exploded into flames. The three watched without much expression.

"Maybe Il Maestro sent that manticore after that guy, but he might have sent him after us as well. And more little goodies could be on the way."

She nodded. Better to be a moving target than a dead duck.

"Okay." She sighed. "It's going to be light soon. Where's the nearest ghost road?"

"According to Antoinette Regnier, there's supposed to be one inside the bell tower in the Cathedral of Notre Dame."

Buffy smiled wryly. "See? I *knew* we'd have a chance to go sightseeing on this trip."

That evening, Giles wandered Sunnydale alone.

" 'The moon was a ghostly galleon,' " he murmured, quoting the poem by Alfred Noyes as he looked up at the sky. He put his hands in his jacket to warm them, remembering another chilly night when he had done so: New York, the librarians' convention, the night he had met Micaela Tomasi.

It was an uncommonly foggy night in Sunnydale, and the shrouded moon loomed huge as its light was thrown against the whirling mists. Thick blankets of vapor covered every street, every storefront and lamppost. Walking through it gave one a sense of swimming through the murk of a fully submerged town. Giles knew of three such. Tonight, Sunnydale could be counted as the fourth.

He thought of London and felt not precisely homesick, for Sunnydale had become his home. Perhaps nostalgic was the better term. Wistful for a time when things had been simpler, and he had not been the Slayer's Watcher. He had worked at the British Museum, biding his time on the chance that he would be called to serve a new Slayer. Done things such as memorize romantic poems about lives that at the time seemed so much larger and more exciting than his own. Not realizing then that his life would become just like that, and that he would long for the relative ease and boredom he was forced to relinquish.

However, he was not complaining. The actual burden of duty rested on shoulders far more slender—and yet more powerful—than his. It was a small thing that was asked of him: to devote his life to helping her.

She was asked to risk her life, hour by hour, minute by minute. And that demand was never rescinded, until she did indeed die.

His footsteps rang on the pavement as he walked, his gaze never resting long on one location. He was on patrol, alone tonight for various logistical reasons, including the fact that he needed to be alone. It was all well and good that Joyce Summers had a safe haven from the breach inside her home, but Giles was unused to sharing his own safe haven with anyone. The need for secrecy about his role as Watcher had isolated him to such an extent that he found that, by habit and inclination, he preferred his own company to that of most other people. Even lovely, intelligent people such as Joyce.

Besides, the last woman who had spent an appreciable amount of time in his apartment had been Jenny. He found himself thinking of her more often, and with a resurgence of his grief, now that another woman was there. Joyce's makeup in his bathroom, the press of lipstick on a glass—the minutiae of femininity served to remind him that what he had once had was gone forever. Now his worry was for

Micaela, and it was difficult for him to entertain the thought that she, too, might be dead. He didn't want Buffy's mother to know that her presence caused such pain for him, and so he kept his feelings carefully hidden. Which made him lonelier still.

Now, in the fog, he was on full alert. Two high school boys were missing, and the kids at school were talking about seeing things down at the beach. Things besides the Kraken, the enormous sea monster which, for all he and the others knew, still lurked beneath the black water. There was the off chance that this fog was merely a trick of the weather, and that the stories were only stories, but he sincerely doubted that. Not here. Not now. They surely indicated another breach. Poor Willow would have to do another binding spell.

He had nothing but the highest admiration for the way Willow had stepped into Jenny's shoes, as it were, becoming the group's spellcaster and researcher of the arcane. Giles had no time for learning rituals and purchasing supplies for them, as he spent his time training the Slayer and researching ancient texts for prophecies about the various demons and other forces of darkness she must battle. That Willow so handily supplemented his work and aided Buffy was helpful indeed, and he was most appreciative.

He appreciated all their efforts, in fact. Over time, Xander had found his place as Buffy's second-in-command, and he could also be an elegant tactician, though he would never believe it of himself if Giles were to mention it. Cordelia, who had once seemed so . . . superfluous, served as the voice of practicality when Giles's own British predilection for tact and discretion hindered the stating of the obvious. Oz was a calming influence, often acting as Willow's second. They were an incredible group of kids, the Slayer's band.

She was lucky to have them, and he was fortunate that they were so loyal to Buffy—

"Help," called a voice. "Oh, God!"

Giles cocked his head. The call was nearby. As were the accompanying footsteps, frantic and uneven.

"No! No!" came another shout.

To the northwest, then. As quickly but as quietly as he could, Giles ran in that direction. He remained silent. The element of surprise might be the most effective weapon he had.

Giles reached a row of warehouses, touching the damp aluminum siding as he felt along the side. This damnable fog. He could see nothing.

There was another clatter of footsteps. The boyish voice yelled, "Oh, God. Oh, my God!"

Farther away this time. There was a muffled cry, followed by a creaking sound that reminded him of something he couldn't quite place.

Then he looked up. His lips parted and his face prickled with alarm.

The moon was descending.

But it was not the moon. It was a large, glowing shape, slowly lowering toward the ground, and his first thought was that it was a UFO.

Giles took a step left. His right hand made contact with something metallic—a Dumpster, he guessed—and he felt along it as he inched backward. There was a space between it and the building; he wedged himself into the hiding place, his head craned upward.

Then a fierce wind whipped up, slapping granules of grit against his cheek. He pressed himself against the building as something flew out of the Dumpster—a piece of cardboard, a torn box—and hit him in the face.

The force of the wind increased, shrieking in Giles's ears, thwarting his ability to hear. For a moment he hoped that the wind would dissipate the fog, but if anything it seemed thicker.

The shrieking rose and fell. After a few seconds Giles realized that voices keened within the shrieking. They were desperate and filled with rage.

The voices blended into the notes of a song; then the notes became words, and Giles's heart thundered against his ribs as he listened:

> *We ride the Dutchman, we,*
> *Damned souls, doomed souls.*
> *We ride the Dutchman we,*
> *As she sails on straight to hell.*

The *Flying Dutchman?* Here in Sunnydale? This was bad indeed. Antoinette Regnier, the ghostly mother of the current Gatekeeper, had mentioned to Giles that the *Dutchman* was bound into the Gatehouse.

The wind continued to blow; then, gradually, Giles was aware that the fog was thinning. Immediately he looked up. Above him floated the rotted hull of a sailing vessel. Barnacles and bones, both human and animal, clung to the decayed, curved timbers. A large chain dangled from the port side; attached to the end was an old-fashioned three-pronged anchor, rusted and covered with more barnacles.

The Dutchman sank still lower until she was eye-level with Giles. Her sails hung in tatters. Rotted corpses strode her deck. The stench of death was unimaginable.

On the main deck, a skeleton dragged a boy in a green and white letterman's jacket by means of a rope around both his wrists. What flesh there was on the skeleton's bones was sun blackened and crawling with worms.

It yanked hard on the rope and the boy fell to his knees with a gasp, wobbling for a moment, then crashing face forward on the deck. Around him, the other ghosts laughed, and the eerie echo made the hair stand up on Giles's head.

Giles doubled his fists, fighting the urge to act. At this juncture, there was nothing he could do. To make matters worse, he recognized the boy. He had come into the library only last week, requesting some college catalogs. His name was Vinnie Navarro, a new transfer student from somewhere in Chicago, and most unhappy about moving to Sunnydale. Yet he had tried to put on a brave face for his family, and for that Giles admired him. The jacket Vinnie wore was from his old high school. Giles felt a rush of sorrow for the lad, who certainly had had no notion of what was to come when his family had moved here.

"Join," said the voice, *"or die."*

It was not offering Vinnie a choice. It was foretelling his future.

Then the owner of the voice stepped forward on the deck, and Giles had to clamp his hand over his own mouth to stifle his shout of fear.

It was a figure dressed in old-fashioned black sea-farer's clothes. But where its face should have been, hung a layer of shadow. It blurred and shifted as the being moved its head, but when Giles looked into that shadow, he saw nothing. But what he felt . . .

Oh, what he felt . . .

Fear beyond reasoning. The kind of terror that devoured thought and left a grown man a jibbering madman. Death wore that face. And worse than death.

The figure approached Vinnie, who sank to his knees and burst into tears. From behind him, another ravaged corpse staggered forward. It held in its hands a noose, and it slipped the loop over Vinnie's head.

"Weigh anchor and string him up," said the ghost with the shadowed face. It waved its skeletal hand carelessly and turned its back on Vinnie.

"Weigh anchor, aye sir," a voice echoed.

The chain began to crawl upward. Mastering his fear as best he could, Giles ran forward and grabbed it. The fog surrounded the vessel as it began to rise back into the air. Through the murk he could no longer see the ground. He lost his sense of direction as he dangled, unsure if they were still rising.

The ship moved forward, trailing him and the anchor slightly behind.

Xander, Cordelia, and Willow stood in the living room of the Summers home and looked at the wobbly circle that hovered waist high.

"I'm saying this is a job for Superman. Or Buffy, as the case may be," Xander said.

The girls nodded. Willow looked tired. She covered her mouth as she yawned, then looked at Xander and said, "I've done all the binding I know how to do."

"And still it lurks," Xander said, "with intent to loom."

"What are you talking about?" Cordelia snapped. She checked her watch. "Let's just call in and tell Giles we did the best we could, but it's still here. Look, one more late night and my mother is shipping me off to a finishing school in Switzerland." She raised her eyes and looked at Xander. "Is that how we want me to finish senior year?"

"Only sometimes," he said earnestly. "Okay, I'm punching in the G-man's number." He picked up the Summers' portable and dialed.

Joyce Summers answered.

"Good evening, Mrs. Summers," Xander said amiably. "How are you?"

"A little worried," she said. "Mr. Giles said he'd check in with me over two hours ago. I haven't heard anything."

Xander scowled, which prompted Cordelia and Willow to start whispering, "What? What?" He gestured for them to be quiet.

"You're sure the phone was on the hook."

"Yes," she said.

"And if you were talking and there was a call waiting, you took it."

"Xander," Buffy's mother said, exasperated, "I deliberately stayed off the phone. You're confusing me with my daughter."

"Hmm. Hold on." He covered the mouth piece and looked at the girls. "Giles is off the radar."

"*What?*" Willow and Cordelia demanded in shocked unison.

Removing his hand, he said, "Mrs. S., did he say where he was going?"

"Yes. On patrol. I think he was going to see about the missing high school students."

"Which ones, out of a pool of, oh, say two hundred?" Xander asked sourly.

"I think he was going to the wharf."

"Ah." He brightened. "That's good. That's something we can use. Anything else?"

"Not that I can think of. He told me not to worry."

"Oh, he's just full of good advice," Xander grumbled. More heartily, he said to her, "We'll go find him and we'll bring him home, okay?"

"That would be good, yes," she said anxiously. "I—I'm pretty worried, Xander."

"Nothing to worry about. We've got everything under control," he assured her.

As soon as he hung up, he turned to the girls and said, "Oh, man, do we have a whole pack o' trouble. Giles went down to the sea again and now he's missing."

"The Kraken," Willow said, horrified.

"Eew." Cordelia sighed. "Switzerland, here I come."

The chain was pulled taut, leaving Giles to cling to the anchor as the ship traveled over Sunnydale. His arms were very tired, and he began to worry that he might actually let go. The fog was so thick he had no idea where he was nor how high up. His arm muscles ached.

After a time, the ghost ship pitched forward. It was descending. He wondered if the fog would lift again, but this time there was no lessening of the damp thickness that filled his lungs and made his hands wet and slick.

Then the rush and roar of the ocean drowned out all other noise. For an alarming instant he wondered if they were going to submerge suddenly, but the vessel glided toward the water with astonishing grace.

Then a large swell hit the *Dutchman*—even some of the crew gave a cry—and to his astonishment Giles lost his grip on the anchor and splashed into the chilly water.

His head bobbed beneath the surface, and all went black.

Buffy didn't like being on the ghost roads again. But it was light outside the catacombs, and she didn't want to lose another twelve hours before Angel could move on. The ghost that had approached them in England had warned her away from using this mode of travel, but she didn't see that she had a choice. Their friend in the catacombs had been pretty certain the Sons of Entropy had been tracking them when they traveled by traditional means.

A short discussion had resulted in this fun new journey, but it was a mission with a purpose: Buffy was looking for help, and she would take it where she could get it. She figured if you could go to destinations you held in your mind, those destinations might include the locations of people.

Fortunately, and to her surprise, the dead were keeping their distance. Most of them were obviously on their way to their final rest, whatever that was supposed to be. The ones that had attacked them before were the lost. But now, even the lost were staying away. *Word on the ghost roads must travel pretty fast,* she thought.

Every once in a while, she would catch sight of a blur of a face or the flash of a figure in the distance. Same with Angel and Oz. But for the most part, they were alone.

At least until the beautiful redheaded Slayer they had met before appeared before them.

"Oh," Buffy said, startled. She was actually trying to get to Kendra, who had fought beside her in life.

"Slayer, I thank the stars that you heard my plea," Maria Regina said. Her expression was grim. "I was unable to come to you, but I desperately need your help."

Buffy was on her guard. She wasn't looking for more to do.

"The fiends you now face are weakening the barriers between Earth and the Otherworld. That much you know. But their dark magick is also weakening the barriers that separate the ghost roads from the Otherworld and from Hell itself. Monsters and demons are invading, racing down the ghost roads, claiming souls for Hell. If they can intrude on the ghost roads, there is an excellent chance they will be able to come through the breaches into your world as well."

"Which is why I can't delay," Buffy said quickly, "and why you have to help me stop the Sons of

Entropy—those are the fiends—from doing all the bad stuff."

"No. You must help me fight now." The Slayer stepped forward and touched Buffy on the forearm. A strange electric sensation passed between them, and Buffy drew back slightly at this evidence that even after death, Slayers were different from other people. She didn't like being different. Except on those occasions when she was wounded so badly a regular person would have died.

Maria Regina took her other hand and stood facing her.

"We are Chosen Ones. We were handed a sacred obligation," she insisted.

"Yeah," Buffy retorted. "To save the world. Not every single world in the galaxy."

"To fight the forces of darkness," Maria Regina insisted.

Buffy groaned. "Do we have to do it now? I am so on a mission—well, actually, you know my mission—can't you find some other Slayers to help you out? I hear Kendra's around."

Maria Regina shook her head. "She's walked on."

"Walked on?" Buffy raised her brows. "To?"

Maria Regina shrugged. "Who can say? The light? I don't know." She added bitterly, "I'm still here, am I not?"

Buffy looked at Angel, who shook his head slightly. "We have to go, Buffy," he said quietly.

Without warning, a horde of demons shimmered into existence, surrounding them. Their faces were hideous—sores bled from the crimson skin of the nearest. A fat, slobbering demon launched himself at

Angel, while two green monsters with glowing hollows for eyes grabbed Oz, their tentacles whipping around him and squeezing tight.

And more were coming.

"The breach has ruptured!" Maria Regina shouted as she went into action. Grabbing the two green, tentacled demons, she crushed their heads together; then, as they swayed, she began ripping their tentacles from their bodies. Green ocher spurted everywhere, covering Buffy and the others.

Oz slumped to the ground. Buffy had just enough time to push him out of the way before the red demon launched itself at her. Buffy contracted into a ball and executed a forward roll as the demon sailed over her. Then she stopped herself with her hands and back-kicked the demon as it whirled around and prepared another attack. As it staggered, it collided with Angel's back. The vampire grabbed it around the neck, stooped, and yanked it over his head like a rag doll. It sailed down on the neck of the hideously fat demon, and the two crashed to the ground. Savagely growling, Angel kicked them until they stopped moving.

Next, Buffy went to help Oz, glaring angrily at Maria Regina, who was having a difficult time with a single, very short monster whose main mode of attack appeared to be hissing.

No wonder she died, she found herself thinking as she grabbed at the blue demon, only to watch his arm dissolve into maggots. She was momentarily startled; Cordelia and Xander had run into a demon like this who'd been an assassin with the Order of Taraka, sent to kill Buffy.

"M.R.," she called, "a little help here, please."

The short demon roared flame at Maria Regina. Perfect. It was a fire breather. Buffy tackled it and forced it down on its stomach, lifted it up, and turned on her heel. The flames shot out at the maggot creature, burning it to a crisp.

"Maria Regina, is this your lunch break?" she asked angrily.

"I'm sorry. I'm . . . I'm somehow sapped," the dead Slayer said, sounding confused. She came to Buffy and touched her. There was another jolt of electricity.

"Hey," Buffy protested, "what are you doing?"

Maria Regina frowned. "I don't know. Perhaps it's because my time is over, and you're the Slayer now. But I feel rejuvenated somehow. I feel that now I can fight!"

"Well, that's just ducky, because there's a lot to do around here," Buffy said, as she jumped into the air, spun completely around, then kicked an oncoming monster full in the face. The creature had a sharp executioner's axe in its grip. When it went down, the axe clattered to the ground. Buffy kicked the weapon out of its grasp, made a double fist, and slammed down hard.

Maria Regina picked up the axe and said, "I'll finish him off." She kicked the monster, and Buffy moved off to get the next guy. She thought about asking for the axe, but Maria Regina needed some kind of extra edge. So far, Buffy didn't.

To her relief, Oz was up and holding his own against a very human-looking demon. Its taloned fingers sliced in the air, reaching for Oz as he pummeled its face. Then Oz kicked it hard in the groin.

The thing went down, and Oz slammed its face into the ground, then stomped on its neck.

"Strong work," Buffy called.

"Buffy, look out!" Oz shouted.

She turned just in time to see the monster she had left to the other Slayer racing toward her with its axe back in its possession.

Buffy backhanded it without even looking, then grabbed the axe and sliced open its abdomen.

"Maria!" she shouted, then turned to see the other Slayer on her hands and knees, her face away from Buffy. "Hey! Are you hurt?"

Buffy ran toward her.

Angel outpaced Buffy, reaching the downed Slayer before she did. He was in full vamp face. Buffy felt a flash of fear for him, not sure that Maria Regina would remember that Angel was on their side.

"Angel, stay back!" Buffy cried.

"Buffy?" he said, but he was looking down at Maria Regina and not at her.

"What?"

He looked up at Buffy.

In that moment, Maria Regina—or whatever had passed for her—flipped in the air and flew straight for Buffy, knocking the axe from her hand.

She wore Buffy's face. Buffy's hair. Buffy's body.

For one second too long, Buffy was stunned. Then, as her impostor launched a full-scale attack—using her battle techniques—Buffy pulled herself together and fought back. The other Buffy parried each blow, blocked each kick.

"You will lose, Slayer," she hissed. *"And Hell will have its day."*

"And it'll be pretty darn cold there," Buffy retorted. Her eyes ticked the merest bit toward Angel, who was advancing on Buffy's double.

"Don't try it, vampire," the doppelgänger threatened. Then she laughed. *"I know everything you will try. I know all your schemes. Your tricks."*

"Then we're not playing poker," Buffy said.

"There's that poker motif again," Oz said numbly, as he grabbed up the axe. "Um, we still have demons." He swung gamely at an advancing monster cloaked in black fur and sporting horns all over its body.

Buffy said to Angel, "Help Oz."

He glared at the impostor. "But—"

"Do it," Buffy said.

He moved away.

The double laughed, keeping her distance from Buffy. *"You blundered, Slayer."*

"Yeah. I should have asked to see proper ID when we first met," Buffy said, assuming a classic fighter's stance as she observed her adversary. Her trained mind assessed the possible attack moves the other Buffy might initiate, planned defensive maneuvers. Played for time. "Too late for that now, I guess, Maria. Or were you ever Maria Regina?"

"This force was once the shade of the dead Slayer. I knew her . . . intimately. I'm the one who killed her."

"There was a *Star Trek* episode like this. Come to think of it, about a dozen of them," Buffy said. "It's a cliché, even in the afterlife, don't you think?"

Her double smiled brightly at her. *"You fell for it. You let me touch you. And now I have your essence. If you destroy this shade, you will kill a part of yourself.*

It is your shade now. You will die even younger than the fates have already decreed."

"Oh, yeah? Well, my future hasn't been written," Buffy said, though she was chilled by the double's words. "Unfortunately for you, yours has. Oz!"

In that moment, Oz threw the axe to her. She caught it, lunged, and in one clean arc decapitated the impostor. The demons disappeared in an instant, as though they had been drawn there merely as part of the doppelgänger's ruse. Her head sailed into the air, then landed with a thud at Oz's feet.

He stared down at it, then at Buffy. "The Chosen One," he said evenly. "I knew her, Horatio."

To her amazement, Buffy burst into laughter. It took a few minutes for her to calm down, and by then, she wasn't sure if she was laughing or sobbing.

Chapter 7

AFTER THE DEBACLE WITH MARIA REGINA, BUFFY pretty much figured it wasn't worth the aggravation of the ghost roads to find Kendra, if she was still walking them. Without a plan, and with too many wicked things that way coming, she suggested they bail.

Everybody agreed, and so they checked back out of the bell tower at Notre Dame cathedral and started wandering around, wondering what to do next.

The three kept to the shadows in the streets of nighttime Paris. It was a truly beautiful city. All the famous monuments were splashed with light—the Eiffel Tower, the Church of the Madeleine, the Hôtel des Invalides. The bistros were crammed with people slightly older than Buffy and Oz, engaged in deep conversations that required lots of coffee in cups as big as soup bowls and many cigarettes. Angelus had smoked. Angel did not.

"Everyone here dresses so cool," Buffy murmured, looking around and feeling kind of skanky. That's what came with clothes you could cram into a backpack and not enough opportunities to shower.

"It's the accessories," Oz offered. "Scarves. Jewelry."

"Yes." She nodded, appraising a trio of girls who were seated at a small round table. Everything matched or blended in some way, from their rings to their patterned panty hose. "You're right." She grinned at Oz. "Career Week? How did they miss your knack for fashion?"

He shrugged. "Devon's new honey reads *Cosmo*. Very heavy on the accessories."

"Yeah, especially on the front cover," she teased. "Big accessories there."

Oz just smiled.

Angel said, "The Parisians have always been known for their fashion sense. At the turn of the century, it was amazing. Those bustles . . ." He trailed off as the other two just looked at him. He shrugged. "They were nice bustles."

"And now we've returned full circle to accessories," Buffy said. She gestured to the throngs of people. "So it's time to tune in once again to the Slayer's favorite topic: Now what?"

For a moment the three were silent. Then Oz said, "Maybe this is too obvious. But how about we be obvious ourselves? They don't know where we're going, either. So if we nose around, make ourselves available for potshots and murder attempts, with any luck they'll try to kill us."

"You're right," Buffy said brightly. "Who'd pass up a chance like that?"

Oz grinned happily, and then the grin slid away like blood draining from a corpse.

Angel glanced around at the lights of Paris. "You know," he said, "I'm thinking if we're going to be obvious, we should be very obvious. We're lost in this crowd. How about we go inside somewhere, have a bite to eat? You two must be hungry."

"Actually, I'm starved," Buffy answered. "How about you?"

"Don't ask," he reminded her.

"Don't tell." She took a breath. "Okay." She looked at Oz. "You in the mood for *le* coffee and *les* cigs?"

"Sure. Well, except for the *les* cigs part."

"Just being French," Buffy said with a shrug.

They headed into the nearest cafe, a place called Bistrot de la Place, and Angel went into his Vulcan mind-meld with the waiter, meaning that they both started speaking rapid-fire French to each other. Buffy could tell that Oz was following at least part of the conversation while she, the one who had actually taken French, couldn't understand a word. It was humiliating. But then, so much about being her was.

The waiter led them to a table by the window. Angel pulled out some francs and the waiter palmed them, inclining his head like a duke and sniffing, *"Merci, monsieur."*

"Now *that* I got," Buffy announced. "You bribed him so we could sit at the window."

"See and be seen," Angel said. He smiled faintly. "With any luck, our friends will show up with another rocket launcher."

"There is that," Oz said flatly. "Hadn't thought of that."

Buffy looked first at him, then at Angel. Her expression was very serious, very determined.

"Look. Both of you. I'm the Slayer. This is my job. But neither of you is under the obligation I'm under. You can go home if you want. I won't blame you."

Completely ignoring her, Angel raised a hand at a passing waiter. *"Garçon,"* he called. He looked at Oz. "Coffee?"

They had croissants and baguettes, and even some delicious, hearty soup. While they mopped up drippy Brie, Angel excused himself and returned about fifteen minutes later, absently wiping his mouth.

"I don't suppose you were reading the paper in the men's room," Buffy said, suddenly finding it difficult to swallow her food.

Angel sat down and picked up her half-eaten croissant. "Do you mind?"

"Not at all."

He nibbled at the croissant, closing his eyes and smiling in delight, as any guy might. Around the room, young Parisians chatted and debated. They smoked like crazy. Everything seemed so serious with them, so much larger than life. Yet Buffy realized that if they had an inkling that a vampire, a werewolf, and a Vampire Slayer sat among them, they would probably be unable to believe it. They certainly wouldn't be able to sit there and smoke and argue about what they believed to be the earth-shattering events of the day.

"Penny," Angel said to her.

She shrugged. "I'm probably one of the youngest people in here, but I feel like one of the oldest."

He cocked his head at her. "You're just tired."

"Yeah. That's it." She looked at Oz. "How many more days do you have?"

"I'm counting eight," he offered.

She sighed. "We should call home, see what's going on. And check in with Jean-Marc, too. I'll go find a phone."

She began to rise, but Angel put his hand on her forearm.

"Buffy, it worked. We have company," he said.

She ticked her gaze left and right without moving her head. "Where?"

"Outside. Across the street."

Buffy saw the shadows thrown across the walls of a news kiosk. No hooded robes. Maybe they were just thieves, but given the circumstances, she had to think they were coming to Mama.

"Wow, good eyesight. You probably get the really big stuffed animals at shooting galleries," she said to Angel.

Oz picked up his coffee bowl and sipped. "That was quick," he said idly. "I'm thinking that idea worked a little too well."

Buffy asked, "Could you tell how many?"

"No." Angel lit a cigarette and took a drag. "They might not be our roadies, but they're skulking around the way those guys tend to skulk."

"They're very skulky," Oz said. "I noticed that before."

"So. We pay our bill, get up, go outside, and get attacked," Buffy said. "You guys with me?"

Oz folded his napkin and laid it beside his plate.

Angel picked up the bill, chuckled. "They charged us extra for the butter. And after I bribed him for the good seats."

Buffy scowled and took the bill. She couldn't read a word. "Get out."

"And you even spoke decent French," Oz added, "at least that I could tell. I thought they didn't take advantage of people who at least made an effort."

"Apparently that's not the case at the Bistrot de la Place." Angel pulled out some francs. "I got some cash with Giles's card at a teller machine, around the corner," he explained before Buffy could ask. "That's where I've been. I'll just deduct the bogus charge."

"Stiff him." Buffy was embarrassed. She'd thought he'd slipped away to hunt. "No tip."

"You're merciless," Angel drawled.

She picked up her new English sweater—having decided, too late, that she was not really a heavy English sweater user—and her backpack. "Too bad we left the guns in the van."

"We've got our secret weapon," Oz said. "You."

The trio filed out of the Bistrot de la Place.

"Thank goodness the fog's lifted," Cordelia said, as she, Xander, and Willow drove slowly down the streets of Sunnydale. They'd gone out last night, gone home to fret until morning, and tried again.

Xander nodded. "Now we'll be able to see Giles if he's around here."

"Oh." Cordelia sounded taken aback. "There's that, too."

"Oh, what?" Xander asked irritably. "The fog's gone so now your hair won't frizz?"

Willow sighed and looked out the window. She was very worried about Giles, and Xander and Cordelia's bickering wasn't helping her mood or her concentration. She couldn't help but feel that this was her fault. If she'd been better at casting binding spells, if she knew how to make them last longer, he'd probably be home in his bed, safe and sound. Well, no, not in his bed, exactly, because that's where Buffy's mom was sleeping, and oh, she did not want to go anywhere near *that*.

Besides, it was almost one in the afternoon.

"There's nothing wrong with my hair!" Cordelia snapped at Xander, then peeked in the rearview mirror. "Is there?"

Then Willow realized that Cordelia was still worried about her new haircut, which had happened because Springheel Jack had set her head on fire. She felt a little more sympathetic—it had felt pretty radical, getting her own hair cut—so she leaned forward and said, "You look good. You always look good."

"Well, I try." Cordelia sniffed. "Not that my efforts are always appreciated."

"I'm sure the football team is grateful," Xander sniped.

"Now, you just stop that!" Willow smacked Xander on the back of the head. "You be nicer to her."

"What?" Xander's eyes had never been more enormous.

"Thanks, Willow."

Cordelia's smile had never been bigger.

When she was through being defender of the vain, Willow fell silent again. The Watcher had been missing since the night before, and they hadn't been able to find a single sign of him yet. Definitely a reason to worry, by any estimation. The way Xander had it figured, Giles was the Jedi master. Without him, the dark side would start to close in. Willow wasn't sure who was who in that little scenario, but she figured as long as she wasn't the Wookie, they were in good shape.

It was past one, though the way the sky was overcast, it was hard to tell the sun was even out to begin with. The days seemed to be sliding by much too quickly. There was no way to tell how long before the Gatekeeper finally expired, but the old man seemed convinced his son was still alive.

For now.

So the world was still in one piece.

For now.

"Um, okay," Buffy said, after they had sauntered down three blocks without incident. "Is it my breath?"

"Buffy, remember," Oz suggested, "in self-defense class, we learned that the person who walks and talks like a victim becomes a victim."

"No, Oz." Angel exhaled in frustration. "I mean, they know she's the Slayer. They're not going to buy it if she breaks a shoe heel."

"But how about if . . ." He stumbled and fell forward, landing on his hands and knees. "Whoops."

"Oz." Buffy reached for him. "You okay?"

"I think I scraped my knees," he said. "No big."

From out of the shadows, men in dark clothes raced at them full tilt, ramming into Buffy and Angel and flattening Oz to the ground.

Oz grunted and said, "Go, Sharks," which made no sense to Buffy whatsoever. Nevertheless, she took on the first two attackers at once—an older man with a circlet of hair and a younger man with a scar that ran over his nose from one temple to the other—and punched each of them hard, dead center in their faces. As their heads whipped back in pain, she fitted the tips of her fingers just under their sternums, cracking their ribcages. With silent gasps, the pair went down.

Angel was pummeling his attacker into a bloody pulp, and yet the man was able to conjure some kind of invisble force that threw Angel back against a chain-link fence and pinioned him there. The metallic links electrified; Angel began to quiver as if he were being electrocuted. His flesh smoked.

"Hey, *le* dirtbag!" Buffy shouted. She launched herself at the man, sending him flying against the fence himself. He screamed and began to convulse uncontrollably. Buffy felt the zing of the electricity and threw herself off him, yanking Angel away and flinging him to the ground.

The acolyte was horribly burned by the time he died.

Meanwhile, Oz had taken a few hits but returned a few more. But he was powerless as two of the Sons of Entropy murmured something at him and he clutched his eyes, moaning in agony.

"Angel!" Buffy shouted, and the two of them

rushed Oz's assailants, Angel matching each of Buffy's kicks and punches until it was like some strange, violent ballet performed to the pulsing of adrenaline through Buffy's body. They were in such perfect synch that it took her breath away.

Soon the two brethren lay unconscious at their feet, and Oz whispered, "My eyes. Can you see them?"

He looked blankly at Buffy, who touched his shoulder. "Yes. They look fine. It's probably temporary," she assured him, but in her heart she was very frightened for him. This was a rough crowd. There was no telling what they could do.

Livid, she renewed her attack on their attackers, ripping into the nearest acolyte, a guy who was actually pretty cute, when Angel shouted into her ear, "We should save a couple."

"Just this one," she said. "I'll just ruin his life and—"

"Buffy." Angel stayed her hand. "One more punch, and he's dead."

She looked down at the ruined man on the floor. "Guess I got a little carried away," she said softly, and then thought about Oz again.

She looked around. There were no other remaining Sons of Entropy. This was the last one, and the others had abandoned him.

She knelt beside him. "How much do you want to live?"

He opened his swollen eyes and stared at her.

"That's not the right question, Buffy," Angel said. "His boss is going to kill him anyway. And soon, if what we've seen before is any indication. The real question is . . ." He joined her at the man's side.

"How much can you take?" he asked, pressed down on a wound in the man's chest.

The man writhed, silently gasping.

"Hey," Oz protested, coming up beside them.

"Hey!" Buffy said back. "You can see."

"Oz, this isn't time for Amnesty International," Angel said. He hurt the man again, and Buffy steeled herself to go with it, go with the torture. Angel was right.

"Where is Il Maestro?" Angel demanded. "Tell me, and the pain stops."

"My life stops," the man rasped.

"Either way," Angel said flatly. "You know it, I know it. You're dead. How much do you want to suffer?"

"Oh, man," Oz murmured. "Oh, God. Angel, this is too much!"

When Angel turned on Oz, his face was contorted by vampirism.

"They just blinded you!" Angel snapped. "They're trying to kill us, to take Buffy, who knows why? And if we don't get that kid back, everything and everyone you love is probably doomed.

"Any questions?"

Oz shook his head slowly.

"Not a one."

Jean-Marc, young, vibrant, and powerful again, kissed his ghostly mother's careworn cheek and flung his arms wide. Energy crackled down the hundreds of corridors of the Gatehouse, sealing breaches, righting angles made terribly wrong. Fearsome creatures in their magickally bound pens shrieked with the knowledge that he was back; the Gatekeeper, their jailer, had resumed control. Ghouls raged; the Medusa cackled with madness. The Minotaur butted his head against the last turn in the maze in which he was imprisoned.

"How long?" Antoinette asked quietly.

"Long enough," Jean-Marc responded.

He stood at the window of his home and sent lightning bolts down among the Sons of Entropy. At least a third of the flashing bolts hit home, burning the enemy to death.

A second volley of bolts hit their mark.

A third.

Soon, only a handful of acolytes ran madly over the lawn.

"You've done it, my son," Antoinette said joyfully, clutching his hand. Only for the Gatekeeper was she formed of solid flesh.

"Mais non, Maman," Jean-Marc replied. His voice trembled, and when he looked at her, he had aged thirty years. It had been that way for several days already, a seemingly endless stream of acolytes of the Sons of Entropy trying to invade his home. It was war on a single front, and yet he was forced to fight it on infinite levels. This was only the most obvious. Day by day, he fought on.

"There will be more," Jean-Marc said wearily.

"I can make it stop," the one named Angel said soothingly. "Just give us an address. Then I'll let you go."

Flat on his back in the dirty, abandoned lot, the acolyte looked up into Angel's feral visage. He had been briefed; he knew the Slayer ran with a vampire and a werewolf. But he had not expected so much pain.

The master would destroy him for his failure. He only hoped it would be soon.

"My master is not forgiving," he managed to say in English, although he was Dutch by birth. How long ago that seemed: Amsterdam, meeting the Master in such an innocent way—a beer in a tavern, a few stories about his life, a very dirty joke about blonds— and then, the sacrificing of young girls, the blood, the degradation—

How far away now, as tears slid down his cheeks.

"It was real," he insisted. "All the magick was real."

"Pain is real," the vampire said, proving it.

In a corner by the fence, the other male companion of the Slayer retched. The young acolyte was grateful for his compassion.

Because he was in a lot of pain.

The vampire knew very well how to inflict it.

The one named Angel said now, "You are going to die. Tell me what I want to know, and it will be quick."

And now, even the Slayer turned white and looked away. And a strange thing happened: the Dutchman—Brother Hans—suddenly connected that she had a mother, and he had a mother, and both of them would mourn the deaths of their children. In that way, she was like him. Because Il Maestro would kill her eventually. It had to happen.

So he said to the vampire, in halting English

because the pain was taking away his ability to think, "A villa, in Florence. Off the Court of the Roses. I don't know it in Italian. I have never been there. But it is where my master is."

"Thank you." The vampire looked down on him, and his eyes were very sad. "Shall I leave you to your master?"

Young Hans blinked. "No," he begged. "I told you what you want to know."

A sharp turn of his head—

Peace.

Buffy and Oz waited around the corner from the alley in which Angel had caused their enemy so much pain. They both knew what was happening there now. It had to happen. Angel hadn't had a choice, and the acolyte was freshly dead in any case.

But Buffy felt so far, far away from Angel just then.

After a time Oz said, "Why didn't Il Maestro fry him?"

Buffy shook her head.

She almost wished he had.

Willow, Xander, and Cordelia had gotten out of the car to walk the streets, hoping for some sign of Giles. There was none. It was almost dinnertime, and their parents would soon begin to wonder where they were.

Giles had been missing for nearly twenty-four hours.

Willow twisted her hands. "This is bad," she said to Xander. "Really bad."

"Can't argue there." He gave her shoulders a quick squeeze. "We'll find him, Will. And we'll put one of those little beeping tags on him like they do with whales, and we'll never lose him again."

"Okay." She sniffled. "Because I hate this. I'm so worried about everybody, and the world might come to an end, pretty much, and if I can't say good-bye to Oz before it does—"

"Willow, shut up," Cordelia barked. "Pull yourself together."

"Cordy," Xander said angrily, "she's suffering."

Cordelia put her hands on her hips. "We're all suffering, Xander. So what? Is that going to help anyone in any way, shape, or form? I doubt it. It's our job to keep our cool and find Giles, okay? We can fall apart on our own time."

She burst into tears. "Which is not now," she said firmly, catching her breath.

"Wow." Xander looked at her with awe. "You are such a fabulous ice goddess."

"It just takes practice." She wiped her eyes. "So, we move on. We keep looking."

"Okey dokey," Xander said. He looked questioningly at Willow.

"Okey dokey," she replied, smiling bravely.

He hugged her. "That's my *chica*. That is to say, Oz's *chica*."

The phone rang a lot of times before someone answered.

Buffy said loudly, "Hello, Mr. Regnier? It's Buffy. Summers," she added. "Um, the Slayer?"

"Yes." He sounded amused. She was a bit affronted. He might know more than one Buffy Summers.

Then he coughed, hard, and began to hack, and she swallowed hard and said, "You're not feeling so great, I take it."

"Have you found my son?"

It was weird. One minute, he sounded like a healthy, middle-aged man. Now, it was like talking to the oldest man on Earth. His voice shook, and she could barely hear him.

"Not quite yet," she allowed, feeling terrible. "But we have an address, finally."

"Ah." There was a long silence. Then his voice was paper-thin as he said, "My son. Find my son. And . . . Buffy?"

"Yes?"

"Hurry."

They had made a grand sweep from the warehouses to the docks. Now Xander, Willow, and Cordelia stood at the harbor, looking out at a black horizon and a blacker sea, coming up with nothing. Xander was truly at a loss.

It was Sunday night, and they were all late for dinner. Xander didn't want to admit that he was giving up hope, but he was on the verge of suggesting that they all sneak back home, deal with screaming parents, and start fresh after school the next day. Grounded, they were no good to anybody.

Then they heard a man say, "Is that the police?"

Willow looked at Xander, who cleared his throat and stepped forward. He moved forward onto the latticework of docks. An elderly man in a dark blue windbreaker and a pair of jeans was standing on the deck of a really cool sailboat. The cabin light was on.

"May I help you?" Xander asked.

"You're not the police. You're too young for the police." He looked irritated. "Some man was hang-gliding in the fog. Very dangerous. He could hurt someone. Or get hurt. Probably drowned."

"I saw him, too," came another voice in the dark.

Another elderly man popped out of a long sailboat beside the first elderly man's.

"Couldn't sleep, so I was reading Melville. I saw him fly by. Couldn't imagine a man like that doing such a thing."

"A man like that," Xander echoed.

The man nodded. "Middle-aged. Well dressed." The man chuckled. "For a second, I thought he was your boy."

"My son's in Malaysia with his wife," the man said, and looked at Xander. "She's a tropical ecologist."

"Kinky," Xander offered.

"It wasn't my boy," he said to the other old man.

"Looked like your boy. Nice brown hair. A bit tweedy."

Cordelia and Willow caught their breaths. Xander did, too. The three looked at each other.

"Tweedy," Willow murmured.

Cordelia added, "Hang-gliding."

Xander said, "We gotta get a boat."

Joyce didn't want to lie to Buffy, but she didn't want to tell her the truth, either. She so wanted to protect her daughter—spare her—but she knew what she had to do. She had to tell Buffy the truth.

"Mr. Giles isn't here, sweetheart," Joyce said softly. "We don't know where he is."

Buffy was silent. Joyce closed her eyes tight.

"They're looking for him," she added.

"Oh, Mom, oh, no," Buffy murmured in a frightened voice, and in that moment, Buffy was her little girl, her very little girl, and Joyce was a young mother again, amazed that this beautiful, tiny thing had actually come from her body into her life. She would do anything for this baby.

"Honey, I'm sorry. They'll find him," Joyce said.

"Yeah. Okay. I'll call again soon, Mom. I've . . . gotta go."

"Honey, wait! Tell me how you are. Tell me—"

The connection had been broken.

Joyce stared across the room.

The fog was so thick she could barely see the house across the street.

Chapter 8

"AND THEN, WHEN WE MADE THE BEACH IN NORMANDY, the enemy gave us hell. Pure hell," the elderly man in the windbreaker was telling Willow and Cordelia.

Seated on his boat as it bobbed at the Sunnydale dock, they nodded politely, holding cups of hot chocolate he had made for them on the propane stove. The boat rocked and creaked while the man droned on, oblivious to their anxiety. Meanwhile, Xander wandered around, his frustration evident to the girls.

"Why, every other boy who hit that beach was killed. The carnage was unbelievable." He shook his head. "First time I saw a dead body, I thought I was going to upchuck."

"Yeah, same here," Willow blurted, then cleared her throat and stared down into her chocolate.

"In that movie last year, she means. We saw the movie," Cordelia told him quickly. "It was intense, wasn't it?" She touched her chest. "I had to go into the lobby for a few minutes." Would he never shut up? She was sweating bullets. The sun was beginning to rise, and though they'd done the whole round-robin "I'm staying at so-and-so's" thing, she was still paranoid that she'd get caught. If her parents found out she'd stayed out all night . . .

Switzerland.

The man scowled. She was pretty sure he had told them his name but now she couldn't remember. She was that tired.

The man checked his watch. "Well, I guess it's time to start the day. Sun'll be up soon, and I'm going fishing." He cocked his head. "Don't you kids have school?"

"Yeah, we sure do," Willow said, shifting uneasily. "But we're doing a biology project where we have to collect nocturnal sea specimens. Our boat . . ." She looked at Cordelia, clearly at a loss.

"Broke," Cordelia cut in. She waved her hand. "Just broke, just like that. The floor part of it, um, we found a hole in it, and we need to borrow another boat so we can go collect the specimens."

"Oh, gee, that's too bad. Where is it?" he asked. "Maybe I can give you a hand with a patch job."

"We left it at home," Willow explained. "We were hoping we could borrow—"

"Hey, girls, time for school," Xander piped up, coming over to them. He stood on the dock and put one foot on the boat. "We'll have to look for my uncle's boat later."

"And the sea specimens," Willow added, eyes wide and innocent.

"Oh, yeah, those elusive specimens. What are you going to do?" He laughed and clapped his hands together. "So. Let's go. Now."

They climbed off the boat and waved good-bye. As Xander hustled them toward Cordelia's car, Cordelia hissed, "Xander, what are you doing? He was just about to lend us a boat!"

He exhaled. "Well, I didn't know that, did I? And it comes a little late. The sun's almost up. We're out of time."

"Now what?" Cordelia demanded.

"Now we go to school so we don't get in trouble, and we come back after school and steal the little red boat that's tied up all by itself next to that promontory over there."

"Promontory?" Cordelia asked, raising an eyebrow.

Willow sighed. "Don't you remember? It was the only word he got right in the fifth-grade spelling bee. I'm sure he's been waiting to use it ever since."

Xander looked a bit downhearted, but pointed to the long pile of rocks that jutted into the ocean. Willow and Cordelia turned. Cordelia squinted, even though that was the straightest road to crow's feet ever invented, except for going out in the sun without at least SPF 25 on.

"I don't see a little red boat," Willow said slowly.

"Good." Xander grinned at them. "Then maybe no one else will."

"Did you put it there?" Cordelia asked.

"Yup. It looked lonely. I befriended it." He rubbed his hands. "So. We go to school, all right? Because if we don't show, either the principal will send the Imperial Stormtroopers to our houses or our parents will ground us for life."

The girls nodded glumly.

"We'll find Giles," Xander said comfortingly. He put his arms around both their shoulders. Cordelia smiled bravely.

"And he won't be chicken nuggets, like that last guy they found on the beach," Xander added.

"Oh, God!" Willow burst into tears.

This time, Cordelia joined her.

"Florence is the ancestral home of the de' Medicis," Oz read from his guidebook. "Interesting. It's where the original Bonfire of the Vanities took place. Wigs, musical instruments, books of poetry, and works of art all went up in flames."

"Musical instruments," Buffy mused from the front seat of the minivan, as Angel took a turn at driving. "They must have heard Glorious Mélange."

Oz smiled at her and flicked his flashlight back on the page.

"The guy who ordered the burning was a fanatic monk who got burned on the same spot a year later. Savonarola."

"The lead guitarist," Buffy said. "Anything about a Court of the Roses? A villa there?" Angel had told them the information he had extracted from the acolyte he'd tortured in Paris.

"No," Oz replied. "I guess we'll just have to ask when we get there."

They were still in France, headed for the Italian

border. Oz had gathered up some books in a small shop near the Cathedral of Notre Dame and occasionally read passages aloud to her and Angel. Sometimes Angel added observations, and Buffy realized he'd roamed all over the continent during his life as Angelus, the Scourge of Europe.

"After the world gets saved, I'm thinking backpacking around Europe. Eurail passes," Oz said. "Willow, me, anybody else who'd like to go."

Buffy looked out the window at the darkness. After this, it would probably be back to Sunnydale for the rest of her natural life. Slayers didn't exactly get time off for exotic vacations. Not even sick days, really.

She thought of the little boy they were searching for. Jacques. His life was similar to hers: he had to live in the Gatehouse, with the occasional foray to gather up some monster or demon. She couldn't imagine having to be the Slayer at eleven. At least she'd had a few good years of blissful ignorance.

A few years of blissful freedom.

Angel made a sudden left into a side road. Badly paved, it led into a thick wood. The beams of the minivan pierced a hole of light in the dense growth of trees that overhung the road. Shadows flashed by, and Buffy sat up a little straighter.

"See anything?" she asked. "Someone following us?"

"Just evasive maneuvers," Angel replied. "I don't think we should trust anyone from here on out. Except each other, of course. No matter what they appear to be, we have to behave as though they are the enemy."

After a few minutes, Angel said, "Let's stop a minute. Stretch our legs."

Buffy, who had to go to the bathroom, said, "Good idea. But we can't linger."

"No lingering," Angel concurred.

"Machiavelli lived in Florence," Oz added, as Angel pulled the van into a particularly dense copse and killed the engine. "All the schemers like it."

"Guess so," Buffy said. "Must have a hellmouth or something. Or a breach."

"Good point." Oz flicked the guidebook shut. "So, maybe with Willow, we skip Florence."

Buffy smiled wistfully. The car ticked noisily as she pushed open her door and hopped out.

"How are we doing on gas?" she asked Angel.

"We'll need some before daybreak."

They had taken to paying for everything they could with cash from teller machines so as not to leave a trail of credit card receipts. But despite all the precautions they took, they had to assume they were being followed. It was the best way to stay on their guard.

Buffy took her flashlight and walked away from the boys, who must have figured out she had private business to attend to and left her alone.

The forest was chilly and smelled of fresh earth. As she walked along, she saw a ring of mushrooms and smiled, delighted. Giles had told her that in England they were called fairy rings and were taken as evidence of the presence of fairies. Once he'd seen a ring and had spent all day looking for magickal sprites. He'd gotten in big trouble with his mother, who had spent all day looking for *him*.

Tears stung her eyes, and she wiped them away angrily. She was worried sick about Giles. She had tried to push her fear for him to the back of her mind so she could concentrate on the task at hand, but it was always there, like a low-level hum from an old TV set.

As they stood waiting for Buffy to return, staring off into the woods, Oz glanced at Angel.

"It's tough for her," he said.

"It's tough, period," Angel replied grimly. "We should get going."

"Miles to go before we sleep. Want me to drive?"

Angel shook his head. "I'm good. You two should get some sleep. We can try the blanket-in-the-back thing again this morning. I'm just a little concerned about crossing the Italian border."

Oz considered. "It might make sense to get you a room someplace. You could catch up later."

"We'll see." Angel straightened as the bushes rustled. "Hey, Buffy, we're going," he called.

The forest erupted.

Dozens of foot-long creatures swarmed at Oz and Angel, crashing down from the trees and springing from the forest floor. Angel flailed wildly, trying to grab one. Finally he caught one around the head and held it into the headlights of the beam as more sprang at him, biting. It was some kind of winged reptile, its blue-and-green head lizardlike, a furl of ridged scales around its neck. Its tongue was very long, and it hissed and spit at him. He ducked, but the creature's saliva ate a hole in his turtleneck sweater. With its sharp claws it dug into the flesh of his arm and tore a stinging scratch from the inside of his elbow to his wrist.

"Damn!" he shouted, hurling it to the ground and stamping on it. "Oz, get in the van!"

But Oz was there beside him, ripping the little monsters away from Angel. For some reason, not a single one of them had attacked Oz. All they wanted, it seemed, was Angel, and they were all over him, nipping and scratching. They never stopped moving.

Then Buffy burst from the bushes, shouting, "Yeowwww!" as she ran headfirst toward the van, then contracted and rammed her shoulders against the door, crushing the three lizard creatures savaging her head and neck.

"What the hell are they?" she asked, kicking and punching for all she was worth. But the creatures could fly, and she succeeded only in stunning a couple as they darted out of her reach.

"No idea," Angel said, moving closer to her and ripping one of the things away from her.

Buffy tried to do the same, but there were too many of them. Their combined weight was almost too much for her. Angel tried to help, but even he was having trouble.

"What the hell are these things?" Oz shouted, tearing the lizards off Angel and Buffy. They still would not go near him.

"They're Draco Volans," came a voice. "Compliments of Il Maestro."

There was an explosion. Then the air above them shimmered with rosy light, and the creatures began to chitter and then to scream. One by one they dropped off Angel and Buffy and fell limply to the ground. The tree above them waved left, right, then disgorged at least twenty of the creatures, their bodies raining down on Buffy and Angel.

Buffy shouted, "Show yourself!"

Someone staggered from the opposite direction, heading directly toward the van. He wore a hooded robe, and he was drenched from head to toe in blood.

He held out his hands and pointed to Buffy and Angel, murmuring in a foreign language.

"Back off, pally!" Buffy snarled, and raced toward the hooded man.

"Buffy, no, it's Latin," Angel said, as the man tried to dodge Buffy. "It's a healing spell."

"Oh, yeah?" She grabbed the man around the neck. Her fingers were slick with his blood. "It must not work too well. Look at him."

The man gazed at her. "Please, I saved you. From the manticore. I shot it."

Startled, Buffy released him. "You're the catacombs guy."

His head dipped forward. He held out his hand, and she guided him slowly toward the van as Oz and Angel moved to join them. Buffy realized that both she and Angel seemed to be mostly healed, despite the blood on their clothes.

"Why didn't they come after you?" Angel asked Oz.

"Garlic breath?" Oz suggested.

"Ask Spooky," Buffy said, then looked the bloody man in the face. "What about it?"

"The Draco Volans have a thing about wolves," the man replied, with a slight smile. "I wish I could do more for you all. Il Maestro is tracking you with magick. I was able to exploit the presence of his spell to follow you myself, but now he surely knows that I am here."

"In other words, you're pretty much history," Buffy said, not unkindly.

"How well you put it." He smiled weakly. "Yes, I fear I am very much history." He winced. "I can't make it to your car. Please, help me sit down."

As Buffy helped him to a sitting position beside the hood of the van, he slid his hand into a fold of his robe. Buffy tensed, on alert.

He pulled out a photograph.

"My name is Albert," he said. "Please tell her I was brave."

Buffy took the picture. The woman in it had lovely honey-blond hair, which she wore loose over her shoulders. Wordlessly she handed the picture to Angel.

"We were misled by him," the man said. "He promised us power in a new world." As he clutched Buffy's arm, blood ran down his fingers. "We didn't know about the evil." He coughed. The light began to go from his eyes.

"That's a lie," he said, gasping. He began to loosen his grip. "We did know. We knew all along. And it didn't matter. But then . . . I fell in love with her. Who wouldn't?"

He coughed again. Great gouts of blood burbled from the side of his mouth.

Buffy turned him over. The back of his coat was ripped to shreds, and pieces of skin and muscle poked from the slashes. She could see pieces of his spine, and wondered how he had lasted this long. If Il Maestro's little remote-control fire was on the way, it would have to hurry to take this poor man's life.

"He's in Florence," the man said, gasping. "You must get to Florence."

Buffy chewed her lip and narrowed her eyes as she watched him dying. Angel shook his head, and she knew what he was thinking. They should trust no one, assume everybody was an enemy. Like Ian Williams.

"No. That's not true," she said slowly, looking hard at Angel and Oz. "He's in Vienna. It was always Vienna. We just got word from . . . other friends."

The man looked bewildered. "Not Florence?"

"Not Florence."

"Ah." He closed his eyes. "That's good. He won't know that you know that."

He mumbled a few syllables and moved his fingers. Buffy felt a tingle over her skin and said, "What are you doing?"

"It's a weak effort," he whispered. "But I may be able to blind Il Maestro to your presence." He lifted his hand and mumbled some more. Then his head flopped forward.

"Micaela," he whispered.

He gasped, and was dead.

Oz looked at her. "Vienna?"

Buffy just shrugged.

Around them, the Draco Volans burst into flames.

Giles woke with a start.

He was lying on the deck of the *Dutchman* in all its ghastly decay. Set against the black velvet night, the spiderweb rigging hung in tatters. The ship herself was little more than worm-eaten planks barely hanging together.

Confused, Giles checked his watch. It should be day now. But above them the night was black as death. *Perhaps,* he thought dimly, *perhaps aboard the Flying Dutchman it's night forever.*

He shifted his gaze, to find ghostly faces peering down at him. Some had no eyes, and yet they stared. The hair rose on the back of Giles's neck. There was a stir among them, and they fell slightly away, clearing a path. A figure appeared, seemingly out of thin air. It was clad in dull black, and its face was . . . its face . . .

Giles was chilled to the bone. There was no way to account for the terror he felt, for he was looking at nothing but blank darkness. Yet the sight stirred more fear inside him than anything else he had ever seen, any demon or monster he had ever encountered. He was certain this was its strongest weapon, and why its captives wept.

Giles knew what he must do.

The element of surprise could still be his.

He cleared his throat and stood with his feet spread wide, and said, in a jocular, easy voice, "Captain, I should like permission to come aboard. I've a terrible thirst, and I know many sea chanteys, and it would be pleasant to pass a few hours with you and your crew."

The faceless specter stared at Giles for a long moment. Then it threw back its head and laughed heartily, but both sound and movement stretched forward slowly, as if emanating from another dimension.

"Permission granted, mortal man. As you are al-

ready aboard. And as you have the stomach of a buccaneer and the sense of an ass. In the centuries I have sailed these wretched seas, no man has ever asked to remain on my ship of his own free will."

"Well, sir, I may be an ass, but I'm a curious one," Giles countered, straining to keep his voice from shaking. "I've heard many stories about you and your illustrious crew. And it would be my pleasure to spend a few hours in your company."

But no more. He had to get off this vessel as soon as he could, hopefully with Vinnie. If he had to leave alone, he must be prepared to do it.

"Illustrious!" The figured laughed again, and the sound rumbled like distant cannon fire. *"A few hours, or eternity?"*

"Grant me a boon, sir," Giles said, licking his lips as he raised his chin. "If my singing pleases you, release me after the watch sets. If I disappoint, I shall join your crew."

"Done." The figure pounded the railing with its fist, its motions blurred and sluggish, at least to Giles's eyes. Somehow, Giles managed to stay on his feet, though his knees had turned to jelly.

Then a flash of movement above caught his attention. He looked up, and would wish for the rest of his life—however long it was—that he had not.

From the yards swung three bodies among dozens of full and partial skeletons and skulls. Their faces were black, their tongues protruding. They had been hung alive. Among them was Dallas Mayhew, one of Sunnydale High's most valued football players; the second was his best friend, Spenser Ketchum, and the third was a young woman with a blond ponytail, dressed in overalls and a green T-shirt. Her eyes were missing, and the sockets were bloody.

For one terrible moment, Giles thought she was Buffy. And he cursed himself for getting himself stuck here, when he should be doing eveything possible to help his Slayer. It had been pure impulse, grabbing the anchor. Or pure stupidity.

Giles swallowed hard and shifted his attention. The ship rocked in blackness; he could see no shore lights, no lighthouse. He had no idea how far out to sea he was. He wondered if soon he would hang from the yards with the others. At least Vinnie was not there. Yet.

Something very cold touched his shoulder, like ice running over his bare skin, and he turned to find the Captain standing behind him. Giles was afraid that if he looked closely into its face, he would completely lose control. So he turned on his heel and cut an old-fashioned bow, which was probably out of date even when the *Dutchman* had originally been commissioned, and a living captain and crew sailed her.

"Captain, Everett Morris at your service," Giles said. There was nothing to be gained by telling this creature his real name.

Giles could feel the figure's gaze on him. It was enough to make his knees wobble.

"Welcome aboard, Rupert Giles," it replied.

"Ah." Giles sighed. "I should have known better, sir, than to dissemble."

"Indeed."

The figure gestured for Giles to follow. It did not exactly float over the deck, but its strange, gliding gait was unlike that of any of the crew. It did not seem to be actually present, rather like a projection of something from somewhere else.

It led Giles up the poop deck and waited regally while one of its dead sailors opened a large wooden door. Then it turned to go down a steep ladderway, gazing up at Giles and saying, *"Custom aboard this vessel dictates that I lead the way."*

"Of course, Captain."

Giles watched it descend. With every fiber of his being, he did not want to follow after. His mind was screaming at him to jump overboard and swim as fast as he could, no matter the illogic of flinging himself into the ocean far from shore.

With supreme effort, he turned around and started down the ladder.

The hatch above slammed shut, throwing him into utter darkness.

He went down another rung.

Something furry skittered over his hand, squeaking. Rat. Slowly he lowered himself to the next rung. He smelled something rotten, and his stomach rolled. He closed his mouth against his gag reaction, took a deep breath, and went down another rung.

Mister Giles, it's a long way down, the Captain said. *It's almost like going to Hell.*

"How delightful," Giles bit off.

He continued on, his muscles aching, his mouth dry as dust. After a time he felt disoriented, as the ship rocked and the ladder stretched for what seemed like forever. They couldn't possibly still be inside the ship. Yet in the darkness, he had no idea where else he could be.

He lowered his foot for the next rung, and touched

something solid instead. Carefully, he lowered his other foot and stood on a hard surface.

He held on to the ladder for a moment, getting his bearings.

As he turned, a light gleamed dully at the end of what appeared to be a short corridor. The door was cracked open.

He took a breath and tried to remember the lyrics to old sea songs he had learned in Boy Scouts. Everything had fled. He searched his memory for a few melodies, but all he could hear was the clattering of the bones as the three fresh bodies swayed from the yards.

He walked down the corridor and pushed open the door. Inside, candlelight flickered, revealing a once-palatial cabin now covered with dust and draped with spiderwebs. The cabin ceiling flared toward the rear, leaving plenty of space for the rotted velvet canopy above a large, carved bed. A large leaded-glass window was propped open, admitting the sea breeze.

On a table, which apparently had been recently cleared of maps and charts, now haphazardly piled at one end, two pewter tankards gleamed in the yellow light. Behind one of them, facing the door, sat the Captain.

Giles made himself acknowledge the figure, trembling as he did so. It inclined its head in turn and gestured for Giles to be seated.

Giles sat and picked up the tankard. There was liquid inside, giving off a smell that reminded him of the hot buttered rum one of the teachers had mixed for the faculty Christmas party.

"Cheers," Giles said, and sipped. He nearly

choked; it was extremely potent, very heavy on the gin.

The figure picked up its own tankard and raised it toward Giles. Then it drank in silence, draining the contents. With a contented sigh, it put the tankard down.

Giles picked his up again. As he took another drink, he realized his thirst was becoming unmanageable This was only going to make it worse.

"If I might," he began, then started when a small, heavy glass appeared beside his right elbow. He sniffed the liquid and tasted it. It was water.

"Thank you," he said. He drank it greedily. As he began to put down the glass, it refilled. He drank that too. It refilled.

"Well, that's convenient," he said.

The Captain chuckled. *There are compensations to being damned for all eternity.*

"I see," Giles said. "Your glass is half full."

The Captain laughed delightedly. *I have missed wit. I have missed companionship. Here, I am only feared.*

"One might venture to say that hanging anyone who comes aboard may have something to do with that," Giles said boldly.

The figure shrugged. *Not all. Currently, three mortals including you draw breath upon this vessel.*

"I see," Giles said, his heart skipping a beat. Who else besides Vinnie, he wondered. He would have to find them both.

No need to concern yourself with them. They'll die eventually, even if I do not kill them.

"Indeed?"

Flowers cannot grow in salt. Mortals cannot live aboard a ghost ship. The Captain leaned forward. *You promised me some songs.*

"Yes, I did," Giles said firmly, and to his surprise and great relief, an old British chantey sprang full-blown into his mind, about blowing winds and harpoons and all manner of nautical things.

Excellent, said the specter, sitting back to listen. *I knew you would not disappoint me.*

Giles smiled and sang.

Screaming would have suited him far better.

"Well, he's not going poof, either," Buffy said, as she, Oz, and Angel stood over dead Albert in the forest. She wanted very badly to bury him. They were starting to leave a trail of bodies. And frankly, it bothered her to think of him rotting here, all alone, after he'd turned to the good side of the force.

"Let's have a quick shovel detail," she said.

"Too bad we don't actually have a shovel," Oz said. "Maybe there's something else in the van we could use."

As he turned to go, Albert's body shifted on the ground. Buffy glanced at Angel. Maybe the man wasn't dead after all.

"Albert?" she said softly.

Then the body rose into the air as if someone had lifted it. It hovered just above their heads for a moment, then continued to rise. Blood dripped from the wounds like scattered raindrops.

"Did that other guy do that?"

Angel shrugged. "Not that I know of."

The body floated higher, out of sight.

"Tell me that's the way we all go to heaven," Oz murmured.

"I hope so." Buffy looked up at the stars. "Rest in peace."

Angel replied stonily, "Somehow I doubt he will."

Giles was a hit.

He was also fairly drunk, which made him an even bigger hit.

The Captain had led him back to the main deck, where Giles had entertained the crew for what seemed like hours, never mind their agreement about spending one watch aboard the *Dutchman*. But Giles's mind was on more than sea chanteys, grog, and his own life.

He had seen where they kept Vinnie and a man who, by the looks of him, was some kind of dock worker. Chillingly, they were imprisoned in the galley, where Giles had been escorted when the Captain determined it was time to decant a very old bottle of port. The shadowy figure made a great show of opening a cabinet above several barrels of desiccated apples and extracting a flask coated with aged grime.

On the other side of the cabinet, the two were literally caged in a lean-to made of planks and rope, and both had been gagged. The Captain made a comment about tiring of "the caterwauling."

When Giles walked into the galley, the eyes of both prisoners bulged above their gags. Their wrists were bound in front of them very tightly, yet as they rushed forward they tried to push them through the slats. He tried to signal them to be quiet, his concern for them increasing as he watched them struggle to conceal their soaring hopes that this nightmare was over. For it was not over yet, and Giles wasn't certain he could end it.

Now, staggering from the effects of the stress and the drink, Giles lifted his voice in song yet again, leading the crew in a rousing rendition of "A Maid from Nantucket," accompanied by a hellish accordion.

The dead grouped around him as the wind picked up, rocking the ship and making the bones overhead clack furiously. Some sang in an eerie, empty monotone, as if their souls had been so consumed that the intangible beauty of music was lost to them. Others were slightly more lively, although Giles could detect no sense of good humor or particular enthusiasm, as if the best they could manage was a respite from suffering, rather than actually enjoying the moment.

After a time, he began to feel rather like a desperate court jester playing to a crowd that would prefer an execution to a song and dance. But it was when he took the bottle of port and drank deeply of it that inspiration hit, for the Captain said, *"Drink up, my lad. There's more where that came from."*

More. In the galley. Where the prisoners were.

With grim determination, Giles polished off the bottle, then volunteered to get another bottle. The Captain consented, and Giles worked furiously to keep his thinking clear as he staggered into the galley, pretending to search for the bottle in the cabinet when in reality he flung himself against the cage and muttered, "I'll get you out. Don't panic. Have you seen a knife anywhere? Any kind of weapon?"

His questions were answered by frantic gesturing by the two prisoners.

Giles said again, "Don't panic."

Vinnie Navarro shook his head and moaned through his gag.

Slowly Giles turned around, the galley spinning as he did so.

The Captain stood in the doorway, its blank face shadowed. Its stance spoke volumes about its fury.

"I should have known," was all it said. *"Ye'll be walking the plank, then, Rupert Giles. And our big ugly lady shall have you for her supper. 'Tis a shame, too. Ye've got a wonderful ear for music."*

The Captain laughed at that.

Chapter 9

WILLOW THOUGHT SHE WOULD NEVER MAKE IT through the school day. When she finally got to her room, she collapsed in a heap and nodded off almost immediately.

In her dream, the Ghost of College Applications Past Due sat at the foot of her bed. He was very sad because she had missed the cutoff date . . . because there were no nice Jewish boys at his college . . . because she was missing so much school that her conditional status at Bryn Mawr was being revoked . . .

"Little Willow."

Her eyes flickered open.

"Spellcaster, awaken now, for you are needed."

She bolted upright to find a man in her room, sitting at the edge of the bed. He was an old man, stooped and shaking, and at first she wasn't sure he was really there.

"Um," she said.

"Jean-Marc Regnier," he said, stooping lower. Bowing, she realized.

"The Gatekeeper?" Of all of them, Willow had never actually met the Gatekeeper. She stared in shock. He looked terrible. He looked like he was a thousand years old.

"Not for much longer." He smiled sadly.

"They're hurrying," Willow earnestly assured him. "They're trying really hard."

"I have a task for you, little Willow." He wheezed, coughing. He seemed to dim. She blinked rapidly. Her heart was pounding. She'd seen a lot of weird things in her life, and this was not the weirdest, but it was the weirdest thing that had ever happened in her bedroom. So far.

"Task, okay," she said, sitting up. She looked worriedly at her door. "But please, um, with the coughing, my parents might hear you. No offense."

A smile flickered across his face, to be replaced by a look of such dead seriousness that she bit her lip.

"A breach," he said shakily, "of such immense proportions even I can scarcely imagine it."

"At Buffy's house?" she asked shrilly, then remembered her own admonition and lowered her voice. "Where?"

"In the sea. Beneath the surface. The *Dutchman* caused it."

"The what?"

"The sailing ship. The *Flying Dutchman*. I bound her and her crew over a century ago. Now they are free, and my runestones tell me she has flown to your skies." He sighed, looking defeated. "First the Kraken, and then that infernal vessel. The breach is wide, and it is growing."

"Oh." Her eyes got huge. "She flies?"

Giles. Hang-gliding.

"You must bind that breach. I will help you," he said. "But it must be done at once. There's no time to spare."

"But I need time to spare," she said anxiously. "I need to find Giles. Buffy's Watcher."

He shook his head. "Impossible," he said. "You must get up from your bed and aid me. *Now.*"

At the top of his lungs, Xander sang, "'It never rains in Southern California!'"

But, of course, it was raining.

It wasn't much, really—a light but persistent shower that had been coming down since early afternoon. They had waited in high anxiety for night to hide them. That would be dangerous enough for three unseasoned seafarers to go boating in. But with the unbelievable fog that seemed to have enveloped the entire town, what they were doing seemed something on the verge of suicide.

With Willow and Cordelia in tow, Xander had sneaked back down to the wharf and retrieved the little red boat he had so conveniently borrowed and hidden away. They were in waters that had been declared off limits by the Coast Guard, at least for now. Their boat was tiny, in comparison to the fishing trawlers that had been torn apart by the Kraken already. But they didn't have much choice. They had to find Giles. They had to seal the breach that the Gatekeeper had come to warn Willow about.

"Hey, Will," Xander said tentatively. "I just had a good thought. A happy. If the Gatekeeper was able to go walkabout and come see you, he must be feeling better, right?"

Willow grimaced, and Xander wished he had never asked.

"Not right," Willow replied. "He's still dying, Xand. It's almost like he's in this weird cycle now, powering up and then draining back down again."

She made a face. "Pretty soon, he won't be able to power up anymore. Used to be, he would have come and closed this breach himself, instead of just giving me the pep talk and saying 'yay, team.' Yeah. Go, Willow, go, but if you don't close this breach before it gets too big, we may not have to worry about the Sons of Entropy because, guess what, it's gonna happen anyway.

"Nothing like a little pressure to relieve the stress, right?"

Cordelia patted Willow's head lightly, smiled wanly, and said, "Yay, team."

Xander frowned at her. "Cor, you're taking this rather well."

"I'm past the whole rational thought stage," Cordelia said. "Monsterama overload. Wake me up when it's over."

"Will do," Xander replied. "But I wish you'd stop saying that to me."

Even Willow smiled at that one.

The waves lapped at the sides of the boat. The rain fell even more lightly now, almost a mist, and Cordelia stopped complaining about being damp. After a while, Xander thought, even she seemed to realize there was little point.

"This is bad," Willow said, gazing around them into the nothingness, the ocean rocking the boat. "We've got to find the *Flying Dutchman*. I can bind the breach all right—at least, I think I can—but we can't do that until we find Giles."

"So we find Giles. It may take a while, but . . ." Xander offered.

Willow shook her head. "You haven't been listening, Xander," she snapped. "We don't have a while. The Gatekeeper said that if we can't free Giles really fast, he and I will have to bind the breach anyway, or it'll get too big. Giles will be trapped onboard the *Flying Dutchman* forever."

Xander didn't have a snappy comeback for that one. Instead, he simply sat in the rear of the boat, using the tiller to steer and wiping the engine dry from time to time. He didn't know a thing about boats, not really. But he suspected that keeping the condensation from the fog from building up on the outboard was a good idea. And if it didn't matter, well, at least it gave him something to concentrate on besides, well, life.

He was sitting in a boat off the coast of his hometown with two of the three women who made his emotional life a circus. Just being alone with them made him uncomfortable. But it seemed like things had been pretty much that way since Buffy had come into his life. It was only really through her that he came to realize, or at least, to admit to himself, that Willow cared for him.

Xander loved Buffy, Buffy loved Angel, Willow

loved Xander. Then Xander fell into whatever this was with Cordelia—not love, at least he didn't think so—and Willow was in love with Oz. And that was how it was supposed to be, right? What the hell was wrong with the lot of them, that's what he wanted to know.

What was worse—and this was a question he had tried desperately not to consider—was that he had to wonder if this insanity would continue into adulthood. Or did people start to get some kind of handle on their emotions as they grew up? He was afraid he wouldn't like the answer.

Willow shivered, and without even thinking about it, Xander slipped out of his jacket and handed it to her. Gratefully, she accepted it and pulled it around her shoulders.

"I'm cold, too, y'know," Cordelia huffed.

Xander raised an eyebrow. "And that's new?"

She rolled her eyes and moved closer to Willow, who seemed content to share her warmth. They went on like that for quite some time until, at long last, the fog seemed to disperse around them. It took Xander a moment to realize that he'd been mistaken. The fog was not going away. Rather, they had come to some kind of clearing in the fog, like the eye of a hurricane.

"This is weird," Willow said, her voice echoing a little off the misty walls around them.

From far above them, a shout split the night.

"God, what is going on?" Cordelia cried miserably.

There was another shout. Louder. Nearer. Then, perhaps fifty yards to the right—the distance difficult to judge in the fog—there came a loud splash.

Then nothing.

Xander looked at Willow. "The voice," he said. "It sounded like . . ."

"Giles," Willow agreed.

"But how can that be?" Cordelia asked. "Librarians don't just fall out of the sky, y'know, not even . . . not even here!"

All three of them began shouting Giles's name into the dark. Into the fog. They could see perhaps thirty feet around them, but beyond that, there was nothing. Xander couldn't even see the lights from shore now.

"Willow, we could use some Gatekeeper help right about now," Xander said.

"He said he'd be here," Willow replied, looking around. "I thought he meant when we'd be, here, but . . ."

Again, they shouted Giles's name.

At last, they heard an answer. "Here!" Giles bellowed. "Over here!"

His voice echoed, but Xander thought he had pinpointed roughly the area where Giles had called from. He pushed the tiller in that direction, and the little outboard rumbled in the water.

"Xander!" Willow shouted.

He turned around, saw the huge, rusted, barnacle-encrusted anchor swing toward him, and he threw himself down in the boat, practically on top of Willow and Cordelia. Lying in the boat, he stared up as it passed overhead: The rotting hull of an ancient sailing ship, dripping seaweed and blood, flooded with mist. The anchor that swung beneath it had nearly taken Xander's head off.

The boat had begun to spin out of control, and now he grabbed the tiller again and turned back toward where he thought he'd heard Giles call out. The same direction the boat was now headed. Xander guided the boat into the fog once more.

"Xander, move it!" Cordelia snapped.

"What do you think I'm doing?" he shouted at her, losing his cool.

"Guys," Willow said softly. "Maybe, ssshhhhh?"

Huffing, Xander held the boat on a steady course. Soon, they heard Giles splashing about and quietly calling for aid.

"Giles?" Xander said softly, his voice thrown back at him by the fog. He couldn't see much above him, but he knew the huge ghost ship was up there. From far off, he thought he could hear dead men singing.

"Here!" Giles said, a bit too loud.

Then he was there, materializing out of the fog, his head bobbing above the surface of the water.

"You look like a drowned rat," Xander said, as he helped the Watcher aboard the tiny boat.

"Yes, pleasant to see you as well," Giles said.

"Uh, Willow, maybe it's time to seal that breach?" Cordelia suggested.

"No!" Giles snapped, turning on them. "You can't send the *Dutchman* back yet. There are still two people alive onboard that ship. At least, they were when I saw them last."

Willow looked at Giles. "The Gatekeeper said the breach was already a questionable size. I really had to fight to buy some time to save you."

"Then fight harder," he told her.

Xander shook his head. "There's no time, Giles.

It's nothing but dumb luck that you fell out of the sky. We never would have found you otherwise."

"I didn't . . ." Giles began to protest. "They made me walk the plank. Said something or other about feeding me to their ugly old lady."

"Well, we're just lucky that they did," Willow said, nodding emphatically.

Xander was about to speak up, when a strong wave lifted the boat. But instead of passing beneath it, the wave caught the boat up and began to carry it along. When it finally passed, they came to rest once more on a calm sea, shrouded in fog.

Then the water began to churn.

They heard the sound of something huge breaking the surface, water tumbling off it. When Xander looked up into the fog and darkness, he saw an enormous green-black tentacle pass in the air above their boat.

"The Kraken," Giles whispered.

"The ugly old lady," Willow said, her voice without inflection.

Xander wondered if it would be now. If it was time to die.

Then, from above, the clanking of rigging and the whisper of ghostly sails came down to them, and the singing of dead men became incredibly loud. The fog seemed to flee from the rotting hull of the *Flying Dutchman* as it lowered itself to sit on the waves, and skeletal buccaneers began to leap from the deck into the water.

"*Ah, Rupert Giles,*" said a voice that chilled Xander to the bone. "*If I'd known ye'd bring yer friends along, I'd have pushed ye overboard hours ago!*"

The dead seamen began to swim toward their boat.

The Kraken raised itself up out of the water a hundred yards away, so huge it was visible through the fog.

Cordelia began to cry.

Willow opened her mouth and began to chant, and Giles laid his hands on her back, as though to give her more than his moral support. It was as though he were giving her part of himself, part of his energy.

"Can she do it?" Xander asked Giles, as the dead men swam closer.

One of the skeletons grabbed the edge of the boat, and Xander used his foot to shatter the bones of its fingers. He kicked another in the head, rocking the boat and causing Cordelia to scream.

Willow's voice rose. She was panicking. The spell was beginning. Beneath the water, the breach far below began to glow. But even without Giles's answer, Xander had already figured out that it was going to be too late.

"No!" roared the Captain of the ghost ship suddenly. *"You can't be here! Get out of here! What are you trying to do?"*

"For my father!" screamed a weak but defiant voice.

"Giles," Xander said, pointing. "Look!"

On the deck of the *Flying Dutchman* stood Jean-Marc Regnier, the Gatekeeper. Somehow he had used his power, used the ghost roads, to appear onboard the ship. Blue magickal energy danced around his hands and shimmered where the rotting corpses that were the ship's crew tried to attack him.

"Great Beast, I call thee, I honor thee, I worship

thee!" cried the Gatekeeper. "Take me, now, swallow me down and let my sacrifice be your sustenance."

"What in God's name is he doing?" Giles whispered.

"If you don't know," Xander said bluntly, "then we have no idea."

Cordelia reached out for Xander's hand, and he gripped it.

The Kraken sprayed water as it submerged again. The little boat rose on an enormous wave and nearly tipped them out. Water flowed in, but the boat righted itself. A tentacle whipped out of the water not far from them. The Kraken was moving beneath the ocean, moving under them.

"OhGodOhGodOhGod," Cordelia muttered.

"He's calling it," Willow said, her voice revealing her astonishment. "He's going to let it kill him so it destroys the ship."

"But he can't!" Cordelia said, panic rising even further. "Without him, the whole thing will . . ."

"Willow!" Xander snapped. "Bind that breach! Do it now!"

Once again, Willow raised her voice. She was sweating, shuddering, and Xander realized for the first time just how much all this took out of her. There was a price to be paid for all this use of wards and spells, and it was taking its toll on Willow. And this was the biggest one of all.

Still, she went on.

"But the Gatekeeper . . ." Cordelia began.

"Is gone," Giles said flatly.

Xander looked up to see that it was true. Jean-Marc Regnier was no longer on the ghost ship's deck.

Then the Kraken's tentacles shot from the water, wrapped themselves around the *Flying Dutchman,* and began to pull the rotting vessel down into the depths.

Regnier had bought them time.

Willow made good use of it.

When the ship was half submerged, Willow completed the binding spell. The water did not swirl, but the breach far below the surface glowed brighter, and the two horrors from the Otherworld were sucked back down to their watery grave . . . down into the breach.

"Poor Vinnie," Giles murmured mournfully. "And there was another fellow, too."

Willow collapsed, unconscious, by Xander's feet. Cursing, he lifted her up so her head was not on the floor of the boat and pushed her hair away from her face.

"You did a great job, Will," he said. "You kicked some serious booty."

Almost instantly, the fog began to clear. The lights of the shore came into view, and all of them were astonished at how close they had been. With Giles now steering and Cordelia hugging herself in silence at the prow, they headed for home.

In Boston, the Gatekeeper lay in the Cauldron of Bran the Blessed. He had barely made it back to the house alive, and now he wondered how long he would have to remain in the Cauldron before its healing properties rejuvenated him again. At the very least, he knew it would be hours.

He rose up on his elbows as a huge bellowing shook

the windows. Down in the yard, the *Dutchman* flickered, two men newly drowned lying on its deck. The Captain roared as the Kraken embraced the bow, gorging itself on wood and ghost. The cronelike figurehead struggled down its gullet.

"For you, Father," Jean-Marc whispered, and gave himself up to the waters.

On the road again, the horizon promising dawn.

Angel studied the sky thoughtfully, then said to Buffy, "Oz is right. We could make better time if we split up. And we have a better chance of success. You can move during the daylight and at least half the night. I'm slowing us down."

She looked away, and he knew she agreed with him. He also knew she didn't want to do it. He understood. Neither did he. But the time had come for hard decisions.

"It's just that you're unprotected when you sleep. We can watch over you, make sure no one gets to you."

As gently as he could, he said, "It's not me you should be worrying about right now."

"I always . . ." she began, then trailed off. She didn't need to say it. He always worried about her, too.

"You're the Slayer," he reminded her. "You've got to do the right thing. I'll get moving as soon as the sun goes down. I'll catch up with you." He grinned lopsidedly. "Maybe I'll even beat you there."

"Hah. Try it," she shot back, fighting hard to smile for him. He smiled back, awed by her, proud of her, and cupped her chin. He couldn't help the soft kiss he gave her. When she closed her eyes and breathed in hard, he wanted to kiss her again. Wanted to give her so much more. Knew he could not.

"I'll find you," he promised her.

"Angel." Her voice broke. She looked down, took a breath, looked back up at him. "You will."

"I will."

"Okay." She turned to Oz. "Let's saddle up. We're taking Angel to the next town and then we'll keep going."

Oz nodded. He said, "How about I drive?"

Angel got into the back and gestured for Buffy to join him. She joined him and said, "When I find this guy, I'm going to gut him."

"I'll hand you the knife," Angel told her.

She sighed.

Oz drove.

"Oh, he's so plump, Spike, and I want a treat," Drusilla said. "Such a pretty lit'l boy. I want to eat him up." She smiled at Jacques, who was sitting in his usual spot on the table in their hideaway. His blood ran cold at the sight of her gleaming eyes and white teeth. Even in her human form she terrified him. She was not only evil, she was crazy.

"Just one bite," she pleaded. "I won't take it all. He's young. He won't even miss it."

"No, pet," Spike said patiently, lighting up a cigarette and taking a deep drag. He flicked his silver lighter shut and put it in the pocket of his duster. "Not one drop. I know you. We've got a bit of a self-control issue, don't we?"

"Spike," she pouted, as he drew her into his arms. She studied Jacques over her shoulder. She licked her lips for his benefit. She was toying with him, and she knew he knew it. "He's been here for days and days, with his ruddy cheeks and his baby fat. It's more than I can bear."

Jacques's heart beat wildly. He had watched these two together. Spike could never deny Drusilla anything for long. If she wanted to suck his blood, Spike would eventually let her. And he knew she would kill him, just for sport. Just to make Spike angry. Jacques would never see his father and Grandmama again. And the world would fall apart, because there would be no new Gatekeeper.

"One lit'l sip," she begged, entwining her hands in Spike's white-blond hair. "Just one. I shall be ever so careful."

"Well . . ." Spike chewed the inside of his lip.

She held up her forefinger. "One."

He sighed. "It's a bit off, you know. He's a special boy, the only boy who'll get us what we want. We don't want to waste him, poodle." He stroked her cheek. "Once we have the Spear, you can have all the chubby lads you want."

"But we don't have it yet, and he's here now." She kissed him and sat on his lap. "And I want a treat."

"Listen, mate," Spike said to Jacques without looking at him. "My baby's got a yen to bite your neck. My night will go a lot easier if I let her. So let's be a sport, eh?"

Now he did turn and look at Jacques, who glared at them both. She pulled out of Spike's arms and flicked her fingers at Jacques in that mad, fierce way of hers, cooing at him as if he were some kind of baby animal to be coaxed into drawing near.

"Come on, come on," she sang. "It's all right, darling boy. It's all right."

"Don't you touch me, you crazy witch!" Jacques yelled, eyes beginning to fill with tears.

He leaped off the table and charged her, ramming into her midsection with his head. She slammed to the floor, laughing, as he pummeled her with both his fists. He had never hit a girl or a woman before, but she was neither. She was a demon. He knew all about vampires. His father had taught him. They were evil, and they all deserved to die.

So he showed her no mercy, ramming his fists into her stomach and chest as hard as he could, but all she did was laugh. Then she covered her face for a moment, and when she pulled her hands away and grabbed him, she wore her true face, the hideous features of a vampire.

"Naughty child," she snarled at him as she flung him onto his back, straddling him, coming in for the kill. "You must be punished for your bad manners."

Jacques forced himself to remain silent, glaring at her.

Spike hurried over and caught her wrists, saying, "Relax, love. Don't want to get carried away and damage the merchandise."

She struggled to free herself. "*I* was polite. I asked nicely. There was going to be tea afterward, but now I don't think I have the spirit left to bake scones."

"All the same, love, let's have a bit of decorum, all

right?" Spike said. Then he pushed Drusilla off Jacques and clamped his hand over the boy's mouth.

"And you. You'd best take care. Spear or not, I'll gut you myself if you misbehave." Spike regarded him levelly. Jacques believed every word Spike said, and nodded.

"Dru, I've got to go out," Spike murmured. He wagged a finger at her without taking his eyes off Jacques. "But no bloody taste tests, all right?"

"Oh, tempter," she whispered. "Mean Daddy."

He patted her. "Be a good girl, then."

She turned her hand palm up and held her nails at Jacques's throat as she gestured for him to rise.

"I killed a Slayer in just this way," she hissed at Jacques. "I can take you just as easily."

She stared at him, and he began to feel his will melting away. He was lost in her eyes, losing track of his thoughts. She was hypnotizing him. All he saw were her eyes. All he felt were her sharp nails.

He had a sense of walking, but he wasn't even sure of that. Of a door closing. Of being made to sit.

Of death, very close at hand.

"Si," Spike said, through the front door of the deserted saloon he'd co-opted for this meeting.

"It's Brother Enoch," someone murmured furtively.

"About time," Spike flung back as he opened the door. "And you're not *my* brother, you silly sod."

Two hooded figures trooped into the room. Spike tried to hide his irritation. Really, what was the point of meeting in secret if these blokes ran about in their ridiculous costumes? He and Dru might as well put on velvet-lined capes and evening clothes. He'd always fancied that Lugosi look, but there were so few occasions to dress these days. Perhaps for dinner, one of these nights . . .

Perhaps tonight, if these two didn't have some good news.

"Tell me what I want to hear," Spike said. "Such as, the Spear's outside in the Beemer and you're ready to swap."

Brother Enoch cleared his throat. "I have the honor of introducing you to my immediate superior, Brother Lucius," he said in an officious voice.

"So you're the big noise around here. Yeah, I'm charmed." Spike took the man's measure as the newcomer flung back his hood. Nice bones. Big veins. Oh, and blue eyes and black hair. Good look, if you were Superman.

"Vampire," the man said dismissively, "we need further reassurances that the boy is in your possession, and that he is unharmed."

Spike blinked and cocked his head at Brother Enoch. "Have you been telling tales out of school, B.E.? Didn't you tell him we gave you the boy's coat and a recording of his voice?"

Spike fluttered his fingers at the new idiot. "I was under the impression you lads could read vibrations off clothes, or some such. Magickal DNA tests. You know it's his coat."

Brother Lucius looked unimpressed. "Which is no proof that you actually have the heir in your possession."

Spike looked down his nose at the man. "Well, it's a

damn sight more impressive than 'Yeah, we've got the Spear in the back room,' which is all we've gotten from you."

A muscle twitched in Brother Lucius's cheek. Spike noted it, filed it away. On its own it didn't signify, but maybe it would fill in a blank or two later.

"So maybe when we have a bit more proof that you've got the Spear, we'll have something to discuss," Spike said, walking toward the door. "But I've got to say, back Stateside we call this situation a 'Mexican standoff.'

"And what usually happens is that the guy who draws first, dies." He smiled pleasantly. "And I'm already dead, theoretically."

His smile vanished as he opened the door. "To cut to it, gents, I don't feature me and Dru putting up with this crap much longer."

Brother Lucius drew himself up. "Now, just a minute. Do you have any idea—"

Spike stifled a yawn. "Who you are? How many Sons of Entropy badges you've collected?" He felt for his pack of cigs and pulled one out. He lit it, and slowly pulled the smoke into his lungs. Held it, blew it out just as slowly. "Between Dru and me, we've bagged three Slayers. As I understand it, your fearless leader has put one and only one out of her misery. So."

He gestured for them to leave.

"Don't let it slam on the way out, right? And have a pleasant evening."

Brother Lucius was livid. "You—"

"—won't regret this one whit," Spike said. "In fact, it's the most fun I've had in days."

"Brother," Brother Enoch said softly, "perhaps we should . . ."

Brother Lucius swept past him in a fury of indignation. Brother Enoch glanced pleadingly at Spike, who winked at him.

"Tell the old boy not to get his knickers in a knot," Spike said. "We've got the brat, and he's alive and well. When you come through, we'll come through."

"Yes. Thank you," Brother Enoch murmured.

"But you'd best hurry things along. We've been talking about changing him. We've always wanted a son."

He shut the door in Brother Enoch's face. For perhaps five full minutes, he stood thoughtfully, smoking, playing out various scenarios. He had no idea why this was taking so bloody long. Still, he was British, and used to the slow wheels of bureaucracy. But that didn't make him any happier about things.

Savagely he kicked the door, then grabbed his duster and headed for home.

"Baby, I'm home," Spike called out, as he entered the cottage. No answer, so he went into the bedroom. What he saw there shocked him only slightly.

Dru had gagged the boy and tied him to the bedpost. Her favorite doll, Miss Edith, sat across from him on the mattress. The dolly was blindfolded, which meant she'd been naughty. Dru sat with her mantilla all askew between the two of them, serving pretend tea from a miniature tea set Spike had stolen from the Victoria and Albert Museum in London, on a dare.

"One lump or two?" she queried the boy, making stabbing motions at his eyes.

"Now, pet, no hitting." He joined the party, perching on the bed and curling one leg beneath himself. "I don't think they've got the bloody thing," Spike said to Dru.

"I don't think they're relaying your messages to the proper authorities," Dru retorted, as she poured him some tea in a tiny bone china cup. "Tell Miss Edith how tasty your tea is, love. She has misbehaved and will not be taking any, and she should know what she has lost."

"It's shatteringly brilliant," he said, flashing his white teeth. "The best. *Numero uno.*"

"Spain," she said sadly.

He set down his cup. "I think you're right. I think we're stuck with some minor Entropy clerk who's trying to make a name for himself in the organization. Thinks he'll come running into the great hall one night with the boy, bow and scrape, 'Look, King Arthur, I've got the Gatekeeper's heir. Make me a knight of the bleeding round table.'" He raised his nose in the air and spoke like an aristocrat, which sent Dru into peals of laughter.

He was glad. He loved to make his baby laugh.

"What do we do if they don't have the Spear?" she asked.

He leaned across her tiny ocean of tea things and kissed the end of her nose. "I suppose we'll eat him."

"Si, matador!" She clicked her fingers. *"Si, si!"*

Chapter 10

T HE BROTHERS WERE UPSTAIRS IN THEIR CLOISTERS, singing their unholy chants. Their voices filtered into the darkness below, as did the screams of the sacrifice. But Il Maestro barely noticed. His gaze was on the corpse of the traitor, Brother Albert, as it hung in the sulfurous, boiling air above the pentagram.

In the shadows, his dark lord watched as Il Maestro waved a hand over the dead mouth and flicked open the dead eyes with a snap of his fingers. From the mouth crawled a spider and a worm, both wilting in the heat. The eyes of the dead man were milky, but something moved beneath their filmy domes.

Sweating and blistered, Il Maestro began the questioning.

"Wretched betrayer, before you suffer the eternal torments of hell, tell me what I wish to know."

"Maestro," the dead man said, *"forgive me."*

"Forgiveness is beyond me," Il Maestro retorted. "Had you need for that, you should have looked elsewhere."

"Maestro, spare me."

Il Maestro only chuckled. He pointed to the dead mouth. "You met the Slayer."

"I met her."

"You told her where I am."

"She did not believe me."

"Oh?"

The shadows shifted. Il Maestro's dark master was listening hard.

"She believes you are in Vienna."

"Why on earth would she believe that?"

"Maestro, I burn," said the corpse. *"I am in agony."*

"It's only the beginning, my friend." Il Maestro smiled to himself in anticipation. "Tell me why she believes I'm in Vienna."

"I do not know."

"Liar!"

From a table laden with instruments of torture, Il Maestro picked up a whip which glowed with a purplish light. He struck the corpse across the face. The corpse writhed.

Again, across the milky eyes, which burst. The fluid began to steam as it cascaded over the temples.

The body gasped and said, *"Maestro, I don't know."*

Il Maestro brought the whip down again.

The corpse groaned dully.

He raised the whip—

"Enough," said the demon in the shadows. *"This is accomplishing nothing."*

Il Maestro was disappointed, but obeyed. "Name your confederates," he said, trying a new direction.

The corpse was silent for a moment. Then it said, *"None."*

"No one?" Il Maestro shook his head. "Not for one moment do I believe you."

The eyeless corpse said, *"No one helped me."*

"But surely, there were those who supported you. Who wished you well."

"Ahhh." Brother Albert twisted in the air. *"Alone."*

The dead man burst into flame. In less than five seconds, he was nothing but a pile of cinders. Il Maestro raised his brows and stared into the shadows.

"I didn't do that. Did you?"

"No, you fool. He did." The demon sounded disgusted. *"And you allowed it."*

"No, my lord," Il Maestro protested. "I didn't—"

"Silence! Oh, you are useless. Useless." The shadows shifted again. The heat in the chamber rose unbearably, singeing the hair off Il Maestro's body. He was terrified that he, too, would burst into flames.

"Please, my lord," he said.

"You promised me the Slayer," the demon said. *"And if she is not here by the full moon, your daughter takes her place. On the altar, and in Hell."*

Il Maestro bowed his head. But in the folds of his robe, his hands were clenched. That would never happen.

Never.

Angel had just awakened. He was in a pension in a small town near Geneva, nowhere on a map. There was an 8:30 P.M. express to Milan. That was the expected rendezvous point with Buffy and Oz. If they weren't there, he was supposed to call Giles. For all the good that would do. If they weren't there, Angel would be on his own in his search for the heir to the Gatehouse.

He wandered across a square, admiring the gargoyle fountain, and saw warm lights through green and yellow bottle-bottom windows.

He pushed open the door and quickly, covertly scanned the bar, but came up with nothing out of the ordinary. Still, he was a stranger, and there was a large mirror over the bar itself. He moved to a table out of range and sat, so that no one would notice that he cast no reflection. It was a form of self-awareness that had been instinctive over the years.

After a few minutes a young woman sauntered over to him. She had short red hair and a large emerald-colored stud in her nose. She eyed him appreciatively, then spoke to him in Italian. He was able to decipher that she was asking for his order, so he told her he wanted a Campari. Then she shook her head and pointed to a short, wiry man seated at the bar, who turned slowly and faced Angel.

Angel's lips parted in shock. He had seen that man before.

In Sunnydale.

The man slid off the stool and walked to Angel's table. He held a glass in his hand, which he raised in Angel's direction. He said a few words to the waitress. She answered, "Campari," then scooted away.

"Signor Angel," the man said, touching his chest. "Small world. I'm stunned."

Angel shrugged. This man had been one of the Sons

of Entropy in the car that had tried to follow Buffy to the airport. They had shot their compatriot rather than allow him to spill any of their secrets to Angel.

"Stunned." Angel looked at him hard. "How long have you been following me?"

The man looked offended. "Truly, I was not."

The waitress came with Angel's Campari. His new companion made a great show of paying for it, but Angel said nothing.

"No, truly, I was not," the man repeated, "but let me take this opportunity to reason with you."

Angel looked at him askance.

"Listen." The man scooted forward on his chair, clearly eager to continue. "As you have no doubt realized, my master is an extremely powerful man with superior knowledge of the arcane."

"Superior knowledge," Angel said dryly.

"Yes, indeed." The man smiled. "He knows of a way to turn you—and only you, because of your soul—into a fully human man who will live out his days in peace, then die the true death." He clapped his hands together. "No more vampire lifestyle. No more bloodlust."

"And in return?"

"Well, of course you must serve him," the man replied. "But it's a small matter, really." He looked thoughtful, then smiled brightly. "For example, as a token of your gratitude, you might explain to us where the Slayer is."

"I'm not with her anymore," Angel said dully.

"Oh?" The man's voice had that quizzical singsong rhythm Angel had always despised.

"She's in Austria, I think," Angel went on. "Vienna. I don't know." He looked away.

"Ah. Lover's quarrel."

As the man feigned sympathy, Angel became aware of movements in the bar. The patrons were shifting their positions, focusing more intently on him. He heard a click at the front door. Locked from the outside, he guessed.

The faces on some of the other customers seemed to blur, reshape. A few looked away.

Angel raised his eyes to the mirror. Seated in a booth to his far right, the scaly, horned face of a demon stared back at him.

"He sees," the demon said.

Angel's companion jumped up from his chair and raised his hands. At once, everyone else in the bar followed suit. Human faces melted away, revealing the truth: Angel was surrounded by monsters and demons, faces covered with scales and bony ridges and sores and hideous distortions. Bodies stooped, grew, cleft, became long, wormlike forms. They hissed, they seethed, they gazed at Angel with hunger and hatred.

The man clapped his hands together once. His voice was calm and soft.

"Accept my master's most gracious offer, or be destroyed," he said.

With demons and monsters making an impenetrable circle around him, Angel remained in his seat. Calm. Bold. He did not stand. Did not raise his hands to defend himself.

Instead, he smiled thinly.

"I've told you where the Slayer's gone, or at least as much as I know," he said, staring at the man before him, one of the Sons of Entropy who had now, to Angel's mind, become just a little too numerous.

Angel laughed a bit, and shook his head. "But you don't believe me, do you?" he asked.

"On the contrary, vampire," the acolyte said. "You have only confirmed what we already knew. The Slayer is expected in Vienna, and she will be greeted there. But there are ways you could help Il Maestro, ways in which you could be useful in deceiving her. Entrapping her."

With a small grunt, Angel narrowed his eyes. The flesh of his face seemed to quiver, and then it changed. His brow grew heavier, jutting out, and the skin around his eyes and nose became rough and callused. His eyes blinked and when they opened again, they glowed a fierce, predatory yellow. He looked around at the monsters and demons. He watched as they snarled at him, moved into a tighter circle, their chests rising and falling as though all that held them back was this acolyte's . . . this human's command.

Several of them were absolutely terrifying to behold, even for Angel.

So fast the acolyte barely flinched, Angel launched himself from the chair, grabbed the man by his thick, graying hair, and slammed his face down on the table in front of him. His nose shattered and blood jetted from one nostril.

"You son of a bitch," Angel whispered into his ear as the demons and monsters screeched a horrid chorus but did not move any closer. "Your boss should have told you to do your homework. I'm a dead man. You can dress that up however you like, magick can do a lot of things, but it can't make me alive again! And even if it could, I'm not a man who can be bought. You should have known that coming in."

With a roar of terrible rage, Angel hefted the whimpering acolyte by collar and belt, lifted the man over his head, and ran at the circle of horrors that surrounded them. They parted for him, staring mutely, and Angel used all his strength to hurl the man over the bar. The acolyte's shout of fear was cut off as he slammed into the mirror, which shattered into a thousand silver fragments, destroying the monstrous image of the room around it.

The shards fell like deadly rain, many of them slicing into the fallen acolyte's body where he lay behind the bar.

A black wave seemed to sweep across the room, invisible but tangible. Angel's hair ruffled with a sickly breeze. He turned, his entire body cold and silent as stone, without even the illusion of life, of breathing and warmth, that vampires so often used to camouflage themselves. He turned to face the monsters.

The monsters. Which were now nothing more than common street thugs and local rowdies. There were several Sons of Entropy among them, he saw, but even they only stared at Angel in horror, stared at the flaring yellow eyes and the lips curled back to reveal gleaming fangs. Angel seethed, furious not only that they would think him a likely traitor but that the idiot spellcaster the Sons of Entropy had put on his tail had actually believed Angel had lived nearly two and a half centuries without being able to tell a real demon from an illusory one.

Demons stank. The only odor coming off these goons was that of stale whiskey and old beer.

Still, they stared.

Angel was stooped slightly, almost like an animal. Now he stood straight and glared at them all.

"You've been led to your deaths," he said grimly, his voice thick with anger and the lust for blood. "The first man I catch dies the fastest. The last is my supper."

He took a single step and they broke and ran, crashing through the windows of the place and battering down the door from within. Only the few Sons of Entropy tried to stay behind, and even they were swept back by the tide of fear. One of the acolytes broke free and brought a long, wicked-looking blade out of his jacket, then swung it around toward Angel's face.

Angel took the blade away, and then gave it back to him. As decoration. It adorned the man's chest amid gouts of spurting blood.

The vampire walked on. Already most of the thugs had fled. Two acolytes remained, shoving aside the others now, the freelance talent they'd hired for aid.

They looked terrified.

A moment later, Angel gave them reason to be.

By the time he relaxed and his face returned to normal, he was alone in the bar.

* * *

"Milano," Oz said. Buffy half-expected him to pull a guidebook from his pack and begin rattling off all the things to do and see in the city. But Oz was quiet, and she was grateful.

They were sitting inside a cafe in a huge park. The cafe was very old-world, crowded with plaster statues and cupids and lots of oil paintings on the walls. It was pricey, too, and Buffy felt out of place in her traveling clothes. It was called Angelina, and it was where Angel had promised to try to rendezvous with them. How he knew of a cafe in Milan, Italy, with an in-joke for a name, Buffy did not know. Maybe he had a lot of guidebooks, too.

The thing was, he'd been due almost an hour and a half ago. And he hadn't shown.

Oz sipped his coffee and said, "He's taking a train. Maybe it was late."

"Don't they all run on time over here?" she asked, toying with her silverware.

"Maybe not." He smiled at her gently. "He'll show."

She flashed him a lopsided smile. "I have a strange feeling of déjà vu here, Oz, only you would be one of my girlfriends back in L.A. and we would possibly be discussing a boy named Tyler. Or maybe Jeff. And we would be at the Cineplex, me officially not caring if he showed."

He smiled back. "You're okay," he said, then shrugged. "I don't mean I think you're okay. Which I do. And you are. What I'm trying to say is that you're strong. Slayer strong and person strong."

She blushed, pleased by the compliment. She'd never really talked to Oz much. It was nice.

"Sometimes I feel pretty not-strong," she confessed.

"So did Superman," Oz replied.

After a time, he said, "It's been bugging me that I don't have a guitar. I keep thinking I should be practicing. It's a mundane thought, but it keeps occurring to me."

She nodded. "Dealing with an end-of-the-world scenario can really make you schizo if you think about it too much. It's like being the Slayer, only more so. But this is me on a daily basis: on the one hand, I'm wondering if that pair of suede boots I want have gone on sale, and on the other I'm wondering if I'll be able to run through the graveyard with them on. Plus if I can get blood out of them. And I'm wondering all this while I'm kickboxing with some demon."

"Hmm. Doubtful."

She leaned forward. "The problem being, of course, that I want the suede boots, just like all the other girls. And none of them are worrying about getting blood out of them.

"And sometimes I wonder if I'll have time to do my homework while I'm staking some vamp." She wrinkled her nose. "But usually not. Usually I'm thinking about suede boots."

"Guitar chords," Oz rejoined. "And Willow."

"You're worried about her," Buffy said gently.

"Full circle." He picked up his coffee. "Angel. Willow. Worrying."

"Giles," she murmured, and picked up her coffee. "Don't you love these word association games?"

They sat together in silence for a moment. Then Oz

suggested, "Walk in the park?" They had been sitting in the cafe for over two hours. Which was actually okay—everyone else had been sitting in the cafe for at least that long. It would make Buffy nervous to live in Europe. They did an awful lot of chitchatting and smoking. No one seemed to get much done.

On the other hand, it would be cool to go to school here and not get much done. If you spoke the lingo.

Buffy rose gratefully. Oz looked at the bill and raised his brows. "This lire thing. It makes you feel like you're spending your life savings on two coffees and one strangely shaped piece of bread."

Buffy peered at the bill and saw what he meant: enormous amounts of 000's. "Are they trying to rip us off?"

He frowned. "Not sure. But let's see . . . if you divide . . . well, it's actually fairly reasonable. For an expensive place."

He pulled out a wad of Italian money and counted it out. "Remind me. Tip is good?"

"I think it's included," she said uncertainly. Then she grinned at him. "Listen to us. We're waiting for a vampire to show up so we can kick some major butt and try to save the world from chaos, and we're worried about the tip."

He grinned back at her. "Like you said. A bit schizo." He counted out the money and left it on the table.

They picked up their backpacks and strolled outside. They'd opted to bring them with. If someone felt the need to break into their van, it would be very bad not to have their stuff with them.

It was nippy, but Buffy didn't want to bother with getting out her new English sweater. Maybe she'd give it to her mom.

There were tons of trees and the grass was lush and green. The air smelled fresh, despite the fact that Milan was a bustling metropolis with a lot of traffic. L.A. was like that on a good night. The surf on the beach, the traffic surf from the highway, a relatively smogless sky.

Nowhere better.

Beneath a streetlight, a fountain shaped like a wood nymph holding an urn trickled water into a circular pool. It was beautiful. There was so much in the world that was. Sometimes Buffy couldn't comprehend why there was so much evil in the world. What compelled the various forces she battled to destroy everything in their path? For her, her worst fury always sprang from her greatest pain. Was that how it was for them?

"How long do we wait?" Oz asked gently.

She sighed. "We'll have to go soon."

"We have a few minutes, then." Oz meandered along, then pointed to a small building beyond the fountain shaped like a miniature Grecian temple. "I wonder what that is."

"Let's check it out," Buffy said.

They crossed the park and reached the building. It was locked tight, but there was a small sign on it that Buffy thought might have something to do with puppets. Maybe it was a puppet theater.

She glanced at Oz, about to tell him her deduction, when she caught a flicker of blue light among a stand of trees about fifty feet away. Tugging on Oz's shoulder, she began to run. After a second or two, he followed her.

There was another flicker, and then, as Buffy crashed through the trees, a large black circle appeared. It hovered about five feet in the air and pulsed dark purple and blue. A figure appeared in the center, and two more sprang up behind it.

"Breach," Buffy said, assuming attack position. Oz stood beside her, bracing himself for a fight.

Suddenly Angel burst from the circle, stumbled but kept his footing, and wheeled around to face the breach. As if they were joined together, two monstrous forms flew from the center.

Buffy darted forward, taking on the one on the left while Angel rammed his fists into the face—if it could be called a face—of the other. They were hideous, oily things that resembled a human form only slightly, and when Buffy kicked hers in the chest, her foot seemed to slide into the creature for a moment before she was able to pull away from it.

Angel grabbed his opponent and threw it back into the circle, where there was a bright flash. Then the creature disappeared.

Buffy did the same, grimacing as her hands were coated with the slippery substance. There was another bright flash.

Then the breach closed. The hole disappeared.

Huffing, Angel said, "Sorry I'm late."

"I thought there was a train," Buffy replied.

"Missed it. So I took the ghost road, which turned out to be a bad idea."

"I'm asking why?" Buffy said.

"Some Sons of Entropy and other assorted garbage were waiting for me in a bar." He shrugged. "No big. They really do think you're in Vienna."

"Good." She gestured to the place where the breach had hung. "So I take it there's a bit of a traffic jam in there?"

"Ghost road rage," Oz muttered.

Angel nodded. "The ghost roads are clogged with demons. At least the one I took was. We'll have to stick to our plan and go overland." He made a face. "Despite the fact that I'm fashionably late."

"At least you're here." She smiled. "Oz was worried about you."

Angel gazed at her. "You?"

She shrugged. "I know you can take care of yourself."

"Good." He frowned. "Damn it. My duffel didn't make it."

"Well, after we destroy Il Maestro, we'll go shopping," Buffy said brightly.

"Where'd you guys park?"

"Down an alley down an alley. Lots of alleys around here," Buffy said. Then she looked at Oz, who was looking up at the moon. "Oh, wow. You okay?"

"So far. But I don't have much time left."

They moved quickly after that.

In Vienna the glockenspiel performed its mad pantomime as it struck noon. Inside a coffee and pastry shop called Gerstner's, several members of the Sons of Entropy sat and blew steam off cups of *Kaffee mit Schlag*. They were dressed as tourists and looked right at home. They looked, for all intents and purposes, normal.

"She's not coming here," one of them said angrily, rubbing his temples before replacing the thick glasses he wore.

Another, an obscenely fat man with sweat pouring down his forehead, despite the cool weather, grunted unhappily.

"How can we know?" he said. "So the seers do not feel her any longer, that could be magick, no? She could be shielded somehow."

"If she were coming here, somehow convinced that Il Maestro made his home here, we would have seen her already. We've been here for hours. Don't forget Paris. They aren't afraid of us," said the bespectacled man in frustration.

The third and last of those gathered, a thin, quiet man called Brother Pino, clucked his tongue.

"Not afraid of us, perhaps," he said. "But afraid of Il Maestro, yes? They must be. Only a fool would not fear for his life."

The obese man laughed gently. "A vampire, a werewolf, and the Chosen One? She is a legend herself. Why would she fear him? It is her calling to face him without fear."

Brother Pino narrowed his gaze, his face like a crow's, and bent forward as if he might peck. "No one is without fear," he said bluntly.

The bespectacled man raised an eyebrow. "What is it, then," he wondered aloud, "that Il Maestro fears?"

The other two men looked horrified, and stared about the room as though they might be struck dead at any moment. As though lightning might shatter the window by which they sat, on the second floor amid the scent of chocolate and hazelnut and caramel.

When it did not, Brother Pino looked at the man with glasses and sneered. "You are an imbecile, Brother," he said. "You might as well have presented your throat to be slit."

"Not at all," replied the man with glasses. "I have heard things, you see. Seen things, in the villa. And I am forced to wonder if all we have been promised will come to pass. I am forced to question a great many things of late."

The others stared at him, but he went on.

"Il Maestro has vengeance in his heart for the Regniers, this we know. He wants the boy alive to train as his own, because the Regnier line has power, and because tainting the son of that house will please him. This I understand."

The obese man nodded, and mopped his forehead with a cloth napkin. Brother Pino only stared as the man with glasses went on.

"The Gatekeeper is failing quickly, very near death. We may not have his heir in hand as yet, but near enough. The boy will never set foot in that house again. So what is our hurry? So many have died already, when we might have just waited for the old magician to die, rather than continue to leech his life away while throwing away so many of our own."

Brother Pino held up a finger. "I must stop you there, Brother," he said, still glancing about warily. "You see, Il Maestro has specifically said that this is a time of great weakness in the walls that hold the worlds apart. As we approach the vernal equinox, the walls thin even further. Afterward, it will be more difficult."

"More difficult than what?" asked the man with the spectacles angrily. "The Gatekeeper would be dead. Once we had control of the Gatehouse, we could simply wait until next year's vernal equinox if necessary."

Brother Pino blinked. He looked thoughtful a moment, then said, warily, "Go on."

"What is more vital," said the other, "if the heir is at least in our control, and the Gatekeeper is dying, what need has he of the Slayer's blood, other than to dispatch her on general principle? What's to be gained from that? Power? When the Gatehouse is his, all the power in the world will belong to Il Macstro. He will be the lord of chaos on Earth when that wall falls."

The obese man gasped, his eyes wide.

"What, Brother Dominic?" Pino said quickly. "What is it?"

"No," Dominic replied. "I can't even speak it. I have no reason to believe it, only that it occurred to me. For Il Maestro has never done anything without specific purpose."

"What is it, Brother?" demanded the man with glasses.

Sweat dripped down the obese man's face, and this time he did not mop it up.

"He plans to drop the barrier between Earth and the Otherworld," he said. "But what if Il Maestro wants to bring down another barrier as well? What then?"

The others only stared at him.

They were still staring when lightning exploded

through the window and baked the three of them where they sat, eyes smoldering and open mouths filled with steam. As for the one who had first spoken his doubts, his spectacles had shattered.

There wasn't a cloud in the sky.

In Florence, alone in his chamber, Il Maestro was frustrated and enraged. His sorcery touched nearly all the Sons of Entropy, and so he could reach out and watch them, through his magick, at any time. All save his own daughter, she for whom he had broken so many of his own rules. She whose life he now wanted to spare.

It was only instinct, luck and curiosity that had allowed him to discover the traitorous conversation of Dominic and the others in Vienna. He had been curious as to the Slayer's whereabouts, and so had looked in on them.

The ungrateful wretches.

He thought now of the occasions on which he had lost track of one or more of his followers, and wondered if that neglect would harm him in any way. However, that was becoming a moot point: his ranks were thinning dangerously after so many attacks on the Gatehouse. He had no choice but to proceed. This was the time that had been dictated by the dark lord whom he served. Belphegor had promised him eternal life or eternal damnation, an empire or the pits of Hell, in exchange for his cooperation.

And for the sacrifice of the most prized blood in all the world. The blood of the Slayer.

Now she had disappeared. She was not in Boston. Not in California. She had been in Europe, but since the traitorous Albert had aided her, Il Maestro could not sense her. She had been on the road to Vienna, that much was clear, but where was she now?

Without her, Micaela would die. Without her, the Gatehouse might fall and the Otherworld be split apart like the ripest of melons, but true power would still elude Il Maestro.

Worse, the demon might take him before the task could be completed. Already it was growing impatient.

Belphegor had once been warmonger of Hell. It did not like to be kept waiting. And, much like Il Maestro himself, it did not suffer failure. Not at all.

No, it was clear that the Slayer must be found once more. It had been his arrogance that had prevented him from personally seeking her before. Il Maestro had not thought such intimate involvement would be necessary. But the girl had proven to be far more resourceful than he'd been led to expect.

Slowly, Il Maestro began to smile.

For he had thought of a way to bring the Slayer into the light where he could lay hands on her. Better than that, he had thought of a way to get her back where he needed her to be.

At the Hellmouth.

Chapter 11

WILLOW LOOKED UP FROM HER BOOK AND SIGHED. Across from her at the study table, Xander and Cordelia were paging through thick, leather-bound volumes, but their hearts obviously weren't into the research thing. She could relate. Neither was hers. All she could think about was what might be going on in Italy. Or Boston. Because nothing was going on here in the Sunnydale High library.

Which was good. Giles had assured her that it meant she had done an excellent job with her binding spells. And she was happy about that, really. But now that she'd had a moment to catch her breath, she felt pretty useless. Her man was off fighting with Buffy, and the Gatekeeper was battling the Sons of Entropy. It seemed like a waste of Slayerettes to be back in Sunnydale, and going to school, of all things.

Although going to school was a good thing in terms

of, okay, making sure she'd be at graduation. The past couple of weeks they'd all missed enough classes to make even the nicest teachers a bit cranky. Willow couldn't blame them. How did they know that there were things more important than calculus?

She sighed and picked up her book, titled *Legends of Italy*. There was nothing in it so far that could help them with this Il Maestro guy. There was nothing in it about an Il Maestro guy at all.

"Willow, are you all right?" Giles asked, as he came out of his office with a cup of tea in one hand and a book in the other.

"Sure." She smiled gamely.

"She's not," Xander snapped. "None of us are." He slammed his book shut. "This is dumb. We should be doing something."

"Yeah," Cordelia said. "Not reading."

Giles paused a moment, then sighed. "And I did so hope that was a joke, Cordelia."

"What?" she said defensively.

"Reading," Willow supplied. "It's doing something."

Cordelia slammed her book shut, too. "Reading is a joke, when everybody else is fighting." Giles, Willow, and Xander stared at her. "Not that I like fighting," she added. "I'm not even any good at it. But it seems way past normal to be going to classes while we're waiting for everything to go pffft."

"I think it will be more like ka-BLAM," Xander said helpfully.

"'Not with a bang, but a whimper,'" Giles murmured.

"Not me, pard. No whimpering here." Xander pushed back his chair. "I'm going to Boston."

"No. You are not," Giles said. He wiped his face, and Willow noticed how tired he looked. There were rings under his eyes and a bit of stubble on his cheeks. "Listen, I know how much you all want to help. But we can't go off half-cocked. Now, I spoke to the Gatekeeper this morning."

"Wow, did he materialize in your bedroom?" Willow asked excitedly.

He blinked. "I beg your pardon?"

"Go on." She nodded at him. "Please."

"On the phone," Giles continued. "He assured me that while he's fairly stretched, he is managing. He specifically asked me to thank you all for your help, especially you, Willow, with the breach. But as the battle being waged is primarily of a magickal nature, he needs to concentrate fully on the matter at hand."

"In other words, thanks but no thanks," Cordelia grumped.

"Because we would be a distraction," Willow filled in. "I can understand that."

"It's not true," Xander said angrily. "Willow's done a lot of magickal stuff here. That breach was a big honkin' deal, and she dealt." He nodded at her. "You rocked, Will."

She dimpled.

"No offense to Willow," Giles said, "but she is a beginner, at best. A cautious dabbler in a war being fought by master sorcerers with decades of experience. She has done exceedingly well with protective and defensive spells, and we may need more of that, right here. But in a war of this magnitude, Willow would likely be killed at the outset."

"Okay, so, maybe no Boston," Willow said, nodding reasonably. "I just wish I knew what was happening with Buffy and Oz."

"And Angel," Cordelia volunteered.

"Angel can take care of himself," Xander said coldly. Then he leaned in to smile at Willow, trying to cheer her up. "Hey, Will. He's okay. Buffy would call if there was a problem."

"If she could," Willow said quietly.

"She *would*. You're her best friend, Will. She would find a way to let you know."

"Yes, Willow," Giles said. "I concur entirely. She would find a way."

"You think?" Willow swallowed hard. She didn't even like to think "Oz" and "problem" in the same paragraph, never mind the same sentence.

"I *know*," Xander insisted, giving the table a little pound. "Buffy's . . . Buffy."

"And *so* perfect," Cordelia muttered.

"Hey, do you mind?" Xander said sharply.

"It's okay." Willow smiled bravely. "I know what you're trying to say, Xander."

"So do I," Cordelia said, giving Xander a look. Xander scowled back at her.

Willow lowered her eyes, pretending to read her book.

Giles felt for Willow. For all of them. The reestablishment of calm was, paradoxically, creating a state of high anxiety. Just this morning, he had had to practically order Joyce Summers to remain in his condo. She had been determined to move back into her home now that the breaches in Sunnydale appeared to be stabilized. As if reestablishing a presence in her home would be an act of strength, and not merely one of defiance.

He knew it might seem paradoxical, but now was when they most needed to stay on their guard. If there was going to be a storm, this was the calm before it.

The last moment of calm any of them might ever know.

"All right, then," he said. "Now that we've all agreed we're actually pleased to be rid of Springheel Jack, the Flying Dutchman, and that horrid sea monster, perhaps you might all continue with your research," he said with asperity. He sipped his tea and went back to his office.

He shut the door and for one moment allowed himself to feel the sum total of his fear. But only for one moment.

It was all he could handle.

Joyce smiled and sipped her glass of chardonnay as she checked the chicken in the oven. The scent of rosemary filled Giles's condo. The sun had just set, and she had lovely new candles for the table. It had been a wonderful idea to invite the kids over, if she did say so herself. She was glad all the parents had agreed, even though they had been a little surprised to discover that the gathering was to be held at the school librarian's home. Joyce had not volunteered that she was staying there, but had casually pointed out during the conversation how special Giles was to all the kids, and that his birthday was coming up. That made sense.

Even if it wasn't true.

Everyone was ragged with worry, and she figured it would help them to be together. With a good meal and a change of scenery, perhaps they would be able to relax just a little.

The doorbell rang. She glanced at the clock. It couldn't be Giles, because he didn't ring—after all, this was his home—but if it was one of the kids, they were a little early.

She checked the peep hole. It was a nice-looking young man, in a delivery uniform, holding a large, attractively arranged vase of flowers.

"Yes?" she said, opening the door.

Brother Forrest thought the deception was going rather well, right up until the woman mentioned that she had never heard of Sherwood Florist, and where was it again?

That was when Brother Dane took out his gun and pistol-whipped the woman, striking her much too hard on the skull.

The youthful Dane caught his breath and muttered, "Chaos' name," as she collapsed into the arms of Brother Forrest, who glared at his fellow acolyte. Both were dressed as florist delivery men, and both were armed, just in case.

"What the hell did you do that for?" Forrest demanded, throwing his arms around the unconscious woman to keep her from slipping to the floor. "We were supposed to scare her, not give her brain damage."

The hand supporting her head came away bloody. He stared at it, then felt the back of her head, moving his way up her scalp.

"I—I—" Dane held out his hands, noted the gun still in his hand, and stuffed it into the pocket of his delivery jacket. "She's the mother of the Slayer. I thought she would struggle."

"And if she did?" Forrest blinked at him. He could not fathom such stupidity. "She's not the Chosen One. Her daughter is."

"Yes, I . . . I guess I panicked, Brother," Dane said dejectedly.

Forrest scowled at him. "I sponsored you. I recommended you for this mission. And now I'll probably die alongside you when Il Maestro hears about this."

Dane's eyes bulged. "Surely we won't be . . . I mean, we have her. It was our job to get her."

"But not like this. We had a plan." Forrest gestured to the limp body of Joyce Summers, draped over his arms. "Put the flowers down. Then help me get her downstairs."

Dane carried the vase into the apartment. He looked around and said, "Where?"

"Just put them down," Forrest bit off. "Come here. Now. Put her arm around your shoulder. I'll do the same. If anyone notices, we'll say she had too much to drink." He laughed bitterly. "As if anyone would believe that. One look at her and you would guess she's dead. And if she dies, she's no good to us, is she?"

Dane swallowed hard. "I'm sorry."

"It won't matter how sorry you are, Brother Dane." At the bottom of the stairs, Brother Lupo waved angrily at the two acolytes he had sent upstairs to kidnap the Slayer's mother.

"You idiots!" he hissed. "Unbelievable! Get her in the car."

The back door of a dark blue Lexus opened. Forrest went in first, then helped pull the woman into the car. Dane gathered up her feet and stuffed them into the car. Then he stood uncertainly beside the vehicle and said, "Ah, where should I sit?"

Brother Lupo, who had been sitting in the front seat with the driver, made a show of glancing at the backseat, where Forrest and the unconscious woman were ensconced.

"In the trunk," he said.

Dane blinked. "Brother," he said unsteadily. "I was nervous."

Lupo stared at him. From his vantage point, Forrest saw the milky white eye begin to glow a deadly blue, and he looked quickly away.

Then he heard Dane cry out. Just once, a strangled shout of pain or surprise that was quickly cut off. Brother Lupo had killed him, destroyed him with magick.

Brother Ariam, who was driving, reached forward and pulled on the lever that opened the trunk. The light from the street was momentarily blocked out as the trunk opened. The car bounced once from an increase in cargo weight. Then the trunk slammed shut.

Brother Forrest heaved a sigh of relief as Brother Ariam slipped back into the driver's seat. He was to be spared, at least for now.

Then he felt a sharp prick at his temple. Something

tore through his head and he moaned low in his throat, once. He understood: Dane had been his responsibility. His failure was Forrest's failure.

The woman who lay next to the dying Brother Forrest on the backseat roused herself slightly. She murmured, "Buffy."

He managed a weak smile. It was a brilliant plan, kidnapping the Slayer's mother to draw the Slayer out.

His smile disappeared just before his soul slipped from his body and went off to receive its just reward. As he died, Forrest's soul knew terror. For he knew what that reward would be.

Chapter 12

Villa Regnier, outside Florence
April 1666

THE AFTERNOON SKY ABOVE THE ROLLING LANDSCAPE was dark and overcast, threatening a spring storm. In the barn, the horses nickered uncertainly and tossed their heads, their eyes widening as Giuliana Regnier, the *signora* of the house, glided among them. She had been restless all day, moving from the bustling kitchen to the clucking henhouse to the more peaceful barn, not finding whatever it was she was looking for, and still having no idea what that was, precisely.

Thunder rumbled. She put her hand protectively over her rounded abdomen. The babe within seemed restless as well, which frightened her. He (for she was certain it was a son) had at least two more months before it was time to greet the world. Her midwife had examined her yesterday, assuring her that all was well. But today Giuliana's back ached and she couldn't seem to stay in one place. She worried that these were portents that something was amiss with her child.

Everyone in the villa was on edge today. Concetta, the cook, had slapped the chambermaid and told her to get her filthy hands out of her kitchen. Two of the field hands had come to blows over a young girl in the village who, it turned out, was betrothed to someone else entirely, a young Florentine from a very good family apprenticed to a banker.

Worst of all was the news from the winemaster: there was something wrong with the fields. The earth contained a type of mold he had never seen before, and he feared it would harm the grapes. He could not be sure; it was outside the realm of his expertise.

Giuliana tried to tell herself that these things happened; there were days like this in every person's life. Other vintners had had trouble with rot and mold, and in fact, some wines had prospered from such things in the past. But, truth be told, she was frightened. Her husband, Richard, was far away, and on a dangerous errand: He had received a missive over five months ago from Kilij Arslan, a great Ottoman sorcerer. She had memorized the letter, so often had she read it:

To M. Richard Regnier, Most Renowned Brother in Magic
Cher Monsieur le Chevalier,
I, Kilij Arslan, send you greetings. As my situation is most desperate, please forgive my dispensing with all the civility due a man of your

illustrious station and allow me to speak quickly and plainly.

I hold in captivity one whom you have sought, namely, that base conjurer of the black arts named Giacomo Fulcanelli. He was already known to me as a most evil sorcerer and a villain before coming to this our beloved Empire, but I, alas, was unable to persuade my master (Allah give him long life!) to shun him and send him away. For he promised My Lord Suleiman many wondrous things, including prosperity for all his people, and thus was my master inclined to listen not to me, but to Fulcanelli, believing my warnings were those of a jealous rival. Not that I blame my master, for he must constantly attend the needs of his subjects, and Fulcanelli assured him that all good things would flow into our Empire.

Instead, as I'm sure you may well imagine, Fulcanelli has delivered only misery and sorrow, most particularly in the form of a most grave insult to My Lord's youngest daughter, who has therefore come to an untimely end at her own hand.

The scales having fallen at last from My Lord's eyes, Fulcanelli has been cast out of favor and sentenced to death. Charged with the wizard's destruction, I bound him within the walls of a remote desert fortress whose location is known only to me and to my master.

When the evil one realized that I had triumphed over him in this small way, he cursed and reviled not only me, but mentioned you by name several times, uttering curses against you and your house. Of course you were already known to me as a Champion of Good, and I have heard stories of your unending quest to dispatch this creature of darkness from this world. Alas, I have myself been unable to do so; save my success in binding him, he has thwarted every spell of destruction which I have visited upon him.

Therefore I beg you in the name of Allah, Who is most wise and beneficent, to come to my fortress and assist me in the destruction of this evil creature. I fear that the time will soon come when he will overpower my binding spell and free himself. My own life shall surely be forfeit in that moment, although if the loss of it could effect his death, I would count it a small price to pay. Yet I fear my end will count for nothing toward his own death, and in desperation—and with great hopes—I turn to you, oh most revered Monsieur Regnier.

I have enclosed a map with Hamza, my trusted confidant, who brings you this letter and who shall escort you. You will in turn be met by a retinue of my guards, who await your arrival at the border of our Empire.

Written in my own hand, and with cordial greetings to my esteemed brother in the arts.

Kilij Arslan, Court Magician to the Ottoman Empire

Giuliana was abjectly sorry that she had encouraged him to go. For things were not right here in Florence, and he was not here to protect his house and his progeny. He had been gone many months, almost five, and she had not had a letter from him for almost two.

Nor had she informed him of her condition, thinking that it would worry him, or worse, bring him home before his mission was completed. But today she worried for her baby, and she wondered if she had been foolish not to insist upon the magickal protection of her husband. To be sure, the midwife had set wards around the perimeter of the property and given her an amulet to wear, but the wisewoman's expertise lay in the realm of old wives' tales, and not in the more enlightened and authentic magick that was the provenance of her husband.

The thunder rumbled again. The horses whinnied uneasily. Giuliana murmured, "Easy, easy, *mi bambini,*" but she herself was not easy. It seemed dishonest to assure any living creature that all was right with the world, and she reflected that a mother's duty lay in part in the perpetuation of such a lie. Every lullaby sang of that lie.

And yet, if a child had a mother and a father who loved him and would die for him, was it falsehood to promise the child safe harbor?

Unhappy with her thoughts, she left the barn and walked across the meadow toward the villa proper. It was called the Court of the Roses, for its dozens of lovely rosebushes. Richard had designed it himself, after the pleasant and airy buildings of Catherine de' Medici's court at Fontainebleau. The de' Medici had been a Florentine also. So the lovely villa mixed his memories of her and her time with that of his wife. "Queen of my conscience, and queen of my soul," he was wont to say.

It was quite something to be the queen of a magician's soul.

"So we should not fear, *caro mio,*" she murmured to her son. "God watches over us, and so does your father."

She crossed herself and entered one of the villa's outbuildings, the fragrant hut where the peasant women dried herbs for cooking and poultices. The entire building smelled of rosemary and lavender, and Giuliana thought she might swoon with delight at the heavy, rich fragrances. Surely naught could be ill in a world that produced such perfume.

Then her abdomen clenched tightly. Groaning deep in her throat, she clutched at it and felt it harden like a rock. Terrified, she took a breath and struggled to stay calm. Too soon, much too soon, she was laboring.

"No," she whispered to her child. "No, my darling, wait."

She groaned as another pain ripped through her, making her shudder and fall to her knees.

"Signora?" a soft voice queried. It was Signorina Alessandra, sent to Giuliana by one of the nuns in the nearby convent. Alessandra had worked for the sisters for three years, and she could keep secrets as well as any priest within the confessional. Giuliana was not naive enough to suppose that her servants did not talk with other servants, but she wished to keep the truth of impending motherhood as private as possible.

"Signora?" the voice echoed.

Giuliana moved her hand to the front of her gown, pressing it against her body. When she saw the blood, she gasped and burst into tears. "My child. God help me. Riccardo!"

Her plea for her husband was a wail lost in the booming thunder, much louder now. As she grew dizzy, she lost sense of where she was. After a hazy passage of time, she became aware of rain pelting her and people carrying her into the house. Of being put into her bed. Of straining and screaming.

And then, of the chambermaid, bursting into the room and shrieking, "Men riding the backs of devils! They come!"

It was then that Giuliana fought hardest against the birth of her child. She wrestled with the Virgin herself to keep him safe inside her body.

But Signorina Alessandra whispered to her, "Lady, if these men are coming to do us mischief, it would be better to give the child to me to hide. I will find safe haven for him. I swear it."

Grunting like an animal, sobbing with fear and pain, Giuliana gripped Alessandra's hand and rasped, "Are you an angel of mercy, then? Or do you mean to deliver my half-formed son into the hands of murderers?"

"I swear, I am God's own child," Alessandra had replied. "On the blood of the One Who died for us, I swear that I will find a safe place for him, my lady."

"They will kill him, as they . . . as they have killed his father," she said, weeping. The pain in her belly caught her off guard, and she screamed. "Riccardo, where are you? You are dead! They've murdered you. Fulcanelli, I curse you! I curse your house!"

"Signora, you must stay calm. Stay quiet," Alessandra said, holding her hand.

"But it is too soon, and they will kill him." Giuliana whispered. "Oh, Alessandra, I had thought to give my husband the fairest rose in his garden of roses. After the horrors that his life has been, I wanted beauty for him. Joy."

Tears spilled down her cheeks, and for a moment, it was six years before, when she was but sixteen, and Riccardo Regnier had come to call at her father's fine home in the bustling metropolis of Florence. She was practically affianced to another, a gallant named Paolo, and she was very much in love with the idea of being in love with a handsome young man.

Then Riccardo strode into her father's house, in his satins and silks, much more colorful than one might have expected, if one knew his age and his travails. His chin, so firm, his eye, so piercing. He had looked at her and she had felt a connection that extended beyond the physical, though in her maidenly way, she wanted him ardently. It was more than a physical attraction. No, this was something that bridged soul to soul.

"I am for you," she had whispered, as they had walked together under the severe gaze of her nurse. "I was created to marry you."

"I believe this as well, I for you," he had replied.

And in time, he confessed all. His age, his explorations into the supernatural, and most of all, his enduring vendetta with the hellspawn, Fulcanelli. With each revelation, she was more sure that Providence had sent her to him.

When they married, she had wept tears of joy.

When she had conceived seven months ago, she had done the same, not realizing that night that he had put a child in her belly.

But now . . . ruin.

"Alessandra," she said, gritting her teeth, as another labor pain wracked her. "If aught should happen, hide him. Shelter him."

"My lady, nothing will happen," Alessandra replied, then hesitated. "But I will do as you ask."

Then, as hoofbeats drowned out her words, she silently inclined her head and nodded.

Pain . . . unimaginable pain . . . and at the last, the plaintive cry of a newborn babe. And Alessandra's words in her ear: "He is very small, but he is well-formed. I think that he will live."

And then, footfalls in the hallway. The door crashing open. And a demon gazing down at her, his face contorted with rage.

"Where is the little bastard Regnier filled you with?"

Giuliana screamed. It was Fulcanelli himself. She recognized his countenance from the sketches her husband had made, so that she would know the face of her husband's most hated nemesis. As she gazed at him in her bed of travail, the blood still wet beneath her hips, she knew the beardless, unlined face, the striking features, the startling crystal-blue eyes.

"You are too late. My child is dead," Giuliana rasped, tears spilling down her cheeks. "And I shall follow him soon."

His fury was terrifying. He raised his withered left

hand and, with a flick of his wrist, sent a whistling wind through the chamber that shrieked of distress and chilled Giuliana to the bone.

"Tell me where your child is," Fulcanelli said, bending over her. "And I will be merciful."

Giuliana swallowed back a scream as something sharp and painful sliced through her breast. She thought it might be a knife, but when she stared down at her chest, she saw no cut, no wound. But she writhed with pain.

"Dead," she whispered, praying that saying it did not make it true. "He was born too soon."

The man blinked, and for the first time, she hoped. If he had already known that she was with child, then he probably realized now that she was telling him the truth. Her child had been born too soon. And yet, Alessandra thought he might live.

That, she would never tell Fulcanelli.

"Where's the body?" he demanded.

Tears spilled down her cheeks. "I know not," she whispered. "They took him away to spare me further agony. He was baptized and then they took him."

"Where's the priest?" the sorcerer asked.

"What?" She caught her breath, realizing she might be caught in her lie. Worrying that she might visit death upon Father Lorenzo, the priest who said mass once a week at the villa but lived in town during the other six days.

"The priest."

"He left." She closed her eyes. "Please, signor, I am so tired and bereft. I need rest."

He slapped her.

* * *

The chambermaid, the cook, and three of Giuliana's other female servants were dragged into the room by men in hooded robes and thrown, sobbing, to the floor.

"Kill the old one," Fulcanelli said carelessly.

"No, stop!" Giuliana cried, raising herself on her elbows.

As she watched in horror, one of the hooded men grabbed Concetta, the cook, and yanked back her head. Lightning fast, the other man pulled a stiletto from his sleeve and slit her throat.

Blood spurted everywhere, cascading over the shrieking women on the floor, the two men, and on Giuliana herself. But Fulcanelli remained untouched.

"Where is Regnier's heir?" he shouted at Giuliana. "Tell me, or everyone in this house dies!"

"Dead," Giuliana sobbed. "He is dead."

Fulcanelli said to the blood-soaked men. "Kill the youngest one."

"No, no!" screamed the chambermaid as they hoisted her to her feet. "My lady, signora, I beg you, tell them!"

"Tell them what?" Giuliana said desperately, staring hard at the young girl, willing her to help, begging her to spare her child.

The chambermaid stared back at her for a long instant. And then she burst into tears and moaned.

"Tell them that he is dead," the girl murmured in a defeated, flat voice.

The slaughter in Giuliana's bedchamber took mere minutes. Afterwards, Fulcanelli's henchmen dragged her from her bed and forced her to stand in the courtyard as every single living creature at the villa was cut down, some by the two dozen hooded men who had come with Fulcanelli, others by hideous monsters the sorcerer called from the air. Giuliana saw the might and strength of the evil he commanded, and wept as her servants and tenants were rent limb from limb, as they were set ablaze, as their bodies were shattered like crystal with a flick of Fulcanelli's wrist.

Men, boys, little girls, it made no difference. They went to their deaths terrified and begging their *signora* to save them.

She did not. She would not. And none of the very few who knew what had happened—that her child had lived—betrayed her.

Alessandra was not discovered, and Giuliana began to hope that she and the child would survive.

Then Fulcanelli's followers mounted strange, shadowy horses and cantered away. Only one remained behind, holding a mount for his master.

Fulcanelli turned to Giuliana and caressed her cheek.

"You were right. You will die soon, from loss of blood," he said.

"And I will be with the Holy Mother, while the Devil waits for you," she whispered.

He laughed. Then he spit in her face. His spittle reeked of the grave as it traced a path down her cheek.

"The Devil and I have a pact," he said, "which includes the assurance that our enemies will suffer at our hands at every possible occasion. Your husband would grieve that you died shortly after childbirth. But many women die in that way. It is a fact of nature."

He leered at her. "But if he knew you were tortured to death, slowly and expertly, while he was away on a fool's errand, well, that would make him suffer."

"A fool's . . ." she breathed.

"Who do you think sent him that letter?"

Then he raised his hands and held them toward her.

The entire villa fell into total blackness. Giuliana caught her breath, and smelled the fragance of roses, withering as if in grief.

Something came up behind her. Something enormous. Something as cold as the grave.

"Ciao, bella," Fulcanelli said jauntily.

There was the creak of leather as someone climbed onto a mount. Hoofbeats rumbled in counterpoint to Giuliana's rapid heartbeat, weak and fluttering as a hummingbird's. She understood: Fulcanelli was leaving her with whatever it was he had conjured to deal her death.

Perhaps, she thought hopefully, *I will die this very minute.*

Because death would be welcome as a lover, she thought, as she writhed in agony. *Dying will make it all right.*

The landscape blazed as brightly as day. In the distance, she saw the Duomo and the city; around her, the beautiful roses. Her eyes filled with tears as she stared at the landscape.

As the pain made her heart stop—

"My God, Buffy!" Angel shouted.

"What!" she shouted back, bolting upright. Then she fell back into his arms, intensely dizzy, and said, "I'm not Buffy. I am Giuliana Regnier."

She blinked. Oz stood on the other side of the saggy mattress in their Florentine pension and said, "Uh-oh."

"Wait. I'm okay," she said.

"You had no pulse," Angel accused.

"I do now, all right?" She frowned. "And why'd you let me fall asleep?"

"You were tired," Oz pointed out.

"What did you dream?" Angel asked urgently. "Tell me, before you forget."

She shrugged. "Like I could forget. Not so pleasant. It was one of *those* dreams." She glanced at Oz. "Something true usually gets mixed up with the weird parts. It happens to me now and then. It's a Slayer thing."

"I know what you mean," Oz assured her. "I dreamed I flunked senior year and had to repeat it. Except there were no weird parts. So that must be the special Slayer feature."

She smiled at him, then turned to Angel. "I was at a villa and I smelled roses. Lots of roses. I'm thinking, Court of the Roses might not be the address, but the name of the villa. And I had a great view of a city." She paused. "A city a long time ago. But I saw a big church dome."

Oz said, "Which Florence has."

"Okay," Angel said, reaching for the phone. "Do you want Giles or the Gatekeeper?"

"Let's go straight to the source," Buffy suggested. "The Gatekeeper."

Angel began to punch in numbers.

* * *

Giles pulled into the parking lot of his condo complex, smiling as Willow shifted the bouquet of flowers in her lap to reach for the door handle. It had been a brilliant idea on Joyce Summers's behalf to invite everyone over for dinner. They needed a moment simply to be together without having to fight monsters or bind breaches. In short, to be kids.

"Y'know, the flowers are going to make her think you have a crush on her," Xander said from the back seat. "Especially since you turned your back on the cheap bouquets with all the daisies and went for the chrysanthemums."

"Ah, yes, chrysanthemums," Giles said archly. "The flower of extravagance and romance."

Cordelia sighed. "Xander, civilized people bring each other flowers all the time. If you had any class at all, you'd know that. Mrs. Summers will know Giles is just being nice."

"Indeed she will," Giles replied, "since she's the one who suggested I pick some up."

"Oh." Xander huffed. "Well, I was just looking out for you. Y'know, it could have been awkward, her being Buffy's mom and all."

"Thank you for your concern," Giles said, getting out of the car. "But it's totally unwarranted, I assure you."

"Yeah, break her heart, Buffy would probably stake you."

Giles decided not to tell Xander that that thought had, on occasion, crossed his mind.

"All right, then," Giles said. "If someone can get the cheesecake, I think we're ready to have a pleasant evening."

They got out of the car and trooped around the building to the main entrance. Giles paused to check his mail while the others went on ahead. He caught up with them, silently grousing at the handful of bills—his credit card bill was bound to be astronomical—and reached for his keys.

"Hey, um," Willow said, tentatively pushing on the door. It swung open.

She looked worriedly at Giles, who stepped past her and swept into the room. The odor of burning food permeated the apartment.

"Joyce?" he called. He took the stairs to the right, his heart clutching as he recalled a similar scenario—going up these very steps, to find Jenny's dead, staring eyes gazing at him from his bed.

Nothing. He sagged with relief as he stared at the neatly made bed. No signs of a scuffle. Nothing in the loo, either.

He hurried down the stairs as Xander pointed to a large ceramic vase of flowers plunked down on the corner of the coffee table.

"What's that?" the boy asked.

"Um, flowers?" Cordelia guessed.

"Joyce?" Giles called again, checking the down-stairs bathroom.

"Maybe she just went to the store," Willow said anxiously.

"Oh, right, and left something in the oven to burn," Xander shot back. Then he cocked his head. "But now that you mention it, that's the kind of thing my mom would do."

"Yeah, but Buffy's mom knows how to cook. And

she wouldn't leave the door unlocked. Even if she didn't have the key to get back in."

Giles shook his head. "She has a key."

He crossed to the flowers. There was a gift card on a plastic stake; he plucked it up and read, *"Thinking of you. Love, Buffy."*

He looked at the kids. "Well, obviously, Buffy didn't send this from, ah, Sherwood Florist." He paused. He had once bought Jenny a little bouquet from the same shop. Coincidence?

"I'd say not," Cordelia sniffed. "Everyone knows Dandelions is the only decent florist in town."

"Really." Giles pushed up his glasses and examined the card.

"Giles." Xander's voice came from the hallway. "Giles, come quick."

"Oh, my God, what?" Willow breathed.

Giles dashed out the door and joined Xander, who knelt on one knee and pointed to some splotches of red on the concrete.

"It's blood, isn't it?" Xander asked shakily.

Giles nodded, a terrible sensation of dread washing over him. "Yes. I'm afraid it is."

Willow made fists of her hands and put them under her chin as Giles placed the call to the florist shop and went through the pleasantries. His eyes on Giles's every move, Xander took the burned chicken out of the oven and doused it with water from the kitchen sink.

Cordelia worried.

She didn't know what else to do.

"And you say a man came in and ordered what kind of flowers?"

As Giles listened, he swiveled toward the bouquet and studied it, his eyes narrowing. He nodded slowly, including the kids in his nod. These must be the ones.

"Missing, you say," Giles said into the phone.

"What, the flowers?" Cordelia asked anxiously.

Xander made a face and turned the faucet off. The charred nuggets of chicken floated in a sea of water, which sloshed over the side as he set the pan to the side of the sink. For some reason, looking at the mess made Cordelia feel slightly ill. Or maybe that was her nerves.

"Who on earth would bother stealing flowers?" Xander said.

Cordelia shot him a look. "Someone who's too cheap to ever buy any."

"Hey." He scowled at her. "I've bought you flowers." He hesitated. "Haven't I?"

"You brought *Willow* flowers when she was in the hospital," Cordelia retorted. "I guess the only way I'll ever get flowers from you is if I perform some bizarre ritual and nearly die."

"Guys," Willow said sternly. She gestured toward Giles, who was hanging up the phone.

"The flowers were purchased by a pleasant-looking man with glasses. When the shop girl closed up for the evening, she noticed that someone had gone through the laundry. She thinks a few items were taken, but she doesn't know what. However, the laundry consisted mainly of uniforms."

"Disguises," Xander said unhappily. "Florist delivery guy. Who wouldn't open the door?"

"I wouldn't," Cordelia said. "Buffy's mom has always been too trusting. I mean, she never figured out that Buffy was the Slayer. And Buffy was coming home with bloodstains all over her clothes. I mean, what was up with that?"

Xander puffed out his cheeks, exhaled, looked very worried. "So they tricked Mrs. Summers, who obviously does not watch very many slasher films, into opening the door. Can you say lowlife scum? I knew you could."

"And then they did something to her that made her bleed," Willow added miserably.

"So now what? I assume calling the police is out. It always is," Cordelia said anxiously.

" 'Cause, y'know, they would be such a big help," Xander drawled.

Giles picked up the phone again.

"We have to tell Buffy," he said. "Perhaps she's already been contacted."

Cordelia frowned. "Contacted?"

"By the kidnappers," Giles explained.

Xander flattened his hands on the counter and stared at the flowers. His expression almost frightened Cordelia, it was so filled with anger.

"It's obvious, isn't it?" he said. "It's not Buffy's mom they're after. It's Buffy."

Chapter 13

A̲t the east end of Sunnydale, still within the town limits but long past anything that actually passed for "town," lay the Sunnydale Twin Drive-In. Or what had once been the Twin. One after another, the nostalgic buyers had come along, dedicated to "doing it right" even if that meant making no money at all. Eventually, reality set in. There were people willing to operate the drive-in purely for pleasure, without any profit at all. But so far, nobody had been willing to run the place at a loss.

Too far out on the edge of town. Too far from just about everything else. Past the desolation that had once been the two-screened drive-in, there were only some thick woods, Route 17, several mom-and-pop stores and then, when you started to get close to the next town over, an ice rink.

Teenagers sneaked in often enough, mostly to drink

or have a bonfire in the lot. One of the screens was ruined, half of it having collapsed during a nasty thunderstorm back in '95. Most of the speakers had been ripped from their stands, swung around some local kid's head by their wires, and thrown at the screens or at the little cement projection booth and concession stand that looked like nothing so much as a bomb shelter.

But there hadn't been any invading teenagers in the past few weeks. Anyone who even came close to the fence had the sudden and irresistible urge to be far, far away from the Sunnydale Twin. It wasn't any one particular thing, but just an overall feeling that drove them off.

It was black magick.

Brother Dando turned off his headlights and then drove his Jeep up through the break in the trees, down a small hill, and through the section of fence that he personally had torn down weeks earlier. Then he was in the Twin's lot, and he headed straight for the concession stand, using only the light of the moon and stars to keep him from slamming into a row of speaker posts.

He braked to a stop, put the Jeep in neutral, set the brake, and pulled his keys from the ignition. Dando was angry as he leaped from the Jeep, but it was an anger he was doing his best to hide.

His best was simply not good enough.

Dando slammed through the door, bringing the two guards lounging inside to their feet, minor magick crackling around their hands. When they saw him, their faces fell, their eyes searching for something, anything, to focus on.

"Brother Dando," gasped the younger of the two, whom Dando thought was named Ramsey. "Our apologies for our, ah, lax security. Your entrance was . . . abrupt, and we . . ."

"Oh, shut up, you idiot," Dando sneered. "Where is Claude?"

Brother Ramsey blinked. "Um. Brother Claude is in the storage area, seeing to the feeding of the prisoner."

With a snort of derision, Dando stormed along a corridor whose decor made it look more like a bathroom than anything else. He reached the double metal doors to the storage area, where the drive-in's owners had kept shelf upon shelf of popping corn, candy, cups, liquid butter substitute, and just about everything else they needed.

As he entered, Brother Claude was closing the opposite door. Beyond that door was the room one owner after another had used as an office. It had held the safe, and so could be locked up quite tightly. There were no windows, and only that one door. It was perfect for holding someone prisoner. Which had been quite convenient, since they had never expected to need to hold anyone prisoner. Not until the order had come from Il Maestro, surprising them, as many of Il Maestro's orders did. Particularly today.

"Claude, what the hell is going on?" Dando snapped.

The other acolyte turned to look at him, and much of Dando's anger fled instantly. Claude was thin and wiry and had delicate features. He had wispy brown hair, a thin mustache, and wore wire-rim glasses. Dando had often thought Claude would look more at home applauding politely in a box at the opera than slipping on a hood and intoning some arcane ritual.

But any time he thought that way, the impression drained away the moment he looked into Claude's eyes. Dando had never seen eyes like that. Not even in the mirror.

"He's upstairs in the projection room," Brother Claude said, and smiled mischievously. "I've done my part, Dando. I called to tell you the news. If you have a problem with that information, I suggest you take it up with him. He is, after all, our commander now."

With an eloquent scowl, Dando turned and retreated from the storage area, then started up the steps to the projection room upstairs. At the top of the steps was another thick metal door. He gripped the knob firmly, felt a peculiar heat in the metal as he turned it, and then he flung the door open and marched straight in.

Three steps, and he stopped, blinking, astounded by what he saw.

His bald pate gleaming in the weird light, Brother Lupo sat at the center of the projection room, magickal blue energy crackling around his blind, white eye and the scars on his brow and cheek. Lupo's single good eye darted around the room, but he didn't seem to notice Dando's entrance at all.

The two square windows through which movies had been projected when the Sunnydale Twin was still in operation showed only the night beyond. Other than the tiny bit of moonlight shining into the room, the only illumination came from Lupo's magick. It spread around the room in a grid of straight and curved lines that Dando took several moments to realize was a map of the town. There were small bursts of energy glowing at perhaps a dozen places on this quivering, floating map that stretched from wall to wall. And, very near its center, not far from where Lupo sat, a large patch of energy glowed savagely red.

As Dando watched, one of the smaller, blue patches began to glow white. Lupo smiled to himself.

"Yes," whispered Brother Lupo.

Just as the white turned back to blue again.

Lupo growled, "Damn!" and his one good eye snapped up to glare at Dando.

"I assume, Brother Dando, that you have some purpose for being here and interrupting me?"

"What are you doing?" Dando asked, his anger having leaked away long ago.

Lupo grunted with dissatisfaction, as though Dando should know perfectly well what he was doing. And Dando could not escape the thought that Lupo had every reason to expect such knowledge from him. However, Brother Dando was nowhere near the magician that Lupo was. This very moment proved that, at least. But Dando still felt slighted by Il Maestro's choice.

"The creatures of chaos, denizens of the Otherworld, have begun crowding the ghost roads, just as Il Maestro planned," Lupo explained with exasperation. "The destruction of that barrier has begun. But unless we can reopen the breaches that were so painstakingly created between the ghost roads and this world, the chain reaction he desires will never take place. It will be quite a task to merge Otherworld and Earth, and this is only the first step.

"With help from the Gatekeeper, and from the Watcher, that little amateur spellcaster who has allied herself with the Slayer has managed to bind these breaches quite well," Lupo said with great frustration. "I am endeavoring to shatter those bindings, but it is no simple task."

Brother Dando nodded, fascinated. Then he remembered his purpose and pulled himself up to his full height.

"That's all well and good," Dando said, "but even more reason for Il Maestro to have chosen me for command. You have too many tasks to see to as it is."

Lupo looked up, brows furrowed with disdain. "That is not for you to decide," he said coldly.

"But why were we not told that the activities of the Sons of Entropy here in America were to be consolidated under one commander? We are used to receiving more personal attention from Il Maestro," Dando complained.

"Perhaps he is simply too busy to hold the hand of each of his acolytes," Lupo suggested, glaring at Dando. "The grand plan of chaos that Il Maestro has spent his considerable life developing is not for us to understand. We have only to obey. Each of us has a duty that contributes to the plan, each of us has been allowed to understand only his part in that plan. Now, as we come together for the final battle, we will all begin to understand far better. So he has vowed to me."

Dando stared at the crackling blue energy, nodded grimly, and turned to go. At the door, however, he paused and glanced back in.

"I still think I was the better choice," Dando said. "My military training gives me an edge you cannot possibly have."

Brother Lupo didn't even look at him this time. Instead, he concentrated on a blue patch on the energy grid. At length, he said, "If you have a problem with this choice, you may take it up with Il Maestro himself when he arrives."

"Here?" Dando asked in astonishment.

"Soon," the other replied.

In the maintenance closet, Joyce came awake slowly, rubbing gently at the spot on her head where she knew there ought to be a great deal of pain. And yet, there was no pain.

None.

Slowly, with unnecessary caution, she rose to her feet and examined her surroundings. The room was a concrete block without windows, and with a single metal door. There were several vents, but none big enough for her to climb through, as they did in the movies. There were several metal shelving units, some of which held half-used bottles of cleaning solution, but for the most part the place was picked clean. There was an old-fashioned rolling iron bucket with a rotten gray mop sticking up out of it.

On the floor there was a tray that she assumed was someone's idea of dinner. The meal consisted of a bowl of plain pasta and two boiled hot dogs which hadn't seen "hot" in a long, long time. She was supposed to eat, she knew. And at first she rebelled at the idea. That was, until she realized how hungry she was. Add to that her understanding that if they had wanted her dead, poison would not be their weapon of choice.

She ate.

When she had finished, she stood up again. Instead of pacing the room, she went directly to the door and began to pound on it, the metal aiding her in her effort to make a lot of noise. There was no way she was going to be in here without at least knowing why.

There came a voice from beyond the door. "Step back," it said.

Joyce steeled herself for something horrible. Vampires. Demons. Evil sorcerers. The man who opened the door was the furthest thing from what she might have imagined. He was well groomed and handsome, in a professorial sort of way. Also, he was smiling, and it wasn't the kind of smile Joyce would have expected from abductors.

"Yes, Mrs. Summers, what can I do for you?" asked the man solicitously.

"You can get me the hell out of here," she snapped. "I don't know what you think you're doing, but you'd better let me go right now."

The man smiled even more warmly. "What I think," he said, "is that we have captured you, and intend to keep you as a prisoner for the foreseeable future. You ought to keep that in mind when you speak to me. I am, after all, the man charged with keeping you fed and alive. You may call me Brother Claude."

Joyce faltered, then. She didn't know what to say. There was no way she was going to fight her way out. Not right now. And this Brother Claude had, in fact, brought her dinner. Then she shook that thought off. These guys had kidnapped her. She wasn't going to be nice to them.

"I remember being hit on the head," she said.

"Ah," Claude said, nodding sympathetically. "Yes. You had a concussion. The brother who struck you has been corrected."

"I . . . *had* a concussion," Joyce repeated, touching her fingers to her skull again.

"Oh yes, quite severe," Claude replied. "But I healed you. I have very little talent with magick, save where it allows for magickal healing."

Joyce raised an eyebrow. "Oh, I'm sure you'll be very useful to the Sons of Entropy once the world ends," she said, her voice thick with sarcasm.

"Despite your tone, I'll take that as sincere," said Claude. "It would not go well for you if I chose to be insulted."

With a shudder, Joyce withdrew into the room. "Well," she said, "I don't want to insult you, but your cuisine leaves a bit to be desired. Plus, it's a bit chilly in here, and it would be nice if I could have a blanket and a pillow, at least."

"I'll take it under advisement," Claude acknowledged, and smiled again. "I like your spirit, Mrs. Summers. No wonder your daughter became the Slayer."

Joyce didn't respond to that. She was shattering inside. All the bravado she had shown this man had been for his benefit, but inside, she was nothing but a quivering mass of fear. *Still,* she thought, *at least he healed me. That must mean they don't plan to kill me right away.*

The thought gave her pause. For if they didn't want her dead right away, then why did they want her? The only thing Joyce could think of was . . . bait.

"You think she'll come for me, don't you?" Joyce whispered in horror. "She won't, you know. She's the Slayer. The world depends on her."

"She'd better," said Brother Claude. "We're all counting on her. Especially you."

After he finished listening to the last cut of Tori Amos, Spike emerged from the room he shared with Drusilla in the little cottage. He'd been half dozing, because he was bored and restless and frustrated, but now it was time to get something done or he would have wasted the entire night.

He had a cigarette halfway to his lips when he realized she wasn't in the main room.

"Damn," he whispered, then chomped on the end and held it in his teeth without lighting it.

Spike went to the door of the room where they had kept the boy prisoner. He figured they'd been pretty easy on the kid. They took him to the bathroom half a dozen times a day, whether he needed to go or not. He got to sleep in a real bed. Even got fed pretty regularly. Just last night, Drusilla had brought home a pair of eager fishermen for supper. When they were drained, and Spike had dragged them down the path to the docks, he'd come upon their haul from the day before.

The kid had fresh fish during the day, and he'd have it again tonight.

If Drusilla hadn't tired of playing baby-sitter.

He saw that the door was still locked, and he was immediately relieved. Which still begged the question of where Dru might be. And he ought to check in on the kid in any case. No reason she couldn't have popped in for a nip and locked the door again on the way out.

But when he pushed the door open, the kid rolled over on his side. His eyes were wide with horror, but they relaxed a bit when he saw who his visitor was.

That pissed Spike off a bit.

He stepped into the kid's room. The boy wore no gag. They'd dispensed with that by the third day. He knew nobody could hear him scream up here, not in time to help him with one of his vampire captors always so close at hand. They'd left his legs free, too. But his hands were cuffed behind him with police shackles, and without them, he wasn't going anywhere. Not locked up tight like they had him.

"I'm thirsty," the boy said.

Spike frowned. He took out his lighter and lit the cigarette dangling from his lips. He went slowly to the edge of the boy's bed and sat down, smiling amiably. He took a long drag on his cigarette.

"You've got it beat, don't you, you little wanker?" Spike asked, smiling.

Jacques blinked. Looked unsure of himself now.

"You figure Drusilla's got bats in her belfry, but I'm a reasonable enough sort, for a vampire," Spike went on. He scratched a phantom itch on his head, then offered an amused nod.

"Not far from the truth, actually," he confessed, and now he stared hard at the boy, his face darting in close, his eyes beginning to turn an odd shade of yellow.

His face changed, brow protruding, eyes sinking back into his face even as his fangs elongated until he flicked his tongue over them lovingly.

The boy cried out in fear and struggled to move backward on the bed, even as Spike crawled after him like a jungle cat.

"Don't start to get the idea that I'm fond of you, Jack-me-lad. If Dru takes a bite, it might make you worthless to us. That's bad. But if we don't get what we want soon, I might just rip your throat open with my own teeth and feed her your life in a fluted champagne glass. She'd like that, my baby. Girl's got class."

He bore down on Jacques.

"You're a unique child, aren't you? Daddy's a bloody magician or whatever, right? But that don't mean much to me, you stupid little sod. To me, you're just another meal."

He stood back, took another drag on his cigarette, and his face slowly returned to normal. He blew smoke at the boy, then went back to the door. Before he closed and locked it again, he took a last look at the terrified child.

"They haven't given us what we want yet, Jacques. Neither one of us is the patient sort. You might want to think on that."

When he stepped into the main room, Drusilla was standing silhouetted in the open door. From outside, the scents of the sea drifted into the house, and Spike relaxed immediately.

"Spike," Drusilla said, in her usual singsong voice. "Are you terrorizing the poor boy?"

"Yes," Spike said, walking toward her and holding out his hands.

She took them and turned him into a little dance, a little twirl, as she said, "Oh, goody!"

Together they walked back out onto the small porch of the cottage. They sat on a bench, and Spike smoked as Drusilla watched the waves roll in. Most of the fishermen had cleared out for the night after bringing their ships back into the wharf area just down the shore. Now it was just the waves and the wind and the calls of the night birds.

"Still thinking of Spain, pet?" Spike asked, glancing sidelong at her.

"I rather think I'm starting to like it here," Dru replied, cocking her head to one side. "I've begun to hear calliope music all the time. Can you hear it, too? There's a carousel in my head, and the horses go up and down."

With a shake of his head, Spike sighed.

"Sorry to hear that, love. I think we're going to have to move on soon, actually," he told her. "Those bloody monks of Entropy are having us on, I think. They've got to figure since we're around here, we wouldn't let the boy be far. It won't be long until they find our little love nest, if they haven't already."

"I'll miss the fishermen," said Dru. "Always so robust."

Then she turned to him with rare focus in her eyes, a look of surprise and pleasure on her face. "Does that mean I get to taste the little veal calf, then?" she asked.

Spike patted her thigh. "Not just yet, Dru darling. I think I'll take a little jaunt over to Florence first. Find out if this Maestro bloke is holding out on us. If he is, I think I might find a better use for that spear than the bit of social climbing we had planned."

Drusilla sighed. "It would have come in handy, wouldn't it, Spike? Never being defeated in battle would be helpful when trying to make an impression on the locals, wherever we decide to settle down next."

They were silent for a moment, and Spike knew that Drusilla was thinking just what he was. There was unfinished business still out there. But that was for another time.

"Ah, well," he said, getting up from the bench. "I ought to get moving."

He went back inside, slipped on the long black leather coat he frequently wore, and came back out again, ready for travel. The battered Mercedes they'd been using since their arrival here was parked just down the road, and he started down the steps without a pause.

At the bottom of the steps, however, he thought better of it and turned to face Drusilla.

"If you get the idea you've got company, love, don't wait. Just get out, and we'll meet up at the bullfights, eh?" he said. "And, just in case our sparklingly charming little magician friend has got his hands on the spear, don't kill the boy just yet, hmm? It would be bad form."

Drusilla sighed and rolled her eyes, then hung her head sulkily. "All right," she replied. "I'll behave."

"Good girl," Spike said, and smiled.

He threw his cigarette to the ground and stubbed it out with his boot.

"So, we're just going to follow your dream?" Oz asked doubtfully. "Sort of a *Man of La Mancha* thing?"

Buffy raised an eyebrow and shot him a look. "Giles's phone machine is full or something and the Gatekeeper's line isn't even ringing. You wolf out tomorrow night. Angel's been living on what we'll kindly call K rations. If we're very lucky, Il Maestro is not certain where we are right now. If we start poking around, he's going to find us in about thirty seconds.

"The dream was pretty clear. So was our information."

"Roses," Oz said.

"Roses," Buffy repeated. "And the Dome thingie."

"Duomo," Angel corrected her.

"Whatever. Would you rather sit around here?" She rolled her eyes. "We'll just go up in the hills until I can match up the landscape—"

"In the dark," Oz pointed out.

"Hey." Buffy narrowed her eyes at him. "If you want to stay here and wait for an open phone line to America, fine. Me, I'm gone."

The three of them stood just outside a trattoria where Buffy and Oz had enjoyed a hearty meal just after dark. Angel had disappeared during dinner, and Buffy didn't ask where he'd been, but she had nasty little visions of him lurking in back alleys and looking for vermin.

She couldn't wait to get home. She wanted her

mother's cooking. Which had never seemed like anything special—unless compared to Xander's mother's—until now.

"So let's go," Angel said urgently. "We're close."

"Keep your pants on," Buffy said with much irritation, just before she registered exactly what she'd said.

Neither of them so much as looked at the other.

Instead, Buffy let her eyes rove over the city. Florence, or Firenze as it was called in Italian, had the most beautiful architecture of any city Buffy had ever seen. The illuminated domes and spires looked as though they were made of marble and mother-of-pearl, and for all she knew, they were. The colors were amazing as well, pinks and oranges and greens and earth tones that were incredibly subtle.

"That way," she said, pointing between twin spires that shot into the sky.

"You're certain?" Angel asked.

"Dream," Oz reminded him.

Buffy led the way.

The city was behind them, and the three of them crouched uncomfortably in what remained of the alternatingly rotten and overrun vegetation that was all that remained of a once vital vineyard. Dead ahead was an amazing, sprawling Italian villa. The architecture was extraordinary. The grounds were expansive. A century earlier, Buffy thought, it must have been one of the most amazing homes in the region.

But now . . .

"It looks like nobody's lived here since Angel was in diapers," Oz said with amazement. "I know, y'know, dream and everything, but is this the same place?"

Angel glanced at her, his own doubt plain on his face.

Buffy only nodded.

"Our buddy the Maestro is in there," she said confidently. "It's exactly as I dreamed. Well, except that in the dream it looked new. And there were roses, which there aren't now. But this is the place.

"Besides . . ." She shrugged. "Can't you feel it?"

Oz cocked his head to one side, then glanced at the house. "I do feel a bit, I don't know, nauseous. I thought that was the clam sauce from my pasta."

Buffy shook her head. "It's coming from in there," she said.

"What is it?" Oz asked.

It was Angel who answered.

"It's chaos."

For about an hour, Buffy, Angel, and Oz watched the villa. Satisfied that no one knew they were there, they crawled closer on their elbows and stomachs like commandos.

Buffy murmured, "Be careful."

"Nothing but," Oz murmured back.

Angel said, "I smell blood. Human blood. And very fresh."

Buffy took a breath and said, "Fresh as in still kicking?"

"Buffy, it's my nose, not a Geiger counter," Angel returned testily. Then he shook his head and said, "Sorry. I don't know."

"Then we have to hurry," Buffy said, and picked up her pace.

They got to the perimeter of the villa, an amazing array of withered vines and foliage, tumbledown buildings, and then the central building itself, a truly lovely ruin of salmon-pink rubble overrun with bougainvillea. It gave new meaning to the word *estate,* and Buffy had seen a few of those when she and her parents lived in L.A. The walls and corners and courtyards seemed to go on for miles, dotted with the remnants of gardens and fountains.

"It's kind of like your place," Buffy whispered to Angel.

"Times twenty." Angel touched her hand. "Look."

It seemed impossible. A trio of figures in hooded robes were sharing a bottle of something. Furtively glancing around like naughty fraternity students— and Buffy knew whereof she spoke—they took turns chugalugging from the curved bottle.

"A million kabillion lire that that's a nice Chianti," Buffy said.

"And another million kabillion that those robes are one-size-fits-all," Oz replied.

Buffy smiled at him grimly. "Great minds think alike."

They stood then and rushed the trio. Before the three had time to realize what had happened, they lay in a heap, unconscious, possibly dead, and Buffy, Angel, and Oz were slipping on their robes.

Buffy pulled her hood over her blond hair and said, "How do I look?"

"Not like Pamela Lee," Oz said.

"I guess that's good." She glanced at Angel.

"It's good," he said. He drew his hood forward. "Okay?"

She couldn't see his face. She said, "Okay." Next she checked Oz. His features were hidden.

"Hey, whoa, there's a knife in my pocket," he said.

"And I thought you were just glad to see me," Buffy quipped. She felt in her own pocket. "Look at this."

It was a rose quartz wrapped with some kind of string.

"I have one, too," Angel said.

"Make that three." Oz held his up.

"Or four," Buffy muttered, as a hooded figure approached them. She tensed her muscles. "Get ready to rumble, boys."

"Buffy, take it easy. These guys are all over the place," Angel cautioned.

"Buona sera," said the newcomer.

Buffy crammed her hands in her pockets and let Angel make the nice talk. He spoke with the other guy in Italian for a few minutes. Then the other guy moved off, saying something over his shoulder.

"It's the rose quartz," Angel said in surprise. "It's some kind of ID. As long as we're carrying, we're considered part of the crowd."

"Maybe that's how Il Maestro knows who to fry," Buffy suggested. "Maybe that guy in Paris dropped his, or something." She took a breath. "Well, let's test that theory."

They walked forward slowly. Despite what Angel's buddy had said, Buffy expected at any moment to be challenged. Her reflexes were on full alert; there was nothing in her that was not ready for a fight.

And yet, to her astonishment, they blended right in

with the clusters of acolytes on the grounds. There weren't as many as Buffy would have expected, but if they decided she and the boys were barbarian invaders, their numbers could pose a problem.

The big test was entering the villa itself. For a second, as Buffy crossed the threshold, she thought they had been discovered. Someone was yelling, and, with all the built-in guilt of a high school senior, Buffy froze.

The yeller was an acolyte with an Australian accent, carping about not having been chosen for something or other. Apparently some kind of ritual.

When they entered, he looked up, and Buffy almost totally freaked, imagining he had seen her girlish face. "Ah," he said conspiratorially, "here come some other second-class citizens. It's standing room only down there, folks. If you want to hold the knife, you'll have to wait until next time. And then you'll have to get in line behind me."

They moved on.

Then Buffy heard a scream echoing up from the lower levels of the ruined villa.

"Here," Angel said, darting into a corridor.

There were more screams, of mortal terror. Buffy bit her lip and allowed Angel to hustle her farther along the corridor. Then they reached a flight of stairs leading down. The stairs were covered with leaves and dirt, and spiderwebs stretched across their entry.

They began to descend, each step punctuated by a shriek. Buffy found herself swearing that she would level this place and sow the ground with salt. She couldn't stand by, and yet she must. How many people had been sacrificed to the war between good and evil, a war she would die fighting and which might never be won?

Down they went, Oz murmuring something about Alice and the rabbit hole, and Buffy shook off her friends' restraining grips as the stairs leveled out to a corridor lit by a single torch. She walked ahead into the semidarkness. She was the Slayer. That was the gig.

There was another flight of stairs, this one very narrow. Her shoulders grazed the walls as she took them slowly yet deliberately, aware of her backup.

Before her, a large door glowed red hot. She touched it, brought back burned fingers.

Angel said, "Allow me."

He pushed the door open.

Again, Buffy took the lead.

She stepped across the threshold and into Hell itself.

The chamber was blazingly hot and stank of sulfur. Buffy felt the hair on her arms singe from the intense heat. She forced down a reflexive cough from the stench, instead hiding behind a large stone pillar that was sizzling to the touch.

About twenty feet directly in front of her, a young girl lay bound hand and foot on an altar. Blood flowed from a deep wound in her chest into a large bowl held in place by a hideously scarred acolyte. To his left, a robed man with striking features pulled his knife from the girl's chest and laid it on the altar.

"Thirteen innocents by thirteen blades," intoned a white-haired man who seemed to be their leader.

Il Maestro, Buffy thought.

In front of the altar raged a fire within an enormous

circle that resembled a breach, pulsing with purple and ebony, billowing with white-hot orange and purple flames that reeked of putrescence, death, and evil.

The white-haired man turned toward the shadows on the opposite side of the room and said, "For you, my lord. The first of many."

From the darkness a voice boomed, *"There may never be enough to appease me. A Slayer's blood is very rich. This blood is thin. It has no life. It will not satisfy."*

"I will give you the Slayer," said the robed man, sounding worried.

"Yes. Or you will give me your daughter, Micaela," the voice replied.

Buffy's lips parted. She couldn't just watch this.

She stared at Angel, who shook his head and pressed his finger to his lips. He took her hand. The contact gave her strength, and the courage to stand by. The courage to be wise.

The courage to endure, as the girl was untied and tossed, summarily, into the fiery breach. It flared. It grew.

"More," said the voice in the shadows. *"Many more, if you wish your daughter to be spared."*

Chapter 14

Joyce woke up to the odor of charred meat. She inhaled sharply, as if someone had popped open a vial of smelling salts beneath her nose, and darted her gaze around the storage room to see if it was on fire.

A pair of large roaches chittered diagonally across the filthy door, which was shut tight. From the ceiling, the weak lightbulb cast more shadows than light, and she was actually glad of that. She didn't want to see the muck that surrounded her. For the moment she appeared to be alone, but she had already learned not to assume anything where these men were concerned. Including whether or not they actually were men. In Buffy's world—now part of Joyce's world—monsters wore many masks.

Her eyes watered and she put her hand over her mouth as she took deep breaths to combat the smoky odor, which was overpowering her. She was afraid she was going to lose her most recent meal, one of a number of rounds of hot dogs and pasta, which lay heavy in her constricted stomach.

Suddenly there were noises beyond the door, a scuffling or a shuffle, perhaps stealthy footsteps. She held herself rigid, afraid but resolved not to panic. She needed to stay focused.

They were footsteps. Very near.

"Oh, God," she breathed, shaking. Twin tears coursed down her cheeks. She didn't know how Buffy handled these kinds of things at all. Because there was no way to stay calm. No hope for focus. The only thing she wanted to do was scream.

A voice cried out, "Chaos' name! Brother Lupo, what has happened?"

"Brother Augustus," someone replied in a voice familiar to her. It must have been Lupo. "What is the meaning of this *immondizia?*"

"Brother Lupo," said the other voice, clearly shocked. "I don't know. Is it not . . . is this Brother Ariam?"

"I have no idea. It could be," Lupo replied, without a trace of concern. "How did the idiot catch himself on fire?"

"It looks . . . it looks like the *Brûlure Noire,*" the other replied in hushed tones. "But only Il Maestro can wield the black burn. Oh, Brother Lupo, is the great one actually *here?*"

"No, he's not. Nor is he expected for another day or two. Now, clean this up before someone trips over it."

"But . . . but Brother Dando should know of this," the second man said tremulously. "No one has ever duplicated Il Maestro's achievement. If someone in our midst has mastered his secret, we should discover who . . ." The voice trailed off, stammered, "Who— wh—"

"By the bones, you're a thick-headed dolt."

"Oh, Brother Lupo, I won't tell," the other man said in a low, terrified tone. "I will never say a word. Only let me follow you. I will be your faithful slave forever."

"I'm sorry, but no. I require someone with a functioning brain."

Suddenly Joyce heard a low, almost subaudible, crackling, as if of fire. The second man began scream- ing in agony, over and over again. Joyce tried to shut herself away, but it was too much. The man's pain was too real, too close. She turned and retched, hard, falling to her knees as she vomited.

Smoke billowed under her door and Joyce crawled to the far corner of the room, heaving and coughing and sobbing.

After less than ten seconds the sounds subsided.

Her door was flung open. A menacing bald-headed man loomed on the threshold in a black cassock with white symbols painted on it. His hood was thrown back, revealing a scarred face and a milky white eye that glowed blue as he glared at her.

"What did you hear?" he demanded.

Wordlessly she shook her head as she looked down at the clear evidence that she had heard something terrible.

Slamming the door behind him, he advanced on her, his fists clenching and unclenching at his sides. He was crazy, she tried to tell herself. Or she was. *He did not set another human being on fire just now. He did not.* No one could do such awful things and be someone who looked at her, talked to her. There was not such evil in the world.

"Tell me this instant what you heard, or I'll kill you."

"I smelled smoke," she answered quickly, her words sticking in her throat. Backing up, she ran into the supply shelf. A rotted pack of paper napkins tipped, the tattered bits of paper fluttering to the floor like dying birds. Biting off a cry, Joyce tried to catch her balance by holding on to the shelf. A can of cleanser splatted on top of the napkins.

"I thought I heard voices," she hedged.

He stared at her, obviously waiting for her to say more. His milky eye was spinning, or the blue light inside it was making it appear as if it were spinning. The veins on his face began to pulsate.

She added, "Someone was in pain."

He narrowed his eyes until they were slits in his doughy face. Then slowly he lifted his hand. Energy crackled around it; tendrils of blue, strobing electricity curled and roiled from his fingertips like sun flares.

"Tell me what you heard," he repeated, pointing directly at her. His hand began to vibrate. A tendril of energy began to uncoil.

"Nothing!" she cried. "I didn't hear anything!"

He smiled. "Very good. If you don't wish to die, stick to that."

He turned his back on her and slammed the door shut.

Joyce trembled, but she did not cry.

And then it occurred to her that he had not un-locked the door to let himself in. It had been unlocked the entire time.

She took halting steps toward it.

The handle turned.

There was a distinct *click*.

She willed herself to find a place of calm. Closing her eyes, she forced herself past the stench of smoke and the realization of what had happened.

She whispered, "If you kill me, your master will be very angry with you."

She shook so hard she slid to the floor.

Giles stopped the car and said to his passengers, "It's almost eleven. Time for you all to go home."

"Are you nuts?" Xander demanded, leaning forward from the backseat.

"If you don't go, your parents will be exceedingly angry with you," Giles said. "They might ground you. And I need you. All of you." He looked at Willow, who was seated beside him. Her eyes closed and her head tipped back, she held one of Joyce's blouses between her hands.

Without opening her eyes, Willow shook her head. "Nothing. I'm sorry. I still don't get any vibrations."

"Then stop, Willow." Giles was clearly disap-pointed, but he mustered a smile when Willow opened her eyes. "You tried your best."

"Psychometry isn't something I know how to do," she murmured.

Xander patted her on the shoulder. "That's cool, Will. Like the man said, you tried."

The problem was, they were running out of things *to* try. Xander was, in a word, freaking. He couldn't get over the idea that somehow Buffy knew about her mom's kidnapping and was already in Sunnydale, doing something that was going to get her killed. Something in the air felt different, like that moment just before a thunderclap. It felt wrong. It felt scary.

"So now what? We go home like good little children and you bust in on the secret floral delivery guys convention? Alone?" Cordelia asked Giles, exasperated.

Xander grabbed her hand and gave it a squeeze, something he would not normally do if she had all wits about her. He wouldn't dare. "Cor, you're joking in a moment of crisis. Congratulations. You've finally become one of us."

"I'm *so* not thrilled," she said dejectedly, shaking her hand out of his grip. "And let go of me. Your palms are sweaty."

"It was the pod I put under your bed. You fell asleep, didn't you?" he said accusingly. "That's when we get you, Cordelia Chase. When you sleep."

She huffed. "Now I know I'm not one of you, because I don't have the slightest idea what you're talking about."

"I know, honey. Feels good, don't it?"

"They must have rented a house," Giles said, obviously not having heard a single word of the Xander-Cordelia Comedy Hour. Or else he had, and he was being all British. "You don't suppose they would have taken over Angel's mansion?"

"Not likely," Willow said. "'Cause, um, some of

them died there. Unpleasantly." She thought a moment. "But maybe that's why they would go there. Because we would think it was too gross for them to. Go there."

"And that exercise of pure and simple logic, folks, is why we take calculus," Xander said. "To the mansion, my good man."

"No. To your doorstep," Giles replied firmly. "I'll go to the mansion after I've dropped you three off." He held up a hand. "I promise you, if there's a need for reinforcements, I'll find a way to contact you."

Xander tapped his shoulder. "Stones against the window. Always a winner."

Cordelia rolled her eyes. "You have my cell phone number."

"And my e-mail address," Willow added. She frowned. "You know, we would have saved a lot of time if the Gatekeeper had been jacked in. A guy like that, you think he would be connected to all kinds of UFO sites and things like that. To check for stuff to bind and talk to people like, well, Buffy. Like those three hackers on the *X-Files.*"

"We'll be sure to tell the heir to get a modem," Xander said solemnly. "When our Slayer brings him home."

"Indeed." Giles smiled grimly. "In fact, I'll take him down to the computer store myself."

"*That*'ll be useful," Xander riffed.

After Giles took the three home, he drove to the mansion and stood in the sunken garden. He shuddered in the night air; a frisson of suppressed memory skittered up his spine. Here he had nearly been tortured to death; here he had been tricked into believing that Jenny had come back from the grave for him. It was a wicked, terrible place for Giles.

And yet, if she needed him to, he would go to Hell itself for Buffy. He was her Watcher; he owed no one greater allegiance. He had no more sacred duty. And yet . . .

And yet, he hated this place.

He stood for a moment, remembering, watching. There was no one here but the dead. Not even the dead.

He turned to go.

And he was so startled by what he saw that he fell backward, smacking against the ruined fountain in the courtyard.

The moon loomed on the horizon twenty times its usual size, and it glowed bloodred. Its beams cast a crimson glow over his hands, the water in the fountain, the small white flowers on the deerweed that had sprouted between the cracks in the cement.

In the distance, thunder rumbled, sucking in all the noise of the night—the rasping of crickets, the query of an owl—and then expelled it in one large sigh.

The air jittered. It trembled. He could feel the tension on his fingertips, along the nerve endings of his body. It was like a mild electric shock; a psychic might define it as a premonition. It was the most stunning omen he had ever witnessed. A portent of horrible things to come.

Giles was shaken to the core of his being.

Something was going to happen soon.

Giles broke out in a sweat.

He had to find Buffy. He had to find her fast.

Willow thought she had stayed awake, until she bolted upright in her bed and whispered, "Buffy?" Her heart pounded furiously; for a moment she was afraid she might have a heart attack.

"I'm too young," she whispered, catching her breath.

She leaped out of bed, sending stuffed animals flying, and checked her e-mail. Nothing.

She lay back down.

But sleep would not come.

Xander heard someone shuffling around in the kitchen. He figured it was his mom, who had this weird sleepwalking-eating thing. Sometimes she'd sit at the kitchen table and devour a quart of Dreyer's ice cream, and not even realize. You could talk to her and she wouldn't remember the conversation. You could get her to sign your report card, no questions asked.

So, weird as it was, it had its compensations.

Now, however, he knew it wasn't his mother.

Yet something was in the kitchen.

Steeling himself, Xander crept out of his room and made it down the hall. He took a breath and flicked on the lights.

Absolutely nothing was out of place. And yet, he had the strong, sure sense that any second, the entire place might blow sky-high. It was like those stories you read about Vietnam, where the guy steps on the land mine and knows that if he steps off, he's hamburger. So he stands there, not moving, sweating.

Xander stood there, not moving, sweating.

Finally he found the breath to whisper, "Something's happening."

Cordelia woke up and said, "Maxie, come here." She stroked her coverlet a couple times, then patted it. "Maxie."

Then she remembered that her Persian cat, Maxie, had died when she was seven.

She caught her breath, totally creeped, and thought about calling Xander. She wanted very badly to call Xander.

Her cell phone, lying on her pillow beside her head, trilled once. She depressed the SEND key and whispered, "Giles?"

"What the hell is going on?"

It was Xander.

Cordelia answered shakily, "I think it's the end of the world."

"I think I missed the announcement," Xander replied grimly.

Cordelia didn't even smile.

In her holding area, Joyce Summers dreamed of a man she had never met, a man who loved her and would take care of her and Buffy. He kissed her once, deeply, and then he whispered, "I will see you in Paradise."

Her eyes popped open. She smelled the smoke and the filth, but she knew the dream had been, in some way, very real.

She did not smile, but she took heart.

* * *

Antoinette Regnier looked up at the ceiling, which was crisscrossed with prismatic light, and touched the wrist of her son. His breath came in labored gasps; he wheezed each time deep in his throat. And yet, the ceiling was layered with auras of colored lights.

Then a shadow fell across the lights and blotted them out, like a piece of black cardboard laid over glitter and lace.

"Maman, je t'aime," Jean-marc whispered.

"My son, what does it mean?" she asked him.

"That love endures," he replied. Then, to Antoinette's horror, he slipped into unconsciousness.

"Help us," Antoinette Regnier whispered, but she was not certain to whom she spoke, or prayed.

Chapter 15

It had taken days, but Brother Sima and Brother Sergei had managed to circumnavigate the protective field that both defended the Gatehouse and made it invisible to outsiders. While their fellow acolytes made repeated attempts at entering the house, drawing the Gatekeeper's attention, they had studied every inch of that barrier in search of a weakness.

They had found none. The Gatekeeper's magick was strong. However, they had been able to pinpoint the spot on that barrier that was most vulnerable. It was there that they now focused their attention.

Over the centuries, the city of Boston had been built up around the Gatehouse. On Beacon Hill there wasn't a square inch that had not been overtaken by those wealthy enough to live in one of the city's most desirable neighborhoods. From the street the house was invisible. To passersby, it would seem as though the brownstones on either side of the manse stood just a few feet apart from each other. Even to the residents of those buildings, that would seem to be the case.

It was magick of the highest order, and it must have taken decades to weave. But once you knew the house was there, it was a simple matter to focus on it.

The twin magicians, Sima and Sergei, had searched the perimeter and found that the rear of the Gatehouse also faced a building. Or, to be more precise, it faced the rear of a building on the next block. It was nearly impossible to reach the Gatehouse from behind.

Unless you were willing to jump from the adjacent building, which was four stories tall.

Sergei and Sima were minor magicians, but the twins were quite powerful when they worked together. They could not fly. They could not even levitate. But they could slow their descent.

Teetering at the edge of the roof behind the Gatehouse, the twins searched each other's blue eyes for a trace of the fear each of them felt. They reached out to join hands, glanced down at the twenty feet of lawn between this building and the Gatehouse . . . and then they jumped.

Both men wanted to scream, but neither of them did. They fell in silence, eyes closed, concentrating as best they could and squeezing each other's hand tightly. For two heartbeats they plummeted toward the ground like stone. Then they began to slow.

A moment later they hit the ground, let their knees buckle, then tucked and rolled across the grass. It had been a hard landing, but nothing like what it might have been.

Both were dressed in dark blue jeans and black T-shirts. Both wore heavy black boots. They were Sons of Entropy, true. But before that, they were brothers. They were family. Slowly and carefully, they approached the rear door that led into the basement and cold cellar of the old house. The Gatekeeper's magickal barrier rippled the air roughly three feet away from the door.

"You have it?" Sima asked his brother.

"Da," Sergei replied, reaching behind his back to withdraw a long, ornate dagger from a pack attached to his belt.

It was called the Blade of Dusk, the name derived from a myth which said that the ensorcelled dagger could cut so finely that it could cleave day from night, light from darkness. The Blade of Dusk had been a gift to their grandfather from Il Maestro, and the twins had never removed it from their home before this mission.

Sergei gripped the dagger in his left hand. Sima wrapped his fingers around his brother's on the hilt. Together, they moved the Blade of Dusk toward the magickal barrier, at precisely the spot where the door appeared on the Gatehouse.

They began to cut. They were slow and methodical about it, and the dagger cut cleanly—so cleanly, in fact, that the Gatekeeper would never realize that his sanctum had been violated. That was the purpose of Sima and Sergei's presence here. The magick brought to bear on the house previously had been far more powerful than this, but it had been like a battering ram, drawing the Gatekeeper's attention, and his wrath. Though he was ailing, his magick was still powerful. And they faced more than his own magick; they faced the power invested into the Gatehouse by the Regnier line for hundreds of years. The house itself defied them.

But not this time. This was an attack so precise, so minute, that the Gatehouse itself would not notice, nor the Gatekeeper. At that very moment, he was being drawn into action to repel an attack on the front of the house, an attack that was meant to draw attention from Sima and Sergei and their Blade of Dusk.

The blade cut. The barrier was sliced open cleanly. Sima was able to slip his hand through and draw the barrier aside as though it were a velvet curtain. A moment later, Sergei followed. Almost immediately, the barrier began to knit itself anew behind them, but it did not matter. The twins had another use in mind for the Blade of Dusk.

Soon the Gatekeeper would be dead, and the Gatehouse would belong to the Sons of Entropy. At last.

The back door of the house was not even locked. Sima turned the knob and pushed it open, and Sergei stared at him with wide eyes a moment before stepping over the threshold and into the basement of the Gatehouse.

"He has placed too much faith in magick," Sima whispered as he followed his brother into the house.

The door slammed behind them with a resounding crack. Its three deadbolts slid into place themselves. The twins glanced anxiously at each other and spun around, their eyes sweeping the sterile room, taking in the stone foundation and the walls of old shelving and wine racks. Sergei waved the Blade of Dusk in front of him wildly, slashing at the air.

From the darkened steps, a voice.

"Too much faith in magick?" it asked, repeating Sima's own words.

Blue light flared around the figure, fighting back the darkness of the cellar and revealing the Gatekeeper. His entire body rippled with energy and he seemed to float above the ground, bathed in that ethereal, electric blue.

"Perhaps I have," the Gatekeeper said. "But then, so have you."

Jean-Marc Regnier reached out a hand and blue electricity crackled from it, tendrils leaping across the room and snatching the Blade of Dusk from Sergei's hand. As Sima watched, the dagger seemed to dance in that magickal light as it carved his brother's body and cut out his heart.

Sergei's corpse hit the stone floor with a wet slap, and Sima screamed in grief and terror as his brother's blood began to flow. He turned his wide-eyed stare to the Gatekeeper.

Blue fire blazed up around the Gatekeeper, his body bathed in it, and he roared at Sima like a ravenous lion.

"Go!" he screamed. "Run! Tell your black-hearted master that the Gatekeeper lives—no, thrives! And that I will cut out the heart of any man who dares invade my home!"

The light winked out, draping the cellar in darkness again. Sima scrambled for the back door, his soles slipping in his brother's blood. He found the door, threw the locks, and ran out onto the back lawn, through the protective barrier around the house. Terrified, he made his way around to the front, where he knew he would receive only the disgusted looks of his superiors, if not some physical censure for his failure.

He didn't care. As long as he didn't have to go back inside that house.

On the cellar steps, Jean-Marc Regnier reached up with a quivering hand and threw on the lights. He was as old as he had ever been. His skin drooped on his bones, his hair was falling out, his vision was nearly gone.

The Sons of Entropy had thought him on the brink of death. While that was not true, it was not far from the truth. Only more and more frequent immersions in the Cauldron of Bran the Blessed kept him from dying.

With the Blade of Dusk grasped firmly in his left hand—yet another trinket for his collection—Jean-Marc began to crawl painfully up the cellar steps. His mother would have filled the Cauldron with warm water.

All he had to do was make it up to the second floor, and into that warm, healing bath. And he was confident that he would make it.

This time.

Over the long years since the Florentine Villa had been violently taken from the Regnier family, the vast subcellar had been used for many dark purposes:

torture chamber, prison, slaughterhouse. On this night, it had become all three.

Il Maestro smiled thinly, to show his acolytes his confidence. But it was a sham, or very near it. Only these few had been allowed to descend for the ritual, thirteen of his most trusted acolytes. For none of them knew the true extent of his plan. Like the fools in Vienna, however, they would soon begin to guess. And those here in the cellar—those who heard the voice of his dark lord Belphegor—anonymous to them, as he had ordered—and the promises that Il Maestro made to the demon—would know after this ritual that he worshiped more than chaos. He worshiped Hell itself.

"I thirst," his demon master hissed from beyond the putrid colored swirls of light that pulsed within the breach that had opened in the room. *"Another life, my servant. Thirteen blades for thirteen innocents. Give me the life that I crave."*

Several of the acolytes seemed to grow anxious at this demand. Il Maestro would not hear of it. This ritual would serve several purposes for him, not the least of which was to lend him some of Belphegor's power. But it would also appease the demon, at least for a short time, so that his acolytes in America could draw the Slayer back into their clutches.

Only the Slayer's blood would stop Belphegor from taking Micaela's. Il Maestro did not want his daughter to die. It had occurred to him briefly that if she did, indeed, end up a sacrifice to the demon, he might be to blame. But only briefly. What the demon demanded, he would have.

Several of the gathered acolytes brought the next

victim to the altar. He was a young boy, perhaps fifteen. He was disoriented because of the elixir Brother Edwin had mixed for them, but when the boy saw the altar, and the acolytes gathered in their ceremonial robes, and the daggers . . . he started to scream.

The screaming continued as they chained him to the altar.

Il Maestro raised a hand and motioned for Brother François to take his turn. To raise his dagger. This was only the second of the night's sacrifices, and it was taking too long. Brother François looked at the writhing boy and then glanced uneasily at Il Maestro. He narrowed his eyes and glared at the acolyte, and Brother François reacted as though he had been struck.

Tentatively, he moved toward the altar and raised his left hand, which held the ornate dagger. He gripped the hilt with both hands and lifted it above the struggling boy's chest.

Brother François raised the dagger a bit higher, closed his eyes a moment, and then forced himself to open them again. The way the screaming boy was moving, he would never find the young man's heart without focusing his attention.

"In chaos' name," he said softly.

Eyes on the boy's chest, Brother François swung the dagger down.

Just about then, there was the sharp *clink* of something clattering to the floor.

"Stop!" Il Maestro commanded.

With a silent breath of prayer, François aborted his

attack. He glanced up at Il Maestro for instructions, but his master was not paying attention to him. Instead, the white-haired man had laid his head back and closed his eyes. His arms were held out at his sides.

Almost by reflex, Brother François said, "Maestro?"

The white-haired sorcerer's eyes opened. With a broad smile, he glanced around at the gathered acolytes.

"What is it, slave of my heart?" whispered the horrid voice from the breach.

The voice of chaos, they had been told. But François knew the voice of a demon when he heard it.

Il Maestro laughed. "My wondrous dark master," he intoned. "Our enemies have been delivered unto us. And now . . ."

He raised his hands and uttered a single word of Latin, and suddenly a dozen torches at distant locations on the walls of the subcellar ignited simultaneously. Firelight bathed the room.

"The Slayer stands revealed," Il Maestro said.

"Damn!" Buffy snapped. There was a hole in her pocket, and her rose quartz had fallen through it to the ground.

The jig was most definitely up.

Behind the nasty-looking breach, the dark thing on the other side began to laugh. The sound alone made Buffy want to throw up. For some reason, whatever it was couldn't come through. She wanted it to stay that way.

"Great! What now?" Oz asked.

"Take them out," Buffy snapped.

She grabbed a torch off the wall, and moved in.

Eyes blazing feral yellow, Angel bared his fangs and tore into the acolytes. Several of them seemed to be working some kind of magick, and multicolored energy began to swirl around them. Angel went after the magicians first. He grabbed the nearest man by the hair, felt magickal energy crackle along his arm, then seized the man's throat and snapped his neck.

With a vicious backhand, he shattered the nose and facial structure of another acolyte, who went down screaming.

Then he turned, and Il Maestro stood right in front of him.

"You're supposed to be in Vienna, vampire," the old man said, in Italian.

"What matters is that you believed that," Angel replied, in the same language, then switched to English. "Where's the boy?"

An acolyte grabbed Angel from behind, wrapping powerful arms around him. The man's hands were locked across Angel's chest in such a way that the hold would be difficult to break, even for him. Angel rammed his head backwards, his skull cracking the man's forehead. His grip fell away, and Angel reached back and grabbed him by the front of his robe.

With a single, powerful thrust, he shoved the man across the room and through the horrid pulsating corpse-colored breach that still burned at the center of the chamber. The demon laughed.

Angel spun to face Il Maestro, but the sorcerer was

already on him. Magickal energy appeared around Angel, its coils encircling his body and tightening around him. Angel didn't need to breathe, but in moments these coils would crush his bones to powder.

Il Maestro laughed. Angel studied the sorcerer's face, the white hair and the cruel blue eyes.

"Where's the boy?" he demanded, struggling against the bonds that were slowly constricting around him.

"What makes you think he's still alive?" Il Maestro asked, curiously.

"If he wasn't, his father would know."

"I have my uses for the heir," said Il Maestro. "They don't concern you, vampire. You're about to die for the second time."

"Yes," sighed a voice from within the breach. *"Give him to me. The balance himself, the demon and the divinity, the vampire with a soul. What a taste that will be."*

"For blessed chaos!" shouted a broad-shouldered, Aryan-looking acolyte who came at Angel with a ceremonial dagger raised above his head. His eyes were wide and crazy; he was rapt in a religious fervor. "For Il Maestro!" he cried.

"Brother Johann, no!" Il Maestro barked.

It was too late. Brother Johann brought the dagger down, its blade stabbing deeply into Angel's shoulder. Angel snarled with the pain. The magick pulsed. It was as if the vampire and the acolyte were one being in that moment, connected as they were by blood and iron. The scarlet coils of magick that surrounded him reached out and ensnared Brother Johann as well.

In that moment, Angel was free. Before the coils could snap together, crushing him against Brother Johann, Angel dropped and rolled out from beneath the magickal field. The coils closed again, and Brother Johann shrieked with pain as they pulled tight. Angel heard bones breaking.

He leaped to his feet and dove for Il Maestro, grabbing the sorcerer by the front of his robe and around the throat. Angel began to squeeze. Il Maestro's eyes bulged from their sockets.

A spear of black flame erupted from Il Maestro's right hand and pierced Angel's abdomen, then jetted straight out through his back. It was as if he had been impaled on a pike.

Angel roared in agony.

Oz was bleeding.

He'd been cut, just slightly, on the left side of his back, and his lip was bleeding where he'd been hit. But other than the blood, he thought he was doing all right. It didn't hurt that Buffy was right beside him.

"Come on!" he said angrily, waving a torch at a couple of acolytes who were moving in on him.

Sick freaks, he thought.

Then he waved the torch again with his left hand. Both men backed off. Oz moved in, shoving the blazing torch into the folds of one man's robe. As the acolyte began to scream and burn, Oz jumped on the other. The man struck him once, hard, in the gut, but that wasn't enough. Oz's fists were flying.

Next to him, Buffy screamed Angel's name.

Oz jumped up, away from the man he'd pummeled

almost senseless, and turned to see Buffy rushing away to help Angel. And three more acolytes moving toward him. One of them had a green glow around his hands. *Different kinds of magick,* he thought, *different kinds of light.* It'd be cool if it was any other day.

With a quick glance around, he caught sight of a heavy thing like a lantern hanging by a thick chain from the ceiling. Incense burned inside it, and that made him remember what it was. A censer. The smell was pervasive, though he hadn't noticed it before. Like rosemary and cinnamon and something else— something not as pleasant.

He ran for it. The acolytes pursued him. Oz grabbed the chain that held the censer and put all his strength into one mighty tug. The hook from which it hung tore free of the ceiling and the censer clanked to the stone floor of the subcellar.

"Die, fool!" one of the acolytes shouted as he rushed at Oz.

Oz whipped the censer up by the chain; it collided with the acolyte's skull, burning incense spilling out and sticking to the man's face. He screamed as he fell, trying to wipe the ash from his eyes. Oz whipped the censer up again, swinging it around his head by the chain and moving toward the other two acolytes, who were backing away from him now.

"Giddyup," he drawled.

"Hey!" Buffy shouted at Il Maestro. In one hand she clutched the torch.

The sorcerer turned from Angel. She took a quick glance at him and saw that, though groaning and holding a hand across the wound on his abdomen, Angel was rising to his feet and turning to meet an acolyte who even now moved to attack him.

"At last, the Slayer!" Il Maestro exulted, striding confidently toward her. The room was blessed chaos now, and he savored it.

Savored her. For she was beautiful, this Slayer.

"Come on, then, pally," the girl said brusquely. "You've been after me long enough. Now you've got me!"

The girl swung the torch at him. Il Maestro raised his ruined, gnarled left hand, and a crackling sheet of red energy shielded him from the blow. The Slayer grunted and turned to face him again.

"You were clever, my young lady," he told her. "Buffy, isn't it? You're not like the other Slayers I've seen. And you're far prettier than the one I killed."

The Slayer blinked.

Il Maestro laughed. "Let me introduce myself," he said, as she beat at his magickal shield. "I am Giacomo Fulcanelli. And I will be your death."

The Slayer blinked again. At first he thought she might be intimidated, and he was a bit disappointed, since he'd thought her made of sterner stuff. She backed away three paces and tilted her head back defiantly.

"You're Fulcanelli?" she asked. "Why are you still alive?"

"Good living, I suppose," he replied.

The Slayer nodded. "Not for long," she said, and she moved to attack him again.

Fulcanelli laughed, truly enjoying her demeanor. Then his smile disappeared into a sneer, he dropped the shield he'd generated, and his good right hand came up, completely covered in crackling flames so dark that they seemed to suck the light from the room.

La Brûlure Noire reached horrid ebony tendrils from Fulcanelli's fingers, and the Slayer was bathed in the black burn, nothing but a silhouette within the magickal blaze.

Dropping her torch, the Slayer screamed.

Il Maestro laughed.

"Hey, Mr. Wizard," said a voice behind him.

But Il Maestro didn't even have time to turn, to see who had addressed him, before the heavy iron censer collided with the back of his head and sent him sprawling to the floor, unconscious.

Without his sorcery, the breach in the subcellar closed instantly, and the black burn also receded. The Slayer slumped to the floor not far from where Giacomo Fulcanelli, Il Maestro, lay bleeding.

"Yeah!" Oz shouted.

Angel was bent over slightly as he moved to stand beside Oz. There were only four acolytes left standing.

"Well done," Angel said. "I think you saved Buffy's life."

"Let's hope so," Oz replied, glaring at the other acolytes. "C'mon, boys. Bring it on, we're ready."

He turned to Angel. "I think we may get out of this alive," he said.

Then the doors at either end of the subcellar slammed open, and the room began to fill with very angry men in matching robes.

* * *

After a long and rather fitful night of half-remembered nightmares, Giles rose at half past six and simply lay in bed for several minutes. It was unlike him to do so. He was normally up the moment he woke, down the stairs to put on a kettle for tea, and then moving on to the bathroom to shower and shave.

Not today. After the portents he had seen the night before, he had little motivation to rise. He began to drift back to sleep.

His eyes snapped open, and he felt disgusted with himself. He sat up, groped for the night table, and retrieved his glasses. He slipped them on, then reached for his bathrobe and stood up.

I'm the bloody Watcher, for God's sake, he thought. *I'm not afforded the luxury of being unmotivated.*

His thoughts turned to Buffy, and then, of course, to Joyce. He could do nothing to help the daughter, not with the task on which she was currently engaged. But he could and intended to dedicate himself wholly to locating her mother. It was all he would think about, until he had found her. Buffy would never forgive herself if something happened to her mother.

Giles wasn't going to let that happen.

Determined, he moved to the winding metal stairs that led down from his loft bedroom to the living room of his small but tastefully decorated apartment. The sun was on the rise, and its rays sliced striations across the air in the apartment.

In the shadows by the door, near Giles's desk, a thin, bespectacled man sat sipping tea from a flowered cup. The cup was from a set willed to Giles on the death of his grandmother.

"Good morning, Watcher," said the man amiably.

"Who the hell are you?" Giles snapped angrily, looking around the room, searching for something to use as a weapon. Several possibilities presented themselves, including a heavy cane that had belonged to his father and even now leaned against the far wall.

Nothing close enough. He moved two steps toward the cane, but in such a way that it seemed that he was moving toward the intruder instead.

"You may call me Brother Claude," the man said. "Though, if you're uncomfortable with the 'brother' part, Claude will do."

"How did you get in here?" Giles asked.

The man named Claude rolled his eyes. "Magick," he said. "What did you think, I was a cat burglar? Please. You've seen too many movies."

"I know who you are, magician," Giles said coldly. "And I know of the fiend you call master. You've invaded my home. You're uninvited . . ."

"I think you have us confused with vampires," Claude said reasonably. "But let's cut to the chase, shall we?"

Giles lunged for the cane, picked it up, spun around, and marched toward Claude. The man didn't so much as rise from the chair by Giles's desk.

"Where is Joyce Summers?" Giles demanded, advancing on the man.

"That's why I'm here," Claude replied.

Giles faltered. He still held the cane up, ready to attack, but he narrowed his eyes.

"You didn't come here to tell me where to find her," he said confidently.

"Well, in a way, I did," Claude told him. "Here's the deal. We want the Slayer, she wants her mother back. She shows up and trades herself for her very attractive and courageous mom, and we're even."

"And then you kill Buffy," Giles said.

Claude smiled, eyeing Giles as though the Watcher were the densest creature on Earth.

"But of course," he said happily. "We're not going to have a slumber party, are we?"

Giles regarded him evenly. He knew nothing would be gained by attacking the man with the cane. This Claude had some magickal ability, and the chances that Giles, alone, might overcome him and elicit more useful information from him were not great. Better to see what he might divine through cooperation.

"All right," Giles agreed. "I'll present your deal to her. Where and when would she show herself for this . . . exchange?"

"Brother Lupo tells me you're familiar with a local club the Slayer frequents," Claude said.

"The Bronze?" Giles asked, with some surprise.

Claude nodded. "That's the place. We'll have the woman there tonight at nine o'clock. The Slayer will be there by nine-thirty, or her mother dies."

"Tonight?"

"The way she's been traveling, she should have no problem with that," Claude said, then shrugged.

Calmly, casually, he rose and walked to the door. He left Giles's apartment, and the Watcher dared not do anything to stop him. They had a little more than twelve hours to find Joyce Summers, or get Buffy home, or her mother would be murdered.

Somehow, he would stop it.

He picked up the phone and dialed Willow's house

as his mind raced down the list of what they knew. Two valuable things:

First, that Buffy was traveling the ghost roads.

Second, and more important, that the Sons of Entropy had no idea whatsoever where Buffy was.

Giles closed his eyes.

As long as the Slayer was alive and free, there was still hope.

On the dank stone floor of the cell where she was imprisoned, Buffy lay unconscious, and did not dream.

Chapter 16

"BLOODY HELL," SPIKE GROUSED, THEN LET HIMSELF OUT of the cellar of the outbuilding where he had spent the entire bloody day.

It had not been easy catching one of those Entropy buggers and torturing the location of the really big noise's HQ out of him. Neither had it been a simple matter to convince Dru that she needed to stay with the kid while Spike drove over to picturesque Florence to arrange for a sit-down. Had to give her the hooded one's little rosy rock from his pocket. She'd sat on the floor like a little child, fondling the damn stone like it was the freakin' Hope diamond.

Then trust that bloody car to overheat. It wore a man down to the nubs, it did.

So, walking in the predawn of *bella Italia,* cursing every used-car salesman he had ever killed, Spike had realized he had to find shelter or his goose—more literally, his arse—would be cooked. That being that, and there was the bloody villa anyway, only he was not sure where exactly all the fun took place—he had done only a slight investigation before it was time to avoid a very disastrous sunburn.

He'd had nothing to eat, and of course he hadn't slept. He was in a fine mood, he was, and if they didn't hand over the bloody Spear of Longinus by the time he counted to ten, some heads were gonna roll.

His duster flying behind him, he stomped across a distant field of dead vines, going the long way around. The villa was still quite a distance away, and Spike stopped once to get a stone out of his boot. As he did so, he scanned for guards. The security around here was worse than the Annoying One's, the little snot-nosed brat he'd replaced—okay, killed—when he and Dru had first arrived in that charming little burg, Sunnydale. Maybe these jumble-sale magicians thought their hocus-pocus was so terrific they didn't need a bunch of wankers standing about with real guns.

But then, getting closer, he saw more and more clusters of hooded chums and nodded to himself, almost relieved.

If the cheese is too easy to get, you have to expect a trap.

So Spike hunted around for a good long while for a way to avoid the guards. Finding none, he took one of those poor bastards out and put on his robe. One size fitted all, and he was off again, barely able to stifle his laughter as he was waved through Checkpoint Charlie. He strolled on down a lane toward what might be a side entrance to the main office and might be the door to the loo, for all he knew. He didn't much care. He'd been invited in, technically, and that was all he needed.

No wonder he and the missus weren't getting much satisfaction from their hostage scheme. These buggers were totally useless.

He started down a hallway, stomp-stomp—you had to act like you owned the bloody place or they'd have you for dinner. At the end of the corridor was a really lovely mirror in a startling gilt frame, and of course he wasn't in it.

But of course the bloke behind him was.

Spike felt something hard in the center of his back as a low voice said, "I have a gun. Don't move."

Spike laughed to himself and said, "All right, mate. I won't."

Then he whirled around in full vamp face and took the poor bastard down.

He found an empty closet and tossed the body in. Then he burped, frowning slightly to himself.

He hoped he didn't get heartburn.

Italians could be so spicy.

"Okay. Now it's time to get serious," Spike announced, and continued on his way.

Buffy opened her eyes but did not raise her head. Her gaze met a stone wall from which studded handcuffs dangled. The stones beneath her cheek were cold and slimy. The air stank. She grimaced as she inhaled. Her ribs hurt.

"You may as well get up," Fulcanelli said somewhere behind her. "I know you're awake."

"Nice place you've got here," she said, not moving. "Who did your decorating, Marilyn Manson?"

He chuckled.

"Rise up, child. You don't have much time left."

Slowly she sat up and raised her head. Seated on a wooden chair on the other side of her barred cell, Fulcanelli sat in a black robe spangled with crimson half-moons and stars. He wore a pointed hat like a witch's, and his long white hair cascaded over his shoulders. He was sipping something from a fancy jeweled goblet in his good hand; the gems caught the weak light from a torch in a sconce on the wall and sent them dancing like dying rainbows over the stones.

He kept sipping. Either it was something that tasted good or he was as thirsty as she was.

She looked around cautiously, the room tilting as she did so. Her stomach lurched, but she fought down the urge to vomit. They were back in the sulfur pit, the altar only a few feet away. And beyond that, the pulsing oval that looked like a festering, decomposing wound. And inside that . . .

Someone was watching her. She could feel it. Something that was hungry for her, would devour her, consume her soul and spit out her bones.

Unnerved, she said to Fulcanelli, "What did you hit me with?"

"Magick. And that's what I'll kill you with."

"Promise, promises," she snapped.

He smiled at her. His eyes were unnaturally blue and his features very sharp. If he really was the original Fulcanelli, he was around five hundred years old. Twice as old as Angel.

Angel.

Oz.

She said in a deadly dangerous voice, "Where are my friends?"

"Soon they won't matter any more. You'll be alone. Briefly."

She narrowed her eyes at him. "They will always matter. When you're in Hell and I'm in living in a Slayer's paradise, they will matter."

"Hell." He chuckled again. "How interesting that you should mention it."

"It was a nice place to visit," she said, "but I wouldn't want to live there."

He chuckled again. Sipped again. Buffy wanted to rip the goblet right out of his grasp, wrap her hands around his neck, and squeeze the very life out of him. But she stayed where she was, scanning her prison, noting the size of the padlock that secured the door, weighing her options. Trying to decide the best course of action.

Then, from the shadows came the clanking of chains and uneven footfalls. A hooded man in a torch led the way, followed by two more acolytes, and then, led by a chain around his neck, Angel. He was naked to the waist, and his chest and back were striped with lash marks. Oz was behind him, also stripped to the waist, also beaten. His hands were tied in front of him, and a chain extended from around his neck to join with Angel's. His face was bruised, and he could barely lift his head.

Buffy bit her lip to keep from crying out. But she let her hatred show as Fulcanelli watched her over the lip of his goblet, clearly enjoying her distress.

The group reached the door of the cell. Fulcanelli casually waved a hand. The padlock clicked open and fell to the floor. The door opened.

Torch flames flickered over Angel's features as he gazed at Buffy. Then he and Oz were pushed into the cell by the two acolytes, who appeared to be very reluctant to enter the cell with Buffy. So she still had a rep, anyway. She guessed she could be grateful for small favors.

Tiny ones, at that.

Oz stumbled and fell to his knees, groaning. Angel bent over to help him up.

"Thanks, man," Oz muttered.

"A man? You think of him as a man?" Fulcanelli asked in an amused tone of voice. "Interesting. I would wager ten thousand ducats that in another few days, he would rip open your throat and drink you dry. But we don't have the time."

"And I'm fresh out of ducats," Buffy sneered.

One of the acolytes took a step forward, as if to come into the cell and strike her. But one look from Buffy and he backed off.

"Yes," Fulcanelli hissed. "The power of the Slayer. You do well to fear it, Brother Andrew."

Buffy exhaled loudly. "Who writes your stuff? Because this kind of dialogue went out, oh, two or three centuries ago."

Fulcanelli snapped his fingers. Immediately, all the lights were extinguished. Then a glow rose from beneath his chin, purple and sickly, lighting only his mouth as he spoke. Behind him, the circle of pulsing gore began to throb.

He said, "I don't care."

Buffy swallowed down her fear.

"Lucky thing."

She walked over to Angel and touched his arm, then to Oz, so sorry for their pain. Angel shook his head and said, "We didn't tell them anything."

"Because they didn't ask us anything," Oz finished. He coughed. "Man, it reeks in here." His skin was blue and he was shivering.

"We already know what we need to know," Fulcanelli said.

"Then we all leave happy," Buffy shot back.

"No." Fulcanelli made a jaunty sort of gesture. "You three don't leave at all. As for the rest of us . . ." He smiled at his acolytes. ". . . we enter a wondrous new world."

The hooded figures stood up a little straighter. Buffy rolled her eyes and shook her head. "That's not what I heard. Word on the street is you're using these guys. They think you're, what, breaking down the barriers between our world and the Otherworld, right?"

He smiled at her. "Very good, Slayer."

"But that's just part of the plan, isn't it? You've got something else going on." She wasn't sure where she was going with this; she was just piecing things together from what he'd said and what Brother Albert had told them. But it was having the desired effect; the acolytes looked uncertain and Fulcanelli looked kind of ticked.

"I'm going to destroy your friends in front of you," he said to her in a low, dangerous voice. "They have power, which I need to prepare my Ritual of Exordium. The lacuna will burst open at last. And my demon lord will leap forward to devour your soul as I send it down to Hell." He spread open his right arm and threw back his head. "And chaos will reign!"

"And you'll be its king."

He shrugged and bowed. "It is a grave duty. Heavy hangs the head that wears the crown."

"Yeah, on my wall," Buffy said, doubling up her fists.

He wagged a finger at her. "Temper," he said. "Don't be so impetuous, young Slayer. Impetuousness got Catherine de' Medici into the worst scrapes."

"Bummer for her."

"Indeed." He looked off into a distance she couldn't see. "At the end, she died defeated and friendless. I could have made her queen of the world."

"Yeah, well, that boat sank a long time ago."

He rose, revealing the withered arm that hung useless at his left side. Then he turned the goblet upside down. Blue flames cascaded to the floor and winked out.

He laughed.

"Enjoy your last moments together. I have arrangements to make, a bit of ritual, a bit of travel. When we return, we'll take the vampire and the boy and flay them alive. Then we'll chain you to the altar, and I will have your life."

Buffy had no retort. She watched in seething silence as he led his followers out of the room.

"Okay," she said, never taking her eyes off the receding figure, not even after he shut another door behind him at the opposite end of the chamber. She glanced up at the stained glass and frowned. "Hopefully this buys us just enough time to come up with a plan. First I'll break us out of here and then we'll . . ."

She paused. "Fill me in. Is it day or night? 'Cause if it's day, we'll have to make sure Angel's got a dark place to be. But if it's night, we're cool. So—"

"It's dusk," Oz said behind her.

"Oh?" She started to turn around. "How do you—"

His answer was a savage roar.

"Buffy!" Angel shouted, diving across the cell.

Where Oz had stood, a slavering werewolf threw back its head and howled with feral madness.

It bared its fangs. Drool dripped down its muzzle.

Then it charged Buffy. *Just enough time,* that's what she'd said, moments before.

And now they were all out of time.

With dawning horror, Micaela Tomasi watched from the darkness of her bedchamber as her adoptive father's acolytes set torches at intervals in a circle cleared from the old vineyard. Only moments earlier eight men had been required to move the three pieces that made up an enormous granite altar out onto the grounds.

Above, the moon shone full and bright, pregnant with power, dark shadows on its face grinning down at these proceedings. There were perhaps thirty acolytes out now, a greater number than she had ever known Fulcanelli to have on the grounds at one time.

She had heard the screams earlier, and the chanting from far below. Locked into her room as she was, there had been little for her to do save cover her ears and fight back the tears. And now, all Micaela could do was thank a God she had been ignoring for most of her life that the screams had stopped.

Micaela blinked. Fulcanelli had emerged from the house and walked around the newly erected altar, then examined the placement of the torches.

"Excellent," he said. "Now, who will offer his own spilled blood for the etching of the runes?"

Two acolytes reacted instantly. Micaela recognized one of them, but the other was a stranger to her. Both offered up their wrists to be cut, and several others began to use their fresh blood to draw symbols on the altar itself.

"With the Slayer as sacrifice, the wall to chaos, the barrier to Otherworld, will fall this very night," Fulcanelli announced. "By dawn you will all be kings in a new world without order."

Micaela frowned. *How can there be any kings at all in a world devoid of order?* It made no sense, and yet these acolytes went along with her father's instructions like obedient pets. Which was, after all, what they really were.

There came a light rap on the door, and Micaela jumped, startled. Someone was there; come for her, perhaps. She glanced around the room quickly. They were spartan quarters, containing little save the bed and dresser. Not even a mirror on the wall. She'd had to make do with an ornate, antique hand mirror instead. It was little more than a disk of mirrored, silver-backed glass on an exquisite handle.

A key rattled in the old metal mechanism.

Micaela grabbed the mirror from her dresser and

went to stand beside the door. The key turned in the lock. The door scraped the floor as it opened, with her behind it.

She ran a finger lightly against the jagged edge of the mirror, where a quarter inch of it had cracked off when she'd set a pitcher of water down on it only days earlier.

When the acolyte entered—a stout, brutish man with gray hair and a thick mustache—she was relieved that it wasn't anyone she recognized. That would have made things harder.

"Pardon me, miss, but Il Maestro has asked that . . ." the man began, before grunting in surprise to find her quarters apparently abandoned.

He was no fool, however. Not like so many of her father's followers. He spun toward the door, already moving into a defensive posture. But he was too late. Micaela struck out with the broken edge of the hand mirror and hacked a long gash in his throat. Blood spurted into her face and across her simple, blue cotton dress.

The man looked shocked, began to reach for his throat, and then his wide eyes lost some of their intensity and he fell to the floor.

Micaela stared at the dying man for a long moment, tears streaming down her face as she held her hands up, half shielding her view of him. Then she looked around anxiously and fled the room, the savagely elegant weapon still clutched in her right hand.

Without hesitation she moved to the top of the stairwell that led down into the horrible subcellar. If the Slayer was a prisoner in the villa, that's where she would be held. Micaela knew that for certain. And thinking of Buffy made her think of Rupert Giles, whom she had betrayed. He was far from the only one, but she had to begin making amends for her betrayals somewhere. And if she could save the life of the Slayer, she might not only redeem herself a little, but—if Fulcanelli could be believed—save the world as well.

Before she rounded the small corner at the bottom of the steps, she could hear the thumps and shouts and growling coming from below. When she turned the corner, she was confronted by two very concerned-looking acolytes. They were staring worriedly at the door.

"What is going on here?" she demanded, though she was still supposed to be a prisoner upstairs.

Both guards looked at her dubiously.

"Signorina Micaela, I don't think you're supposed to be—"

"No! You don't think!" she snapped. "I have been released to participate in this ritual, and I mean to do so. Now what's going on here?"

They hesitated a moment, and Micaela prayed silently that her lie would work.

"We're not sure," the other guard, a young man whose head was completely shaved, replied. "We thought it might be a bluff."

Inside the chamber, a female voice screamed, "Oz, no!"

Micaela sighed. "Does that sound like a bluff to you? Open the door, you idiots. If the Slayer is killed, there can be no sacrifice, can there?"

After only the slightest hesitation, the two guards obediently went to open the door. It was barred with a huge plank of wood, just as it had been when the centuries-old villa had first been built.

The guards removed the plank and began to open the door. The moment it had opened a crack, a huge, slavering, fur-matted beast slammed against it and the door flew open the rest of the way. The beast—a werewolf, she saw—fell on one of the guards and began tearing into him with its massive claws.

She shrieked, and then looked up as the Slayer burst through the broken door at high speed. Micaela had never seen Buffy Summers before, but she took one look at this girl, at the way she moved, and knew she could not be anyone else.

"Oz, stop!" the Slayer screamed at the wolf, who ignored her.

The werewolf kept attacking the guard, but now a vampire emerged from the subcellar, his face contorted into a reflection of the demon within. This was Angel, she surmised from Rupert's talk with her while he was in the hospital. Micaela could only stand and stare as the other guard rose to his feet, took one look at the werewolf, and ran screaming up the stairs the way Micaela had come down.

So shocked was she at what she was witnessing, it didn't even occur to her to go after him.

The Slayer leaped on the werewolf, trying to choke him, but the enormous beast reached around, grabbed her and threw her across the corridor to crash painfully into the stone foundation. Then the beast turned toward Micaela.

She whipped the mirror up, realizing even as she did how ridiculous it was. There was no way a sharp-edged piece of glass was going to hold back a moon-driven wolf-man. It salivated as it approached, and then it lunged for her. Micaela lashed out with the mirror, and it cut through the werewolf's left arm.

The beast howled in agony and stumbled backward.

"What did you do?" the Slayer yelled, as she came up next to Micaela.

"I don't know, I . . ." she began, then looked down at the hand mirror. "Of course! The mirror is an antique. Its back is a thin, flattened bit of silver."

But then the time she'd had to appreciate her luck ran out, and the werewolf lunged for them again, wary of Micaela's right hand. Buffy used both arms to repel an attack by the wolf, crashing her joined fists across its snout. But it would be back, seconds later. The beast was hungry.

It reared up.

Angel cracked it across the skull with the heavy plank that had been used to bar the door. The wolf staggered. Angel hit him again.

The Slayer screamed, "Angel, no!"

But the vampire hit the wolf again, and finally it went down, sinking into an unconscious heap on the stone floor.

Buffy stared at Angel.

"What the hell's the matter with you? That's Oz!"

Angel snarled, his vampiric features in full bloom, yellow eyes flashing.

"No, it's not," he said. "That's a werewolf that

wanted to kill us both. When he's in this form, he's almost impossible to kill. When he wakes up, he'll probably feel like he has a killer hangover. That's it."

Angel bent down and lifted the huge werewolf and slung him over one shoulder. Buffy blinked, reminded once again how strong vampires actually were. Oz's bulk was a burden for Angel, but that he could carry the werewolf at all was amazing.

Something shifted to her left, and Buffy turned and stared at the pretty blond woman who'd slashed Oz with the broken mirror. "What's your deal?" she demanded. "Spill it fast. We don't have any time to spare."

The woman looked around nervously, then seemed to deflate. "I'm Micaela Tomasi," she said.

Buffy stared at her. Of course. She was the woman Albert had shown her in the photograph.

"You're Micaela? Giles's Micaela? So he was right to be suspicious."

"Yes," she admitted. "But I'm afraid it's much more complicated than that. Maybe I can explain it to you while we're getting out of here. He was planning to sacrifice you, you know?"

"Fulcanelli?" Angel asked, as he hefted Oz and followed them as they started up the steps.

"Yes," Micaela agreed. "My father."

"Oh, I can't wait to hear this one," Buffy said, sighing.

Before they'd reached the top of the steps, Micaela had quickly told them an abbreviated version of her life story. Adopted by a sorcerer with seemingly noble intent toward Earth, and a convincing philosophy—*if you're into cults,* Buffy thought—she'd infiltrated the

Watchers' Council and later realized what a huge mistake she'd made.

"Why are you still alive if he knows you're not on his team anymore?" Buffy asked.

"Maybe he loves her," Angel suggested.

Both women looked at him oddly.

Buffy shrugged. "Anything's possible, even for mad wizards who want to destroy the world."

"Is Rupert all right?" Micaela asked, eyes wide and vulnerable.

Buffy didn't want to buy her shtick. Any of it. But she seemed so earnest.

"He's fine," she said. "And we'll all be a little better once we get Jacques Regnier out of here."

Micaela stopped her before she could charge out into the corridor. Buffy turned to look at the woman, and didn't like the fear in her eyes.

"The boy isn't here," Micaela said.

"What?" Angel snapped.

"But the Sons of Entropy took him," Buffy said. "Where else could they be keeping him?"

"You're wrong," she said. "I've learned a great deal in the days I've been captive here. My fath . . . I mean, Il Maestro often uses creatures of the dark to do his dirty work. In this case, he bargained with a pair of vampires. They stole the child away from his school in England, and in exchange, my father was to provide them with an artifact called the Spear of Longinus."

Buffy and Angel exchanged a glance. Then she looked back at Micaela. "But the Spear isn't here," she said.

It was in Boston, at the Gatehouse, but she didn't

trust Micaela enough yet to tell her something she might not already know.

"And that's why the boy isn't here," Micaela said. "Il Maestro said that without the Spear, he would have to use force to take the child away from this vampire, this . . . what was his name?"

Micaela's brows knitted, and Buffy stopped paying attention. What difference did it make? The boy wasn't here. That meant it was time for them to not be here either.

"What's the best way out of here?" she asked.

"They were preparing to sacrifice you in the vineyard," Micaela said. "We should probably go right out the front."

"The wolf's getting heavy," Angel said. "I vote for the front. Anybody gets in the way, they'll regret it."

"Let's go," Buffy agreed.

They popped out into the corridor, glanced around, and started for the front of the villa. No one appeared to bar their progress. All of the acolytes must have been with Fulcanelli or guarding the buildings at regular posts outside, Buffy reasoned.

Moments later, they were approaching the door when they heard the sounds of a struggle outside.

"God, what now?" Buffy asked.

Micaela snapped her fingers. "I remember the vampire's name now. An odd one, which was what confused me."

Angel reached for the door.

"It was Spike."

Buffy turned to stare wide-eyed at Micaela. Angel nearly dropped Oz's unconscious form as he turned, letting his hand fall away from the door.

From outside, a man screamed in agony—a long, high, keening wail.

The door tore off its hinges as two acolytes slammed against it from outside. They fell to the floor, one dead, one nearly so. Framed in the open door, in the moonlight streaming in from outside, Buffy saw three Sons of Entropy attacking the tall, lithe, familiar figure of Spike. He'd grown his white-blond hair out a bit, but there was no mistaking him.

"Look, boys, I'm here for the Spear, and I mean to have it," he said, sounding entirely reasonable, just before he snapped one acolyte's neck.

Yep, Buffy thought. *Same old Spike.*

"You've gotta be kidding me," Angel said, his voice raspy and dangerous.

Spike looked up, blinked in surprise, then laughed as he crushed the face of another acolyte beneath his boot heel.

"Well, isn't this lovely," he said, "it's a bloody reunion. Not that it doesn't give me grand spasms of pleasure, but what brings you lot here? Don't tell me you're after the Spear as well?"

From behind them, deeper inside the house, Buffy heard shouting. Something about the Slayer having escaped. That was bad.

"We're gonna have company in a second," she said, glancing at Angel. Then she looked at Micaela. "How many are there?"

"At least thirty."

"How many magicians?" Angel demanded.

"I don't know," she said nervously. "Most of them are new faces to me. The ones who are most skilled have already been sent off on other errands, I think. In America, and here as well."

"Yeah, but there've gotta be a couple who know the hocus-pocus."

Spike stepped over to stand in the doorway, hands on the frame as he leaned in and cleared his throat.

"Hello?" he said angrily. "Have you forgotten someone? What is going on?"

Buffy shot him a withering glance. "The Spear isn't here," she said. "We're not here for that. We're here for Jacques Regnier."

Spike grinned broadly. "Ah. All right, then. I'll make you the same offer I made old Lefty inside, all right? You get me the Spear, and . . ."

Buffy spun and kicked Spike in the chest, sending him tumbling back out of the doorway and clearing a path for them.

"We've got to get out of here," she told Angel.

Footsteps pounded through the house behind them. They emerged from the house onto the broad expanse of land beyond the front door. A dirt road led away from it, winding down toward the city, and they didn't even have a vehicle.

"You know what we're going to have to do," Angel said.

"Ghost roads," Buffy agreed.

"There they are!" shouted an acolyte, who had just come around the front of the house holding a flickering torch. Several others with torches appeared behind him.

"What about her?" Angel asked, and nodded at Micaela. "Only beings touched by the supernatural can travel the ghost roads."

"I can take care of myself," Micaela said. "In fact, I'm sure I can find you the entrance you'll need."

They looked at her.

Spike lunged up from the ground, hands reaching for Buffy's throat. He clamped them around her neck and began to squeeze.

"Now you listen to me, you little tart!" he snarled. "We had a brief association by convenience. That's not going to stop me ripping your bleedin' heart out!"

Buffy pried his fingers from her throat, matching his strength. She glared at Micaela.

"Open it," she said, as even more acolytes came around the house and began to surround them.

"What are they waiting for?" Angel asked, glaring at the acolytes.

"Il Maestro," Micaela replied as she began to weave a spell.

Then Buffy looked into Spike's yellow eyes and said stiffly, "You're not going to get the Spear, Spike. Get it through your head. Fulcanelli never had it. But if we don't get that boy back to his father soon, it'll be Hell on Earth. The very thing that got you to back me up in Sunnydale. And you know who'll be the only human left alive? The guy who ripped you off."

Spike only glared at her. An acolyte thrust a torch at him, but Spike grabbed it out of his hand and gave him a backhand to the face that sent him sprawling. He tossed the torch at the villa; it crashed through a window, immediately setting the curtains on fire.

"Good shot," he told himself, and went on with his conversation.

"I want the Spear," he insisted. "For Dru."

Buffy blinked, remembering what Micaela had said.

"You can't have the Spear," she told him, "but if you don't get back to the boy, Drusilla won't be there. Fulcanelli's sent some heavy hitters to take him back. She'll be roasting on a spit in no time."

Spike swore loudly, looked around, and then turned back to Buffy.

"I've got no way to get back there," he snarled.

"Stick with us," Buffy said.

"Slayer!" Fulcanelli shouted.

Buffy turned and looked back at the villa. She could see inside the open front door, where the flames had begun to spread to the rest of the house. Fulcanelli was striding purposefully down the corridor toward them, ignoring the flames creeping up the walls.

"Hurry," she said to Micaela, her eyes still on Fulcanelli, who held his withered left hand against his body.

"How did you learn to do this?" Angel asked Micaela.

"I can do a few things," she said, her voice filled with urgency. "I can reach out and touch the ghost roads, and make them open up for me."

"Bloody hell," Spike whispered to himself, as a breach into the ghost roads began to form.

It wasn't like the other breaches they'd seen, Buffy realized. Rather than a circle in the air, it was more like a rip in the air, almost like a door that Micaela was pushing open.

"Micaela?" shouted Il Maestro, as he saw the girl he thought of as his daughter, standing with the Slayer.

Buffy smiled at him. Felt the urge to stick out her tongue, but didn't.

"No!" Fulcanelli roared, as he emerged from the

house. "Stop them!" he demanded, as black flames began to blaze around his right hand.

The acolytes, who had been awaiting his word, surged forward suddenly. Buffy spun, saw the open breach, reached out and shoved Angel through, with the unconscious Oz-wolf on his shoulder.

"Look out!"

Buffy whirled again and kicked an acolyte in the face, then turned to look. There were monsters within the ghost roads, just as there had been the last time Angel traveled them. Creatures with faces like blisters, with no faces, creatures of bone and insubstantial wraiths that flailed and screeched at the intruders.

This is crazy, Buffy thought. Suicide. But they didn't have any other choice. It was the only way to get to Jacques Regnier in time.

"Here!" Spike said.

Buffy turned to see him hurl the corpse of a dead acolyte through the breach. The monsters left Angel alone and set upon it like a pack of wild dogs.

"Go!" Buffy snapped.

Spike and Micaela followed Angel into the breach.

"Damn you, Slayer, for taking my daughter from me!" Fulcanelli shouted, and now the sorcerer began to run toward her.

They were closing in on all sides now. Buffy broke the arm of an acolyte who reached for her. She grabbed the torch from his hands and shoved it into the face of another, who began to scream. She waved the torch around, and then Fulcanelli was standing there, in front of her.

That burning black magick had engulfed his entire arm. His eyes pulsed with blackness so dark it seemed like ragged tears in the night. Beyond him, she could see the villa burning, flames ravenously consuming the place.

"Die," Fulcanelli said, and pointed at her.

Oily black energy reached out for Buffy and struck her body, and she spasmed as though electrocuted.

And tumbled back into the breach. Into the ghost roads.

Micaela drew the breach closed behind her.

Chapter 17

DUSK HAD FALLEN, TAKING WITH IT THE BRILLIANCE OF the sunset and draining the town of Sunnydale to shades of gray. The cool, still twilight hung like the calm before the storm, a breath held before the plunge. Panthers and leopards growled and paced in the Sunnydale Zoo. Swings in the park swayed ever so slightly. An owl hooted plaintively.

Gravestones shifted as the restless dead waited for night to fall.

For most of the citizens of Sunnydale, it was a twilight like any other.

For Joyce Summers, it seemed as though it might be the beginning of her last night on earth.

"Now, remember, Mrs. Summers," the one named Brother Claude said pleasantly over his shoulder, raising his brows like a college professor reminding a student about homework. As he stood beside the ratty couch where she sat in the basement, the dim light-bulb suspended from a chain cast demonic shadows over his features. "Make a sound, and you are dead."

Surrounded by hooded figures, Joyce nodded numbly. Although the music from the band upstairs was making the walls throb, the beating of her heart was so loud in her ears that she was half prepared for Claude to kill her for it. She had never known that it was possible to be this afraid and still function. That she could nod her head. And that her heart would continue to beat.

Since learning that Buffy was the Slayer, Joyce had known fear many times. Seated on Buffy's bed, clutching a pillow or some prized possession of her daughter's, she had stared for hours into the darkness. Soundlessly she would stroke the fur of a stuffed animal—that silly, fat pig, Mr. Gordo—her forehead beaded with clammy perspiration, willing her child to come home safely from patrol. She'd practically worn tracks in the kitchen floor, pacing, reaching for the phone, with no one to call. It would do no good to alert the police if Buffy was overdue. And it would be little comfort to speak to Giles, who had no way of telling if that night would be the night Buffy wouldn't be coming home at all.

It was a mother's job to keep her daughter from harm, but in the case of the Summers women, the roles were reversed. No matter how much Joyce wanted it otherwise, Buffy, and not she, was the Chosen One. Buffy and Buffy alone stood against the forces of darkness.

Joyce prayed to any god who would listen that Buffy would stay away from this place tonight.

As the figures parted and Brother Lupo, the one with the milky white eye surrounded by scars, approached her, Joyce Summers was shaking from head to toe. She was afraid to die. It was only with supreme effort that she did not cry out. But she was more afraid of Buffy's death than her own. If, as they planned, she were to be the bait in the trap that caused her daughter's death, she might as well be dead herself.

Without realizing it, she moaned deep in her throat as Brother Lupo came over to the couch.

"Be quiet!" someone snapped.

Joyce closed her eyes.

"Okay, so where are they?" Cordelia said to Xander, straining to be heard over the latest thrash offering from You Killed My Brother.

"They must be inside already," Xander said unhappily. "They're in there sneaking around, those sneaky SOE's. How'd they do that? I hate magick guys."

He, Cordy, Willow, and Giles had shown up hours before dusk, waiting at their hiding places, fully expecting to have beaten the Sons of Entropy to the Bronze. Together, Xander and Giles had worked out a strategy for guarding the "entrance and egress" to the Bronze, although Xander had no idea what any of that had to do with baby eagles. He figured they should just call it "securing the perimeter" and be done with it.

But apparently they'd been tricked, and Xander was monumentally frustrated. With a few more soldiers, they could take down any number of Sons of Entropy and rescue Joyce. Provided their side knew a little something about magick. That had not been on the roster of military knowledge he'd acquired when he'd been transformed into a soldier a couple Halloweens ago.

But he and the others did have a little magick on their side. Willow, who was currently on patrol with Giles on the opposite side of the building, had provided everybody with scapulas, which were protective talismans with all kinds of stinky herbs in them. Giles had muttered a few words in Latin over them, and that was supposed to keep the four of them relatively camouflaged from the creeps who were holding Buffy's mom hostage. Off the magick radar, as it were. But it didn't make them invisible. Just less detectable.

Before they'd left for the mission, Giles had tried to phone the Gatekeeper for some words of wisdom, but the connection had not gone through. Not a good sign. They should have left someone there to help the old guy, no matter how much he protested that they'd just be in the way.

As the shadows lengthened and the crowd grew, Xander and Cordelia crouched behind a row of overflowing trash cans, facing the entrance to the Bronze. Xander had moved the trash cans there himself from their regular location in the alley. He figured the Sons of Entropy wouldn't realize that the cans were not normally here. He hoped like crazy they wouldn't think to look behind them, but just in case, he planned to move Cordelia and himself to a new hiding spot behind the Dumpsters flush with the exterior of the Bronze itself once true darkness fell.

"Do you think there's a ghost road into the

Bronze?" Cordelia said directly into his ear. The music was very loud. "Is that how they got in without us seeing them?"

He shrugged. "Who can say? Maybe they've been in there for a while. Maybe they were already there when Brother Claude stopped by for tea at Giles's place. Y'know, maybe they're using the element of surprise. The way we aren't," he added bitterly.

They sat without speaking for a while. Cordelia had on some new perfume. It smelled great, and it masked the odor of the garbage fairly well. He inhaled it, savoring the spicy scent, and let his mind wander back to happier times, happier places. Happier activities.

"Are you nervous?" Xander asked. He looked at her. "You're holding your breath."

"Only a moron wouldn't be nervous," she said. After a few moments, she said, "Can you imagine having to save your mother from religious fanatics?"

He pondered a moment. "No. Avon ladies, maybe."

She sighed. "Our lives are so weird."

"True." He shrugged. "But at least we live in interesting times."

"Give me boredom any day."

"It's my constant desire." He patted her arm. "What I wouldn't give for an Uzi right now."

She rolled her eyes and frowned at him. "All guys ever want to do is shoot things."

"Wrong."

"And *that.*"

"Sums it up." He gave her a wink. "And that would be a problem why?"

"Oh, Xander." Cordelia shook her head like a weary older relative. "There *is* more to life."

"Yes," he replied earnestly. "In your case, shoes."

They heard a noise and ducked.

Xander peered around the side of the trash can. In the crush by the entrance, this guy stood out by the mere fact that he was trying not to stand out. He wore a hooded sweatshirt, and he was obviously looking for something. Not a date, however, unless she had told him to meet her behind the Dumpster; he wandered over there and dum-da-dum looked behind it. His face was hidden by his hood, and at the moment, he was looking downward.

But if he snooped on over to the trash cans, they were dead meat.

Here he came. In the dim light, Xander saw a face striped with scars.

"Oh, my God," Cordelia whispered. "I don't think he goes to Sunnydale."

"Me, either."

Sweatshirt guy was halfway to the row of cans.

"Looks like we're going to have to do something, aren't we?"

"Looks that way, sugar," Xander said. He licked his lips as he watched the potential SOE. "Somehow I doubt he'd fall for the old distracto routine. You know, where you wander over and ask him if he has a light, preferably in an exotic foreign accent. I'll bet he'd set you on fire just for spite."

Cordelia shivered. "No way am I trying it."

He nodded. "Okay, too bad. Then let's think of something else."

He watched the guy walking nearer and nearer. Then he realized he was watching the guy through a colored filter. On top of his garbage pile, an empty green beer bottle stood at an angle.

Xander smiled and fished it out of the garbage, showing it to Cordelia. He hefted the bottle in his hand. He would have only one chance. If he missed, they were in big trouble.

If he missed and they'd made a mistake, they were in bigger trouble.

For a few seconds, Xander waited. Maybe the guy wouldn't come too close. Maybe some of his buddies would call out to him—his plastic surgeon, maybe—and they'd go into the Bronze and have a cappuccino and talk about anesthesia options.

The guy made a right and sauntered away, whistling the love theme from *Armageddon*.

Xander put the bottle back. He cocked his head and looked at Cordelia. "You don't think they have protecto fields or whatever, do you?"

She grimaced. "Good point. Then what good are we?"

He wagged a finger at her. "That's not a good question for Slayerettes to ask, Cordy. I think we've all proven by now that we're effective members of a team. Well, except maybe you."

"Hey!" She stiffened. "Uh-oh. Here comes another one."

This time, the sweatshirt hood was thrown back. This time, the guy was not whistling and staring at the ground. A tall, dark man, he was smoking a cigarette.

Then he was tossing his match into the trash can.

And he was looking straight at Xander.

"Hey," the acolyte blurted, more surprised than anything.

Xander shot up from behind the trash can, grabbed the man by the front of his sweatshirt, and shattered the green bottle across his forehead.

The guy collapsed face first into the trash can. No one appeared to notice yet.

"Ouch," Xander groaned. "That had to hurt."

"Good," Cordelia said firmly. "C'mon, we've got to hide him."

She ran around to the opposite side of the cans and grabbed the acolyte around the waist.

"How do they do it in the movies?" she asked. "You put one arm around your shoulders and I'll put the other one around my shoulders. Like he's drunk."

Xander did as she said. Then they staggered back behind the trash cans with their burden.

"Well, now we know, in case it ever comes up in conversation," Xander said, "it's a lot harder to prop up an unconscious two-hundred-pounder than it looks."

"Try being under—" Cordelia started to say, then shook her head. "Forget I said that."

He grinned at her, but she wouldn't look at him. "I don't weigh two hundred pounds."

"Yes, I know."

They lowered the guy to the ground and leaned over him. Xander said, "Let's get the sweatshirt off him. It might be useful later."

It was also a lot harder to yank a hooded sweatshirt over the head and arms of an unconscious two-hundred-pounder than it looked. But as Cordelia crouched with the sweatshirt balled up in her lap, they surveyed the guy's jeans and Savage Garden T-shirt with something akin to amusement.

"You always think they're going to have a pentagram branded into their chests or something," Xander said. "Then you find a nice, normal ensemble direct from the pages of *Teen*."

"Yeah," Cordelia said hoarsely.

"But I'll bet they dress nicer for their ritual sacrifices," Xander said. "Tuxes."

Cordelia nodded. "At least."

Cordelia started rolling up the sweatshirt. Then she gasped and held up her hand. It was streaked with blood. She held up the sweatshirt and together they examined it. In the light from the Bronze's doorway, dark stains ran across the upper section of the back, slightly below the hood. The back of the sweatshirt was soaked with blood.

Gingerly, Xander rolled him over.

The back of the T-shirt was bloody, too.

Using his thumbs and forefingers, Xander peeled the stretchy cotton up around the guy's armpits.

"Eew," Cordelia said.

His back was carved between the shoulder blades, if not in the shape of a pentagram, then in the shape of something very like it.

"These hazing practices have got to stop," Xander said tiredly. "It makes recruitment so much more difficult."

"Which is a good thing," Cordelia reminded him. "Difficult recruitment."

"Hi," said a voice behind them, and Xander whirled around, his hand in a fist.

"Hey." It was Willow, who blinked. "It's just me." She gestured at the sky as she sank to her heels. "It's dusk."

"And they're in," Xander said.

"They're in," Willow confirmed, staring at the guy on the ground with the bloody wound and the T-shirt. "Wow. Which you can take to mean 'gross.' What happened to him?"

"Someone got all crazy with the Ginsu," Xander said.

"Xander knocked him out," Cordelia announced proudly. "With a beer bottle."

Willow looked both impressed and concerned. "Did anyone else see it?"

"Nope," Xander said.

"Well, they might start to wonder where he is," Willow ventured. "And look for him."

"My guess is they sent him outside to have his cigarette," Xander replied. "You know how strict the management is nowadays."

"She has a point," Cordelia said uneasily.

"Which occurred to me." Xander knew he sounded a little defensive, which he was not. The guy had needed to be knocked out. "But there wasn't much choice."

That dear old British voice said, "Oh, dear."

Xander looked behind Willow. Now Giles had joined the party behind the trash cans. Xander was not happy about the fact that in the last ten seconds, two separate people had sneaked up on him and Cordy and he had not had a clue.

"He'll be missed," Giles said.

Then, "Good Lord, he's bleeding." He examined

the carved wound. "Perhaps they needed to perform a ritual to keep their magick strong."

"Or for when they killed Buffy's mom," Cordelia filled in. She widened her eyes and glared at the three of them. "Oh, *what?* That didn't occur to anyone else?"

"Actually, no," Willow said.

"Oh." Cordelia cleared her throat.

Giles pushed up his glasses. "I wonder if we should abort Plan B."

"I haven't been looking forward to Plan B," Cordelia admitted, wiping her hand on the front of the sweatshirt. "Plan B is not my favorite plan."

Xander had to agree, especially now that they had taken out the Illustrated Man. Plan B required them to infiltrate the Bronze and try to quietly observe where Joyce Summers might be. Could be the attic, could be the basement. Could be Mr. Plum in the conservatory or the ballroom. They wouldn't have a lot of opportunities to guess wrong.

As the last of the light disappeared and true darkness fell, Giles's glasses reflected the moon. Something tugged at the back of Xander's mind, but he didn't know precisely what.

Then he was distracted by heavy footsteps and a deep voice calling, barely loud enough to be heard over the band, "Brother Tibor?"

There were more footsteps, directly toward the line of trash cans.

"Brother Tibor?"

Well hidden by the trash cans, they all held their breath. Xander felt cold fingers of dread crawling up his spine. He glanced left to see if Giles had a Plan C he was working on, but the last of the light had fled. The moonlight was too dim, and the street lamp overhead was not working.

"Brother Tibor?"

Xander hazarded a peek and saw the guy silhouetted against the lights in the Bronze. He murmured, "Hooded sweatshirt."

The man departed.

"Leaving," Xander added. "Left."

"We're out of time," Giles said grimly. "He'll report back that he couldn't find the missing acolyte."

"Wouldn't they assume that the Slayer would take out one or two?" Xander asked. "For form's sake?"

"We can't make that assumption," Giles said. "We've got to go now."

"What, after all this hiding, we just walk in?" Xander asked.

"Yes." Giles stood and gestured for them to follow. "They don't expect us to attack them. What are we, four against so many? They'll think we're fairly harmless."

"And oh, boy, do we have them fooled," Xander shot back.

"So, we do attack," Giles finished. "There's a window in the basement that looks fairly breakable. I suggest we split up. Two of us will break that window and the other two will go directly into the Bronze. That way—"

At that moment, a ball of fire struck the ground inches from Willow's foot. She cried out and looked up.

On the roof of the Bronze, a hooded man stood

silhouetted against the moon. He threw back his hand and flicked it at them. Another ball shattered two of the trash cans.

Bronze patrons milling around by the entrance began to scream and scatter. Someone shouted, "There's a live electric wire!" and pandemonium struck.

"Attack," Giles yelled.

He grabbed Willow's hand and together they dashed into the Bronze.

"Looks like we get the window," Xander told Cordy.

"Oh, my God." Cordelia raced to keep up with him. "I can't believe this is happening!"

Xander bobbed to his left and picked up a heavy rock. Then, as they rounded the corner of the building, he saw half a chunk of brick and handed it to Cordy.

They dashed to the little window and threw their ammo at it. It shattered as if a bomb had hit it.

Xander took a deep breath and said, "We're going in."

A face appeared among the jagged pieces stuck in the window. Xander pulled back his leg and gave it a good, swift kick. With a shout, it disappeared.

Xander looked at Cordelia over his shoulder. Then he dove for the window.

"No!" she shouted. "Xander, don't!"

The Bronze was on fire. Smoke choked Willow as she and Giles pushed their way against the stream of people fighting to get out.

A guy in a Sunnydale High sweatshirt raced through the Bronze, shouting, "There's a live electric wire outside!"

He ran up to Claire Bellamy, the manager, who had a portable phone against her shoulder and a fire extinguisher in both hands. She nodded at him and shouted back into the phone. Then she gestured to the guy to take the fire extinguisher from her.

People were running in panic all over the place. They clattered down the stairs, pushing and shoving, dervished out of the bathrooms and poured out the front door.

They were coming from everywhere except the basement.

And while there was a lot of smoke, Willow had yet to see flames anywhere in the Bronze.

As patrons swarmed around them, Willow pointed to the basement door and Giles nodded.

"My thinking exactly," he shouted.

Together they fought their way through the terrified crowd. Someone hit Willow in the face. She cried out, reeling for a moment.

"I'm okay, I'm okay," she assured Giles. She got her bearings as Giles grabbed her wrist and urged her behind him, acting as her shield. Her lip throbbed and her cheekbone was stinging.

Then it was Giles's turn to fall back slightly. Willow pushed her way through, fighting a rising tide that threatened to catch her up with it.

She bellowed, "Coming through!" and elbowed a couple of jocks from school out of her way.

At last she reached the door. Giles was behind her.

Willow wrapped her hand around the knob and yanked. Nothing happened.

"It's locked," she said.

The journey along the ghost roads was harrowing. The monsters were distracted by the dead acolyte's corpse at first. But then it was up to Spike and Buffy to keep them at bay, while Angel tried to keep Oz safe.

Micaela explained that she had learned some magick as a child, and she had been skilled in talking to the dead. In fact, she had helped Albert travel the ghost roads to warn them in the catacombs. Now she aided them by speaking to the dead, to the spirits, by explaining their plight in terms the dead could understand. And when she was through, the ghosts began to aid them, to hold the monsters back and clear their way.

"That's amazing," Buffy told her.

"No," Micaela said, shaking her head, the gray, eternal twilight of the ghost roads surrounding them all. "It's horrible, actually. They hate it here. While they're walking these roads, they don't know where they'll end up. That's why so many of them never move on to their final destination. They're afraid of what that destination might be."

Spike tossed a scaled beast toward Buffy, and the Slayer got it into a choke hold and broke its neck.

And the journey went on like that, until Micaela told them all to halt.

"Here," she said. "We're here."

"How the bloody hell do you know?" Spike asked. "I didn't even tell you where we were going."

"The ghosts know," she told him. "And besides, I can feel the boy. The Gatekeeper's son. He's here."

Another door opened, and moonlight spilled into the gray of the ghost roads, along with the sound and smell of the ocean. Buffy was the last one out, and she heard Spike shouting even before she emerged back into the land of the living.

Ahead of them, a little cottage was already under siege by Fulcanelli's followers.

It was a massacre.

With Buffy, Angel, and Spike outside, and Drusilla on the inside—less than pleased—the Sons of Entropy never stood a chance.

The moment Xander dove through the open window into the basement of the Bronze, colliding with an acolyte and crashing to the floor in a tumble of limbs, Brother Lupo knew that the Slayer was not coming.

Something had gone wrong.

"Chaos' name!" he cursed. "Kill the fool!"

Immediately, several acolytes moved in on the teenager. He fought back, and he fought well. Better than Lupo would ever have expected.

"Xander!" shouted the mother of the Slayer. "God, no!" She turned to Lupo, eyes wild as she pleaded with him. "He can be useful to you. He's one of Buffy's best friends. Don't kill him!"

Lupo struck her, hard, across the cheek. One of his knuckles popped with the force of the blow, and he swore. That was the cost of resorting to physical violence instead of sticking to magick, he thought.

But there was something very fulfilling about the feeling of flesh on flesh, bone on bone.

The woman fell back and stared up at him in fury from the basement floor. She held a hand to her cheek where he'd struck her, and Lupo smiled at her pain.

"My daughter's going to kill you for that," Joyce Summers said. "Unless I get a chance to do it first."

Lupo only laughed. Then he looked up as a girl's scream ripped through the basement. At the shattered window, Cordelia Chase shouted at the Sons of Entropy to leave her boyfriend alone.

Two of them. And there would be more, Lupo knew. At the very least, the Watcher and the little spellcaster. They were probably upstairs already. And who knew what others had been convinced to align themselves with the Slayer.

Yet, without the Slayer, there was no benefit to this battle.

"You!" he shouted to a particularly brawny acolyte. "Take her and come with me!"

Joyce Summers screamed as the acolyte pushed her arm up behind her back and held her in that position—in great pain and inches away from a broken limb—as they hurried up the basement steps, leaving the others behind to deal with Xander and Cordelia. It wouldn't take long, Brother Lupo knew. Four acolytes against one boy.

He was as good as dead. And the girl, too, if she continued to scream at them.

There was no fire in the Bronze. It had been nothing but smoke. Giles was uncertain whether it had been achieved through magick or technology, but either way, it was a hoax meant to empty the Bronze of all staff and clientele. And it had worked.

Save for him and Willow, of course.

With a loud curse uncharacteristic of the Watcher, Giles reared back and kicked the basement door once again.

"I hear screaming," Willow said. For the third time.

"I know!" Giles snapped. "I'm doing my best."

He took several steps backward, determined to put his shoulder into it this time, to try to tear the door right off its hinges.

"I wish Buffy was here," Willow said quietly.

"No," Giles replied. "That's exactly what they want!"

Then he ran at the door.

A moment before he would have crashed into it, the door opened. Giles was taken off guard, and instead of throwing himself at the bald, scar-faced man with the blind white eye, he hesitated and moved to one side to avoid him.

"Giles!"

He looked up and saw Joyce Summers being forced past him by a muscular acolyte. Without another thought, Giles attacked. He reached for the man's arms. The acolyte hauled back and snap-kicked him hard in the abdomen. It all happened so fast that Giles was unprepared for the kick. He was thrown backward where he sprawled into a table and several chairs, then lay on the ground and began to vomit up everything he'd had to eat that day.

Through the haze of pain and nausea, he saw the white-eyed man—Brother Lupo, he surmised, from earlier descriptions—face off against a courageous but obviously terrified Willow.

"Get out of the way, little spellcaster," Brother Lupo snarled at the redheaded girl.

"I can't do that," Willow replied, and reached for an aluminum folding chair that stood nearby.

"Willow, do as he says," Joyce Summers snapped, her voice taut from the pain in her arm, where it was held almost at the breaking point.

Brother Lupo smiled. "Yes, listen to the woman, Ms. Rosenberg. She is wise. Though she will be dead if her daughter does not appear in Sunnydale soon to claim her."

Willow stood straight, hefted the chair and stood as if to attack.

Joyce Summers dropped her voice. Her tone stern, she said, "Willow, listen to me. You can't help Buffy if you're dead."

"Hmm, now that's true," said Brother Lupo.

He raised a hand, whispered a few words, and sickly blue energy crackled from his fingers and struck the metal chair. Willow shuddered as though she were being electrocuted, and then she and the chair were thrown back against the coffee counter.

"Oh, God, no," Joyce Summers whispered.

Lupo left the Bronze. In moments, he knew the other acolytes would follow. But his mind was not on his men. He thought of one thing only: what Il Maestro might say when he discovered that they did not have the Slayer.

Brother Lupo was afraid.

* * *

Cordelia slipped into the basement of the Bronze with a length of rusty metal chain in her hands. It was the only thing she could find in the alley outside that vaguely resembled a weapon.

"Hello, sweet one," said a leering acolyte as he turned his attention from beating the crap out of Xander to this new intruder.

"Oh, please," Cordelia sneered.

Then she whipped the rusty chain around and it slapped him hard in the face, breaking his jaw. The man screamed in pain.

The others looked up and stared at her wide-eyed. The guy with the broken jaw mumbled something unintelligible and pointed at Cordy.

"Xander!" she shouted. "The cavalry needs the cavalry!"

With a tremendous effort, Xander threw off one of the acolytes and got to his feet. He was bleeding from several cuts on his face, which was a mess. His clothes were torn. And he looked very pissed.

"Come on!" he yelled.

The acolytes turned to look at him again and started to laugh. Then they moved toward Cordelia. With a shriek, she swung the chain to keep them back. Xander leaped on the back of the acolyte nearest him and began to choke the man, who spun around and around trying to get him off.

Finally Xander was thrown, and he landed painfully by Cordelia's feet. He jumped up just as the three other acolytes were lunging at him. The fourth, with the broken jaw, stood a short distance away.

"Give me that!" Xander bellowed, grabbing the

chain from Cordelia's hands and then stepping in front of her and swinging the chain out to drive them back.

They moved back.

But only for a moment.

The closest acolyte charged Xander. The chain whipped out and wrapped around his neck, and while Xander was occupied with him, the other two moved in, surrounding the teen. They were fast. But not fast enough. He yanked the chain off the throat of the acolyte he'd been choking, and it tore skin off as well, its jagged rust ripping open veins.

"Come on!" he screamed again, and swung the chain.

The guy with the broken jaw mumbled something else. Then he reached inside his jacket and pulled out a gun.

"Whoa," Xander said, even as he ducked a punch. "You guys are supposed to have swords and knives, right? Maybe some magick?"

The acolyte whose jaw Cordelia had broken leveled the gun at Xander and shot him in the chest.

Cordelia was shrieking at the top of her lungs as the four acolytes went up the stairs from the basement and disappeared. She crouched down by Xander, tears flowing freely, and tried to find something clean with which to staunch the wound in Xander's chest.

A pool of blood was forming on the ground beneath his still form, and his eyes were glazed with shock.

She stopped screaming only when Giles and Willow came down into the basement, both in bad shape from whatever scrape they'd gotten into upstairs.

"They . . . they *shot* him," Cordelia said, in a voice that sounded to her as though it were coming from somebody else.

Giles quickly knelt and examined the wound.

Cordelia stared up into Willow's face and realized that the shock and the horror and the tears there, the mute despair, were just a mirror of her own face.

"There's too much blood," Giles said, breaking that connection.

Cordelia stared at him, but it was Willow who spoke.

"What do you mean?" she asked.

Giles glanced from one girl's face to the other. When he spoke, his own voice sounded as hollow as theirs had.

"Xander's going to die."

Chapter 18

THERE WAS A LULL IN THE FIGHTING, FOR WHICH JEAN-Marc was most grateful. He crawled on his elbows to the Cauldron and fell in, immersing himself. He would have to stay here many hours to find a small measure of relief, and what would happen if the Sons of Entropy renewed their assault?

His agony was mental; his body was so old and aged now he could scarcely feel anything. He remembered as a young man how vigor had surged through him. The joy of living, the joy of moving. The joy of making love to his wife. But even then, he had begun to age. The Regniers married old. He did not understand why.

The joy of creating his son within her. The feeling of power that gave a man. Any man, but especially a sorcerer.

Gone now. He could barely create within himself the power to breathe, much less to procreate.

"Mother," he whispered, his arms outstretched. "I'm so tired."

"I know." She leaned over the Cauldron and looked into his eyes. *"Soon you will rest, my darling boy."*

"Soon, it won't matter how long I rest in here," he told her. "I'm losing more than I'm gaining. I can't recapture a tenth of what I was. I could stay here for a month, and yet I'll die within a fortnight. Sooner."

"Death is not so terrible, my sweetling. I promise you that."

He was exhausted from talking, and yet it was practically all he had left. "Defeat is, Mother. It is odious."

"There are others. The Slayer, and her friends. The Watcher. Most capable. Very brave."

"But what of my Jacques?" He coughed hard. "What of my son?"

Soon, darling. Soon all will come right.

Her tears fell into the Cauldron.

As she wept, she sang a lullaby.

It proved to be the most soothing balm of all.

For the first few moments after his daughter closed the breach behind her, Fulcanelli could not move or speak. His icy fury froze him in place.

Then, with no notion of the passage of time, he watched the scene around him as if he were not present in it, as if the rage had transported him to another plane of existence. He staggered and lost his breath, and then he whispered his daughter's name: "Micaela."

352

The flames from the burning villa flickered on the faces of his terrified acolytes as they ran like mindless barn animals through the crackling vineyards and fields. Smoke roiled like a fog above the roofs of the buildings, and as he stared up at it, he could plainly see the face of his old nemesis, Richard Regnier, father of the Regnier dynastic line of sorcerers, laughing at him.

"I killed your true love here, on this very spot," Fulcanelli whispered to the smoke. "I made her suffer agonies you can scarcely imagine."

But Regnier continued to laugh. The past was over. The dead were buried. He had an heir, and Fulcanelli did not. And not only had the Regniers an heir, but Fulcanelli's chosen heiress had stolen the Slayer from beneath his very nose.

Fulcanelli swore then that when he found Micaela, he would kill her.

He was so enraged he could not breathe.

"Fulcanelli," came the call inside his mind.

Fulcanelli roused. Belphegor was summoning him. The breach through which he communicated was in the subcellar, and the house was on fire. He didn't think that would matter; breaches could be found underwater, and within stone. So this breach would survive fire.

"Fulcanelli," the demon called again.

"I come," Fulcanelli replied aloud.

He made signs and signals of protection in the air, then walked back toward the inferno. One of his acolytes, Brother Eric, ran right into him, grasped him, and gasped, "Master! Don't go in there. It's Hell itself."

Fulcanelli stopped, bemused. "Oh?"

"The villa is burning, Maestro," Eric said, sobbing. "It's the end of everything!"

Fulcanelli's wrath was unleashed.

"Bastardo," he flung at the boy. He caught the idiot by the sleeve and dragged him along. "You have had no comprehension of the vastness of my power, and yet you have imagined yourself my follower."

"Master, please," the acolyte pleaded, his voice rising. The flames roared ten feet before them, walls of fire that skyrocketed into the night sky. *"Please!"*

Then Brother Eric did the unthinkable: he laid his hands on Fulcanelli's arm and tried to make him let go.

Fulcanelli glared at him. "I, who began the Great Fire of London! I, who walked the streets of Chernobyl. You have the temerity to doubt me? You can insult me to my face?"

"Master, I am only human," Brother Eric pleaded, tugging, not able to stop. His skin was beginning to blister. "I will burn."

Fulcanelli narrowed his eyes and smiled evilly. "Yes," he said. "You will."

Then he shook the acolyte off like a bothersome insect and flung him into the conflagration. The child's screams were short, but sincere.

Fulcanelli stepped into the fire.

The flames did not touch him.

Around him, inside the lovely villa, the walls cracked. Statuary tumbled. Mirrors exploded. So much beauty. But like all things of this earth, fleeting. Better to lay one's treasures up in the hereafter.

He stared, watching a man writhe on the floor.

Watching him burn and bubble as he stepped over his body, unaffected.

It never ceased to amaze him that so many had clamored to follow him, yet so few had benefited from their proximity. Where were the ambitious, power-hungry lads who aspired to greatness? It certainly wasn't like the days of the de' Medici.

He shook his head, pulling a sad face as he listened to the shrieks of the barnyard animals. It occurred to him that a cat had recently adopted him, and he wondered briefly what had become of it.

But only briefly.

Then he was down in the subcellar, where the sulfur smell competed with the odor of roasted meat, and ah! he remembered that there had been a few captives down here besides the Slayer and the other two abominations. Just a few locals, to add spice to tonight's aborted proceedings.

Remarkably—or perhaps, not remarkably, for he had expected it—the breach hovered in the smoke and contagion. He thought of the wonder that was to have occurred tonight, and tears of frustration welled at the corners of his eyes. Fulcanelli wiped them away. For Micaela, no tears. No mercy. For his own plight, only resolve. Strong men survived everything. Weak men perished at the first obstacle.

He knelt on the white-hot stone, gritting his teeth against the pain, and lowered his head.

"My Lord Belphegor," he said, "I am here."

"Your bastard child attempts to take them to the Gate."

Fulcanelli closed his eyes, completely humiliated.

"We must stop them."

"Is it possible?" Fulcanelli asked.

"How can it be that you have served me so long, and yet have not divined one small portion of that which is available to you as my follower?"

Fulcanelli flinched as his own words were hurled back at him. He murmured, "I have been remiss. It will not happen again."

"Then cast your power with me against the ghost roads. The Gatekeeper cannot last much longer. His heir must not reach the Gatehouse."

"So shall it be done," Fulcanelli said.

Belphegor chuckled.

"Who writes your dialogue?"

"So, no Spear," Spike finished as he helped Dru stack up the broken and bleeding bodies of the Sons of Entropy acolytes they'd taken out.

"Then take the lit'l bastard," Dru said with a sneer at one of the two pretty blond girls. "He's been nothing but trouble and proud of it, eh, you?"

She boxed the boy's ears and he clamped down hard not to cry out. Jacques began to walk with great dignity toward the two blond girls, then ran for all he was worth and flung his arms around the nearest one. To his intense relief, she hugged him tightly.

He whispered to her, "She's crazy."

The girl whispered back, "I know."

He decided to tell her everything. "She's a vampire."

She patted him. "No news there."

She held him at arm's length and smiled at him. "We haven't been introduced, but my name's Buffy.

I'm kind of in your line of work. I'm the Slayer. And I know you're the Gatekeeper's heir."

He took a deep breath and stared at the girl. He could see the fear in her eyes, and the sadness. He braced himself for the horrible news she was going to give him, bursting into heavy, wrenching sobs.

"My father," he moaned.

"No, no," she said. "He's alive. We think," she muttered. Then she patted him. "Alive, yeah. It's okay, Jacques, we're going to get you home."

Spike ambled over to Jacques and gave him a mock punch. "Last chance, Jack the lad. You can stay with us. We'll fix you right up with a big kiss and then you'll run with us for the rest of time. What do you say?"

Jacques looked at Spike, then at Dru, and then at Buffy Summers. He was ashamed to let her know, but he was a little tempted by Spike's offer. Just a little. He didn't want to be the Gatekeeper quite yet. He wanted to have some fun. To live, and have friends, and play. He was only eleven years old.

"Does it hurt?" he asked, and then Buffy was laughing uncertainly and giving him a little punch.

"You're so funny. Ha ha ha," she said, sounding very nervous and phony.

Then, almost before he realized it, he was outside the little cottage for the first time in what seemed like years. There were bodies everywhere out here. The battle had been horrible.

Jacques looked up at Buffy and said, "You didn't tell them that my father has the Spear, did you?"

She raised her brows. "Are you kidding? No way."

They walked on a little way with the other blond woman. No one had introduced him to her, but he knew that she was very troubled.

He drew back when he saw another vampire, this one carrying a dead werewolf over his shoulders.

"Friends," Buffy said. "Trust me."

And since Jacques had no one else to trust, he did.

Cordelia cradled Xander in her lap.

"Oh, God, Xander," she whispered. "Xander, you can't die. Because it would be so . . . stupid." She reached out to Willow. "He'd do that, wouldn't he? Die, because it would be so stupid and he's so stupid oh God Willow can't you do something?"

Willow looked down at Xander and felt her entire life draining away in the river of blood flowing out of his chest. His face was gray. His lips were white. She fought to pull herself together but she could feel pieces of herself floating off in a white haze of panic. She could vaguely hear Cordelia sobbing and babbling, and she wanted to tell her to be quiet but it didn't matter if she was quiet. Maybe it would help. Maybe it would irritate Xander so much he would sit right up and tell Cordelia to shut up.

Giles leaned over Xander, taking off his jacket and laying it over Xander's chest.

"Call 911!" Cordelia screamed, batting at Giles "Call an ambulance!"

Sirens wailed in the distance. Emergency vehicles coming to check on the nonexistent fire and the nonexistent live wire, Willow realized. An ambulance would come.

But Willow knew deep in her soul that it would not help.

Finally she dug down deeply enough to find the focus to speak. She looked hard at Giles. "There must be something I can do. We can do."

He pushed up his glasses. "You may be right. We must take him to the Gatekeeper."

"Right!" Cordelia cried. "He can heal Xander!"

Willow held up a hand. "Giles, how can we go on the ghost roads? We aren't touched by the supernatural. I mean, I've cast a few spells, but I'm a long way from witchdom."

Giles hesitated, then said, "Before our raid tonight, I tried to read up on everything I could find about the Sons of Entropy and anything connected to our situation."

He swallowed hard and looked at each of them in turn. "I found an incantation which may allow a human being access to the roads. There was no documentation about its effectiveness, which led me to conclude that we were better off not attempting it unless we had an emergency."

"Which this is," Cordelia said. "Come on, say it! Say it now!"

Willow looked directly at Giles and nodded. "Say it."

Giles said, "It may fail. None of you may make it."

"Say it," Willow told him. "Damn it, Giles, say it!"

"The Cauldron," he added. "Go straight to the Cauldron."

"Giles!" Cordelia shrieked.

"I'll go," he said. "You two stay here and—"

"No, Giles," Willow said. "You have to stay here."

He blinked at her. "No, indeed. I—"

"You are the Watcher," she said. "You have to stay here for Buffy. And get her mother back."

He lowered his head and nodded.

"We'll take him to the breach immediately," he said. "I'll do the incantation on the way."

They stood in the darkness across the street from the high school. Giles was still uncertain how they had managed to slip past all the fire trucks and police cars, and how Xander had survived the short ride from the Bronze to the breach in Cordelia's car. There was blood all over her backseat. Incredibly, she hadn't complained.

But they were here now, and Giles finished the incantation in Latin as he helped Cordelia and Willow carry Xander out of the car:

Souls who wander, free of form,
Allow these passage safe from harm.
Do not make them tarry, these three yet breathe,
Do not cause them mischief, they've no power to
relieve.

The breach hovered in the air, shimmering and pulsing. Willow looked at Giles and said, "Angel saw Jenny." He saw that she tried to smile, but she just couldn't pull it off. "She'll make sure we're all right."

Giles could not respond to that. It would be too easy to believe that some part of Jenny still lived, just out of reach, beyond the veil that separated the world from the ghost roads. It would only cause him pain to consider such a thing.

He was terrified. There was no other word for it. All of them knew that there was a good chance this wouldn't work. If it were possible for humans to travel the ghost roads, someone would have done it by now. Il Maestro would have sent his followers traveling that way. Surely the Gatekeeper and his mother would know of any instance where a normal human being had walked the roads and lived to tell the tale.

He hated sending these young people on this journey. Everything in his being cried out for him to go himself, but Willow was right. His first duty was to the Slayer. And for her, he had to find a way to rescue Joyce.

This was the only way.

He looked down at Xander. Willow took Xander's ankles and Cordelia took his wrists. Just for them to lift him was an enormous effort. There was no other way for them to carry him, and no time to fashion a travois or any other sort of stretcher.

Giles had no idea what it was like to walk on the ghost roads, nor for how long they would have to actually carry him. How they would manage.

It was the best he could do.

But it was not very much at all.

"Come on, come on," Willow said frantically. "We have to go!"

"Take care," Giles said to Willow. "Willow, I . . . I want so badly . . ."

She nodded.

"We'll be okay," she said.

They stepped into the breach.

In case they could see him, Giles stood facing it and stared straight ahead into the void.

Okay, just for the road, one last pack of desperate dead people.

The dozen or so wraiths were so out of control that not even Micaela could calm them down. Maybe they'd heard rumors about the impending arrival of squatters from Hell, or that they might be stuck in here forever, but whatever their deal, she and Angel took them out one by one, battering at the fragile creatures, who disintegrated with each roundhouse kick or one-two punch.

Finally the way was clear; except for onlookers, who lined the rows here and there like people cheering on marathon runners. Angel had draped Oz back over his shoulder, and Micaela was holding Jacques's hand. *The complete Dorothy foursome . . .*

"Drizzle, drazzle, druzzle, drome, Mister Wizard," Buffy said cheerily, smiling over her shoulder at Jacques, who, she supposed, had grown up watching the Cartoon Network; then again, maybe not if he was raised in England. Most of the decent shows never made it there.

"Here we are, Jacques, safe and sound," she said, running for the breach that led to a spot directly across from . . .

"Sunnydale?" she asked in complete confusion as she burst from the breach and stared across the street at her high school. It was supposed to be Boston. But it most definitely wasn't. It was dark out; the fat, round moon shone above the silhouette of the roof.

"Buffy?" someone called to her.

She took one look at the figure by Cordelia's car and loped toward it.

"Giles!" she cried. "What's going on?"

He took a step backward, then grabbed her and gave her a tight hug. "Oh, thank God. You're alive!"

"Looks that way," she said, staring at him. In the moonlight, his face was chalk white. She wasn't sure she had actually seen someone's face so pale. Someone who wasn't dead, anyway. She added slowly, gingerly touching the bruises on her face, "But looks can be deceiving."

He frowned. "Where have you been? Are you returning from Boston? Did you see—"

"We thought we were *going* to Boston." She turned back around, to see Angel with Oz draped over his shoulder. He was holding the heir's hand, and she gestured them forward to show Giles. "Rupert Giles. This is Jacques Regnier."

As the group approached, Giles held out his hand. "Thank heaven. I'm so glad you're all right." He sounded about as thrilled as a guy who'd been fired from his job.

"Thank you, sir," the boy replied.

Angel came up behind Buffy. "What's going on? How'd we get here?"

Buffy frowned at Giles. "You're not exactly cheering our arrival," she said. "Which I assume means adbay ewsnay."

Jacques tensed. Buffy made a face and said, "And I'm guessing you speak pig Latin."

"Buffy," Giles said, and then he must have seen Micaela, for he hesitated a moment. He bowed his head and blinked. When he looked back up, Buffy saw tears in his eyes.

"Oh, God, what?" she cried.

"You didn't see them, then. On the ghost road. And if you couldn't get to Boston, how can they?"

"See who?" she asked, frantic.

"Oh, dear Lord, Buffy," Giles said. "It's Xander. Xander's dying."

"What?" Buffy shouted. "Giles, what—"

Then the sky erupted with thunder. Lightning stabbed the ground in half a dozen different places. The earth beneath them shook so hard that Giles staggered and fell to his knees. The others followed suit, crashing to the ground.

Icy rain pelted them, and then slimy, cold toads plummeted from the sky. As Buffy got to her hands and feet, she heard screams. She didn't know where they were coming from, but they were filled with terror.

From the breach, a pair of hideous demons lurched out. They raced across the street, making for Buffy and the others.

Buffy leaped to her feet. Angel did the same.

"It's happening!" Micaela cried. "The barriers between Hell and the ghost roads have opened. They're tearing their way through to Earth!"

Buffy looked around wildly, then said, to Giles, "Protect the heir. Do whatever you need to do to save him."

"He must go to Boston!" Giles shouted, above the gale winds that had erupted. "Now! There's no time to lose!"

* * *

It was like a very bad day at the beach, only with no beach, just the slate sky above and below her. Overcast, dull, gray. It wasn't hot, it wasn't cold. It was nothing.

Cordelia caught her breath and fought like crazy to stop from going completely nuts. Something was wrapping around her like a ghost, an evil fog or a fingertip or something. Shadows crossed over her, only there were no shadows.

Ghosts, she thought. *It's a place of ghosts. Antoinette was a ghost and she was nice to us.*

Then suddenly, the ground beneath her became solid, and she stumbled slightly.

"Don't drop him!" Willow cried anxiously.

"Of course I won't," Cordelia retorted, although she had almost let go of Xander's wrists.

Slung between them, his body was completely limp and his eyes were closed. If she didn't look at the wound in his chest, she could pretend he was asleep.

No. She couldn't.

Anxiously she glanced from his face to Willow's, to find Willow also staring at him.

Then they gazed at each other, and if Cordelia looked like Willow, then she looked nauseous with fear.

"Cauldron," Willow said. "It's magickal. It'll restore him."

"If they let us use it," Cordelia replied.

Willow's face softened. "They will. They're on our side, Cordy."

"Yeah, well, if the Gatekeeper needs—"

A rumbling drowned out the rest of her words. It

grew louder and louder, and Cordelia gasped as they were shaken from side to side.

"Willow?" she asked, her voice shrill. "What's happening?"

Without warning, a blinding white flash burned away all the gray. The road beneath Cordelia turned to charred ash. She covered her eyes, blinking, as her eyelids glowed red.

Then suddenly, she, Willow, and Xander were surrounded by blurred bits and pieces of people. Faces. A hand. An arm. Most of the people were crying. Others looked blank, as if they had seen something they just couldn't handle. There were a few at first, but as Cordelia focused on them, she realized there was hundreds of them, maybe thousands.

They began to take shape.

They began to close in on the three of them.

"Um, we're just passing through," Cordelia said, smiling brightly. "Right, Willow?"

"It is the last days," said a young girl dressed in a sort of toga. There was a huge, gaping cut down the center of her face. "It is over."

"Willow?" Cordelia said.

"Safe passage," Willow said firmly. "We said the ritual of safe passage. We're alive."

The girl shook her head. "It is the end."

There was another rumbling, and the girl looked terrified. A high keening filled the air, like one sad, lost person. Shivering, Cordelia remembered her uncle's funeral. She had been nine; it was her first funeral. Now, after so many years in Sunnydale, she'd been to a lot of them.

But at nine, the crying and the grief had frightened

her. Her uncle had lain in his coffin with the lid open, and all through the service she could barely see his profile.

Then everyone got up to file past him, past the dead body, and her mother had whispered to her, "What a terrible makeup job. Your aunt must be devastated."

And Cordelia had thought, *Yes, that must be it,* when her aunt was led to the coffin and she began to cry so hard it was like screaming.

That was what this was like.

Only now it was worse, because deep within the foggy distance, Cordelia saw some kind of shading in the gray, and within that shading, a huge, glowing circle appeared. It pulsed and throbbed like a breach, only flames poured out of it. And inside the circle, something huge, mottled, and slimy tumbled out and flopped into the gray. It rose on its hind legs and let out a horrible roar.

The girl turned in its direction, screamed, and pointed. "It is Hell! They are coming!" she shrieked. Then she turned to Cordelia, panting with fear, and said, "You must go quickly, you who are living. You who can leave," she added bitterly.

"Okay. Thanks. And, don't worry. We're going to the Gatekeeper," she assured the girl. But as she spoke, another fiery circle appeared. "He can stop this stuff." To Willow, she gritted, "Let's go."

They began to move with Xander between.

"No," the girl said anxiously. "Only the living may leave."

"Right." Cordelia blinked at her.

From the second circle, a tentacled creature flopped out and rolled into the fog. A ghostly scream seared

Willow's nerves as she nervously tightened her grip around Xander's feet.

The girl said, "These are the ghost roads. The dead travel here." She gestured toward Xander. "He travels here."

Together, Willow and Cordelia looked down at Xander.

His eyes were half open, as if he were looking at her, but they were vacant and unseeing. His lips were tinged with blue, and the hollows in his cheeks were dark gray.

"Willow?" The charging demon's roar almost drowned out Cordelia's voice. The ghost in the toga screamed again and disappeared.

The monster lunged for them.

TO BE CONTINUED

About the Authors

Christopher Golden's latest novels include *Of Masques and Martyrs* and *X-Men: Codename Wolverine*. With Nancy Holder, he is the author of several previous *Buffy the Vampire Slayer* novels, including *Blooded* and *Child of the Hunt*. The team also wrote *BtVS: The Watcher's Guide*. Christopher is currently writing a new series of young adult mysteries for Pocket Books entitled *Body of Evidence: The Jenna Blake Mysteries,* and has recently completed a new, original novel, *Strangewood,* which will be published by Signet Books in fall 1999. He is also a comic book writer, whose latest projects include Marvel Comics' *Punisher* and several *Buffy the Vampire Slayer* specials and miniseries from Dark Horse Comics. Please visit him at his web site: www.christophergolden.com.

Nancy Holder is a four-time Bram Stoker Award winner for her supernatural short stories and her novel *Dead in the Water*. She has sold thirty-five novels and over two hundred short stories and edits a column for a writing newsletter. Her most recent novels include the science-fiction novel *Gambler's Star: The Six Families* and the upcoming *Sabrina, the Teenage Witch: Scarabian Nights*. She received the Amazon Sales Report Award for *Buffy the Vampire Slayer: The Angel Chronicles, Vol. 1,* which was also on the *Locus* magazine bestseller list. She has written computer game fiction and *manga* and TV commercials in Japan. She and Christopher have also written a number of short stories together, including "Ate" for *Vampire Magazine* and "Hiding" for *The Ultimate Hulk.*

Christopher and Nancy started working together when Nancy sold an essay to Christopher's Bram Stoker Award-winning collection, *Cut! Horror Writers on Horror Films.* They write together via the Internet. Christopher lives in Massachusetts with his wife and sons, and Nancy lives in San Diego with her husband, Wayne, and their daughter, Belle.

Buffy the Vampire Slayer
OFFICIAL FAN CLUB
www.buffyfanclub.com

1 YEAR MEMBERSHIP INCLUDES:

4 Issues of the *Buffy* Official Magazine

Official I.D. Membership Card

Exclusive Cast Photos

Exclusive *Buffy* Poster

Official *Buffy* Bumper Sticker

JOIN
NOW!

PLEASE FILL OUT THIS FORM AND SUBMIT PAYMENT OPTION INTO AN
ENVELOPE AND MAIL TO: P.O. BOX 465, MT. MORRIS, IL 61054-0465

CHECK ONE ▶ ○ CHECK ENCLOSED   ○ MASTERCARD   ○ VISA

CARD#:   EXPIRES:

SIGNATURE:

NAME: (PLEASE PRINT)

ADDRESS:

CITY: STATE: ZIP:

MEMBERSHIP RATES: APK78K

1YEAR-$29.95 U.S., CANADA AND MEXICO ADD $6.00 PER YEAR U.S. FUNDS ONLY

TM & © '98 FOX   ALLOW 6-8 WEEKS FOR DELIVERY OF THE FIRST ISSUE

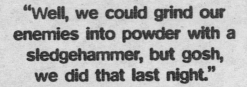

Buffy the vampire slayer™

"Well, we could grind our
enemies into powder with a
sledgehammer, but gosh,
we did that last night."

—Xander

As long as there have been vampires,
there has been the Slayer. One girl
in all the world, to find them where
they gather and to stop the spread of
their evil...the swell of their numbers.

LOOK FOR A NEW TITLE
EVERY MONTH!

Based on the hit TV series created by
Joss Whedon

™ & © 2000 Twentieth Century Fox Film Corporation. All Rights Reserved.   2400

Everyone's got his demons....

ANGEL™

If it takes an eternity, he will make amends.

❖

Original stories based on the
TV show created by Joss Whedon
& David Greenwalt

Available from Pocket Pulse
Published by Pocket Books

© 1999 Twentieth Century Fox Film Corporation. All Rights Reserved.

TV YOU CAN READ

Your favorite shows on  are now your favorite books.

Look for books from Pocket Pulse™ based on these hit series:

ANGEL™

Buffy the vampire slayer™

Charmed™

Dawson's Creek™

ROSWELL™

Angel ™ & © 2000 Twentieth Century Fox Film Corporation. All Rights Reserved.
Buffy the Vampire Slayer ™ & © 2000 Twentieth Century Fox Film Corporation. All Rights Reserved.
Charmed ™ & © 2000 Spelling Television Inc. All Rights Reserved.
Charmed books written and produced by Parachute Publishing, L.L.C.
Dawson's Creek ™ & © 2000 Columbia TriStar Television Inc. All Rights Reserved.
Roswell ™ 2000 Twentieth Century Fox Film Corporation. All Rights Reserved.
™ & © Warner Bros.2000   For more information on your favorite shows check out THE WB.com
                                                                        WB-1

POCKET PULSE

Published by
Pocket Books